JASYN AND THE ASTRONAUTS

THE SEA OF STARS

II

GWENHYVER

A NOTE FROM THE AUTHOR

SAPPHIC
SWORDS & SORCERY.
IN SPACE

If you'd like to hear more about my writing adventures and tales of sapphic swords and sorcery in space (and more!), new release announcements, special offers, behind-the-scenes insights, and bonus materials – including a free e-book of *Theseus and The Sky Labyrinth* – find the sign up information at the end of this book.

In the meantime, it's time to begin the adventure!

To all the people
Who make our worlds
Perfect

CREW

HELM

Herakles	SKY CAPTAIN
Castor	FLIGHT TECH (FIRST MATE)
Pollux	FLIGHT TECH
Tiphys	NAVIGATOR
Lynk	METEOROLOGICAL AND COSMIC FORECASTER
Gus	CHIEF ENGINEER/ SKY SHIP DESIGNER
Orpheus	MEDICIAN (DOCTOR)
Kalais	ENGINE TECH
Zetes	ENGINE TECH
Hylas	INTERPLANETARY INTERPRETER
Peleus	SUSTENANCE CO-ORDINATOR a.k.a. CHEF
Atalanta	SPARE/SHIP UPKEEP/TBD
Jasyn	SPARE/SHIP UPKEEP/TBD

PART I

[C]ARGO

1

GRAVITY

ATALANTA

Relentless ropes of hail lash the hull. Metal *groans*, air filters *gasp* and pipes *strain* as the [C]ARGO ship *roars* to the skies. That the dented-chrome vessel hasn't yet folded in on itself like a dying star is — to Atalanta's mind — a surprise and a nerve-jangling relief.

Pushing beyond her own terror, she signs words designed to help Jasyn calm. And, as their fingers thread together, as Jasyn's tension melts away, the skies respond. Curtains of storm part, unveiling star-studded oblivion.

"Clear skies ahead," confirms Cosmic Forecaster Lynk, the awe, relief, and disbelief in her voice echoed by the gasps and laughter of the crew and the captain's question:

"Is this you, Ice-monger?"

As they drift above the main deck, the torn patchwork of burgundy and purple of Jasyn's cape undulates. Even the loose locks of her ash-blond hair reach for the vista beyond the glass.

The chaos of crew orbits them. The threat of the unknown tugs at the ship. But in this moment all is still.

If only Jasyn's abilities extended to freezing time itself, Atalanta would capture the wonder and possibility before everything — inevitably — unravels and Jasyn discovers the hard way that the heavens care little for explorers. Even ones with charming, lopsided grins, powers of ice, and the best of intentions.

As they break from orbit against the odds, the star-studded twinkle in Jasyn's eyes suggests the skies are made of magic and mystery.

If only that were true.

How Atalanta loves to see the sparkle in Jasyn's eyes. How she fears it too. She'd never want to dampen Jasyn's sense of adventure. She'd never want to see her lost without direction, or scared of what lies ahead. But there's something to be said for a healthy dose of apprehension. It's an unwelcome lesson never to trust the skies.

The ship shunts.

"Gravity adjusted," the ship informs them as they all drop with punctuating thuds to the deck. Not that Atalanta minds. Even with her breath knocked from her, she'd much prefer the bruising of solid ground to being lost to the tide between stars.

That her fingers are still entangled with Jasyn's, that they'd instinctively gravitated to each other, warms her more than any therma-stone or fire-pit could. It's hardly any time since the sky ship workshop, where mouths, tongues, fingers and feelings had all aligned, and Jasyn's ice-created stars had crystallised into galaxies around them. The sensations still crackle beneath Atalanta's skin.

That Jasyn's eyes connect with hers sparks a smile.

"Remember how you wanted adventure?" Atalanta signs. And in that moment, she feels Jasyn's drive toward the skies, her happiness at finally reaching them, as her own.

The sensation departs, and her smile falters. Because the *actual stars* reflected in Jasyn's eyes tug at the fraying threads of Atalanta's calm, threatening to unravel her and weight her down like an overactive gravity console.

The controls must be overcompensating. The air around her squeezes too tight, forcing the air from her lungs. For a moment, even her knuckles, knees and teeth hurt.

"You okay?" Jasyn signs with one hand as they fight against gravity and help each other to their feet.

Atalanta manages a nod, but she's fooling neither of them.

"The gravity console is calibrating," the smooth and outwardly calm voice of the captain announces to the helm. Her words snake through the open comms, pulling Atalanta's Transonic focus with them in a dizzying vertigo, down through the layers of the ship until they spill out through the open comms on the floors below.

As if a sudden escape to the skies isn't enough to churn her stomach, dizziness lingers as she retrains her Transonics on her immediate surroundings.

A silken sound steals her focus — curls *spring*. The *scratch* of the shorter hairs catching against thumb. The furrows of the design shaved into temples — as the captain sweeps a hand through her sculpted neon purple-blue hair.

With a shake of her head, Atalanta takes a literal and Transonic step back. Captain Herakles might be a masterclass in chiselled looks, muscles, and confidence, but that doesn't mean Atalanta has any desire to experience her up close. Transonically, or otherwise.

Why the captain is frowning at Atalanta and Jasyn, and their linked hands in particular, Atalanta has less than a clue. Captain Herakles stands tall, defiant, as she surveys the ether-screen above the two helm-wheels — but her gritted teeth and straining sinews confess that she's just as susceptible to an overexuberance of gravity as the rest of them.

"Don't panic, snowflakes," First-mate Castor jeers from her flight-technician station, with a flick of her silver hair. "Don't go melting just yet."

Adept at entertaining crowds in The Games arena with weaponry, her toned physique and athletic prowess, Castor apparently also has enough confidence in her role aboard the ship, and enough no-confidence in the new arrivals, to make fun of them. But — *ba-boom-ba-boom-ba-boom* — the flight-tech's thundering heart lets Atalanta know she's shielding behind bravado.

Atalanta can hardly blame her heart — and the rest of the crew's — for stumbling. Her own is doing a mighty job of the same as her Transonics sweep through the layers of the ship, pulling at threads of sound, knotting into panic in her gut.

Sounds on Iolcus at least had the good grace to dissipate into the atmosphere, but the innumerable noises on the ship insist on echoing within its shell. Each taking form, *rattling* on every surface within until it loses energy and dies, taking a piece of Atalanta's sanity with it.

Nausea slides within her veins.

A groan... A strain... Metal complaining...

Somewhere in the ship...

Something is wrong.

Before she can locate it, the sounds whip away.

In amongst the Transonically-audible blizzard, rasps and wheezes are familiar, but their quantity and formation are different. Enough to give her a migraine.

Perhaps it's just her panic colouring her perception...

But dismissing potential chaos is as ill-advised as taking to the skies aboard a faulting vessel.

"There are sounds," Atalanta signs, perhaps the least useful sentence she's ever shaped.

"Don't worry." Hylas, the ship's interplanetary translator, aims a kind smile at her as he signs: "You'll get used to sky travel in no time."

Probably looking like she's about to vomit, Atalanta doesn't have the mental dexterity right now to tell him that she knows more than she cares to about sky travel, thank you very much. She knows — viscerally — what the proximity and threat of *the nothing* a mere sky ship shell away can do to test and trick the mind.

If she weren't so preoccupied by the onslaught of straining ship sounds, audible to her ears only, she might be more responsive to the recent discovery of the only other person (aside from Jasyn) who signs her language.

"Something's out of alignment," Atalanta manages, despite her rising nausea, but Hylas, Jasyn, and every other person on the helm deck is focused on the strutting presence of the captain.

"Chief?" Captain Herakles throws a summoning look to Gus, the Chief Engineer, busy at her diagnostics station. "Ship's not much use without its shell." Herakles indicates the area of the apex that had ruptured on take-off. The break Jasyn had fused back together with her ice. "Do what you need to do. Castor and Pollux will assist."

"Aye, Captain." Gus begins her inspection of the apex, Diagnostic-Shard in hand as Castor and Pollux "Aye, Captain," their acknowledgment. Gus's neat silver-blonde hair has evaded its pins, and though there's repressed stress clear in her eyes, thankfully so too is a commanding intelligence.

Atalanta would spell out the underlying threat lurking in the ship, only it's slipped from her grasp like electrical viscera drenched in insulation goo. In her state of whiplash, she's not sure she trusts her instincts.

Not only are they in space, not only are Castor and Pollux — Herakles's foes in the arena — apparently willing to follow her to the end of the planet and, evidently, beyond, but Gus, an elite Ice City engineer *(a literal sky ship scientist for hail's sake),* is deferring to *Captain* Herakles, who Atalanta had until far too recently known only to be a Gladiator spilling blood for entertainment.

Yes, in the arena she'd been known as 'Captain of the Skies,' but Atalanta had assumed that was hyperbole for the sake of questionable entertainment.

If the crew's penchant for turning to Herakles and following her commands is a marker to go by, she seems to know what she's doing.

"Now." Herakles raises her voice, the wall of sound blocking Atalanta's Transonics from searching. "Let's assume this ship isn't going to suddenly crumble and send us all sailing to our deaths..."

Atalanta's stomach sours. The captain really needs to work on her rousing speeches.

"There's no point in risking our lives and more for this journey," the captain turns to the apex framing the star-dappled darkness, "unless we're heading in the right direction." She turns to the boy, Tiphys, who instinctively scoops his mop of hair out of his eyes and stands a little taller. "Tiphys. We'll need your map. And to go over the co-ordinates."

Tiphys nods. The very essence of obedience. Witnessing Tiphys accept something without a question uttered, Atalanta could be convinced the impossible is possible. Perhaps they'll triumph on this journey, after all.

"Lynk?" Herakles turns to the always-smiling woman who's mid-way through de-steaming the lenses of her magnification ether-goggles with the corner of her cardigan. "You'll ensure there are no obstacles blocking our course."

"Aye, Captain." Lynk rubs her blinking eyes.

"Wasn't someone in the middle of sedating an ice-monger?" First-mate Castor growls as she struts in Jasyn's direction.

Captain Herakles steps into the flight-tech's path. It doesn't take a sky ship scientist to figure out that Jasyn will have to do a lot more than unravel a deadly storm, and mend the ship's shell at a crucial moment, to gain Castor's respect. She probably blames Jasyn for the tumultuous weather in the first place.

"Castor. Once the ship's secured, get Orpheus to check that out." Herakles nods to Castor's ice-burned forearm, the result of her attempt to wrestle Jasyn to the deck mid-take-off. To Atalanta's ear the scorched skin fizzes as Castor's body rallies to deal with the injury.

Doctor Orpheus — the personification of a scowl — huffs possible agreement as she tucks the sedation-syringe in question up her dark sleeve.

Atalanta could tell her where to stick her damn syringe. The signed words would be fairly self-explanatory. But she settles for clenching her fists at her sides instead.

Jasyn glowers at the doctor with understandable suspicion, while the captain observes Jasyn in a similar manner. Any awe at parting the life-threatening hail is clearly as changeable as the weather.

Perhaps the captain isn't even looking at Jasyn. Perhaps she's looking past her to Atalanta, likely turning a shade of Corinthian green. Or to Peleus making a show of getting ensnared in his own un-clasped seat-harness. Perhaps Herakles is just doing what a captain does and assessing all the components of their situation, which now includes them.

"If further hands are needed," says Herakles to Gus, "use the new recruits. Whoever you think less likely to cause chaos." Her judging eyes sweep across Jasyn, Atalanta and Peleus, returning to linger on Atalanta.

Why is the captain's heart stuttering like that? It's certainly not doing Atalanta's building headache and unsettled equilibrium any good.

"You." The captain swerves to Peleus.

Peleus's eyes widen and his heart jumps, either in panic or

joy. Atalanta had almost forgotten about his hero-worship crush on Herakles. Peleus opens his mouth to respond, but fails to form words. Atalanta would smile at his buffering, if she wasn't currently so fragile herself.

"All weapons are locked away in transit." The captain holds out an expectant hand.

Peleus stares at it for the longest moment.

Just as his hand twitches, as if he might reach out and hold the captain's hand, Herakles rolls her eyes and clarifies:

"So hand them over."

To Atalanta's surprise, likely to Peleus's too, he unbuckles the axe-knife harness criss-crossing his chest and hands over his precious weapons. The disquiet at being parted from them seems to be outweighed by the thrill of being addressed by the hero of the arena.

"Food supply crates are in the cargo hold." Herakles continues, apparently unfazed by his lack of verbal response. She's probably used to rendering mere mortals speechless. "Unless Gus needs you," a brief shake-of-the head exchange between Gus and the captain confirms she does not, "take inventory, make sure you know what we've got. We have a thirteen strong crew, and — apparently — *that*." She points at the fawn attempting to stand but getting tangled in his own legs.

Atalanta breathes an inward sigh of relief that the creature is being fed as *part of* the crew and not *fed to* the crew.

"Two meals a day," Herakles continues. "Figure out how long our supplies will last and report back. Then find your way to the galley. Get familiar with the facilities and make the first meal."

Peleus gapes at the captain, as if awaiting the next moment of glacier-house fiction to unfold.

"*Now*." Herakles's emphasis startles him into action. He exits the helm deck via the metal staircase, his footsteps ringing out, audibly flagging his spiral downward journey through the ship.

"Really?" Flight-tech Pollux scoffs. "We have limited resources and we're feeding that thing?"

"Pipe down, Pollux," says Herakles. "If our resources become that limited, *that thing* might become one of them. Or you will. Depends who best follows my orders."

Atalanta's teeth grind and her fingers twitch at the threat before noticing Pollux and Castor's smirks. *Oh good. No cannibalism on this ship!* Still, for the sake of the fawn, Atalanta and Jasyn share a look that confirms they'll supervise the animal for his own safety.

"You." Herakles turns to Jasyn and Atalanta. It's so sudden, Atalanta isn't sure whether the heart-stutter belongs to her or the captain. "Unless Gus needs you," a glance at Gus assessing the apex sees them waved away, "get yourselves down to the engine chamber. Hylas will show you the way. Kalais and Zetes will get you trained."

Jasyn is quick to heed her orders, matching Hylas's strides towards the metal stairway. A wave of nausea rolls through Atalanta's gut, flooding panic through her veins, holding her back.

A groan... A strain...

Something about to burst at the seams...

A repetitive high pitched squeaking of metal against something unfamiliar, piercing... annoying — irrelevant?

With effort, Atalanta sets that sound aside. Her shallow breaths and thumping heart, too. Because in amongst the tangle, deep in the ship, there's a snag. She hones in on it, only to have the thread snatched beyond her reach. Something isn't right, but whether it's the buckling of the ship or her self, she can't tell.

Herakles is scowling, possibly at her, or at whatever Doctor Orpheus is saying. The doctor's mouth is moving, but Atalanta can't identify the words. Her Transonics are too busy tripping from floor to floor, through varying timbres and intensities, from air vents to umbilicals snaking up and across and through the ship, tying it and her in knots—

Her lungs rebel. Her heartbeat races beyond control. The *chirps* of her own stats monitor in the medical quarters three floors down underscore her inner chaos.

She doesn't want to be this person. The person who can't breathe right, or keep her own heart rate in check. She must be doing a poor job of hiding it, because the captain's amber eyes are on her, annoyance or concern scoring her brow.

She should have trusted her gut...

There's something terribly wrong...

Atalanta tries to shape the words, but her hands tremble. Not that it would do much good anyway, with Jasyn and Hylas far enough away, their backs turned.

Blazing blue light hurls across the helm—

Blaring ship alarms soon follow, doing all the speaking for her. *(As if she needed more sensory input!)* Atalanta's eyes clamp shut. The ship's screams turn her thoughts to mush. Her brain might just be being whisked inside her skull with serrated metal paddles through her eardrums.

There are a thousand ways to die in the depths of space...

It looks like they're about to discover one.

2

BENEATH THE WAVES

ATALANTA

The warring symphony of sounds bleated by the ship — the shrill squeak of metal struggling, heartbeats jolting sonar-like across the helm — are a web formed by an overzealous and inebriated spider, each new addition a silken rope yanking Atalanta's thoughts in a new and jarring direction.

She can only assume the ship and its diagnostics aren't functioning as they should. And that the *please switch off the alarm now* button isn't working.

When Atalanta opens her eyes, Captain Herakles is gesturing in a controlled, authoritative manner, saying something to Gus and the flight-techs — each focused on the information scrolling in the ether above their stations.

"Engine to helm. What in the hailing heavens is happening?" Kalais's voice ricochets up through the ship, fighting a screaming wall of sound that has Atalanta's ears drenched in the fuel-flames of the engine chamber.

Nausea crashes through Atalanta, threatening to pull her under. The onslaught forces her to her knees. She reaches behind her ears but her fingers are clumsy.

The captain's concerned face occupies her swimming vision.

Her mouth moves, but Atalanta can't identify the words. It's all strangely distant, like she's above water and Atalanta is submerged.

The captain's deep breaths deliver air into the fast thumping stream of her blood. Atalanta shakes her head. She hadn't meant to land her focus anywhere near the captain's chest, never mind within it.

The helm is slipping on its axis. Or Atalanta is slipping on hers.

Before Atalanta can do something useful, the captain is reaching down, thumbing her Transonics closed, enabling her to retreat to silence.

Relief.

Only the echoes of pain remain. But the calm that follows is limited, thanks to the tremor of warning lights and the overall impending doom in progress.

As Jasyn skids to Atalanta's side, Captain Herakles returns to the helm. Worry buckles Jasyn's brow and she's asking if she's okay, but Atalanta's attention is elsewhere:

A silhouette forms shaped words at the edge of her vision. "*Be the hunter, not the prey.*" The familiar words smart like a reopened wound.

But no-one else responds to the presence. Perhaps they're all too busy with the state of the ship, and Jasyn is too busy with the state of her.

No. It doesn't make sense.

Everything aches, as the doctor had warned it would after her return from death. The doctor had warned, too, of 'after-effects.' And this, this impossible silhouette from her past loitering beyond her sight but in her thoughts... must be such.

Atalanta breathes deep, or tries to, uncertain whether she wants it, *them*, to stay or go. Whether they're real or not, their words ring in her thoughts. How tempting it is to remain in her cocoon of silence, to close her eyes until someone else has turned their situation around.

But that is not a strategy for longevity.

Atalanta pushes herself to her feet and takes the unwanted but necessary step of sliding her thumbs over her Transonics, opening the floodgates and inviting mind-crushing chaos back into her ears.

The drilling of her brain through her eardrums resumes. The ship in three-dimensions pulses sharp through her mind's eye. If the alarm has one benefit it is that — if she grits her teeth against the agony — every aspect of the ship is audibly-visible at once.

Beside her, Jasyn's body is a comforting wall of breaths and heartbeats, wrapping around her like a blanket. Beyond that, in amongst the network of humming cables and components, connecting and powering flight deck consoles: the impressive contours of Herakles, muscles expanding and contracting with every decisive gesture.

"*Focus*," scolds her inner voice, and she's not sure whether it's the familiar silhouette's or her own. Yes. *Focus*. Now is not the time to be dwelling on the shape of the captain, no matter how aesthetically pleasing.

Atalanta closes her eyes, as if that may help.

From the stomach of the ship, the flaming crackle of deforming fuel-ice sears through her every nerve. Perspiration drips from two lithe figures. *Kalais and Zetes. Engine-techs.*

The skittish rodent population offer their own sparkler-like circulatory crackles into the mix, lighting up the narrow spaces between floors and in every gap possible. Heavens above. Just how many vole-rats can one ship house? Their writhing en masse movements have her stomach threatening revolt. She'll deal with them later.

The cavernous cargo hold adds another human shape.

Peleus?

The roar of the engines floods her auditory vision. That's how it goes. Flashes of clarity buried by a confusion of details. Just as she's able to grasp a particular origin point, just as the contours of the room take shape — the sounds reverberating off walls, giving definition — others interrupt and overshadow.

"Breathe, Atalanta," insists the familiar shaped-words that must only be in her mind.

Indignant, transported back to the mindset of a child, Atalanta manages to remind herself that she's a grown-up who shouldn't throw a tantrum when being told to do the obvious.

After a stuttering breath, she endeavours to take their advice. Breathing in... and out... in... out...

Like a dance or a piece of music, a ship has its own tempo, and a well-trained, Transonic-augmented ear might hone in on any mis-step or fluffed note. But, having only been aboard this ship in its down-beaten, malfunctioning state, the task of seeking out what should and shouldn't be there could be as impossible as traversing the galaxies of the Seven Suns in search of the fabled Golden Fleece.

By Iolcian standards, Atalanta had spent around seven sun-orbits in the great expanse on the sky raft, the only home she'd known before Iolcus. Her parents' ship had been all organic sleek lines and lava-like circuitry veins, not so different from her Transonics. She'd learned to listen to its beating heart and figure out whether it had lost its rhythm; whether the air-circulation ducts needed cleansing, or the water filtration system required another tune up. She grew to know that raft, its every sinew, its orange-electrical viscera, as precisely as a horologist knows every cog of a ticking timepiece.

This ship... Qualitatively different, it boasts an unapologetically mechanical base layer augmented by pipe and cable bundles, each housing a patchwork of electrical and ether components. A chimera of different times, worlds and technologies. A ship created of a world open to the skies and maintained by a closed borders junk yard planet forced to make do with its own dwindled resources.

Even so, the function is the same: to keep its inhabitants breathing and safe. She clings to that idea more tightly than a space walking astronaut to their tether.

Breathe in...

Sounds launch themselves at her, as if desperate for her to hear what they can do. With a concerted effort, she reaches beneath the surface of the scalding, crashing waves and into the depths. Under the heavy weight of the alarm, air *gushes* up and down and along and within the tunnels of pipes, crisscrossing at junctions.

Breathe out...

The *thwack* of air hits filters, segmenting and funnelling out of vents and into lungs. Echoes bounce off walls, reflecting back on themselves, fading, eventually. Her own sweat trickles loudly down her brow.

Breathe in...

The furnace burrows its flourishing ice-flame into her mind. She identifies the sound, assesses its size and shape, its consistency, then isolates and discards it. The pipes fizzing air old and new throughout the ship. Identified. Assessed. Isolated. Discarded.

Breathe out...

With each sound piercing into her consciousness, Atalanta performs the same process, peeling away the auditory layers of the ship, one by one. As she digs deeper, as her breaths even out, she hazards careful Transonic steps. It's not unlike venturing across a lake of thin ice. Any misstep, any cracks, and she'll plunge into a flood of overwhelming sensation.

Beneath the clinking of metal and the squelch of oil gunked

mechanisms, there are sounds that do not fit. She strips through the layers to discover a low kind of *groan,* as if the ship itself is in the throes of an epic and unshifting headache. There's a *strain.*

There. The point in the ship where mechanical innards are clotting, blazing as bright as a storm flooded river about to burst its banks.

"CATASTROPHIC FAILURE IMMINENT." The ship's voice crashes unhelpfully onto the shore of her mind.

"*Move,*" the proactive voice in her head instructs and Atalanta wastes no time making a break for the core stairway.

Footsteps thump metal. Jasyn is quick to follow as Atalanta forges her way down the spiral stairs. Jasyn reaches for her and signs "Are you okay?" as she simultaneously asks aloud, "Where are you going?"

The nearby engine chamber *howls.* Atalanta manages only to heave in a couple of breaths and sign "there's a blockage" before squaring up to the corridor. Jasyn's footsteps rattle away from her, but she can't focus on that right now.

Time is running out.

From the audible distortions shuddering her equilibrium, the corridor sways like a rope bridge in a storm. Of course, she's painfully aware of the irony that sounds as her way to 'see' can show intricate detail, all the layers of the universe, or in their crowding combination be as blinding as staring into the sun. She'd like to greet nature with an eye roll on the subject. But, later.

Because, *there.*

The pulsing thrombosis that threatens them all.

The deck nestled beneath the engine chamber. A rupture here would punch a hole through electrical arteries, and rip through the chamber that powers the ship *and* the ship's outer shell. A promise of oblivion. *Dark undertows. Choking silence.*

Atalanta buckles, but manages to keep her bodily mutiny to

retching only.

Don't think about that...

She braces herself against the smooth, cold metal of the ship's corridor, each step a monumental challenge.

Purposeful footsteps. The ship's audible fluctuations give shape to three figures winding down the stairwell towards her. *Could they run a little quieter, please?*

Sweat drips from her brow, *whistles* through air, *clinks* on metal, slipping between the triangular mesh, before *whistling* down through air again. The audible descent presents a new wave of vertigo, and Atalanta imagines all that might be left of her soon is a soup of a person, dripping down through the layers of ship.

Jasyn fills her tilting vision, her frown overlayed at several angles. The doctor's gloved hand reaches for her, but Atalanta stumbles away. Her heartbeat tremors as she folds against the point in the corridor where the angry bulge is kicking up a storm. Blue goo, sour and sharp, pools out from under the wall panel.

Her hands shaking, Atalanta uselessly thumbs the rivets at each corner of the panel. A sleek arrow head could solve this in a second. If only her bow and arrows hadn't been lost to the Iolcian scrap heap.

The alarm drills her skull. The gravity of sound shoves her from all directions, knocking her to her knees.

When chief engineer Gus steps in to work on the rivets with a motorised screwdriver, Atalanta should be relieved, but the metal against metal and winding mechanisms dig in and churn her audible landscape.

It's too much.

The alarms within her body sound all the louder and the final thread of her inner-tether snaps, plunging her into silent darkness.

3

SPY

ATALANTA

Either her world has ended, or someone has closed her Transonics.

Jasyn's worried eyes gazing down at her would suggest she's to thank for that. There's a calming warmth in her tempered smile that lets Atalanta know two important things. One — if Jasyn could banish her discomfort, she would. And, two — the ship-annihilation crisis has been averted. At least for now.

"You saved the ship," signs Jasyn as the blue alarm lights finally fade.

Atalanta would argue — if she were feeling up to it — she merely pointed in the right direction.

Beyond Jasyn, Gus wields her screwdriver, a mildly startled expression, and wears a considerable quantity of blue goo on her sky-blue overalls. A once over of the open wall panel confirms for Atalanta that the partially split pipes are patched up.

She thumbs her Transonics open, lowering their intensity to more manageable levels. The steady flow within the pipes suggests Gus has done a good job.

The ship gurgles in coincidental tandem with the uncomfortable sensations in her stomach. She gulps extra air as *somewhere* metal grinds.

What could have happened...

Dark undertows. Choking silence.

She lurches forward and ruptures like a blocked pipe, puking across the doctor's left boot — "fucking yuck," the doctor grumbles — and down through the gaps in the metal grate and, apparently, onto the perfectly coifed curls of Captain Herakles.

Though there are other thoughts that should be more pressing, Atalanta's first is: *what is the captain doing down there?*

In the corridor below, Herakles wipes the contents of Atalanta's stomach from her sculpted — now soggy — blue-purple hair. She doesn't look angry, or annoyed. Nor, understandably, does she look thrilled. The captain, her amber eyes flashing up at Atalanta, is apparently difficult to read even when covered in bile.

"The lift is working," says Captain Herakles with a nod to the doorway she must have just stepped out of. "Could do with some oil, though."

"I'll get to it," says Gus. "Looks like we've got a sniffer-hound for ship faults," she adds, with an impressed smile aimed at Atalanta.

Herakles blinks up at them. "Yes. Good. You should... um..." She swipes a hand through her hair, hesitating when it serves as a reminder that she's covered in ick. *Why is the captain being awkward?* Her heartbeat is practically tripping over itself. The woman who can remain calm taking to the skies during a worst case scenario, is only now struggling to function? Perhaps her adrenaline has worn off? Perhaps she really doesn't like being puked on. Fair enough. "Work together... Yes... You two should work together."

"An excellent idea, Captain," says Gus, sounding genuinely pleased.

The captain pulls her attention to her own corridor. "Guess I'll go check the ice-melt facilities next," she mutters, opting to take the stairs.

"That'll need clearing up." The doctor nods at the offending patch of floor while sounding like she, too, might puke. She sprays something from a vial onto her blemished boot. "I'll be in my medical quarters," she adds, probably to Gus, before striding away and not looking back.

"I'll clear up," says Jasyn, so automatically Atalanta is grateful, and too churned up to be embarrassed.

"You're expected in the engine chamber," Gus reminds Jasyn. "Captain's orders."

Atalanta forces herself to stand tall in an attempt to fool both her body and Jasyn that she's cut out for this adventure. She gives her best *don't worry about me* smile as she signs for Jasyn to: "Get going, I can deal with this."

Jasyn opens her mouth, definitely to object — of course she does — but they've known each other long enough to decipher when to dig heels in and when to not. A look from Atalanta is enough to nudge her, reluctantly, on her way.

Jasyn's footfalls carry through the ship and Atalanta's thoughts.

"USE A DECON PACK." Gus's voice is sudden and loud, more due to Atalanta's lack of recalibration than the chief engineer's volume.

She opens a wall panel that's — apparently — a floor-to-ceiling storage cupboard. Spiders and their webs have asserted ownership of the space, but beyond the mesh of silk is the item needed.

"Clean this up. Then, if you're able and willing, we'll work on getting this ship into shape."

Atalanta nods, appreciating Gus's direct but gentle tone.

"You can change into overalls if you want to protect your

clothes," adds Gus. "Follow the yellow lights to the crew quarters. You'll find clothing options there."

Atalanta looks down at her tunic. The patchwork of blues and greens are dulled and the fabric ripped by all the events since the Ice King's military attacked their village. There are gaps where pellet shots stole her life in The Games arena. If anything, she should want to burn them, along with all the events that blemished them. But they are *her* clothes, their style reminiscent of a pattern her mother taught her, a fashion from an ancestral home she has never known. They are a piece of her unknown past. She could repair them. If her own body can heal from death, she can wield a needle and thread.

Gus glides to the stairwell, clearly on a mission.

It takes no time at all to decipher the mechanisms of the decon pack: a solid shell backpack with a couple of tubes. She suctions up the mess with one nozzle and sprays the offending patch of floor with the other. With each sweep, she forces herself to breathe slow and deep to keep her remaining stomach contents within.

Breathe in... Breathe out...

She tries not to think about the chaos of the skies. This trip might be different... It needs to be. And a negative attitude won't help her or anyone else, will it? She *knows* this, but — judging by the tension in her neck and every other muscle — the notion of positivity isn't resonating just yet.

Breathe in... Breathe out...

She tries to ignore the sparkler-like flutters within the walls; the heartbeats of vermin crawling through the ship. Their presence scratches beneath her skin, unwanted memories scored into her thoughts and flesh. She'd escaped swarms of them in the Unforgiving Mountains, so of course irony would see to it that the creatures are now her unwelcome travel companions.

Deep breath in...

Layers of sound peel away...

Jasyn's heartbeat blazes into her mind's eye like a locator beacon. Atalanta follows the familiar echoing footsteps, making sure Jasyn reaches her destination without event. The engine hisses, each fuel-ribbon in the mined ice flaring to flame.

"Well, hey there Snowflake," says a muffled voice at the end of the footstep trail. Why is it that when Kalais calls Jasyn *Snowflake* it sounds like she's flirting? A strange, challenging kind of flirtation, as if she's testing Jasyn, seeing how far she can push her. It has Atalanta's hackles up.

"I'm here to be useful."

Atalanta can practically hear Jasyn's winning smile. Turns out she'd travel the universe for that smile. Or brave an intergalactic adventure at the very least.

"Oh good," says Kalais, with a bite of frost, clearly not so enamoured. "I'm sure we're thrilled."

If Atalanta were in the same room as them, she'd tell Kalais to back off and *play nice*. (Though, not *too* nice...).

A rogue Transonic-jarring sneeze from the helm knocks her focus—

Sounds jumble—

Details snatched—

New sounds thrum in the echo chamber of her skull.

"The fuck?"

A new conversation. A new location. She's not familiar enough with the ship layout to know exactly where the voice is coming from, but the words and gruff voice are undoubtedly those of Doctor Orpheus.

"I thought you were going to shower? Sort yourself out..."

"Yeah, yeah," replies Herakles, now more quietly confident than overtly commanding. "This conversation couldn't wait. Suggesting to the entire crew that there's a spy amongst us?

Really, Orpheus?" Herakles tuts. Her hushed tone makes clear this is a private conversation.

Ordinarily, Atalanta tries not to encroach on privacy, but there's nothing ordinary about their situation. Finding out as much as she can about this ship and its occupants — some of whom aren't thrilled to have Jasyn aboard — could be a matter of life or death.

Especially if there is a spy. That must be what the doctor was saying on the helm deck when Atalanta was lost to the sounds strangling her and the ship.

It's the doctor's turn to tut, and Atalanta can practically hear the rolling of eyes as she spews a selection of swear words.

"Morale won't count for much if there's someone amongst us intent on ripping us from the skies," continues Doctor Orpheus. "*Euryproktos*, Herakles. No-one on board is thick. Well, apart from—"

Atalanta's fairly certain from their previous exchanges that the doctor is about to say the captain herself, but a third voice interrupts.

"Will you two give over?" *Gus*. Her footsteps are lighter than the doctor and captain's. "Even my children don't squabble as much as you."

"You think we're squabbling?" Herakles's tone is suggestive and the air displacement in the region of her left eye highlights for Atalanta the captain's cheeky wink.

The doctor tuts and grumbles. Fabric rasps against skin as she crosses her arms. But there must be some detail that the captain and doctor observe, because instead of more banter (or whatever this weird dynamic is), a weighty silence with uncomfortable heart rates follows.

"Shit. Sorry, Gus," says the captain.

"Fuck. Yeah. Sorry." Even the doctor sounds contrite.

Clearly the comment that had been intended as a mild

telling off has highlighted the devastating fact that Gus's children, her family, have been left behind. Or rather, Gus has been whisked away on a journey that she was only ever intending to manage from afar. And now her family are left to deal with the consequences from an Ice King and a Warden General known always for cruelty, never for fairness, should her role in the treasonous plot to the skies be known.

Muscles expand and contract; Herakles reaching a comforting hand to Gus's shoulder. The captain's mouth opens, her vocal cords already shaping to speak, but Gus interrupts.

"I don't want to talk about it," she says, giving the captain's hand an acknowledging squeeze before rolling the tension from her shoulders. "Right now I want to focus on getting this ship safely to and from its destination, and I welcome the distraction of knowing why Orpheus saw fit to make accusations that can unravel our crew and destroy this voyage." Despite her words, her tone is more curious than accusatory.

"Okay." The doctor's footfalls suggest a slight swagger. "It won't have escaped your notice that we left under a hail of bullets from an entire platoon of the Iolcian guard?"

"It did not." Gus sighs.

"Obviously." Herakles.

"The Ice King's military knew we were there. Someone either got sloppy, or they purposefully shared information about our mission."

The doctor's footfalls lead the way across the room, joined by Herakles's surefooted but surprisingly light step, and Gus's graceful strides. The reverberation of the footfalls gives shape to the stack of chunky cube monitors along one wall of the medical chamber. Atalanta recalls seeing them not long ago, when they'd made a brief detour to medical on the way to the helm deck. The screens had been bursting with each of the crew's vital statistics, fed from citizen Permits embedded in flesh, or, like

Atalanta and Jasyn, the cuffs now clamped about their left wrists.

Apparently Atalanta isn't the only one with the ability to quietly keep watch over the goings on within the ship and its inhabitants.

"Take a look," says the doctor.

For Atalanta's Transonic reach, the monitor screens have no discernible information. "This is the time-frame when I prattled on about the possibility of sabotage. The engine comms were still open, so engine crew heard, too."

"You were trying to uncover a guilty conscience," says Gus, understanding.

"And?" asks Herakles.

"Every heartbeat spiked. Apart from yours, Herakles, because you're clearly dead inside."

Herakles grunts possible agreement at that.

Atalanta subconsciously rubs her cuff. That it can be used as some sort of lie detector is useful, but the idea that someone can see the details of her inner workings makes her skin crawl. Though, who is she to find issue with such things? If she tries, she could hear every breath taken, every heartbeat and chemical reaction aboard this ship.

"I'm sure you're not saying everyone apart from Herakles is responsible..." Gus hedges.

"I'm saying there's nothing in the stats other than what you'd expect from the stress of an unplanned take-off."

"No saboteur." There's relief in the captain's voice.

"Or they're exceptionally good at hiding it," adds the doctor.

The captain sighs, audibly less relieved.

"What about the spike here?" The captain's sleeve scrunches. The shape of her pulsing circulatory system suggests she's pointing at one monitor in particular.

"That's the archer," says the doctor.

Atalanta practically stops breathing.

"Oh." The captain's heart does a double step. *Odd.*

"I think it's safe to say she was suffering sensory overload," continues Doctor Orpheus. "And saboteurs tend not to hone in on catastrophic malfunctions in order to save the ship." Yes. Exactly. *Phew.* "Besides, she'd have had no opportunity between learning of the plan and it all going abysmally wrong."

"Are we going to talk about the archer?" asks Gus.

Why would they talk about 'the archer'? What does that mean?

"Not unless she's a saboteur," says Herakles, more stand-offish than before. Has Atalanta done something to offend the captain? Do they know of her potential to be spying on their conversation right now?

"So, in conclusion," continues the doctor, "we don't know for sure if there is a traitor on board. But if they are, they'll be risking their own lives if they try anything."

Gus sighs and so does Atalanta. *That's something, at least.*

4

FLEDGLING

JASYN

It turns out that being trained in the engine chamber involves repetitive backbreaking work, shovelling fuel-ice into the furnace while her 'instructors' expect her to keep their pace. It is both disconcerting and impressive to watch the two engine-tech siblings in full flow: their shoulders and angular-winged tattoos protruding from their vests, undulating with such intensity they might themselves take flight.

Meanwhile, Jasyn — stuck in the middle — is the fledgling struggling to fly.

She had been told to "Watch what we do, and copy, okay?" Well, she'd actually been told by Kalais to "Take off that stupid cape, unless you want it snagged. If engine mechanisms chew you up, I ain't risking my other hand to rescue you," and "Watch what we do, and copy, okay?"

With Kalais's shovel affixed to her right arm via a buckled harness, Jasyn questions whether engine work is how she lost her right hand. Or is Kalais just trying to scare her?

Either way, Jasyn unhooked the decorative metal clasp that holds her cape in place and tucked both away.

The engine roars, blazing teal-fire more scorching than ice-burn reaching through the hatch. Jasyn retreats, but Kalais and Zetes roar right back. If this is where Kalais lost her right hand, she's no more cautious as a result. For the two engine-techs, fuelling the ship appears to be some kind of unhinged dance.

Even the white powder smudges from the fuel-ice have the engine-tech duo looking like they're adorned in war paint and fitting right in. Jasyn just looks like she's rolled around in the snow.

She'd never before have thought herself unfit, but the ache in her back from a short stint of shovelling begs to differ. Give her a cliff face or a tree to climb, or a weather system to upend, and she'd run rings around them, but unfortunately there's little need for her particular skillsets right now.

It's astounding how much heat a fuel that's mostly ice can kick out. She strips out of her mottled woollen over-shirt, down to her collared long sleeve, using the material to mop her brow. Her shirt and vest are already soaked.

"Just keep shovelling, Snowflake," Kalais shouts above the blue-flames, without breaking her fuelling stride. Her piercing jade eyes judge her, making Jasyn's skin prickle even more than the stifling heat.

Why is it, when Kalais calls her 'Snowflake,' it sounds like a not-so-veiled insult?

Kalais follows her order with a threat to throw her into the brig if she doesn't pick up speed. Her last threat was to throw her out an airlock. Zetes buries his knowing smile. Though what the hail that's about, Jasyn has no idea.

Seeing the engine-techs side by side, Jasyn is reminded how similar they look: both lithe and muscular, with Zetes a little bulkier, his jaw squarer. There's no question they're siblings. Clearly Kalais is the more vocal of the two.

Just keep shovelling.

Her palms smart where she grips her shovel. As she heaves

one load after another, her thoughts turn to what the crew's approach to order might be. *Military? Pirates? A little of both?* It would be useful to know whether Kalais's threats are idle or not, and thus whether Jasyn should be wary of any airlocks.

If Kalais's threats weren't enough, a few 'accidental' elbows to the abdomen gives Jasyn the distinct impression the engine-techs don't want her here. Probably not thrilled with having to supervise the *unknown quantity*. And why should they be? She's the ill-starred child, the offspring of the untethered and fallen Ice Queen. Jasyn can hardly blame them, after her own sky-splitting display in The Games arena.

That Kalais and Zetes had helped her in the arena now feels a distant memory. Her performance there must have cemented her status as dangerous, useless or both in their minds. Whatever they wanted her to prove when they gave her the ice-sword to fight the Gladiator Princess, she's clearly disappointed them.

Another elbow—

Jasyn's jaw strains with the effect of biting her tongue and keeping her temper in check.

It's not been the most promising start to the voyage. The 'welcome' to the ship has been as abrasive as their sudden launch. Adventure, exploration, discovery, that's what she'd dreamed about when staring up at the stars. Not being the resident pariah.

What a way to steal the fuel from her engines.

A breeze or a breath...

...it caresses Jasyn's ear, her neck. With a shudder, she turns. But there's no-one there. Kalais and Zetes are shovelling and glaring at her as though she's more peculiar than any creature in this galaxy or the next.

Kalais starts barking something about what she's "playing at" and calling her a "fucking liability," but Jasyn's senses fill with a strange yet familiar whisper-song: *lyrical, sweet and full of warning.*

No... It can only be her imagination, because there's not a chance under the Seven Suns that her ice-sword is on this ship. It must be an after-effect of death that the doctor warned her about.

The thickening in the air — is that in her imagination, too?

The haunting whisper could be sound shaped by exhaustion and shame. Jasyn winces at her own internal gut punch. Because only someone utterly useless would lose a *fabled ice-sword* twice within a few days. The first time, ironically, to Kalais and Zetes (until they'd returned it to her in the arena to witness her unspooling, terrifying capabilities). The second, when the Ice King had forced the sword between her ribs before reclaiming it.

A twist of blade within her gut, slicing her from within. Her chest aches as every muscle in her torso revolts at the memory.

"Are you even listening?"

Sharp green eyes confront Jasyn, along with the choking arrival of Kalais's shovel shaft crushing her throat. Something digs into her back — a gauge or dial? Likely something more crucial to this engine chamber than her.

Instinctively steadying herself against the wall, ice webs from the epicentre of her touch.

No, please. Not now.

Nothing good will come of losing control aboard a sky ship. And — catastrophe aside — how's she ever supposed to fit in if the crew all think she's about to freeze them to death, or tear their ship in two?

Her palm aches with the effort of reeling in her inner ice.

A breeze...? A song...? A whisper...?

Something shifts within her, fraying the fabric of her mind, making her dizzy. *Why?* Why now, when she's in no position to follow its trail?

"You've got two of these —" Kalais flicks Jasyn's ear (ouch!), "— so, use them. When I tell you to shovel, you shovel."

With so many sun-orbits spent play-fighting with Atalanta, she can give this idiot a run for her therma-stones, but would the ice crackling at her fingertips know when to stop?

The frosting plume Jasyn exhales, and the crystalline formations webbing from her palm along her shovel sours Kalais's grimace to disgust as she discards Jasyn as quick as she'd struck.

"Snowflake's got some bite," says Kalais. It's not a compliment.

Jasyn draws a chilled and shaky breath and barely a moment passes before a buzz cuts across the hiss of the engine, accompanied by a green flashing wall-light.

The harness affixing the shovel to Kalais's right arm pivots at the stump of her wrist as she lets loose with her left to punch the intercom and press the receiver to her ear.

"What do you want, Doc?" Kalais demands, followed by a series of vague responses and a second punch to close the intercom. Without looking at Jasyn, Kalais nods her to the exit: "Doctor's orders. Go be her problem for a while."

Jasyn downs her shovel with a clang at the chamber edge, not lingering in case the offer to leave is retracted.

✦

WHEN SHE REACHES THE CORRIDOR WHERE ALL GREEN CABLE LINES meet, Jasyn's relief is doused with ice as a familiar silver shimmer emerges from the medical quarters: Castor, her forearm wrapped in a bandage.

On their chaotic launch, Jasyn hadn't wanted to burn her, but the flight-tech/first-mate had tried to knock her out. Before Jasyn can change course, Castor's dark and unsympathetic eyes find her. Her features twist to something bitter as she heads

Jasyn's way. With the even steps of an athlete adept at entertaining an entire arena, Castor veers to bodycheck Jasyn as she passes, leaving her momentarily stunned and without breath.

"Watch it, Ice-monger," Castor warns, without looking back.

What is it with this crew? Anyone would think being a new recruit and an 'ice-monger' was some sort of contact sport.

Jasyn pauses at the sickly green doorway of the doctor's domain. It occurs to her, then: what if the doctor witnessed the *icy* exchange in the engine chamber and is about to reward her with a dose of sedative? She's tried it once already...

The last time they interacted, Doctor Orpheus had tried to sedate her against her will. Yes, they were hurtling into orbit. And, *yes*, there was an assumption that Jasyn was the source of the storm hindering their planetary escape. If she were in the captain's position, if she had thought someone responsible for the weapons-grade hail raining down on them, perhaps Jasyn would have given the same order.

But that doesn't mean she likes it. Having her faculties and freedom claimed is more chilling than her own ice.

Doctor Orpheus might have invited her to the skies in order to study her and her ice abilities, but Jasyn hadn't thought to clarify whether she'd need to be conscious to do so.

She sighs. It's not as if she's got anywhere to run to. And with an identity cuff clamped about her wrist, hiding is likely a lost cause now, anyway.

Something tickles at the base of her neck. Is she being watched?

Perhaps it's the thought of the overseers. She checks over her shoulder. She's getting the feeling *looking over her shoulder* is something she's going to have to do a lot on this ship.

The shadow shape at the end of the corridor doesn't fit. The woman's form isn't subject to the corridor's green glow. Her fine ebony gowns and hair drift in a manner suited to lower gravity, not the slightly oppressive gravity settings of this scrap heap ship. When she steps closer, her indigo eyes illuminate with the kind of smile that could light up a sky or inspire a solar system into orbit.

Medea.

Guardian of the Golden Fleece. She'd guided Jasyn, Atalanta and Peleus to safety on their journey across Iolcus. Now, with graceful movements, she beckons Jasyn. Her direction would have them retracing Jasyn's path, down into the belly of the ship.

The air undulates around the woman, as if a breeze is winding around her and reaching for Jasyn, pulling at her on an invisible string.

That whisper. That song. It's faint, but there. She'd been listening for it on her journey up from the engine chamber — but as with most things under the Seven Suns, ethereal songs and lost keys in particular — it usually disappears to nothing when sought out.

As curious as Jasyn is, she's not sure it's wise to trust the suggestions of apparitions. Nor is it wise to roam on an unfamiliar ship occupied with people who aren't enamoured with her presence.

The dilemma is short-lived as Medea whips her attention over her own shoulder, as if she can hear something Jasyn cannot. As Medea's image collapses to nothing, the song of her sword dissipates, too.

Well, that decides that, then...

Returning her attention to the sickly green medical quarters doorway (an odd colour choice!), Jasyn reminds herself: despite the doctor's prickly demeanour, she did bring her back to life, which isn't something someone hail-bent on her demise would do...

So, with a deep breath, and a scrape of metal against metal, Jasyn pushes open the door.

5

MEDICAL

JASYN

Despite Jasyn's less than subtle entrance, Doctor Orpheus doesn't turn around. She stares out at space, leaving Jasyn standing awkwardly. Instead, she marvels at the ice-plagued planet that's been her home her whole life, suspended in the inky darkness and framed by a sizeable porthole.

That a massive hunk of metal can even leave a planet is nothing short of astounding. She can hardly believe they're here. *In the skies.* Her thoughts have always been rooted in the stars, and now she's sailing amongst them.

The doctor's attention seems affixed on another, smaller porthole: the one framing the green-hazed moon Corinth, which the Ice King would have Iolcians believe is a planet stealing their sunlight. The celestial body hangs there, dwarfed by the ice-planet beyond. A perfect reminder that if this mission fails, Iolcus and Corinth and all their inhabitants will pay the price.

Before they took flight, Gus had mentioned that the doctor's family are from Corinth, or perhaps *on* Corinth. Jasyn opens her mouth to say something — perhaps words of comfort about the journey ahead — then she remembers the doctor knows considerably more about this journey, and the doctor doesn't like her, so anything Jasyn can offer is unlikely to help.

Jasyn snaps her mouth shut.

Much of the room's perimeter is in darkness. Perhaps to conserve vital ship resources? It doesn't look like the room of a ship that has rushed to the skies. It looks... functional. Lived in, even. Perhaps the sky ship was the doctor's office even before their impromptu voyage?

A third of the medical quarters is occupied by a clear walled chamber marked with the words DANGER and QUARANTINE. An outer clear-walled corridor wraps around an inner chamber. The set-up likely to enable medical professionals to make close observations without having to enter the den of whatever beast or contagion is caged within. There's scoring (*scratch marks?*) blemishing the inner shell... enough to make Jasyn gulp.

Bathed in the warm light of a lamp, the doctor's medician case atop a large desk draws her closer. Unclasped and open, it's too much of a lure...

Jasyn reaches for the case, only for the desk's potted plant to sway towards her. Instinctive dread coils in her stomach at its serrated leaves, reminiscent of jaws and fangs. It has her questioning which of them is higher in the food chain.

If Atalanta were here she'd be rolling her eyes at Jasyn's inability to curb her curiosity.

Now that Jasyn's closer, she catches the doctor's reflection in the porthole. Her glazed expression speaks volumes, but not in a language Jasyn understands. Is it sadness? Detachment? Something else? The question is snatched away as the doctor's eyes lock with hers in their reflections. Any vulnerability that might have been there a moment before has been swallowed up by the monster of her personality. Her scowl communicates *What the fuck do you want?*, as if she hadn't been the one to summon Jasyn in the first place.

Doctor Orpheus overrides her expression with something more neutral (though still uninviting) as she leads the way to the corner of the quarters occupied by a medical examination table. Metal and clinical, it has the air of undertaker about it, as per the doctor's general style. She might not be wearing her black hooded gown right now, but her slacks and long-sleeved shirt, even her boots, are in-keeping with her colour scheme of shadows.

Not compelled to be any closer, Jasyn stays where she is and watches as the doctor's brow battles irritation.

"I'm not stood over here for my own amusement." The doctor's voice is muffled by the black fabric mask covering the lower half of her face. She sighs, as if it's the worst inconvenience to have to actually explain what's going on. "I need to examine how your injuries have healed."

Jasyn must admit, her injuries have been rather too numerous of late. Being checked over by someone with the right knowledge, well... that sounds sensible. Her scowl relaxes, if only a little. "So long as 'medical examination' isn't code for sedating me against my will?"

The doctor looks away, perhaps pondering whether to feel bad. "It is not." She gestures for Jasyn to sit on the gurney. "Remove your shirt and vest," she instructs so matter of factly, Jasyn almost forgets to be bashful. "Unless you expect me to examine you with my imagination?"

Jasyn's jaw drops, because — *what the hail to say to that?*

That the doctor's eyes widen recategorises the moment from *possible flirtation* to *misjudged sarcasm.* Rather than being offended, Jasyn can't help chuckling to herself at the abrasive doctor's misfire. Serves her right for being so... *her*.

With a sigh, Jasyn reaches for her shirt buttons.

"Wait." The doctor clicks something on a nearby console and looks up at the overseer lens in the corner of the room as it blots out. "Don't want the helm watching in, do we?"

No. No, we don't. Why didn't she do that first? Is the doctor messing with her? Or did she really just forget?

"Do I get naked now? Or are there other overseers giving the crew a good view?"

"You're annoyed." The doctor squints as if the concept confuses her.

It looks like *stating the obvious* can be added to the doctor's skillset, accompanied by *being infuriating*. Jasyn's fingers fumble from indignation.

"Do you need me to show you how buttons work?"

At the doctor's irritation, Jasyn inwardly questions how many days in a closed environment together the two of them will be able to endure. Tracking down an impossible and mysterious power source might well be the simple part of this voyage.

"Don't worry," adds the doctor, inspecting her cuff that could be a time-piece. "I'm sure I can contain myself. Nothing I haven't seen before."

Was that the doctor's attempt at being reassuring?

With a huff, Jasyn unbuttons her shirt and pulls her vest over her head. *Best get this over with.* The doctor adjusts her face mask, her hands covered by black medi-gloves, as if Jasyn might be infectious.

Her gloved fingers hone in on the scarred tissue on Jasyn's shoulder. A bloom of pain pierces Jasyn's thoughts. That's where she'd been hit by the ice-spike from the military raid on the village, when Atalanta had shielded her from the projectile as best she could.

The doctor moves on to the blemished area between Jasyn's ribs where her own ice-sword had — with the Ice King's instance — sliced through her like a hot knife through snow. She flinches as her chest aches.

The doctor's eyes flit to hers. Probably about to scold her for daring to move a muscle. Jasyn reminds herself again that if it hadn't been for Doctor Orpheus, her body would still be ripped open, her life-force cascaded out of her. Atalanta and Tiphys, too. Somehow, with music, the doctor has returned them to life. Which, Jasyn begrudgingly admits, is really rather impressive.

She's about to thank her and ask a thousand questions on the topic (naturally!), when the doctor presses on her healed chest wound.

"*Heavens above.*"

A dull ache radiates through her like a full body period cramp. It's not as bad as when she'd first been retrieved from death, but, still...

"Considering the depth of the wound," the doctor breezes on as if she hadn't just made Jasyn curse, "it's healing well. There's scar tissue. It'll ache every now and then."

Depth of the wound? You mean *the sword that went right through me?*

"Like when someone pushes on it?" Jasyn asks, pointedly.

"You can put your shirts back on." The doctor turns away, perhaps to give the illusion of privacy.

Jasyn resists pointing out that she's already seen her half-naked. Instead, she wastes no time in pulling her vest back on. Being naked in front of someone so sullen and sarcastic is making her itchy.

"How did you do it?" Jasyn is genuinely curious and relieved to have finally unleashed one of her many questions. "How did you bring us back?" Bringing one person back is miracle enough. But three people? That has to be a mix of talent and magic, doesn't it?

Though, technically, Jasyn doesn't believe in magic...

The doctor sighs, as if she's been asked this question many times before and it's incredibly mundane for her to even consider. "I could tell you. But it'd take too long and you won't understand."

Jasyn frowns, but the doctor either pretends not to notice or just isn't interested as she makes notes on the rippling screen of her... cuff? ...time-piece? Annoyed eyes flit to her before returning to her wrist-tech.

"Have you noticed any side-effects since your return?" the doctor asks, as if the question is supposed to make sense.

"Return?"

The doctor's eyebrows raise as if she's accusing Jasyn of being simple. "From death."

Oh. "Side-effects?" Like speaking with her father who had died by the rifles of the warden general's military? Her father calling to Snowdrop, their claw-goat, who'd suffered the same end. Or like imagining a mountain bear as tall as a sky ship? Seeing silhouettes in the dark? Imagining her lost ice-sword calling to her?

"There are a range of death after-effects," says the doctor. "Headaches. Nausea. Cramping. Disorientation. Sensory disturbances."

Sensory disturbances? So... That's her answer? That's why she'd seen her father and Snowdrop? Though, why hadn't she seen her mother, too?

Jasyn nods, but gives nothing away. Her feelings around the 'disturbances' are real — the loss of her family, her village, aches and sears like a chest wound — but the actual manifestations have been benign. She self-diagnoses that it's nothing to worry about because she's hardly going to tell the doctor who tried to stick her with a syringe that she's hallucinating. Especially not when there's a quarantine chamber that could all too easily have her name on it.

"No. Nothing." Jasyn shrugs.

The doctor pauses, her fingers hovering mid-notation.

"As we were taking off, you mentioned seeing things, hearing things. You were..." The doctor makes brief eye contact. "...distressed."

Hail. She'd forgotten about that. She recalls the doctor being none too helpful at the time. Though, in her defence, an impromptu ship launch probably wasn't the best time for Jasyn's thousand questions under the suns.

"So your launch outburst was...?"

"Stress?"

The doctor offers a non-committal "hmmn," as she turns her back. She's saying something, but Jasyn isn't listening as the quarantine chamber grows larger in her awareness, its internal bars more prominent. The perfect location to house an unhinged ice-monger with inconsistent control over her abilities and a fraying hold on reality.

Keen to remove the focus from her mental state, Jasyn's about to ask about being a medician and how the life-restoring V-iolin works. But then the doctor turns, brandishing a glinting syringe and — without preamble — pierces her arm.

A flare of cold floods through her—

Blood emerges — crystalline — cracking the vial—

Muscles react—

Jasyn plants a punch square against the doctor's nose—

Her knuckles protest—

But the sting is overshadowed by a slamming burst of pain as the doctor plants a solid right hook against her jaw.

The syringe clatters to the floor.

They reel from each other.

"What the hail?" snaps Jasyn.

"Fuck's sake," scolds the doctor, glaring daggers.

6

SAMPLES

JASYN

"What kind of doctor punches their patient in the face?" Jasyn rubs her smarting jawline. The doctor clearly gives as good as she gets. *Good to know.*

"What kind of patient punches their doctor?" The doctor's voice is muffled through her medi-mask and the gloved hand cradling her nose. "I'm just taking a fucking blood sample. I literally just told you."

Oh. It's entirely possible Jasyn hadn't been listening...

Blood trickles down the doctor's chin. Where it meets the dark medi-mask, the fabric turns neon blue.

"Is your nose...?"

"It's fine." The doctor wipes her face with a decon-cloth and replaces her mask without fuss. "I suppose I've no need to get you ice for that?" Her glower targets Jasyn's bruised jaw.

Jasyn presses the ice thickened on her palms against her injury. Her palms ache with the chill. If the doctor didn't think her a liability before, she certainly does now. Jasyn grimaces. But she may as well put it to some use.

"Do you want me to...?" she asks, lifting her other hand, hazing ice. The doctor flinches, which is hint enough that she doesn't want Jasyn anywhere near her. She probably thinks she'll get carried away and give her frostbite or literal brain-freeze.

Jasyn takes the hint and stays within her own personal space. After what just happened, she can hardly blame the doctor for being on edge.

"You've had an ice-sword cut through your chest, what looks like a spear through your shoulder, and you react like *that* to a little needle?"

"Little needles look more than a little threatening when someone wields sedative against your will."

Doctor Orpheus scowls. It's difficult to decipher: it could be annoyance, or guilt, or something else entirely. "I see." Her words are less abrupt now, but Jasyn's wound too tight to find calm.

Her shaky breath hits the air in a plume.

With a wary eye on Jasyn, Doctor Orpheus collects the fallen vial, knives of blood straining at the glass. Jasyn hadn't expected her blood to turn to ice crystals. *Who does?* The doctor mutters "interesting," before placing the sample onto a small metal tray. "I was following orders."

"Do you do everything Captain Herakles tells you?"

The doctor scoffs.

Jasyn's not sure what to make of that, but before she can make head or tail of it, Doctor Orpheus sighs.

"Look. I can't force you to trust me. But I wouldn't be risking my life taking to the skies, going against an Ice King known to freeze dissidents from the inside out..." Jasyn's healing scar tissue aches at that, "...if I wasn't invested in this mission. Understanding your abilities is part of that. Figuring out the logistics of your hold over ice will help me, will help *us*, diffuse the Ice King's powers or battle against them. Unless you're a threat to others on this ship, it wouldn't serve me or the mission to do anything to your detriment."

Jasyn nods. The last thing she wants is to negatively impact people's lives... Perhaps it doesn't make sense to hold onto this grudge.

"Do you need an ice sample too?" Jasyn stretches her aching palms.

"That depends." The doctor narrows her eyes. "Does it involve punching me in the face?"

"There's one way to find out." Jasyn stifles a smile.

The doctor's eyes brighten, and Jasyn could swear she must be smiling beneath her mask, but as quick as the expression arrives, it departs like a cloud shrouding sunshine, and her usual scowl takes its place. Never mind figuring out her ice powers, how about deciphering the doctor?

Jasyn upturns her palms for the doctor to see, and the scowl is replaced by fascination as Doctor Orpheus cautiously leans in for a closer look.

A layer of inconsistent ice clings to Jasyn's palms. A haze drifts above, like an ice plain in a fog. The doctor inspects each palm and mutters words like "extraordinary" and "fascinating," and a few that aren't Iolcian but don't sound critical.

Then again, ice-devils had once been extraordinary and fascinating, before the extreme weather had almost decimated everything Jasyn knew and loved. Such superlatives are not necessarily a good thing.

"What are you expecting? Mutant snow?"

"You make the weather with your body. You create ice, seemingly out of nothing. It's not the most *usual* of skills."

"Neither is bringing people back from the dead with music."

The doctor's focus remains on her task. When it's clear she's not going to engage, Jasyn shrugs and continues:

"Weather and ice: it's a great party trick. Makes everyone

hate you." *Well, almost everyone.* Atalanta had never stared at her as though she were an anomaly.

"I'm sure that's just your winning personality."

The doctor's quip is so sudden, Jasyn doesn't know what to do with it. The doctor's eyes flit to hers, perhaps in apology, or perhaps trying to gauge her reaction, but either way she quickly returns to the safety of her scowl.

With the doctor's focus firmly on Jasyn's palms, Jasyn takes the opportunity to observe.

In the shadows of the death-tunnel back on Iolcus, she'd assumed at least ten sun-orbits between them, but now she's not sure. Perhaps Doctor Orpheus had just been tired, or aged up by her perpetual scowl. Her dark hair pulled back in a practical manner, Jasyn would guess preening isn't one of the doctor's priorities. But, judging from her medi-mask and gloves and repetitive use of a vial that Jasyn guesses holds disinfectant, hygiene clearly is.

There's already a blush of bruise forming at the bridge of her nose, tightening the knot of guilt in Jasyn's stomach.

"Can you heal that with your V-iolin?"

The doctor's eyes sparkle with interest as she scrapes palm-ice into a vial, and Jasyn can't decide whether she feels special, or like a frost-ant under a magnifying glass.

"Some things are best left to time." The response is somewhat more mysterious than necessary, in Jasyn's opinion. "Does it hurt?" The doctor nods to the residue of ice on Jasyn's palm. Her question could be perceived as caring, but is more likely medical curiosity.

"Sometimes. If it happens suddenly, it's sharp. And if I try to stop it, it aches."

The doctor nods, absorbing the information. "You reinforced the helm's apex with your ice."

Jasyn's palms haze at the memory of thickening air to ice to maintain the ship's barrier between them and the thrashing skies. Under the military's rifle fire, the splitting window had threatened to stop their journey before it'd even begun.

"Standard ice would have sublimated on launch... but yours has held. And yet, the ice on your palms is melting?"

"You didn't want *figuring me out* to be easy did you?" Oh, hail, why do half the things she says to the doctor emerge as an awkward flirtation? Jasyn clears her throat before adding, more serious: "I wish I could explain it." The questions of how she ticks and how what she does *works* has been troubling her her whole life. "Probably best if the ship engineers patch the apex with better understood materials."

She expects the doctor to say something sarcastic, but she only nods.

The promise of knowledge and the calmed nature of their conversation has Jasyn's palms drenched with melted ice. She wipes them on her trousers and for some reason mutters an apology, as if she's been caught with excessively clammy hands.

"From what I've seen so far," offers the doctor, "your ice-abilities are tied to your emotions." *No kidding.* Jasyn is tempted to offer a healthy dose of sarcasm herself, but refrains to keep the peace. "But I'm sure you've already figured that out." The crinkling at the corner of the doctor's eyes suggests she's smirking.

"To start studying your abilities," the doctor continues, more carefully, "I do need a better blood sample..." She reaches for a syringe, not turning her back this time. "Shall we try this again? And try to remember I'm the one with the sharp implements?"

7

SAFE IN THE SKIES

ATALANTA

It's been a few hours since Atalanta buckled, so she's almost convinced she can keep it together. All she has to do is keep moving, not look out the portholes, and not think about what happens when a sky ship critically malfunctions.

Joining Gus in assessing every aspect of the ship and working towards solving any issues is a good distraction. With each solution, Atalanta can breathe a little easier.

It's no mean feat, given that a ship like this isn't static. A pipe or connection might be functioning perfectly one moment, and then be blocked the next. Careful listening, along with guidance from Gus, enable her to precisely adjust the shuddering pipes in the hatch before her. In fact, now kitted out in standard issue astro-mechanic attire — a set of cerulean-grey overalls with a patch over the breast pocket with the AE of the Athena Enterprises insignia — Atalanta is hopeful she could be a functioning and useful part of the ship.

Though judging by Castor's withering glare as they pass each other in the corridor, she's not an entirely welcome one. *What's her problem?*

Still, Atalanta is pleased that she and Gus work well

together. The Chief Engineer seems to have no problem working in silence, though Atalanta can't decide if her silence is sombre, or concentrated. When necessary, Gus speaks up. But otherwise, she remains quiet and industrious. It's been a matter of hours, but they already work in sync, preempting the other's requirement for particular tools and passing them across without a word. It's perfect.

Well, as perfect as it can be when Atalanta's nerves are crackling with a constant, base level terror. At least their synchronicity and focusing on the task at hand provides a measure of calm. And the fawn's enthusiasm for being wherever Atalanta is provides a welcome distraction.

Perhaps he remembers it was her who saved him from Peleus's axe, back in the Iolcian Dead Woods. Perhaps he appreciates she's kept him safe ever since.

His tail wag propels him after Atalanta and Gus in winding through the ship. The metal grate stairs are a challenge for spindly fawn legs, but he perseveres and catches up. The way Gus glides through the wire-bulged corridors, no-one would guess her to be almost thirty sun-orbits Atalanta's senior.

A buzz rattles Atalanta's teeth as a nearby wall-light flashes green. Gus presses the intercom and lifts the receiver to her ear, but Atalanta can hear it anyway.

Not wanting to make a show of listening, she waits until Gus informs her of the doctor's request to see her in the medical quarters, and tells her she'll carry on here and keep an eye on the fawn. When the fawn tries to follow anyway, Gus shrugs and tells her: "I'm sure the doctor won't mind."

Atalanta's not sure what to make of that. She might have known the doctor hardly any time at all, but *not minding* doesn't sound like her. But, Gus knows the doctor better than she does, and the fawn is keen to follow.

Being summoned to the medical quarters likely has something to do with vomiting on the captain (and the doctor's boot). Equally, it could be because her heartbeat is intermittently attempting to punch through her eardrums and stress hormones are doing their damnedest to drown her.

As she makes her way down into the midriff of the ship, she pulls at her identity cuff. She doesn't want any fuss. She'd rather carry on suffering in silence, thank you. Or as close to silence as she can manage when her body is echoing even her own sounds back at her.

Footsteps in the shadows.

She tries to ignore them. They're not really there. They can't be, because real footsteps reverberate in their surroundings. These footsteps, they don't align. Besides, it's impossible for this particular shadow-figure to really be here.

It's the last thing she needs: the jarring sounds of the ship being joined by those of her frazzled mind. Not knowing whether their intent — if it's possible for an imaginary silhouette to have intent — is to protect or to haunt, their presence has Atalanta's skin breaking out in goosebumps.

Just like the headache throbbing behind her eyes, it should be endured until it goes away.

Approaching the medical quarters corridor, Jasyn's footsteps resound like a familiar knock on a den post. She's on the stairway, heading down. Probably back to the engine chamber. Atalanta is tempted to follow, but she doesn't want to keep Jasyn from her tasks. And, the quicker she gets her medical visit over and done with, the quicker she can get back to making sure the ship doesn't fold in on itself.

Still, she lets her auditory reach wash over Jasyn a moment longer, appreciating the contours of the person she's taken to the terrifying skies for. The thump of Jasyn's heart always has her own responding. Unusually, Jasyn's blood flows heavy around her left jawline. It sounds like swelling.

Atalanta frowns.

How did that happen?

She presses the intercom at the medical chamber entrance.

"YES?" The doctor's voice crackles loudly through the speakers. Atalanta winces as the sharpness needles her eardrums.

With no other way to respond, Atalanta raps on the door, not enjoying those sounds either. A sigh of annoyance catches her ears as the doctor's footsteps pound towards her.

The lock clicks. The *screech* of hinges as Doctor Orpheus swings the door open are about as welcoming as the doctor's: "What the fuck d'you think an intercom is—" She stops when she sees who it is. "Oh. Right."

She steps away, leaving the door open in invitation.

Hinges scrape as the door closes behind her, fraying Atalanta's nerves and tripping her focus to within a decorative plant on a shelf above the doctor's desk.

The percolating gurgle of a fly being digested within the trap of its pronged petals isn't something she'd wanted to hear. *Yuck.*

Atalanta observes the doctor with suspicion, because her nose suffers the same throb of swelling as Jasyn's jaw. It's unlikely to be coincidence...

As Jasyn's footsteps fade, so too does the erratic beat of the doctor's heart. *Is she afraid of Jasyn? Annoyed? Angry?* Whatever the doctor's scowl means, it softens when she sets sight on the fawn. Atalanta hadn't expected that. Nor does she expect the doctor to reach into her desk and produce a morsel of something: a treat.

The fawn's tail jiggles with joy as he accepts the offering.

Gus was right. The doctor can't be entirely grumpy and unapproachable if she's kind to animals, can she? Though there's the matter of Jasyn's injury, and Atalanta is unlikely to forgive the doctor for attempting to sedate Jasyn on take-off, so she remains suspicious, nonetheless.

Probably most people wouldn't notice the door locking. But to Atalanta's ears it's as clear as an arrow shot. At the click of the desk button, electrical signal sails along the embedded wire, down the table's leg, along the under-floor cabling and up into the door's casing before the mechanical latches bite into place.

Atalanta has never welcomed being contained. Being confined within the ship is bad enough.

The doctor pulls on her face-mask and gloves and gestures for her to head over to the gurney. While Atalanta's attention snags on every rivet of the portholes, assessing their integrity, she tries not to look at the shroud of darkness beyond. Nor the fast fading ice-planet and its green-hazed neighbour.

Finally, nudged by the doctor clearing her throat, Atalanta perches on the gurney.

"If you want to say something to me, you can write on this." Doctor Orpheus places an ice-tablet within her reach. "You were shot in the back," she says, matter of factly.

Sharpness and heat, bullets burst through —

Atalanta's memory coughs up the sensations. Her hand gravitates to her sternum. The bullets had punched the life from her and star-dappled oblivion had filled her, had drawn out time and tortured her with terror and lack of breath. Then a haunting song had grasped her with a firm grip. Gold had danced in the darkness and flames had flooded through her. Her own flesh had sizzled on a molecular level as her torn insides threaded themselves — impossibly, suddenly — back together.

That had been something.

Thanks to Doctor Orpheus — as medically and musically gifted as she is adept at scowling — Atalanta had escaped the drowning depths of death or space, the untethered tangle of her troubled mind. She should thank her, really.

She nods and writes THANK YOU on the ice-tablet. At the

doctor's perplexed scowl Atalanta adds: FOR SAVING MY LIFE. At that, the doctor simply grunts and waves away the idea.

"To check how you're healing, I need you to remove the top half of your overalls and any undershirts."

Atalanta has never been bashful about undressing. Probably because she's lived in the wilderness for most of her life. She'd always found it a little amusing that Jasyn would blush so profusely when she'd happen upon her swimming naked in the Glowing Woods lagoon. But now — perhaps because she and Jasyn have discovered physical intimacy together — it's strange to remove her clothes for someone else. Never mind her anxiety over her space being occupied by a stranger.

Hesitating will only prolong things, so she does as the doctor requests. The doctor's manner in examining her is no different than if she were inspecting an engine and its parts.

"You have an injury to your shoulder." It sounds both a statement and a question. Perhaps she's seen Jasyn's shoulder injury, the mirror image of her own. One injury likely isn't intriguing, two that are the same but opposite must tell a story.

She stays still as the doctor traces the outer edges of shined skin on her sternum, overlapping each other like the contours of a scruffily drawn map.

Sharpness and heat —

Atalanta flinches. Enough to startle the fawn into skittering on the spot and the doctor into leaping away and cursing a stream of words (*kèpfos-katàratos-keràstes!*) Atalanta hasn't heard before.

A stats monitor chirps, loud and insistent. There's no chance of hiding her stress from the doctor, is there?

"Are you going to punch me, too?" The doctor's fists are ready at her sides, the stance so natural Atalanta would guess she's won a few sparring matches in her time.

Atalanta does her best to apologise with her eyes and the

doctor seems to understand as her fists unclench and she returns to inspecting Atalanta's back. Her gloved hands trace the three points where the ice-bullets had entered.

Sudden. Stabbing. Searing.

The pressure against each scar pierces the memory of the pain through her, hot and angry and beyond her control. Atalanta steadies her breath and briefly closes her eyes to try to stop herself from flinching.

The doctor hands Atalanta's vest back to her and turns away. Atalanta takes the hint to get dressed.

"You've healed well," the doctor says as she makes notes on the device at her cuff and proceeds to ask her about any after-effects since her return from death. The doctor might have brought them back, but it's because of her they're on this voyage, which — Atalanta is fairly certain — is its own death sentence. It's just a matter of how and when. *The skies will find a way.*

When Atalanta denies any after-effects, she expects to be caught in her lie, and for some sort of lecture, but the doctor just nods. She clears her throat, which adds a certain gravity to her words:

"Jasyn doesn't know the full extent of what she can do, nor how to control it." She does her best to make eye contact but fails. "In time, I hope we can change that." She pauses, as if gauging Atalanta's reaction.

Atalanta nods, because yes, Jasyn confident in her abilities is what she wants for her. *Of course.*

"She trusts you," continues the doctor. "To look out for her, to keep her safe. And that's all I'm asking of you."

The doctor places a capped syringe within Atalanta's reach.

"It's nothing more than a sedative. I hope it's never needed. But if it is, she won't let anyone else close enough. We all saw what she's capable of in the arena." She tilts her head, ponderous. "Well, I suppose you didn't..."

That's right, Atalanta was mostly busy *being dead.*

Doctor Orpheus taps her fingers against her palm. A nervous habit? "When you were gone, Jasyn tore at the heavens. Her pain, it was... powerful."

The way her eyes have widened, Atalanta can't decide whether the doctor is impressed or daunted.

"I'm sure you can appreciate that in a closed environment, we have to be careful for the sake of everyone's safety, for the sake of the mission itself."

Atalanta inwardly nods. She can at least appreciate that.

"Should there be a figurative or literal storm, all I ask is that you help her find calm."

Atalanta considers scribbling on the ice-tablet her own selection of curse words, or that if Doctor Orpheus wants Jasyn on an even keel, perhaps those aboard could antagonise her a little less. But it's a lot of effort for likely little result.

Instead, she claims the syringe, slotting it into the pocket up her sleeve to keep it from others' hands, knowing the universe will have to freeze over before she ever considers using it.

8

MESS

JASYN

How is it possible for every muscle and bone to ache at the same time? Jasyn buries her frustration and ups her pace, not wanting to give Kalais in particular the satisfaction of her struggling to keep up as the two engine-techs stride towards the mess hall.

That they were able to down shovels and leave the engine chamber so swiftly once the captain summoned all crew, has Jasyn suspecting that there had been no need for her to be breaking her back shovelling without pause in the first place.

Helm crew are already at the mess hall's main table. First-mate Castor and Flight-tech Pollux are sprawled and slouching at one corner, with Cosmic Forecaster Lynk diagonally opposite, rubbing her eyes, free from goggles.

A porthole framing shimmering stars punctuates the far end of the table. *What a view.*

"Rolling in engine dirt again, Kalais?" Castor has a mischievous twinkle in her dark eyes as Kalais and Zetes claim the bench seats beside Lynk.

"Keeping sparkly clean at the helm, Castor?" Kalais fires back.

Are the barbs and buried smiles camaraderie, flirtation, or venom? *Hail.* Never mind figuring out her ice-abilities, or the doctor, the whole crew need their own instruction manual.

"Hey, Lynk," says Zetes, as he perches next to her.

"Hey, Zee." Lynk's smile seems to be her default setting.

As Jasyn's eyes lock with Castor's, the twinkle in Castor's eyes dies. At least she's not body checking her this time. Though that's either because there's a table in the way, or because they have an audience.

While Zetes and Pollux offer each other easy nods, Jasyn considers whether it'd be weird to draw a diagram to keep track of what each of the crew do aboard the ship, who they get along with, and who might have an inclination to push her out an airlock.

Yes, that would be weird. Useful, though.

"Someone show you what they really think of you, hey?" Castor's stomach-churning glare lands on Jasyn, turning to a smirk at her smarting jaw, swollen despite the iced palm she'd pressed to it.

Jasyn decides she doesn't at all like this woman. That can be noted on the figurative diagram, weird or not.

"Something like that," she mutters as she scans the seating options. Common sense should place her as far from Castor and Kalais as possible, but instead pride sees her opting for the seat at the head of the table, precisely in between the two.

"You can't sit there," Castor says through gritted teeth.

"You should move," agrees Kalais, but in a manner more detached.

Even Pollux and Zetes are frowning at her. The tension could be cut with a knife, which has Jasyn worrying she might be, too.

"What's happening?" asks Lynk, her blind eyes blinking, and Jasyn agrees with her perplexed sentiments entirely.

Zetes opens his mouth, but Castor gets there first: "Ice-monger thinks she rules the damn ship."

Kalais chuckles as she casually reaches for a bottle. Aware of her one-hand situation, Jasyn instinctively asks: "Want me to open that?"

Kalais eyes spark like reacting ribbons of ice-fuel as she pointedly uncaps the bottle by knocking the cap against the table edge with her stump in a smooth motion.

Jasyn tries not to squirm under the fiery-green stare. Her cheeks flame instead. She hadn't meant to patronise Kalais, she'd only wanted to help. Perhaps she shouldn't have assumed...

Pollux and Zetes watch with mild detachment, Castor with a mixture of amusement and disgust.

"Damn do-gooders," Kalais mumbles, as she pours herself and Zetes a drink, her flashing eyes more annoyed than anything else.

Jasyn doesn't expect her to pour her a drink, but she does fill a third cup. She braces for it being thrown in her face, but Kalais pushes it towards her. *A peace offering? Common decency?*

"Keep it up, if you want a matching set," Kalais threatens with a light slap to Jasyn's bruised jaw. It smarts in protest, made worse by her blushing, no doubt.

Just as Jasyn is considering whether to retaliate, explain, or walk herself to an airlock, Doctor Orpheus swaggers in with a sigh, not unlike when Jasyn was a teenager and had been told she must eat dinner at the table. Without breaking her stride, the doctor's eyes sweep across Jasyn and states, "That's the captain's chair," before heading to the far end of the table.

"Oh," is all Jasyn can think to say. They could have told her. It hadn't occurred to Jasyn that the chair has any authority about it. *It's a chair.*

If only Atalanta were here, they could share *a look* about all this.

"There's a seat beside me." Lynk's voice is so chipper Jasyn wonders whether she's meant to be part of *this crew.* In fact, it's an apt question, because — as the Iolcian Meteorological and Cosmic Forecaster — Lynk had been the one spouting lies to the citizens of Iolcus about the trajectory of Corinth, even calling it a planet when it's a moon. Jasyn wants to ask about that. And particularly how Doctor Orpheus, a Corinthian, feels about that.

But it's unlikely a comfortable question. Perhaps one for when she has a more solid grounding. For now, grateful for the invite, Jasyn takes Lynk up on her offer, while the doctor settles into the seat opposite.

"Damn." A smile curls Castor's lips, her eyes flitting between Jasyn and the doctor. "You two look like you've gone ten rounds in the arena." The doctor's bruised nose is more purple now.

"I'd have paid to see that," adds Kalais with a raised eyebrow, which is either ill-wishes or innuendo.

The doctor grumbles and mutters swear words Jasyn doesn't recognise. Castor and Kalais seem to accept that as a valid response.

"Friendly crew," Jasyn mutters to herself.

"Yes," beams Lynk, her smile so genuine Jasyn could almost be convinced Lynk must be right and Jasyn must have misunderstood every barbed comment and body check. "So..." Lynk pauses and angles away from the table to sneeze into the crook of her arm, muttering something about "damned allergies," before asking: "What's your favourite weather?" It's either some masterfully veiled dig, or the instinctive conversation of a merry meteorological and cosmic forecaster.

"Um..." Before Jasyn can think of a response, Lynk is already telling her that she loves all types of weather, and is particularly thrilled to share her top five cloud formations. Her top being cumulonimbus clouds and any weather that produces a good rainbow.

While the crew chatter amongst themselves, and Lynk chatters at her, Jasyn steals a glance at Doctor Orpheus and her darkening bruise. Not wanting to be caught staring, she considers the contents of her cup. The liquid is thicker than she expected, and warm, with a flavour combination of berries and mint with a metallic and bitter tang. It's not unpleasant exactly, but it is odd.

"What is this drink?" Jasyn asks, and Lynk takes a moment to realise she's been interrupted. She doesn't seem to mind.

"Vita-milk," says Lynk. "Full of vitamins. It also cleans your teeth."

Jasyn runs her tongue along her teeth. They are fresher.

With Lynk being the first person on this ship to actively volunteer information, Jasyn asks a selection of follow-up questions, including: *What's it made from? How is it made? Why does it taste like metal? etc.* — only for Lynk's answers to be interrupted by Castor scoffing as she asks Kalais:

"Does she ever stop with the questions?"

Jasyn's face burns again, more-so when she notices the doctor watching her with a curious expression. *Hail.* Is Lynk the only person at this table Jasyn isn't annoying?

An excitable young voice precedes the arrival of Tiphys with Hylas, the former telling a kindly smiling and politely nodding Hylas about how sky maps work (even though this isn't Hylas's first stint to the skies). The boy quietens when they enter the mess hall and he claims the seat beside the doctor. Hylas claims the one by Jasyn.

"Evening, all," says Hylas in his affable way, and receives raised cups and nods in response.

"What is *that* doing in here?" says Pollux, as the fawn trots into the room, ears twitching as he sniffs at the air and observes them all. He about-turns and retreats until Atalanta accompanies him, the fawn practically leaning against her knee.

Hail, that's cute.

When Jasyn's focus traces up from the fawn to Atalanta kitted out in ship-tech overalls and a tool belt slung about her hips, her pulse picks up. Because, *hail, that's hot.*

Atalanta must notice Jasyn's elevated heart rate or the breath caught in her throat, or understand the quirk of her eyebrow, because when their eyes lock, there's a definite *something* in the way her eyes narrow and her mouth twitches into an almost-smile.

That *mischievous Atalanta smile* has Jasyn's thoughts leaping back in time to what the two of them had accomplished in the darkness of the sky ship workshop: hands, fingers, mouths, tongues, all seeking to know more of each other. If they were alone right now, Jasyn would reach across the table, draw Atalanta to her, invite those overall buttons open, and —

Doctor Orpheus clears her throat, bringing Jasyn back to reality. She must have been staring, or, worse, *ogling*. Atalanta buries her smile as she settles in the seat opposite. Her shoulders aren't so raised now. Working on the ship must be calming her.

That's something.

The doctor clears her throat again. This time, it's Tiphys who's staring in open mouthed wonder at Atalanta. He, too, is blushing. Jasyn narrows her eyes. *Oh yeah.* She'd forgotten about his little crush.

When the entire table stand, Jasyn lags behind. The cause is, apparently, Captain Herakles striding in with the kind of confidence that must have paved her way to occupying the captain's chair. Standing for the captain. Okay. That's apparently something they do.

There's been a costume change for the gladiator-captain,

who's now making slate-grey breeches and a midnight blue waistcoat with silver buttons and detailing look good. Her light grey shirt is unlaced at the collar and her sleeves are rolled up, enough to reveal the tattoos winding around her forearms. They must have been covered by her brace-armour in the arena.

Jasyn squints to try to decipher the intricate designs. Are they purposeful or just decorative? Either way, they're about as distracting as the captain herself, and Jasyn reminds herself — before the doctor is compelled to cough again — it's rude to stare.

Keeping pace at Herakles's side, Gus is demonstrating something on her ice-tablet. They're both muttering and nodding, probably solving ongoing ship issues or summarising things that need attention.

"Looking sharp, Captain," says Pollux.

"Yes, well..." Herakles's gaze snags on Atalanta. "A change was necessary."

Atalanta's cheeks colour at that.

And that's something more distracting than the captain. Because... *What's that about?*

Tension. There's definite tension in Atalanta's posture, her jaw. Is she just embarrassed about puking on the captain? Or is it something else?

Something like panic fizzes low in Jasyn's stomach.

Waving for the crew to take their seats, the captain claims hers at the head of table. Kalais automatically shuffles over to make space for Gus to sit beside the captain. On the other side of the captain, Castor sits a little straighter in her seat.

Herakles's alert eyes sweep over the crew, lingering on Jasyn before glaring at Kalais. "*Hail*, Kalais. What did you do?"

Kalais snorts — a mix of unimpressed and offended. Holding Kalais's glare, Herakles runs her hand through her sculpted hair, her mighty impressive bicep flexing as she rubs the back of her neck.

Yeah, if Atalanta has a crush on the captain, it's not hard to see why. But never mind that. There's something simmering between Kalais and the captain, but *hail* if Jasyn knows what. Reciprocal resentment?

Heavens. This crew.

"Yeah, no. That was me," says Doctor Orpheus, raising her hand.

Herakles's eyes widen at the doctor's bruised state. The doctor merely peers into her mug, shrugging the situation away. "It's not a thing. Do your updates, or whatever."

The captain looks between Jasyn and the doctor before obviously deciding it's not something worth pursuing.

"Okay." Herakles clears her throat. "I'm sure you'll all agree this has been one long night." Mumbles around the table confirm. Is it still night when they're not *under a sky* but *in it*...? "You'll all be pleased to know we have enough food to sustain us for the planned duration of our voyage."

Several of the well-seasoned crew cheer, followed by the doctor's "thank fuck for that."

"It's not news to you," continues the captain, turning more sombre, "that in rushing to the skies, all of us have left part of ourselves behind..."

The crew quieten down. Jasyn's thoughts turn to Gus and her husband, their children. Who and what else have this crew left behind?

"Sailing the skies is not a quick fix. There will be time to adjust our plans as needed. We also need to understand why we're in this situation, of course: why we were forced to the skies ahead of schedule. How the Ice King's military found us... But for now, we take a breath."

And that is exactly what several of the crew do. The captain lets the moment stretch, as if she herself is taking her first breath in the longest time.

"Now that the ship's ticking over, we'll start adjusting to flight routines. Once we're done here, we'll have skeletal crew watching over each station to allow rest and recovery. For those of you new to the skies, we'll be following the Circadian Rhythm. Day and Night cycles will be tailored to each of you via your I.D.s or cuffs. Meals will be every twelve Iolcian hours. Your cuffs will let you know where to be. When you should be sleeping, stick to sleep quarters —"

Captain Herakles stops, because the fawn has chosen this precise moment to charge the length of the mess hall and headbutt her just below the knee. His exuberance is so ineffectual, the wall of Herakles so unmoving, all the fawn can do is topple to the floor and shake off the fall.

Stifled laughs around the table are punctuated by Kalais's more open laughter.

"I think we found our saboteur." Kalais wipes away her laughter-tears.

"Think he's trying to tell you something, Captain?" asks the doctor, grinning into her cup.

The fawn's interjection has at least broken the tension.

"Keep that up and you'll be on the menu," says Herakles, peering down at the creature. Her words contain amusement rather than threat. "Anyway. Before I get a mild bruise..." She turns to the table, her final words on the matter: "Follow the Rhythm and we won't have a problem."

She claims her cup and sinks back into her chair.

"So, Captain... Did you lure us to the mess hall under false pretences?" Kalais pauses for dramatic effect, meeting the captain's questioning eye. "I personally only obeyed thinking there'd be food involved."

Herakles smirks. As if on cue, Peleus trots out from the

adjoining chamber, his flat hair stuck to his sweaty forehead, lugging a massive metal bowl. His half-untucked shirt and the mixture of alertness and exhaustion in his eyes suggests he's perhaps wrestled an epic beast and only just survived.

"Ta-da!" he says, as he heaves the vat and ladle to the middle of the table.

Pollux takes the lead in serving, passing each bowl along until they all have their own supply of unappetising grey-green gruel.

Peleus claims the remaining bench seat between Pollux and Atalanta, as he says to no-one in particular: "Food pouches have no instructions."

Tiphys prods the food as it it might bite him, earning him dagger eyes from Peleus. *Great. There's a reciprocal grudge that keeps on giving.*

"As ship doctor, I'm not sure I can condone the consumption of whatever this is," says Doctor Orpheus, and Jasyn *thinks* she's joking. She must be, because she doesn't hesitate to dig into the culinary nightmare.

Jasyn and the rest of the crew follow suit. The reconstituted mush is too bland to be an assault on the senses. It's not a delight, but it's not terrible either. Even the fawn devours his portion from the bowl the doctor places on the floor for him.

That Doctor Orpheus would think to feed the creature surprises Jasyn. She doesn't exactly give off caring, empathetic vibes. More likely she's just trying to fatten him up...

Either way, the fawn snuffle-snorts his way through the meal, his mouth chomping in an odd sideways motion as he raises his head at intervals to observe everything around him.

For a while, the crew focus only on their food and drink. With Atalanta's serious expression trained on her food, Jasyn seeks out her foot beneath the table. When the doctor's scowling attention swerves to her instead, it's clearer than ice is cold she's misjudged her foot's trajectory.

Withering under the doctor's glare, Jasyn concentrates on her bowl.

This is going to be a long voyage.

9

ARROWS IN OUTER SPACE

ATALANTA

The ship's diagnostics are functioning more consistently now. There are things to be seen to — *so many things* — but nothing imminent. Which means, according to Gus, having a meal with the rest of the crew won't be the end of the world. Or, in this case, *the ship.*

But Atalanta's not so sure. Ship issues aside, she's never even been in a room with this many people at once. Back in the village, she'd even avoided dinners at Jasyn's house where there would've only been, apart from Jasyn, two other people and one claw-goat.

Twelve other people and one fawn is a lot.

Gurgle-growl-waahhrrrr. Stomachs are starting to digest, which adds a whole other level of sound to filter out. At the far end of the table, Gus is telling Captain Herakles:

"Vole-rats are occupying every hidden gap within the ship, outnumbering the crew by at least one hundred to one. But it's not something to be too worried about."

Atalanta's own stomach gurgles protest.

"Thanks to their dexterous noses and inbuilt barometers for survival," the doctor raises her voice across the table, "they seldom chew through wires or cause havoc with electrics." *Good to know.* "The main threat is that they become so numerous they start to block pipes. But they're carnivorous, and they mainly keep their own population in check."

Yuck. Atalanta's not certain she'll be able to keep her dinner down.

"Why don't they eat us instead of each other?" asks Tiphys, as if that weren't a harrowing concept.

"They're territorial," the doctor replies, "but people were on this ship first, so they don't see it as their hunting ground."

Still, the idea that there are so many of the creatures on board... Atalanta's skin prickles with discomfort. Of course going to the skies — one of her worst nightmares — would involve a mass of hitch-hikers that also feature in her nightmares. She's experienced first hand what vole-rats can achieve when hungry. It's not something she wants to encounter again.

Their squeaks echoing within the cavities of the ship, the constant scratching and pitter-patter of tiny claws against metal, needle her tired brain. It's all making the mess hall conversations difficult to follow and her own sanity a challenge to maintain.

Along the table, Peleus is saying something... complaining about the lack of knives in the kitchen and being parted from his axe-knives. Pollux's matter of fact response centres around "a blade not caring whose hand it's in when it causes harm," and Castor backs him up: "voyages like this can do strange things to the sanest of minds," and that it's "best if the sharp objects are locked away."

Peleus grunts before scooping food into his face. He probably thought the two athletes would've agreed with him.

Zetes and Lynk (between the latter's Transonic-*screeching* sneezes) are talking in-depth about the use of weather to parallel emotions in fictional works and when and how it can be effective. Every now and then, they make an effort to include Jasyn in the discussion. Though once Lynk and Zetes get animated about something, it's difficult to get a word in edgeways. Lynk in particular has a habit of talking over people, though she does with such a smile it can only be accidental.

Jasyn's bruised jaw and the doctor's bruised nose are both loud with the *thump-thump-thump* of blood flow; their bodies working to heal. Observing rather than engaging, Jasyn's enthusiasm seems as bruised as her jaw. Atalanta's chest aches at seeing her so subdued.

Tiphys is now exuberantly telling Atalanta, Doctor Orpheus and Hylas something about his father being "a noble explorer" and how he was meant to be called Agnius, after his father, but his mother preferred Tiphys. Hylas is his usual polite, kind-eyed self. And the doctor, despite her default gruff setting, seems to nod in the right places, and if she's exasperated by the boy, she doesn't show it.

Gus exudes a certain serenity, while Kalais jerks from conversation to conversation, laughing and joking perhaps a little too much.

Another pulse of healing draws Atalanta's Transonic gaze directly through the captain's chest. Or, more precisely, beneath her left shoulder blade, just beneath the left lapel of her waistcoat. A repeating whoosh pinpoints a recent injury. She hadn't noticed that before. It's small, and not too deep: perhaps a bullet graze. Did she get nicked when they were loading the ship?

The fabric fibres sighing as they stretch across the captain's admittedly impressive shoulders is distracting. Almost as much as the uptick in Atalanta's own heart rate.

Only when the captain's heart stutters does Atalanta tune in to the fact that she's staring. And not only that, Herakles is staring back.

Before she can question why, Hylas is signing to her, so she tries to block out everything else. He's signing something banal about the food and asking what she thinks. People do this, she is aware, as an avenue into a conversation. It's never been one of her strong suits. In fact, it takes her so much mental energy to tackle small talk, it's rarely worth it. She certainly hasn't the energy right now, but she does want to know:

"How do you know my language?"

Like her mother before her, Atalanta had been born to silence. Her auditory capabilities had only unfurled when augmented by the sliver of a Transonic — its formation not unlike electric lava-veins through smooth volcanic rock, latched behind her ear when she was too young to count sun-orbits as a measure of age. Apart from her parents, apart from Jasyn — who she taught — Atalanta has never met anyone else who can form the shapes of her language. That Interplanetary Translator Hylas is signing intrigues and unsettles her.

"I'm not fluent, I admit," signs Hylas. "But when I crossed paths with someone from your home world, they were kind enough to teach me."

Home world is a strange term for somewhere she's never even been...

"What world is that?" The question is given shape before she can stop herself. She'd been raised not to be curious about this topic. And the tension of her upbringing remains.

The look Hylas offers is one of curiosity. *You don't know your own planet?* But she's not going to tell this new acquaintance, no matter how personable, anything of her past. Not only can other people not be trusted, it wouldn't be right to answer his questions when she's evaded so many of Jasyn's over the fourteen sun-orbits they've known each other.

Jasyn — who's currently doing her best to not stare at their conversation, no doubt a thousand questions held on her tongue.

"Arcadia," Hylas signs, and it's not a word she's seen before. At her puzzled expression, he shapes the word more slowly.

Her parents' evasiveness about their past led Atalanta to surmise early on that they hadn't taken to the skies for fun. No-one invites a lengthy voyage in an escape raft for *fun*. She wishes she'd had the foresight to press her parents on *what* they were escaping. It's been a source of gnawing regret for her ever since. She was brought up not to dwell on the past. But, in losing her mother, she'd lost her link to their hidden history. Where they were from. What their origin world was like. Why they had left. Before losing her, she hadn't considered there would be a time she would no longer be able to ask.

"What's it like, Arcadia?" she signs, trepidatious.

The incessant chatter of the mess hall crew assaults her senses. Each hack of laughter scrapes past her ears. All the cranking machinations of the ship seek her out. Each sound taking a detour through the shell of the ship, tying itself in knots before returning to her ears.

The *flutter* of rodents roaming, air filtration *hissing*, percolating ice *fizzing* up from the engine chamber. It all churns her thoughts.

She tries to concentrate on what he's signing, but discomfort seeps into her gut. She has so many questions, but questions result in answers. Knowledge can be all kinds of good, but good or bad, it can never be undone.

Her legs itch to be elsewhere. She stands, knocking the table. Jasyn's eyes flash with worry. Hylas arches his brow in concern.

"Refills are needed," announces Zetes in a jovial manner that has Atalanta suspecting some of the cups might be filled with fermented fruit. Or, it could just be the intoxicating relief of not being torn from the skies. "Someone needs to go to the cargo hold."

"Perhaps that someone is you, Zetes," suggests Castor with a flirtatious smile that has him gulping and his heart skipping. Each thump hits Atalanta right in the skull.

Kalais rolls her eyes.

"I'll go," signs Atalanta, claiming the jug from Zetes.

Jasyn looks like she'll go with her, but Lynk has her locked in an enthusiastic, if one-sided, discussion about cloud composition. Atalanta gestures:

"I'll be back soon. Don't worry."

Jasyn's nod is reluctant, but Atalanta manages a *Really, I'm fine* smile. The fawn hazards to his spindly legs to follow, but Atalanta gestures for him to stay too.

Someone cheers "points for volunteering," but Atalanta doesn't look back to find out who. In need of a break, she closes her Transonics as the gentle pulse of colour coded lights leads her down into the depths of the ship.

Finally, she can breathe...

Being trapped with a bunch of strangers on a sky ship wading through the endless skies is hardly her idea of fun.

In the intermittent darkness of the ship's tunnel-like corridors, a silhouette haunts the periphery of her vision, darting from shadow to shadow with fluid grace. She can sense it. She can even picture the bow-wielding shape, the Transonic on show like a firefly in the dark. Its presence aches like an old injury.

She doesn't dare give the silhouette a name, because to do so would be to give it power over her. And that way danger lies.

It's just a lingering after-effect of her dalliance with death, she reminds herself. It's nothing to be afraid of. Though, her knotted stomach doesn't appear to be entirely in agreement.

Tap-tap—

Atalanta's insides clench.

Refusing to look at the portholes, she knows the sound. The

sound that should not be here. Nor should any sound be heard with her Transonics closed.

Tap-tap-t-tap—

She knows what it is. Can picture it as clearly as a bad dream. The arrow pinging off the porthole glass like the discarded toothpick of a giant. Without even a glance, she knows the arrow is tethered to twine, coiling about the nothingness of space like a lost serpent looking to bite.

Tap-tap-t-tap—

It's not there. Not really. It can only be the twine of her mind, tying her in knots. Like the silhouette following her, it can only be a conjuring of imagination, a memory tapping at the porthole of her mind.

Arrows don't drift in outer space.

She shakes her head in an attempt to be free of her delusions. Can't she have a moment's peace? Blocking out sound isn't enough? Her mind has to conjure sounds to haunt her, too?

Breathe in... Breathe out...

Arriving at the airlock entrance to the cargo hold, Atalanta hesitates. It makes sense that a door like this would be locked. She reaches for the keypad but her cuff lights up and so too does the keypad. It unlocks with a *thunk*. Guess she has permission, then.

She hitches open the sturdy metal drawbar, closing the door behind her before heading along the airlock tunnel. Once through the secondary door and into the hold, awareness that the emptiness of space is only one hatch away trips her heart rate.

Breathe.... Just breathe...

Spotlit by the illumination from the tunnel's inner porthole, the hold's floor-hatch takes centre stage amongst the shadows. She be giving the porthole a wide berth. She has no desire to stare into the depths of space, nor to have it stare back.

She seeks out an illumination switch, and light floods the hold. Vehicles, similar to the ice-engine bi-ice-cycle Gus impressed them with when rescuing them from the hungry hoard back in the Ice City, are anchored to the floor and walls by netting. These ones, though, have paintwork more overtly in line with the Iolcian colour scheme of blue, white and grey and the shaped AE logo of Athena Enterprises. The surfaces aren't chipped, but the vehicles look tarnished, exhausted, as if they've been waiting to perform their function for too long.

Similar vehicles sport three rather than two wheels. One at the front, two at the back. The markings on their rear chassis suggest them capable of unfurling a trailer of some sort. She can't help being a little fascinated by how the machines work, but that's not what she's here for. The crew will be getting thirsty.

But before she can get a good look at how far the chamber extends, the lights dim.

She tries the illumination switch but that only has the option of *off* or *dim*. She's one step away from removing wall panelling and tackling some rewiring when her cuff bleeps. A simplistic depiction of an arrow illuminates beneath the surface of the band. *What does that mean?*

Its timing would suggest it has something to do with the lighting. There must be some sort of override, but now's not the time to be toying with an item that's clamped about her pulse point, nor mysterious wall switches one hold-hatch away from an ocean of emptiness.

Her eyes adjust to the half-light, to the room's maze of hastily loaded crates, to the winged vehicles that she can only assume, by their design, are for exploring skies rather than terrain. Life rafts, perhaps?

It's so easy to get distracted deciphering the components and purpose of machines. In amongst the shapes and shadows, a selection of crates are branded with a semi-circle. It's the same symbol that marks the mess hall entryway. At a guess, these are the right crates.

With just enough glow from the corridor's porthole and the dimmed lights to see by, she lifts the lid and rifles through. The drinks pouches aren't labelled with words, but with droplet symbols in different colours. What will 'blue' flavour taste like? Its vibrancy puts her in mind of the captain's neon hair.

And on that topic...

Why *does* the captain keep staring at her? It's kind of pissing her off. If she's never seen Transonics before, she could at least hide her curiosity better. She'd have assumed a sky ship captain, a *hero of the skies* no less, would be better at concealing such ignorance.

Atalanta's parents were both departed by the time she was twelve Iolcian sun-orbits old, and even she knows it's rude to stare.

Though, she might have to admit to the crime herself...

Unwilling to go down that vole-rat burrow, she digs through the crate for the other flavour options. She doesn't hear the voice, she only sees the hand reaching from the shadows—

10

TREMORS

JASYN

The irony that Jasyn has had her sights set on the skies her whole life and is proving to be as useful as a crumbling sky ship, is not lost on her. At no point in her star-gazing had she considered being elbows deep in suds and water that keep cooling at her touch. *She can't even get the washing up right.*

The doctor had been the first to escape the table, followed by Gus and the captain, leaving the rest of them to socialise until the Circadian Rhythms kick in. *Whatever that looks like.*

Castor had kindly declared her vote that "the ice-monger does the washing up," and the remaining crew had cheered their agreement, almost disguising Kalais's mutterings about it being "the only thing she can be trusted with."

Well, at least she's getting cheered on for something.

While battling grease that won't shift in the cooled water, Jasyn tries not to think about how she's hardly on course for making the universe a better place, and instead observes the remaining crew through the galley hatch. A hatch that seems purposefully designed to highlight how she's separate, on the outside looking in.

At least Atalanta is being useful. Jasyn hadn't considered

how in-tune with the mechanisms of the ship she would be. She should have guessed. Atalanta has always been good with materials and engineering.

Speaking of which... *Where is Atalanta?*

The engine-techs and flight-techs are asking the same question, but their concern is more centred around their lack of drinks.

The lights tremor, undulating from dim to bright and back again, as if the ship itself is gripped in the tendrils of a migraine. The Circadian Rhythms are kicking in, according to Hylas who stops by the hatch to tell her as much.

According to him, if you have two or more people on opposing schedules (Day and Night shifts respectively) in the same ship-space, the result is lighting that's intent on being both on and off. Though apparently the tremors aren't usual, but likely the result of a ship in need of attention.

Hylas encourages her to check her cuff for what she's expected to be *doing*. Her cuff has a simple, angular depiction of a pair of wings. The design seems to be a simplified version of the tattoos the engine-techs have been mesmerising her with. Well, she's not sure what to do with that information...

"You're on Day shift," explains Hylas. "That's the symbol for the engine chamber."

Oh good. Because Jasyn has no desire to be *doing* either of the engine-techs. But, also, *really?* Because she could do with whatever the symbol for bunks and sleep might be.

Epic sigh.

Others, according to the symbols lit up on their cuffs or under the flesh between their thumb and forefinger, have a downward arrow — *wind-down*, apparently — followed by two dots signifying the Iolcian moons. That's the Night schedule.

The idea of staying awake for even another few hours has Jasyn fighting a yawn. It's not as though she's gotten much rest since being brought back to life. A few hours, at most. Atalanta is partially to thank for that, but before Jasyn can soothe her budding headache with amorous thoughts, the mess hall illuminates as the captain strides in. The room dims to half-light and repeats.

Herakles observes the lighting fluctuations and mutters something about Gus needing to sort that out, before turning her attention to the rest of them.

"Those of you scheduled to *Night* need to head to the bunks." She folds her arms. "Old timers know this and should be setting a better example." She aims her words at Castor, Pollux, Kalais and Zetes in particular.

"What?" says Kalais, "and miss an opportunity for you to fold your arms?" She winks at the captain, but seems to be taking the order, standing and checking the cuff on her left wrist. She mutters a few swear words at what she sees, while Zetes claims victory at it being his turn to sleep.

Kalais lets a glower settle in Jasyn's direction and Jasyn swallows, hard. Is there anything either of them want less than spending more time together? Jasyn fully expects her sky voyage to be ended by a quick shove and the jaws of an ice-furnace.

"Come on, Snowflake." Kalais doesn't look back as she heads for the door. "You've got shovelling to do."

A tickle of something familiar burrows into Jasyn's thoughts...

A breeze... A song... That whisper...

Its sudden interruption has her vision swaying. She rubs her temples. It's just a trick of her mind, brought on by one of many causes. Recovering from death... The stress of a military attack and a subsequent rush towards the stars... Lynk's excessive talk of weather fronts... A migraine from the tantrum of lighting...

The breeze becomes a gale... The song a lyrical scream... The whisper a shout...

Jasyn grips the sink edge as a mix of hot and cold burns through her veins. Her insides quake. Her heart climbs into her throat. Her stomach free falls. Water crackles to ice. Hazes to steam.

In the mess hall, the lift doors scrape open and *the breeze, the song, the whisper,* all disappear as fast as mist in the wake of an ice-devil. Did the room get smaller? Did her knees grow weaker?

Shocked silence chokes the room as they all observe the impossible.

"Why is everyone's stress spiking?" asks Doctor Orpheus, swaggering into the mess hall before following the stares aimed at the open lift. Her scowl soars in surprise.

"Fuck me, it's the Ice Princess."

PART II

SHIPWRECK

11

STOWAWAY

ATALANTA

A lift journey, a corridor, an airlock tunnel and a cargo hold earlier...

"Watch out." Those are the signed words that form at the periphery of Atalanta's vision. She's ready to dismiss them as an echo of her tired and unspooling mind, but the wall-shadow before her has thickened.

A reaching hand—

Atalanta whips around, elbow raised. The strike is solid. Enough that her own forearm protests.

Her assailant stumbles back.

On instinct, Atalanta's left hand flexes, her right reaches over her shoulder — but she's not carrying a bow, and her quiver of arrows has been lost to the Iolcian scrap heap.

Her eyes comb the gloom, deciphering the new and imposing silhouette. In spite of the cape that blends her attacker with the shadows, the long blonde hair sparkling like frost gives her form. The flash of white shirt buttoned up but for a V at her neck frames the skull-quartz pendant. Eyes so blue they could be a glacial crevasse threaten to swallow any trusting traveller.

All details confirm her attacker to be none other than the Ice Princess.

Atalanta's heart rate sails to the stars. *How did she get here? What does she want?*

Atalanta refuses to be fooled by pleading eyes. She'll not sympathise or feel guilt for the perforation at the bridge of her nose and the blood spilling from nostrils. She will not be tricked by the hands raised in retreat.

With pliers from her tool belt, she lunges.

A well-timed knock to her wrist casts the makeshift weapon into the shadows. She grasps a screwdriver next, wielding it dagger-like. The *Gladiator* Princess disarms her next strike with similar efficiency.

Heart hammering, breaths tripping, Atalanta lunges again, foregoing any weapons.

The Ice Princess sidesteps. Instead of grappling, she puts distance between them, rounding the labyrinth of supply crates, making a break for the airlock tunnel.

Don't let her loose in the ship...

Three strides and Atalanta grasps the princess's cape, her long hair, too, and tugs, sweeping her off her feet, landing her on her back. Though she can't hear the *oof* from the fall, that the Ice Princess is still lying there would suggest she's at least a little winded.

She recovers quickly, though she hazards to her feet with less finesse than Atalanta expects from the royal athlete whose murderous reputation very much precedes her.

As the Ice Princess wipes her bloody nose on the back of her hand, with her features hidden by crate shadows, it's difficult to discern the level of glower being aimed Atalanta's way.

She must have lead the assault on their ship. As Warden General of the Iolcian Guard, she could've orchestrated it from afar, but here she is, in the thick of things, creating chaos first-hand. Though how she managed to get into the cargo hold before they took flight, Atalanta cannot fathom.

The Ice Princess stumbles for the airlock again. The decorative metal swirls of her scabbard catch the light.

If she touches her ice-sword, none of us will stand a chance...

Clamping arms about torso, Atalanta tackles her from behind. Solid, strong, and warm. Though she knows the Ice Princess isn't actually made of ice, she hadn't expected *warm.*

"Go for the back of the knee," suggests the silent silhouette at the edge of her vision and Atalanta rolls her eyes, because she was *just about to do that.*

Buckling her at the knees, Atalanta wrestles the thrashing ice royal to the floor, pinning her with the length of her body. Despite having grabbed her from behind, her insistent squirming somehow has them face to face.

Atalanta's thighs have the princess's hips pinned. Her hands anchor her wrists by her head. And her forearms press against her clavicle, leaving her neck inches from the deadly princess...

Hail, I hope she's not a biter...

Though she shifts, the ice royal's resistance isn't as strong as Atalanta expects. She should be better than this. She should be *winning.*

Perhaps the cargo hold hadn't been properly pressurised on take-off and she's still suffering the consequences. Perhaps that's why she hasn't reached for her ice-sword. Or perhaps even an Ice Princess is wise enough not to toy with the elements when there's only a few layers of metal between herself and the stars.

"Or perhaps she's toying with you so you'll drop your guard..." Atalanta's not sure whether the thought is her own, or the words of the silent silhouette.

The Ice Princess's mouth is moving. She's saying something, but Atalanta has no idea what. And she's not about to give up her superior position to open her Transonics. It'll only be sour words and trickery anyway.

Sweat prickles at the nape of her neck. She can't maintain this hold forever. The exertion of attempting to make herself heavier than she is has her pulse knocking the inside of her eardrums.

The angry wound across the Ice Princess's throat jolts Atalanta's thoughts back to the confrontation in The Games arena. *Jasyn vs the Gladiator Princess.* From Jasyn's contact, the ice had crept up her throat in lightning formation. Jasyn could have killed her — Atalanta was convinced she would — but chose not to.

Would the Ice Princess have afforded Jasyn the same mercy? Would she show mercy now, if Atalanta let her go?

Unlikely...

It would be so easy to grasp her neck, to press down and open the wound that's barely starting to heal.

"Be the hunter, not the prey."

The words, her own re-opened wound. Bile burns her throat. She doesn't want to be that person. *That's not who she is.* But—

The sudden hooking of her neck — the dizzying motion — the upending — swiped sideways — it's as startling as it is impressive. The princess must have used her leg, toppling her, stealing her upper hand in one fell swoop.

The full weight of the Ice Princess pins her.

A confusing mix of panic and admiration infuses Atalanta as the Ice Princess restrains her with the solid insistence of someone who's spent a lifetime training to best their opponent.

But the mechanics of the manoeuvre and Atalanta's feelings about it are overwhelmed by something far worse. Worse than being confronted by the potent chemical-grime of the cold metal floor. Worse than staring into the devious eyes of an Ice Princess in the floor-hatch porthole reflection.

There's a vibration against her ear and a warm tickle that suggests the woman is saying something. But Atalanta can't hear her, and even if she could, she's as much use as a vole-rat caught in a trap. Because there's no escaping that the porthole is aligned perfectly, jeeringly, beneath her.

Untethered — suspended in space — oxygen depleted — choking breaths—

Her stomach revolts, retching. How can she concentrate on getting out of this death grip when the *grip of death* taunts her?

"Be the hunter, not the prey," signs the hidden silhouette, loud in her thoughts. Atalanta would gesture for them to leave her the hail alone, if her arms weren't constrained and she weren't drowning in adrenaline.

But the familiar words are enough to ground her, for her to squeeze her eyes shut and block out the nothing beyond. They're enough to remind her that she has something her attacker does not.

12

GLADIATOR PRINCESS

JASYN

As the lighting stutters around them, Atalanta deposits the unconscious Ice Princess over the lift's threshold as if she were dragging nothing more than a sack of rotten filament fruit.

The grime and blood are stark against the ice royal's pale skin and crisp white shirt. The barely-crusting blood across the bridge of her nose, the crimson cascade across her lower face, it's all underscored in adrenaline-fuelled clarity as Jasyn rushes out from the galley.

Her palms ache with ice-burn, but her eyes are drawn to Atalanta. *Hail. Is she okay?* She looks intact. A little scuffed with grime, but standing tall.

"I'm okay," Atalanta's eyes tell her, but Jasyn knows that *end of her tether* look. If they were still in the village, Atalanta would retreat to her woodland den and Jasyn probably wouldn't see her for days. Jasyn wishes she could give her the solitude she needs.

"What the fuck?" says Doctor Orpheus, gravitating to the heap of unmoving princess.

"Just another day in the skies," mutters Kalais.

"What...?" Herakles splutters, her fists at her side as if she can't decide whether to fight the galaxy or run from it. Jasyn can certainly relate, clenching her own cooled fists.

Interesting that Herakles, *captain of the skies, hero of the arena, slayer of monsters* can keep her cool when launching into the unknown against the odds, but show her one Iolcian Ice Princess and she wilts like a flower suffering frost. This only confirms in Jasyn's mind that the Ice Princess is the worst kind of monster, terrifying even when inanimate. Even with her eyes closed, her body limp and drenched in blood, she has a royal arrogance about her.

Blood or not, it's a face that'll forever be imprinted with Jasyn's hatred. Her throat already bears the mark. Jasyn's parents, her friends, would all still be alive if it weren't for the Ice Princess and her army. That they are gone reverberates like a full body gut punch, amplifying to anger trained entirely on the woman at Atalanta's feet.

She is death and destruction.

Jasyn's iced palms protest. The stare Atalanta aims at her warns her to *Be Calm*. It won't help her situation to be sparking like a live wire in a bucket.

Drawing a steadying breath, Jasyn melts her instinctive and unsettling combination of panic and contempt, and gives Atalanta a *Don't worry, I've got this* nod.

The fawn totters over and snuffles at Atalanta. Perhaps checking on her, or deciphering what grime is blemishing her overalls. Atalanta shrugs, stretching her shoulders. She signs, but before Jasyn can find her words and relay the information, Hylas translates:

"She snuck up on me in the cargo bay."

"And whose bright idea was it to bring an ice royal to the upper decks?" Castor's words are laced with venom. "Perhaps you'd like to place the helm console in the palm of her hand?"

What is her problem?

Before Jasyn can put Castor in her place — or regret trying — Herakles steps between them and aims her words squarely at Castor:

"Check the attitude at the airlock."

Castor splutters, a flash of hurt or frustration in her eyes, as if she'd thought the captain would have her back. Castor's muscles remain tensed for so long, Jasyn expects the first-mate to snap. Instead, she holds her hands up and backs off.

"Is she unconscious, or...?" Herakles's attention swerves back to the doctor and ice royal, betraying her nerves by rubbing the back of her neck. The question hangs there, awaiting the doctor's verdict.

Jasyn can only assume that the captain's concern stems from the need to keep the crew and ship safe. And, perhaps, because a sky voyage to seek the solution to Iolcian ills might struggle to keep the ethical high ground if its crew killed the Iolcian ruler's daughter.

"Pulse and breathing are steady. She's been knocked out," determines Doctor Orpheus, and the captain's muscles un-tense a little.

"I was in the cargo hold getting supplies," says Peleus, visibly flustered. "I didn't see anyone..."

"How did she...?" Doctor Orpheus checks over her patient, puzzling something out. "Was it the knock to her head? Or...?"

Atalanta offers up her palm with an empty syringe.

Jasyn's nerves prickle. Her palms, too, because why Atalanta has a syringe, and why the doctor's guilty eyes are flicking to her right now, she can hazard a guess.

The doctor and her sedatives, that's no surprise. That Atalanta would take on the task... Jasyn doesn't know what to feel about that. She gives herself enough of a *breathe, breathe* pep-talk that she's able to let it go. For now. But it's there, occupying her stomach worse than Peleus's cooking.

"Right." Doctor Orpheus nods. "That'll do it. She'll be out for a few hours at least."

"Let's get her to medical." Herakles steps forward, but before she can assist with the task—

"Are you serious? The *Ice Princess* getting the royal treatment on our ship?" Castor spits the words, as if there might have been doubt around her feelings on Iolcian royalty.

"Tending to injuries is not being treated like *royalty*." There's a fire in Herakles's eyes.

"She's hardly here for fun and games, is she?" Castor's fists strain at her sides, and Jasyn could be convinced they're not in the mess hall of a sky ship but in the Iolcian Games arena. "She's here to steal us from the skies. An offence worthy of an airlock if ever there was one."

"She didn't, though, did she?" Herakles squares up to Castor, both contenders' patience worn thin.

"I wouldn't put it past the Ice King to send his daughter to knock us from the skies," says Kalais from the side-lines, her tone more matter of fact. "We should check she hasn't rigged something."

The captain nods, her countenance calmer.

"Push her out an airlock and be done with it," Castor mutters. "Better we're rid of her. She's an *Ice-monger*." The room bristles at the words, undoubtedly aimed not just at the Ice Princess.

Jasyn's fists clench so hard, she crunches the ice already formed. If Castor wants to see some ice, she can show her some ice—

"That's enough," Herakles commands as she places herself as a pre-emptive barrier between them. "On this ship, we are not Ice City low lives." She aims her words at Castor but makes sure everyone takes note. "Should anyone harm the Ice Princess, or intentionally harm anyone else on this ship..." Even the fawn stares unblinking up at her. "...*they* will be rewarded with an airlock. Is that clear?"

"Yes, Captain," are the mumbled responses.

"Castor, Zetes, do a sweep of the cargo hold. Then report back. The rest of you, get on with what your Rhythms tell you. And, yes, that is an order."

After a few "Aye, Captain"s, the crew shuffle for the exit.

"Capturing the Ice Princess? Quite the achievement." Kalais grins as she passes Atalanta. "Looks like you can handle yourself in a scuffle." The air of approval, Jasyn agrees with, but the flirtatious grin and wink churns her stomach.

Is murder always wrong? Jasyn shakes the thought from her mind. She's been around too much death lately to even pretend to be flippant about such things.

As Tiphys passes, he grins and blushes up at Atalanta, as if discovering *yes, his crush can expand to fill the universe.*

Atalanta's frown suggests she'd welcome a black hole to swallow her right about now. Jasyn steps closer to comfort her, distract her, or perhaps even to grill her about her possession of the sedative, but—

That breeze... That song... That whisper...

The sounds, the sensations, they crawl under her skin, upending her equilibrium. The whooshing whisper-song lassoes her thoughts.

Jasyn grabs the galley hatch for support as Atalanta hands a scabbard and sword to the captain. Even with its blade contained, with the snow-globe ensnared in its hilt, the sword itself is unmistakably fabled Iolcian Ice. The Ice Princess's sword.

Is that what's calling out? That whispering song rustles against her eardrums. Air fluttering. *Free-falling.* A rug pulled from under her. It's enough to make her lose her breath.

The doctor and captain lift the Ice Princess, draping her

arms over each of their shoulders. The captain's barely buried wince suggests this is her nightmare.

"Jasyn...?"

The doctor's voice is distant. And Jasyn can only stare as a wrapped swathe of familiar fabric tumbles from within the ice royal's cape, landing with a punctuating *clunk*.

The burgundy and purple patchwork scrap material... the missing puzzle piece to the rip in her own cape. Jasyn knows what's contained within, even before Atalanta steps in to unravel it.

Her sword.

That curious sensation, of connection, of a completed circuit flowing, it echoes through her veins, her muscles, her every singing synapse. Her fingers twitch at the memory: holding the sword had been like speed-sledding down an ice-ravine with no idea whether it'd end with exhilaration or obliteration.

While Jasyn's fingertips buzz, it remains inert in Atalanta's grasp. Jasyn's hand lifts as if of its own accord. Which is probably why the doctor is staring at her as though the sword is frost-berry gin and Jasyn an alcoholic. Is it distrust? Curiosity? Jasyn's experiencing both herself right now.

She pulls her hand away, buries it in her pocket. Because as much as her every cell is vibrating to the tune of her sword, completing the connection — a lightning rod for her ice — is probably as dangerous and unpredictable as the Ice Princess herself.

Jasyn might not be answering her visceral need to possess her sword, but within all this there is a balm of relief. Her parents had hidden the item from her her whole life. Then she'd found it and lost it — *twice* — within a matter of days. Though she has no intention of grappling with such a weapon as they sail between stars in a breakable vessel, at least it's no longer lost.

The doctor opens her mouth, probably to say something scathing—

"Oh." Gus pauses in the doorway, squinting up at the juddering lights. "I'll add that to the list." Her eyes drift down, taking in the components of the situation. "Okay. We'll need to adjust the sustenance quantities." She nods decisively, as if it isn't weird and unexpected to have a cut-throat Ice Princess on board. "And those weapons need locking away."

13

ICE-MELT-STEAM

ATALANTA

Where's a Glowing Wood lagoon when you need one? Atalanta grumbles as she tightens connections between the ice-melt-steam pipes. Thanks to her adjustments the tanks are quick to scald the ice. The pipes creak — she'll have to look at that later — but the purpose is fulfilled. She lets the shower seep through her overalls, her underwear, down to her skin. She dreads to think what ancient cargo grime she's rolled in.

Splish-splosh —

The fawn makes a spectacle of himself splashing about in the water. In spite of her built up stress, Atalanta can't help but smile at that. He wanders to the air-blast hallway where a whirlwind of warm air boggles his eyes as he dries. It must be a cosy experience, because he curls up beside the gentle *whoosh* of a leaking air-funnel, basking in its warmth.

At least *he's* relaxed.

Atalanta's nerves jangle from her recent confrontation. The aftermath of adrenaline has her on high alert: muscles coiled and ready to run, with nowhere to go. Her Transonics roam. Beyond the cascade of water and steam, from the depths of the ship a series of *clicks* and *clunks* puncture into her consciousness, followed by the *screech* of un-oiled hinges. The echoes give shape to a lock and the rhythm of internal mechanisms as they manipulate into alignment — *clunk* — and etch into her memory. The *whoosh* and *thump* of blood circulating give shape to Gus as she stores the two inert ice-swords in the weapons lock-up.

A further auditory sweep finds the sedated *thud-thud* of the Ice Princess's heartbeat and her languid breaths locating her in the medical quarters, behind two further walls. The quarantine chamber. *Good.* Now that the weapons and ice royal are where they should be, Atalanta can Transonically roam in search of more positive things.

Jasyn's heartbeat is as easy to identify as a comet blazing across the sky. The manner in which she's weaving through the ship, checking each chamber, Atalanta can guess she's looking for her. At least she's headed in the right direction.

Atalanta hadn't exactly intended to slip away from the mess hall when Gus arrived, but she'd needed to escape the person who'd brought out the hunter in her.

She could have killed the Ice Princess. If the choice was for only one of them to emerge alive, she wasn't willing to lose that battle. Especially so soon after being retrieved from death.

She has never wanted to end a life. When the village had been attacked, she'd taken lives of soldiers with her arrows. Perhaps it had been the shroud of mist that morning, or that her arrows dealt the deadly blows, but ending those lives had felt, and still feels, distant. Like it happened in a dream. *A nightmare.*

The altercation with the Ice Princess may have been in the shadows, but it had unfolded in searing hi-definition. If she had killed her, her hands, not her arrows would have been the weapon.

When her face had met the metal of the hold-hatch porthole, she feared she'd run out of luck. *Untethered — suspended in space — oxygen depleted —*

Atalanta squeezes her eyes shut. She doesn't want to think about that.

A deep breath in...

She'd much rather think about...

The whirlwind blizzard of the nighttime Iolcian Glowing Wood... Orbs of colourful fruit suspended in familiar darkness... The unsuspecting rainbow backdrop to the mechanisms of her world clicking into place... In their village, she'd thought Jasyn was going to leave her behind, to seek out her own new adventures. But Jasyn had chased after her. And amongst the chaos of churning emotions, they'd confessed the adventure they wanted most was each other. As gentle snowfall pulsed the air, their mouths had met and fingers entwined, and —

A deep breath out...

Atalanta raises an eyebrow at herself, intrigued to discover that even at times of disquiet, her attraction to Jasyn blazes bright. Thoughts of Jasyn unwind the stress from her muscles, while the sprinkling-soap and water entice the grime from her clothes, her skin.

Her overalls dealt with, she strips and hangs them over an ice-melt-steam pipe. Adding more soap, she starts on her under layer, lathering her vest and shorts, before running her soap-covered fingers through her hair, massaging her scalp and rinsing.

She peels off her sodden vest.

Thump-thump-thump-thump — The heart that's a comet has crashed into her orbit and found something to accelerate about.

Atalanta washes the soap from her eyes.

Beyond the chamber's threshold, Jasyn's features flicker with several emotions. From her dropped shoulders, the first can be labelled *relief*. Mouth agape, her gaze explores Atalanta's bare skin, only partially blanketed by billowing steam... The sudden intake of breath and the blood thrumming through veins... well, that would be *desire*.

But there's a cloud shadowing Jasyn's eyes. Her cheeks tinting, Jasyn looks away. How many times in the Glowing Wood lagoon had she averted her eyes, her cheeks glowing brighter than the filament fruits? Has she forgotten being naked together is something they do now?

Jasyn opens her mouth to speak, but as Atalanta slicks the hot water through her hair, her biceps tensing and torso lengthening, Jasyn's ability to use words appears to be severely dampened. A satisfied smile tugs at Atalanta's lips, but when Jasyn doesn't venture closer and a light scowl disrupts her features, Atalanta lets the smile drift away. They need to talk. And Atalanta can guess what about.

"Yes," signs Atalanta, a nervous tremor in her hands, "the syringe was meant for you." She may as well come out with it. They've spent too many sun-orbits not addressing issues directly. The last thing they need is for a misunderstanding to knock them off-course.

Jasyn's brow looks like it's battling thoughts.

"Doctor Orpheus asked me to take it." The ice-melt's steam envelops each signed word, simultaneously accentuating and hiding them from view. "Just in case. To keep you safe." Atalanta's signed words are quicker than Jasyn's forming objection. "If I didn't, she'd find a different way, or assign someone else the task. So I took it." She pauses, giving Jasyn a moment to process, before adding: "Turns out a syringe of sedative can come in handy."

Jasyn's brow raises and her head tilts, as if she's thinking: *I can hardly disagree with that.*

"Now," Atalanta's nerves calm as the tension in Jasyn's

features unravels, "if you've quite finished gawping, are you just going to stand there, or are you going to join me?"

Jasyn's heart rate stumbles over itself. Atalanta grins as a playful smile brightens Jasyn's features. Grey eyes with threads of black and silver, lit up with possibility. *Hail... that look...*

The second Jasyn strides over the threshold, the lights stutter. The Circadian Rhythm must be protesting their opposing schedules, but Atalanta could be convinced it's their pulsing heartbeats in illuminated form.

At the precise moment their mouths meet, the ice-melt sensors kick in and a slush of water, a confusion of hot and cold, cascades onto them both. Steam envelops them in a welcome embrace as Atalanta seeks beneath the soaked material of Jasyn's shirts, simultaneously wanting to rush and to take all the time under the Seven Suns. Heartbeats dance, roaring through them like wildfire.

"The hail is this?" *Castor*. A figurative ice-bucket to their flames.

They pull apart, retreating from the new arrivals. Atalanta had been too focused on Jasyn to notice the approach of Castor and Zetes. She tamps down her instinct to run, to drag Jasyn with her, because... well, they're naked and they'll get water everywhere.

Her heart thumps with irritation.

"It's not enough you're here on the ship, you're chilling our showers, too?" Castor sneers, picking at the drifting snowflakes at the shower's perimeter.

Atalanta hadn't even noticed the weather orbiting them. Jasyn's cheeks blaze. It's not the cute, bashful cheek-tint Atalanta loves, but something more like shame. *Stupid Castor.* She needs to mind her damn business.

"You're supposed to undress before getting in," adds Castor

as she confidently strips at the edge of the chamber. Her smug smile suggests she's mighty pleased to have ended their fun.

"All clear in the cargo hold, by the way," says Zetes, conversationally, as he undresses, wades into the steam and sprinkles soap into his hair. "Apart from the grime. So much grime."

Atalanta turns her back, hiding her body from the interlopers. *Urgh.* Is there anything less intimate than communal showers? At least there's a blanket of steam to cover them.

Zetes keeps his eyes to himself, getting on with the task of cleanliness, but Castor scours her gaze over Atalanta and Jasyn as if she's personally offended.

"*Hail.* Whichever of you isn't on the wind-down schedule," Castor squints up at the inconsistent lighting, "get lost so you don't give the rest of us headaches."

"Jasyn. You might want to hurry along..." says Zetes, not unkindly, "...if you don't want Kal to throw a shovel at your head."

14

WHAT TO DO WITH A PRINCESS?

ATALANTA

The lights dim in each corridor Atalanta traverses. The stresses of the ship — metal *groaning*, gears *grinding* — scrape at her tired mind as the eardrum-rattle of *snores*, and the *whoosh-sigh* of sleeping breaths, guide her towards the sleeping quarters.

Apparently, she's on the wind-down schedule, which means her next task is sleep. Why Jasyn is on an opposing schedule when she's a novice in the skies seems harsh... but the captain — or whoever's in charge of the schedules — must know what they're doing. Hopefully. Or this trip is more doomed than Iolcus itself.

The fawn lags behind every few paces. The stairs that spiral around the lift column, the spine of the ship, is difficult for little legs to conquer. Though his intermittent acceleration and apparent enthusiasm to be at her side has her smiling.

Two large dots — identical to the icon on her cuff — glow on the door ahead. Metal claws at metal as she pushes it open, making her nerves scrunch. After a wince, she sorts the offending hinges with a quick spray from a grease can. As she does so, she latches on to Kalais's barking voice two floors down, giving Jasyn a piece of her mind. Something about being "...on thin ice. No pun intended."

Kalais really needs to calm the hail down or she'll burst a blood vessel. Or Atalanta will burst one for her.

The fawn looks up at her with curiosity, adoration, or perhaps just for a clue. He can't hear what she's hearing, but it seems like his blinking eyes are asking: "And what are you going to do about it?"

She could march down to the belly of the ship to give Kalais a run for her therma-stones. But Jasyn would only have to translate. And the lights would tremor. It'd all likely add up to further angering the beast. There's no reasoning with the unreasonable. By the sounds of it — with muscles *flexing*, breaths *gasping* and the repetitive engine *sizzle* — Jasyn's already shovelling, taking the level-headed approach of *just getting on with it.*

Atalanta sighs. Jasyn has wanted adventure for so long. If only this impromptu voyage and the people on it would treat her better.

Atalanta has never been enamoured with other people. And for her, there was no point in seeking out the horizon and beyond, because she had already found what she was looking for: a quiet life with Jasyn. Jasyn's hunt for adventure would have changed their lives eventually. Of that, Atalanta has no doubt. But she wishes they'd had more time; a few more shots at the perfect life before their world changed.

The door sorted, Atalanta steps into the dimly lit room, followed by the fawn. The grid of bunks lining the lefthand wall puts her in mind of stacked coffins in a funeral hut. With each square hatch only just tall and wide enough to crawl through, she estimates sitting up in the bunk might be possible, but only just.

Being packed in so tightly with strangers above or below her (albeit in their own bunks), has her itchy all over. She's tempted to find her own hideaway, somewhere in the depths of the ship. But she doubts her hermit tendencies can even be entertained with overseer lenses everywhere.

For now though, she just needs sleep.

Several of the bunks have already been claimed; their hatch doors closed. Atalanta selects a bottom bunk, which is fortuitous because the fawn assumes he's invited. Poking his spindly legs up into the bunk, he's trying to scramble in but getting stuck halfway. Not knowing the crew and therefore not trusting them to treat him well, she hoists him in and closes the hatch.

The tubular bunk doesn't allow for much manoeuvrability, and adding another creature to the small space doesn't help. Though, she hadn't considered that wouldn't be the worst of it.

Pin prick stars needle into her line of sight before she's able to close her eyes, look away, or close the shutter. *Of course this damn ship would have portholes in the bunks.*

Tap... Tap...

Her eyes are closed, but she already knows what's there.

Or what isn't.

Untethered—

Suspended in space—

Oxygen depleted—

Choking breaths—

Cursed to spend eternity drifting in the sea of stars—

The sounds, the sensations, can only be within her own mind, but that doesn't stop her heart racing and her hands clamming.

A warm and furry face nuzzles against her, comforting her. With a deep breath, she opens her eyes, and instead of being confronted by the horrors of the heavens, she's distracted by the fawn wobbling across the thin mattress and curling up against the porthole, so tight he's practically swallowing his own tail. Apparently the vista of space isn't so terrifying when there's a fluffy white and grey-dappled fawn bundled up in front of it. She runs her hand affectionately over the fawn's fur.

There's just enough room to kick off boots at the bunk's entrance. Atalanta wriggles against the mattress, stretching her back, attempting to loosen her muscles and decompress. Strangely enough, a claustrophobia-inducing tubular bunk does little to alleviate her tension.

A deep and steadying breath...

Seeking calm, she sifts through the sounds beyond the bunk. She hunts through the tangle, peeling back the layers. Flame-like contours — *roaring* — give shape to the engine room. There, beside the furnace, the pulsating *thump-thump-thump* of the heartbeat she's been listening for ever since she lived in the Unforgiving Mountains.

Judging by the tempo, Jasyn's working hard. Sweat slides down her neck, slicking against fine hairs, capturing the heat of her skin. The droplets join forces, some meeting material and wicking into the fibres, others licking down her skin.

Hail. Never mind the engine's fire, Atalanta's own has plenty of fuel. How she wishes that thumping heartbeat was next to her right now. A series of *groans* from the belly of the ship have her blushing in case the sounds are her own. It trips her focus and she tries to recalibrate, but her Transonic targeting misses its mark, reeled in by Gus instead.

"You've sparred opposite her in the arena," says Gus, her voice reaching from the medical quarters one floor down. "How much do we need to worry?"

The stutter-step of a nearby heartbeat gives sonar-like contours to crossed arms. Defined and particularly muscular arms. *That'll be the captain.* Atalanta allows herself another deep and steadying breath. For no particular reason.

"She'll cause no havoc of the ice variety, if that's what you mean?" Herakles's voice angles towards Gus. "The princess can't conjure ice. Not without her sword."

Interesting. The Ice Princess's abilities aren't the same as Jasyn's.

"She was on board before the arrival of the Ice King's hunting party," Gus's muffled voice and steady heartbeat give her shape from within. "And before all of us. Look." Atalanta can only guess they're watching overseer recordings. "She seems to know her way around, too."

"Why would the Ice Princess climb aboard our ship?" Doctor Orpheus's voice lights her up as the third corner in the triangle of this conversation. "Ice Princesses don't tend to turn up on renegade sky voyages for no reason."

"I'm not an oracle, Orpheus," says Herakles, annoyance personified. "How about I ask her once she's conscious?"

"I'll reel back through the overseer records," says Gus, "See whether she's been aboard before and —"

"I'll do it," says Doctor Orpheus. "You haven't slept yet."

"Neither have you," says Gus.

"I've got to keep an eye on the stowaway, anyway. I may as well do something useful with my time. And... well... to be honest, while I've been occupying the ship with no-one else aboard, it's entirely possible I developed an enthusiasm for being butt-naked. *So freeing.* But, if you want to see me in all my glory, by all means..."

"Naked? Really?" Gus doesn't sound convinced. In fact, she sounds outright confused. "You don't even like not wearing gloves, how do you —"

"Leave the overseer recs to me," says Herakles, decisive.

"Aye, aye, Captain," says the doctor in exaggerated flirtation to which Herakles's response is a grumble of exasperation. "I knew you couldn't resist gazing upon —"

Gus interrupts with a sigh, pinching the bridge of her nose. "Sleep would be good..."

"You, doctor," says Herakles, "have a patient and the health of the crew to be focusing on. I'll check the overseers and will avert or scratch my eyes out at appropriate points."

Just as the doctor grunts her response — *CLUNK-CLUNK-CLUNK* — obnoxiously loud footsteps in the deck above whip the conversation from Atalanta.

She hasn't been in this thicket of sounds long enough to identify the steps, but she's sure it won't be long before she'll know every footfall, whether she wants to or not.

A gentle *snuffle-snore* from the fawn reminds her she really should get some sleep. She's already encountering things that aren't there: arrows at portholes, the dead in the shadows... Not giving her mind a chance to repair its fractured state would be inviting chaos.

Planting her foot against the bunk hatch (so she might be jolted awake should someone open it), Atalanta closes her Transonics. Relief washes over her, as cooling as the Glowing Wood lagoon, and it's not long before the heavy waves of sleep pull her under.

15

AMONGST THE STARS

ATALANTA

Z

Z Z

Light pinpricks into the darkness until the vista of stars has you surrounded.

In space, you can stretch, you can play.

Out here, you can fly.

Today, the name of the game is to hit the target. Mother has made a point of making the game more complex, introducing several targets and moving them in unpredictable patterns, daring you to miss. When the game was first introduced, you hadn't thought to question it. You hadn't thought it odd to brandish a bow and arrow in space, each item in your arsenal tethered to you, just as you are to the raft.

Mother created the game when it had become too arduous keeping you entertained within the confines of such a small ship. Or, perhaps her motivation was in teaching you a skill, and the only way to wield a bow and arrow safely is to do so away from delicate ship instruments and moving mortal targets.

The target sails to the left.

You aim. You calculate. You release.

You smirk.

The target stops, your arrow lodged in it.

✦

ATALANTA GASPS AWAKE SO SUDDENLY, SO THOROUGHLY, ANYONE listening might think her lungs had just rejuvenated from death. Her heart thunders.

The only saving grace is that the fawn — balled up as small as its possible for him to be — continues his slumber with gentle snores.

Atalanta rubs her sternum, willing her heart to slow. It's ridiculous, she's aware, to have such an over-reaction to what must appear a pleasant enough dream. Though anyone who would suggest so doesn't know what happens next.

It's something she never wants to revisit.

Tap-tap —

Atalanta sighs. Nightmares in her sleep, imaginary arrows knocking at the porthole of her mind when she's awake... *Hail. This is going to be a long voyage.*

16

CIRCADIAN RHYTHM I

JASYN

Her vision and concentration are so hazy, Jasyn could easily be convinced her repetitive manoeuvres of ice into furnace are just some bad dream. But the burn of her muscles and the rebellion of her lower back insist the task is real. What she wouldn't give to be sleeping right now.

Instead, she's enduring the longest of days in the scorching engine chamber, shoulder to shoulder with a feral engine-tech who's on a mission to convince her she's a misshapen cog jamming a machine.

The constant roar and crackle of the engine makes communicating a challenge. Not that she has the energy for that, and it's clear Kalais doesn't welcome the interaction anyway.

With each heap of ice-fuel, the clock hands of Jasyn's mind tick over on the topic of the Ice Princess. Why is she here? Why has she brought Jasyn's sword? Has she claimed it for herself? *Is that even possible?*

As time drags on, Jasyn eventually catches on that she is doing the heavy lifting. Kalais even has the audacity to raise a challenging eyebrow when Jasyn catches her just *watching her.*

Her cool green stare reminds Jasyn of a snow-hawk's predatory gaze.

"Why are we both here if only one of us needs to shovel?" Jasyn calls above the ice-flames.

"*Hail if I know.*" Kalais takes an important moment to check the dirt beneath her finger nails.

"Won't we run out of fuel if we keep feeding the engines at this rate?" The stack of ice-fuel must be finite... constantly adding fuel can't be a good way to conserve their resources. "And doesn't this thing have an autopilot setting?" Okay, so maybe Jasyn's curiosity hasn't been entirely nixed by exhaustion.

"Don't you have a mute button?" Kalais presses her palm to her forehead as if Jasyn is giving her a headache.

Rude. She can't be worse than an ever humming ice-engine, can she?

"Surely we don't need to be doing this the entire way across this galaxy and the next?" Jasyn's not sure whether she means *this* as in 'shovelling ice', or *this* as in 'Kalais's atrocious attitude.'

Just as the fire in Kalais's eyes flares, Jasyn's and Kalais's cuffs bleep, vibrate and flash all at once, alerting them to *something* with a luminous yellow shape of a... half-circle?

"Thank the Seven Heavens for that." Kalais unhitches her shovel and harness and affixes them at the edge of the chamber, more gently than Jasyn would've expected given her general persona "And wouldn't you know it?" Kalais makes a show of consulting various gauges and pressing a series of buttons. "The engine is ticking over nicely."

Is she serious? Pushing her, running her into the ground, it's all just to make a point about who's in charge?

Jasyn would give her a piece of her mind if her every fibre wasn't buzzing, her muscles and bones surely out of alignment.

Jasyn reclaims her cape from the corner of the engine-chamber where she'd left it about a million muscle-aches ago.

She keeps a safe distance from Kalais as they follow the yellow blips of lights arranged in uniform constellations.

Pedantic glow-worms.

The strange thought makes Jasyn chuckle. She must be a little delirious. Kalais casts her a glare as they reach the mess hall, where the illuminated half-circle on their cuffs matches the glowing symbol above the mess hall door.

Atalanta isn't there. According to Lynk, she's been and gone. No doubt doing something crucial to the functioning of the ship and the crew's survival, while Jasyn is struggling to even lift her mug of vita-milk.

Once she's consumed an imitation of food, now on the wind-down schedule, Jasyn heads for the ice-melt-steam facilities. Kalais is there too, her angular winged back tattoo on show, the rest of her shrouded in steam. Either she's as exhausted as Jasyn, or she can't ever bring herself to have a normal conversation, because the two of them don't say a single word as the water washes away sweat and grime.

Once clean, Jasyn lingers in the ice-melt to give Kalais a head start. When Jasyn does reach the dimly lit sleeping quarters, the fiery engine-tech is nowhere to be seen. She must have claimed a bunk already. *Good.*

Pollux and Zetes are already dressed and ready to start their shifts. There's hardly room to move with the three of them in the gangway.

"Everyone shares this space?" Jasyn asks.

Pollux barely acknowledges her, and she's not sure if that's better or worse than how Castor and Kalais treat her.

"You want your own space, you gotta be captain," says Zetes as he presses apologetically past her, shrugging as if to say *that's just the way it is.*

Hail, he looks so much like Kalais they could be twins.

Though, the green of his eyes is calmer than the tempestuous engine-furnace of Kalais eyes.

Jasyn inwardly chuckles at that strange thought — *tempestuous engine-furnace?* — stranger even than *pedantic glow-worms*. She could do without thinking about Kalais's eyes right now.

Or ever.

Heavens above, she needs some sleep.

Pollux outwardly scoffs, leaving little doubt that it's aimed at her. Does he think she's complaining?

Indignance rears its ugly head. He doesn't even know her. It's not like she's lived her life in some ornate Ice Palace. She wants to correct him, but she also can't be bothered.

She drags herself into an unoccupied bunk. Once she shuts the hatch, only the vague burble of Pollux and Zetes reaches her. The porthole punctuating the far end of the bunk captures her entire attention. Framing shimmering space, it's a perfect view and she can't help grinning.

Logically, she shouldn't be fascinated because what she's really staring at is a whole lot of *nothing*. The view is technically less eventful than the Iolcian ice plains, which she'd always criticised as boring. But there's something about a skyscape akin to polished granite and quartz glistening in specks and ribbons that make it seem alive.

It takes her breath away, and she wants to keep staring, but — unhooking her cape's clasp and storing it on the porthole's ledge, and bundling up her cape as a second pillow — it's not long before her body sinks into slumber.

Z

Z Z

Darkness and stars undulate as though reflected on a lagoon. From the confusion of light and dark, a figure emerges. Ethereal tendrils of dark hair drift to their own gravity and rhythm.

Medea.

Indigo eyes light up like beacons as she sets sight on you. Her lyrical voice weaves on an unseen current, just as fluidly as her flowing gowns formed of midnight sky.

"I invited you to follow," says the echoed translation as her silken words caress your ears.

Yes, she'd beckoned you to follow her to the lower decks. It seems so long ago, and yet it's a matter of hours, only.

"I still don't know if you're real," you say, as fascinated by her presence as you are uncomfortable in it.

As much as she appears to have led you to safety before, the raw power rippling in her eyes has you unsettled. It reminds you of the kind of campfire that promises warmth, but could unleash a wildfire if you fail to keep a careful eye.

If that weren't enough to put you on edge, she'd stolen a kiss from you once before, in your dreams. As much as she fans the flames of your curiosity, she ignites your suspicions, too.

Medea's inviting smile tones down from magical to vaguely unimpressed.

"I led you to safety in the ice-labyrinth. Must I move the heavens to prove myself?" There's a war of fire and ice in her eyes. You don't know whether to be awed or afraid. You should be cautious...

"I mean no offence. It's my own mind I don't trust."

"The Iolcian Princess, she was at risk of losing all breath," says the echo of Medea. "I intended to lead you to her."

That catches you by surprise. How does she know the princess is on the ship? The timings align. The Ice Princess would have been locked in the cargo hold when Medea had beckoned you to follow. But that doesn't mean she's real. Especially given that you're in the middle of a dream! Perhaps your own thoughts are just trying to force the puzzle pieces to fit.

"You disappeared," you say, recalling Medea's brief appearance in the corridor, and your hesitance to follow.

Medea's attention flits over her shoulder. "As always, I do not have the luxury of time. Follow me, Jasyn of Iolcus."

Your choice in the matter is apparently an illusion as Medea's hands shape the air, conducting stars to her will, as a familiar tapestry of colours and forms stitch into existence. Mountain air wraps around you. A chill shivers down your spine. Your stomach knots.

You know this place. You wish you didn't. You only encountered it once, but it has haunted your thoughts and nightmares since.

The runway of grey-green and navy blue tufts — bell-poppies — amongst the stark white of snow, is punctuated by the gateway to the mountain bear cave. The Unforgiving Mountains. This is the last place you want to be.

You take an instinctive step backwards and it's plucked from your view—

Your stomach drops, your world upturns, as your sudden misstep sends you over the cliff edge—

17

CIRCADIAN RHYTHM II

JASYN

Jolt. Jasyn wakes with a start, sweat crystallising on her brow.

What just happened?

Her waking hours hammer her with physical exhaustion and now her sleeping hours pummel her emotionally, too. It's a sorry state of things when she can't even take refuge in her dreams.

Suspicious of sleep, she drifts until her cuff flashes and beeps and buzzes. An upward arrow glows, letting her know it's time to get up.

At each corridor turn, she's suspicious, as if Medea might be loitering in her path, on a mission to make her waking hours a nightmare too.

Taking to the skies and keeping her innate ice-abilities in check is challenging enough without having an apparition creating chaos in her thoughts.

Speaking of chaos, the universe must be having a laugh at her expense, because the only people in the mess hall are Castor and Kalais. *Seriously?* Their joint welcome is decidedly icy (and yet they have the audacity to call her Ice-monger and Snowflake!). Before Jasyn's even halfway through her breakfast sludge, Kalais struts past and clips Jasyn's ear, telling her "ice won't shovel itself."

Once in the engine chamber, Kalais stretches silence to eternity. Not welcoming another shift like this, Jasyn enquires whether the schedules are set.

"Take it up with the captain," Kalais snaps. Just as Jasyn deflates at the idea of having to wait an entire engine shift before being able to do so, Kalais adds: "File a Rhythm request through your cuff."

She doesn't offer to show her how, but she doesn't stop Jasyn when she pauses shovelling to investigate her cuff settings. A submenu allows her to input a request for 'reassignment'. Though once the request sends, there's no obvious outcome. Apart from Kalais barking at her to get back to work.

When Castor turns up to do a "steam check," Jasyn assumes it must be a routine flight-tech thing, checking helm records are accurate or something. She carries on shovelling, keeping her eyes down in the hope of not angering either beast.

It's only when Castor raises her voice above the roar of the ice-furnace to ask whether the "ice-monger has brain freeze" that Jasyn turns and notices (whether she wants to or not) Kalais and Castor pressed into a shadowed corner, halfway through pulling each other's clothes off.

Hail. Not the kind of 'steam check' Jasyn had assumed. Her gaping, buffering presence doesn't deter their roaming hands. *Double hail.*

"She always this slow?" asks Castor, pausing to speak before running her tongue along the length of Kalais's neck.

"Time for a break, Snowflake," calls Kalais, her focus understandably more on Castor nipping at her earlobe.

Practically tripping over her own feet, Jasyn shows herself out. It doesn't help that their laughter and moans crest above the growls of the engine. Jasyn hurries along. *Heavens above*, she's not sure she could feel any more out of place.

At least she's not trapped in the engine chamber for a while. If she could find Atalanta in the bunks... If Kalais and Castor can have some fun... well, perhaps she and Atalanta can too... But Jasyn has more than an inkling that opening and closing bunk hatches in search of someone isn't the done thing. And to venture into the sleeping quarters while her Rhythm is on the 'day schedule' will cause its own kind of chaos.

So she takes her opportunity to explore the ship.

With a skeletal crew split across different schedules, it's apparently possible to travel from one end of the [C]ARGO ship to the other without crossing paths with anyone. It wouldn't take much to convince her she's on a ghost ship drifting between stars.

And she doesn't get far before things turn a little strange.

It takes her a moment to catch up to the fact that she's stopped, on instinct. The lights trip. Bright to dim, to bright. Over and over. She checks her cuff. She's definitely on the day schedule. The captain hasn't confirmed her request. So why is the corridor acting as if she shouldn't be here? It would be just her luck if even the ship turned against her. *(Can ships do that?)*

In amongst the strobes of clashing Rhythms, a shadow shape grows larger, closer. *Medea?* Jasyn holds her breath, considering whether it's possible to outrun an apparition who can visit her while awake or asleep.

Only when the silhouette is within six feet of her does Jasyn decipher the features of Doctor Orpheus encased in her hooded black gown. Her face is more relaxed than usual, lacking its usual scowl or frown, confirming that the doctor is younger than Jasyn had first assumed her to be. There's probably only a few sun-orbits between them.

Jasyn's tempted to give her a piece of her mind. *How dare she task Atalanta with her sedation.* But as she approaches, the doctor looks through her, as if she's not there. Jasyn is ready to be offended, but as they get closer, about to pass each other, there's something different about the doctor's demeanour. Something missing… something vacant.

Is she sleep walking?

Jasyn waves a hand in front of the doctor's glassy stare.

No response.

"Doctor?" Jasyn backtracks to stay at her side.

The doctor inhales suddenly, her body tensing. She glances around and looks precisely as someone might if they'd just been woken, their mind catching up to their surroundings. Her focus swerves to Jasyn and, in classic Doctor Orpheus fashion, her scowl awakens and her features return to their usual setting of *pretty pissed off*.

"*Katàratos-kèpfos-moikalìs,*" the doctor swears, retreating from Jasyn as if she were infectious. *(Rude.)* "What the fuck are you doing?"

"Checking you're okay?"

"Why the fuck wouldn't I be?" The question must be rhetorical because the doctor makes quick work of swaggering away. She obviously doesn't want to talk about it — whatever *it* is — so Jasyn carries on her idle exploration until she braves a return to the engine chamber.

After minimal clashing with Kalais, she refuels herself in the mess hall, then attempts to unknot her muscles under the scorching ice-melt.

This place. She refuses to let her spirit be crushed, but she might have to admit to it being more than a little dented. She's lifted more fuel-ice than she'd have thought possible. She hasn't seen Atalanta in too long. She's seen and heard more of Kalais and Castor than she'd ever wanted. And the doctor? She's not sure what to do with that encounter.

By the time Jasyn returns to her bunk, her body and mind are so frazzled, sleep is easy, until she gets there —

Z

z Z

— because you're on that cliff edge again.

A precipice in one direction. The cave mouth in the other, inviting you towards it as though by an invisible thread. From your last encounter with this nightmare of a place, you know well enough the way out, but falling from a cliff on purpose — even in the realm of your imagination — is almost as intimidating as the gateway to your fears up ahead.

Mountain air chills your nerves.

A hand wraps around your bicep, seeking your attention, or preventing your escape. Amethyst eyes greet you with a mix of invitation and warning.

"Do not run from me, Jasyn of Iolcus. Do not run from this place."

The words drift past your ears as if delivered by a melodious breeze. You blink, trying to focus on their meaning. *She wants you to be here.* She wants you in this place that has terror crawling under your skin with the ferocity of fire ants.

Momentum floors you, upending both you and your thoughts. Bell-poppies shudder as you land amongst them as the forbidding mass of mountain bear shrouds the sky.

Your every atom quakes as the air shakes, shuddered by the creatures' almighty growl. Bile burns. You might vomit as a double row of claws *clack-clack-clack-clack* against rock underfoot, scratching at your sanity.

You run. You have to. That's what you did then, so that's what you do now.

The next roar swipes you from your feet, reminding you of your place in the food chain.

You land, impacting something solid. It slices your palm and blood smears across metal. Hail, you wish you didn't, but you remember this.

What you don't remember, what isn't part of what happened, is the presence of the woman who apparently wants you here, who wants you to "not run from this," whatever in the heavens that means.

Why she's hunting the blur of your surroundings, seeking something in the snow rather than reacting to the mountain bear charging your way, you have less than a clue.

Something in her demeanour has changed. On Iolcus she'd been flirtatious, playful. Not that you would invite that. But it had perhaps been preferable to the seriousness she now possesses, the skittishness to her search.

What is she looking for?

The question is overshadowed somewhat literally as every detail of the fast approaching creature crystallises. Every bristle of fur. Every gleaming fang. Every scrape of rock under claws. Its shadow floods across you—

The air shifts under the force of its swiping paw—

You gasp now, as you did then—

18

CIRCADIAN RHYTHM III

JASYN

Heavens, this is stressful.

Another jolting nightmare. Another confusion of sweat and ice. Jasyn exhales a plume of ice-air. Her cuff bleeps and buzzes and taunts her into action. And so it begins, another day of discomfort and exhaustion.

At shift end, hoping she might cross paths with Atalanta, or at least make eye contact with someone who doesn't hate her, Jasyn peers into the rec room. There are track-mills and weights, boxing bags, an area set out for bounce ball, and even a miniature Games arena. Though the arena-circle isn't kitted out with silver sand like the real thing on Iolcus, but with mats. Makes sense. Sand must be a nightmare for ship instruments when gravity is doing its own thing.

On an area of mats off to the side, Gus makes slow, controlled work of... strength training? Yoga? Her bodily contortions are a perfectly poised example of quiet strength and control. At her side, performing similar feats of athleticism — albeit with more distracting muscles — is the captain. Both the chief engineer's and captain's eyes are closed.

A sudden pain at Jasyn's earlobe has her turning. Kalais

follows up her earlobe flick with a light slap to Jasyn's healing jaw, making it ache all over again.

"Don't stare, Snowflake. It's not proper."

Anyone would think Kalais is on a mission to get a rise out of her. No wonder the captain thought her responsible for Jasyn's jaw injury. Also, how *bold* that the person who had her hand between Castor's thighs, *right in front of her*, only one shift ago, is telling her how to act "proper."

All Jasyn can do is scowl. She might have been staring, but she wasn't leering. She's just impressed at the athleticism is all. And she has a matter to raise with the captain.

"You said to take up my request with the captain."

"Through your cuff, Snowflake. I wouldn't disturb her while she's—"

But Jasyn has had enough. Her Rhythm request has done nothing. She's not afraid of hard work. Far from it. She's not even that bothered that the work is breaking her a little and the company is testing her more so, but not being able to see Atalanta, without good reason — that's too much.

The closer she strides to the captain, however, the less sure she is of herself. There had been talk of airlocks and being pushed out... and brigs, too... What punishment might there be for pestering the captain? She guesses she's about to find out.

"Captain?"

In some sort of rigid plank position, Herakles supports her weight with her right arm while stretching her left to the ceiling. Jasyn's abdominals tense just watching. The captain opens her eyes. Her expression is cool and uninviting, but it's too late now.

"I sent a schedule request... I'm not sure if... I've not used —"

"Your request has been received."

"Oh." Good? Though the captain's tone doesn't suggest that it's good. "So... Atalanta and I can be on the same schedule?"

"I didn't say that." The captain's words are curt and her eyes are closed again. Is that the end of their discussion?

Even Gus has opened her eyes. Her brow is almost as furrowed as Jasyn's own. Perhaps she can also sense the captain's mood. Sky-travellers from the next galaxy could probably sense the captain's mood.

It's odd. Jasyn and the captain had briefly tussled in the sky ship workshop — on account of Jasyn thinking her an intruder. The captain entirely had the upper hand in strength and agility, but even then she'd seemed friendlier. More playful. Welcoming, almost. Has something changed? The only thing Jasyn can think of is her perceived role in the weather chaos during take-off. But didn't she unravel the storm, too?

"You can occupy the same schedule when it's logistically viable to do so." The captain must have peeked, or assumed her to still be there.

"Um. But —"

"Um. But." She does open her eyes then. Amber eyes bore into Jasyn, challenging her to question her authority. "This room is for relaxing. For exercising and blowing off steam. Not for bringing me your problems."

Okay, so the captain can be an asshole. That's... disappointing.

Jasyn retreats, doing her best to ignore Kalais's "I told you so" expression, and quietly cursing the captain and her situation in general. She sighs. The heavy kind of sigh that lets the universe know its conspiracy to dampen her enthusiasm might just be working.

Unease and irritation have a headache blooming, tiredness has tears prickling behind her eyes. She mustn't let Kalais see, she'll never live it down.

Six quick steps into the corridor and Jasyn startles, stumbling back.

Glowing amethyst eyes and impossible drifting gowns so dark they could be created of nothing and everything occupy her path. Little about the presence makes sense.

"Heaven's hail."

Medea is right there. No preamble. No slow approach or beckoning. Just. *There.*

"What do you want?" Jasyn doesn't mean to snap, but Medea is the reason she's now suspicious of sleep. Sleep she could do with right now to reduce this raw and vulnerable feeling.

"I need you to listen to me." Medea's words are out of step with her movements, as always. The leading notes of her voice are less melodious than usual. Honey and silk has been soured and snagged. It's enough to give Jasyn pause. "You possess information crucial for the journey ahead, and we do not have much time."

What is she talking about? Does she enjoy speaking in riddles?

Jasyn opens her mouth to object, but—

"If you listen, Jasyn, I will tell you." Medea's quirked eyebrow underscores that Jasyn is delaying this. Whatever *this* is.

Jasyn sighs and rubs her temple, hoping no-one's watching her on the overseers. Knowing her luck, it'll show her talking to herself like someone in need of a quarantine chamber.

"I assume this has something to do with my nightmares?"

"Not your nightmares. Your memories." Medea pauses, checking over her shoulder where there's only a ship-wall with horizontal wire-bundles.

What does she keep looking at? Where is she? The Golden Planet? That's what she said in the sky ship workshop, isn't it?

"There's an artefact locked away in your thoughts," Medea continues.

"Artefact? What? How do you—?"

Yeah, not asking questions isn't Jasyn's strength.

"Already lost the plot, Snowflake?"

Jasyn spins around. Arms crossed, Kalais leans against the rec room doorway. Hawk-eyes watch her, cooly. Suspiciously?

When Jasyn looks back, Medea is gone. If she was even *there* in the first place.

Jasyn scrubs her face.

"You should get some sleep." There's a smirk in Kalais's tone that has Jasyn biting her tongue. *Yeah, no kidding.*

As Jasyn settles into her bunk, she quietly wishes Atalanta "Goodnight," in the hope that, wherever she is she'll hear her. She'll know she's thinking about her. It's that warming thought that encourages Jasyn's eyes to close...

Z

z Z

Frost-filled air bites your nostrils as the gateway to your fears takes formation. That invisible tether encourages you closer, but all you want is to run the other way.

You land amongst the bell-poppies as the mountain bear blocks the sky. Bile burns. Your insides quake. The air vibrates with the creature's growl.

"Let it play out," Medea calls out, as if you aren't in the middle of something horrifying, as if the creature's scratching claws aren't *clack-clack-clacking* against rock and shredding your nerves.

You run, but the roar knocks you from your feet.

You impact the solid metal that slices your palm. Blood smears across the D-o-VE emblazoned metal, hidden in the snow. Medea hunts the metal scraps as if they might hold the answer to her questions.

It's a blur. All you can think about is the beast barrelling towards you. Its undulating fur. Its saliva-dripping fangs. Its claws, and the ease with which they'll tear through flesh. The chaos and grief those moments lead to. And the part you played in it all.

All you want is to push this moment away, bury it in the past and never let it loose.

"Stay focused," that lyrical voice implores, but as the creature swipes, your every nerve bristles and bell-poppies, snow powder and a mighty mountain bear all blizzard to nothing as you wake.

19

DON'T LOOK

ATALANTA

Jasyn's "Goodnight," whispered from her bunk had reached out to Atalanta through the ship layers like a welcome embrace. She was minded to down tools and seek out Jasyn's bunk, but she'd been midway through untangling a nest of wire within a wall cavity that vole-rats had turned into... well... *a nest*. Once that was sorted, she'd headed for the crew quarters, only to be directed back to the door by the crew on the wind-down schedule as her day-Rhythm tremored the lights.

Atalanta sighs. She's aware the universe does not *technically* have a sense of humour. But, given that she and Jasyn have spent their lives within each others's orbit and have only recently discovered intimacy together — and are now stuck in a ship and routine that conspires to keep them apart — it feels a little like the universe is having a laugh at their expense.

Atalanta would raise two fingers to the universe if it would do any good, and if her hands weren't busy adjusting ship components.

Still, at least they're on this journey together.

As Atalanta tackles a leaking pipe, the fawn watches on, either taking in the particulars of what she's doing, or observing the shiny objects. His black marble eyes sparkle as Atalanta selects tools from her tool belt. When she lies on the floor to get a closer look at screws that need attention, he lies down too. With the fawn so focused on her, and his frequent attempted theft of useful items, Atalanta has taken to including him in the process.

Each time she reaches for the adjustable wrench, she clicks her fingers twice and signs W. Each time she claims a screw-driver she clicks her fingers twice and signs S. The fawn watched on, and it seemed futile, until he *finally* retrieved the right item. It could have been a fluke, so Atalanta repeated and he did the same.

When she reaches out to stroke his muzzle, he wiggles with glee, pressing into the contact. When he's not fetching tools for her, he divides his time between watching her work and staring out the portholes. He seems to enjoy watching the stars. It gives him a literal twinkle in his eyes, which would be cute, if the source of the twinkle wasn't so troubling.

Tap-t-tap-tap...

Atalanta refuses to look out the portholes in case what isn't there might trick her into thinking it is. She focuses on returning the inspection panel to the wall and seeking out sounds within the ship.

The quiet voice of Gus skitters up from two floors below: "... you've never had a problem with your crew being in close proximity before." There's a note of gentle caution in her voice. The *splosh* that follows gives shape to the water bottle she's drinking from.

Atalanta concentrates on the shape of the sounds, placing them in space. The rec room. Another heartbeat beside Gus. *The captain.* Her heart rate is a little elevated, perhaps from a work-out, perhaps from the conversation.

"It's not her fault, you know," says Gus. Atalanta might not possess Jasyn's insatiable curiosity, but she's intrigued enough to wish she knew what and who they're talking about.

"Yeah," is all the captain says before the beacon of her heart signals her leaving the room. Boots strike metal as she winds down the stairwell to the medical quarters level, while Gus's lighter footsteps head to the ice-melt-steam facilities.

A short while later, there's a *scuffle*... A *thud*... An "oof." And a *gasp*.

Wired to seek out drama like a radio dial tuning past the static, Atalanta hones in on the quarantine chamber. Scuffles and thuds form a confusion of shapes in her mind. Two hearts *hammer*, breaths *whoosh* and blood *pulses hard*, sending ripples through the quarantine chamber, highlighting the close proximity as Herakles wrestles the Ice Princess to the floor.

From how Herakles had reacted to the arrival of the unconscious princess in the mess hall, Atalanta would've guessed she wouldn't venture within arms' reach of the murderous ice royal. Particularly after however many sun-orbits of losing battles to her in the arena.

Though a quarantine chamber where the odds are stacked in the captain's favour might have something to do with her 'bravery'.

Now that she thinks about it, in the cargo hold her assailant hadn't been as overbearing as Atalanta assumed she would be, given her unblemished record of arena triumphs. Either the princess let Atalanta win — *ridiculous!* — or her skills in the arena have been far exaggerated for dramatic and political effect.

Perhaps the captain, after countless thrown arena battles, can now — finally — let the Ice Princess know what she thinks of her.

A masochistic gasp tumbles from the Ice Princess's lips.

Atalanta swallows her discomfort. If the stories are to be believed, the Ice Princess is a sadist, too.

Is this an interrogation? Or punishment? Misguided therapy for the captain? Or just the captain being a thug? Whatever it is, Atalanta's sure she doesn't want to listen. Herakles might want to get answers, might need them, but starting an interrogation — or whatever it is — dialled to ten seems unnecessary. Even if the princess is enjoying it.

Gross.

MEEEHHHH - Atalanta's attention snaps back to her corridor, and the fawn who's either trying on a tantrum for size, or is trying to tell her something. Either way, it rings in Atalanta's ears.

Serves her right for spying.

The fawn springs up, bouncing as if his feet aren't convinced he's going to land. Atalanta reaches to calm him, to stroke his muzzle and ruffle his ears. Only when he stills does the dread seep in.

Because there's nothing reflecting in his wide eyes. And the uninvited silhouette at the edge of her vision is throwing shapes louder than any sounds:

"Turn around. Look where you're going."

She doesn't want to look...

As she turns to the portholes she'd been avoiding, body rigid, heart racing, her focus tumbles through the ship, instinctively seeking Jasyn and the gentle breaths and heartbeat that can quiet her panicked mind.

But she clumsily overshoots the sleeping quarters and lands back in the quarantine chamber just as the breathless Ice Princess asks:

"Where did the stars go?"

20

WHAT THE—?

JASYN

Jasyn's not sure which woke her: the nightmare, the ear-piercing alarm, or the ship shunting. Her cuff vibrates and bleeps and flashes the angular wings of the engine chamber at her, just as the tannoy voice of Castor summons: "Captain to the helm," and "All hands on deck."

The Ship chimes in with: "Rhythm override."

Panic propels Jasyn out of her bunk, into her overalls and down two flights of stairs. Kalais and Zetes are already in the engine chamber, playing the dials — checking levels, making adjustments — as if their lives depend on it. Even without the obnoxious alarm, even if the chamber weren't filling with steam, the distress etched in the engine-techs' brows underscore that there's something terribly wrong.

Jasyn lingers at the door, entirely certain that to go any further won't help.

"What's going on?" she calls above the chaos, but Kalais is already punching the comms, demanding: "Engine to helm. What in the Seven-bloody-Heavens is going on?"

"Helm to Engines. Stand-by for further." Castor's voice crackles through the comms.

"Further?" Kalais responds sharply. "Further to what? You've not told us anything."

When there's no response within three seconds, Kalais instructs Jasyn to: "Get to the helm. Find out what's happening. Report back." At the urgency in her voice, Jasyn about turns and launches along the corridor. "And tell the flight-techs to get their heads out of their asses," Kalais calls after her.

Jasyn probably won't quote her word for word.

With the cube-lift lingering on another level, Jasyn strides past and winds up the central stairs. Four flights to climb...

Along with her feet, her heart and mind race. At each level, she scans the corridors in the hope of evidence that Atalanta isn't suffering from the insistent alarm.

But they don't cross paths.

The captain joins Jasyn in the upward journey. She's more disheveled than Jasyn has seen her before, adjusting her waistcoat and tucking in her shirt as she goes. Before Jasyn can put her brain in gear to ask what's going on, the captain outpaces her, two steps at a time, reaching the flight deck several strides ahead. She could at least pretend to be a little out of breath, while Jasyn is busy losing a lung in her race to the top deck.

The captain is already mid-flow through a string of no-nonsense update demands by the time Jasyn reaches the helm deck. The crux of which boil down to the question they're all wondering: *What the hail is going on?*

Jasyn pauses at the edge of the room, watching as Herakles commands the helm deck.

"Why has no-one responded to the engine room?" Herakles points to the pulsing blue comms light.

"We don't know what to report," admits Pollux, his concentration divided between their way ahead and the flight consoles. "We're being pulled in but can't see anything."

Castor mumbles her agreement.

The captain steps up to the station at the centre of the flight deck, wrapping her palms about the spokes of the two perpendicular steering wheels. Each gentle adjustment of the wheels has the ship groaning, shuddering as the captain and her ship attempt to pull from an invisible maelstrom.

"Whatever this is, it's not letting us go." Herakles strikes the comms and the overseer console displays Kalais pacing the engine chamber. "Helm to Engines. Status update."

"Whatever you're doing up there, it's fighting our engines." Kalais raises her voice above the epic hissing of protesting machinery.

"Helm to engines, stand by for further," Herakles responds.

Kalais's mumbles are sure to evolve to curses, but her feed cuts out.

"Tiphys, Lynk — where's Lynk?" Herakles scans the flight deck — "Hylas, find Lynk." — before honing in on their navigator. "Tiphys, what are we looking at?"

"There's nothing on our map," says Tiphys, sifting through the 3-D mesh of cosmic topography streaming around him, originating from his coin-sized sky map reader. A neon purple locator dot signifies their place in the sea of stars. He scratches his head, visibly confused.

Herakles turns to Castor. "Switch off those bloody alarms, will you?"

"Aye, Captain." Castor's sneer suggests she's biting her tongue.

The silence in the wake of the alarm is unsettling, leaving space for the groans of the ship to echo from its depths. Metal under stress. Sinews straining.

Alongside Tiphys, Herakles studies the map's grid lines in three dimensions, manipulating the information hanging in the ether.

Jasyn gravitates to the immersive map, the data rippling at her touch.

Tiphys swallows thickly. "We checked the co-ordinates."

"How are we so far off course?" asks Herakles to a flight deck response of stunned silence. Sure enough, the streaming map-mesh depicts the chasm between where they should be and where they are. "*It's not rhetorical.*" The words are aimed at her flight-techs, both of whom pale.

"It doesn't make sense." Castor somehow looks both more indignant and cowed than Jasyn has seen her before. "The input co-ordinates were correct..."

"What is *that*?" Lynk's voice cuts across the deck, uncharacteristically loud as she guides herself onto the flight deck, tapping her cane, trailed by Hylas. Her goggle-augmented eyes are trained ahead.

Jasyn takes another step forward, following Lynk's line of sight to the apex.

"What is *what*?" asks Castor.

"You can't see that?" Adjusting her goggles, Lynk casts the visual feed of scrolling data so it hangs in the ether for all to see. The data streams so thickly with chemical formulae and labels and a thousand other details it's impossible to see anything through the info-blizzard. She makes further adjustments. The crowding details fall away and it turns to a hazy image, shaped through the rainfall of data.

"Skies above," the captain swears.

Jasyn's breaths pause in tandem with the gasps of the helm crew.

No wonder they can't see any stars, with the behemoth black disc of a planet in the way. So close, it's almost impossible to see its edges.

"Chief...?" says Herakles, almost in a whisper.

That those in charge look like they've stumbled upon a nest of sleeping mountain bears, isn't inspiring calm.

"Well, that's... interesting," says Gus, her hand paused above her ice-tablet.

New alarms spring to life and, despite Castor and Pollux's efforts, as soon as one alarm is extinguished, another screams into existence. How long until the ship's cries turn to irreversible silence?

"*Chief*," says Herakles, a little more forcefully.

Gus's attention snaps back to her ice-tablet. "If it's gravity pulling at us, the reverse thrusters should free us, but...."

"Surface gravity is low..." Lynk interjects, before announcing in an *aha!* manner: "Magnetism." Her eyebrows quirk above her goggles as a series of equations scroll in the ether. "A concentrated burst. Strong. Too strong. If we keep trying to change course, it'll pull us apart."

Another mournful groan shudders the ship.

The calculation in Herakles's eyes is immediate.

"Get strapped in," she announces to the flight deck, before taking to the comms: "Ship-wide. All crew, secure for landing."

Without delay, Castor and Pollux secure themselves into landing harnesses with the ease of pulling on an extra layer. Lynk gravitates to her station and does the same, while Hylas guides wide-eyed Tiphys to their seats at the edge of the deck.

Hylas gestures for Jasyn to join them, but she's glued to the spot, fascinated by the captain's control in the face of chaos.

"*Eskòrakas* Captain," Doctor Orpheus's voices unleashes through the comms, "have you lost your mind?"

"Captain," Gus's tone hints agreement with the doctor, "the ship is in better shape than it was, but—"

"Either we break apart in the skies, or we risk the landing," explains the captain, attending to the helm console and the many flashing alerts vying for attention. "Surface gravity is weak. It's better odds."

Gus nods — "Aye, Captain," — and anchors herself at her diagnostics station.

"Helm to engine room," says Herakles into the comms. "Close the hatch and get secured."

"Engine to helm. Aye, Captain." *Kalais and Zetes in unison.* Kalais's agreement seems easier than Jasyn would have imagined.

"Helm to medical," says the captain into the comms. "Orpheus, confirm status ready for landing."

The doctor must have overheard the captain's reasoning, or — in spite of her brusque manner — trusts her, because she replies with an official: "Medical to helm. Medical and quarantine, status ready. Confirm."

"Helm to galley. Peleus, confirm status ready for landing."

"Uh...?" Peleus's voice crackles out of the comms. The captain calls up the overseer feed for the galley where Peleus is tangled in the wall tethers.

"Near enough," confirms the captain. "You need to get strapped in," she says to Jasyn, but Jasyn can't tear her eyes from the data cascading above them, including blueprints of the ship and what must be various locator beacons.

"Where's Atalanta?" she asks, stepping closer. She expects the captain to tell her to back off and shut up — or something scathing and dismissive along those lines — but instead she hones in on the map.

Most of the beacons are on the flight deck. Two are in the medical quarters. *Doctor Orpheus and their captive.* One is in the galley — *Peleus.* And one is only one floor down, but in the far reaches of the outer corridor. *Atalanta.*

Apparently, being tracked by their cuffs does have its uses.

"Helm to Atalanta. Confirm status ready for landing?"

The captain nimbly calls up the overseer feed showcasing the corridor in question. Jasyn's stomach drops. Atalanta is slumped on the floor, against the wall, her eyes closed as she she clutches the bright white fawn.

"Her Transonics are closed," says the captain.

Jasyn's too frazzled to question how Herakles knows that. All that matters right now is it's true. Where there should be a glow of orange, there's nothing. Atalanta must have switched them off to escape the alarms — or to give herself a break. She might have an idea of chaos in motion, but she'll have no idea that they're about to drop from the skies.

Jasyn runs, not pausing for permission.

"Six seconds to atmospheric entry, Captain," says the distant voice of Castor, as Jasyn leaps three stair rungs at a time to reach the next level. If the captain is protesting, she's not listening.

Once within the central spiral stairs, the ship shunts. Up and down swap places. *Oof!* Jasyn's back pins against the stairwell grate. Air coughs from her lungs.

That'll be the atmospheric entry, then.

Six seconds?! More like three.

The stairs that should have been a downward journey into the ship now require upper body strength to conquer. Clutching the metal grate of the stairs, she fights the forces working against her. Forearms, biceps, shoulders and core: if they weren't burning before, they are now. One rung at a time, she climbs until she reaches the corridor.

Portholes frame the flaming entry as the ship hammers through the atmosphere. She drags herself up and along the wall railings as though they're rope, because — *Atalanta*. She has to get to Atalanta...

21

SKYFALL

ATALANTA

Not many survive once they know the sound of ripping metal. Of ship entrails snapping. Of what a sky looks like from within the crumbling shell of a falling ship. Of the relentless bite of air against cheeks as it gnaws away any calm and hope.

Atalanta's chest tightens as the whisper of the memory grows to a scream. It might have been over half her lifetime ago, but the time passed will never be enough to forget being shaken so hard that collapsing to atoms felt inevitable.

Bile scorches her throat and copper coats her tongue. This is what she'd been afraid of.

Panicking helps no-one, she knows that, but it's difficult not to in the circumstances. She could open her Transonics, to make sure the ship is functioning as it should, but, at this point, if anything clogs or twists or breaks, the G-force won't let her do anything about it. She could open her eyes, but she has no wish to see how imminent their demise is.

A hand grasps her shoulder and Atalanta's eyes jolt open to Jasyn's worried brow.

For a moment, Atalanta forgets the chaos around them as

Jasyn presses against her, wrapping one arm around her and the fawn while clutching the railing with her other.

If the look of the explorer, the adventurer, could ever be captured, that expression would be Jasyn's as her focus shifts to the porthole opposite. The silver-threads in her irises dance as the planet's mists part.

She must know hurtling towards a planet in a ship that's seen better days guarantees catastrophe, but the glint in her eyes says: "I can't believe this is happening." Only without the undertow of terror that's claiming Atalanta.

Even if Atalanta cannot fully grasp how to achieve such a state herself, Jasyn's ability to manifest wonder is something she admires. If she were to ignore the impending doom, if she were to face the planet with Jasyn-like enthusiasm, she'd observe the swirls of parting clouds, the planet starting to show itself below them. Or above them. It's difficult to tell which way is up when you feel like you're falling *and* being shoved backwards all at once.

Colours and contours are taking shape. Emerald and forest green interspersed with grey and white, woven together with ropes of glacial blue.

Pristine. Stunning. Breathtaking.

As they fall closer, crystal blue arteries of rivers and the veins of streams disappear into the mosaic of green and white.

It takes her fast thumping heart longer than it should to decipher that the ship is no longer plummeting in the manner she imagined, but is falling, gently.

When the ship's trajectory changes, veering in a controlled manoeuvre towards a clearing amongst the dense jungle, Atalanta lets herself breathe.

With the lower gravity cushioning their decent, her nerves are cushioned too. She braves a return to open Transonics, and as the ship sets down, the landing gear decompresses as if it too is breathing a sigh of relief. And there's not a single person aboard who doesn't breathe that same sigh.

The possibilities of falling, of all the things that could go wrong, of all the things that have gone wrong in her past, still scrapes at her nerves, but amidst all that, she can admit that whatever this world is — with its towering trees rivalling even the ship's height, rich depths of greenery, and blanketed snow — it's beautiful.

Where in the heavens are we?

PART III

THE SNOW JUNGLE I

JASYN

22

HOOKED

JASYN

"Well," says Kalais, lounging in the captain's helm chair, stretching like a cat in the sun. She almost looks *bored*. "Isn't this the galactic equivalent of taking to the open road and landing in a ditch?"

With the entire crew gathered, observing the vista beyond the windows, the lush green foliage, fresh white snow and purple skies, Jasyn loiters at the edge of the flight-deck in the hope of not getting under anyone's feet. She grumbles to herself. Sure, she should be focusing on the more pressing matter of cheating death while being pulled from the sky by unknown forces. But why Kalais can recline in the *captain's helm chair* without anyone making comment, when Jasyn couldn't even sit at the mess table, well... life under the Seven Suns isn't exactly fair, is it?

"Don't be so negative," says ever sunny Lynk to Kalais. "We'll get there in the end."

"The end is what I'm worried about," says Kalais.

Jasyn glances at Atalanta beside her, checking she's okay. There's a sharpness in Atalanta's eyes. She's still on edge, but at least she's channelling her energy into patting the fawn —

comforting herself, the creature, or both. Though if she continues too long like that, the little creature's going to end up with a bald spot.

"How the hail does an Iolcian sky ship veer from its course and wander into the net of a planet that's not even on our maps? How are we so far off course?" The captain's words are aimed at Castor and Pollux, both sitting a little straighter at their flight-stations under her gaze.

If Jasyn had to describe Herakles's body language, she'd call it *pissed off captain*. She'd be surprised if the purpose of the gathering is to humiliate the flight-techs. The captain might have been an asshole to her, but it doesn't seem her style. But then, what does Jasyn know?

"Like I said when we were busy being pulled from the skies," says Castor, "it doesn't make any sense. The input co-ordinates were correct..."

Pollux nods. "We both checked. Like always. But — somehow — the course changed."

"No shit," Kalais mumbles.

"When?" Herakles apparently sees fit to ignore Kalais's comment.

"Two shifts ago," says Pollux, his focus on his monitor.

"Two shifts and it wasn't detected?" The reprimand in the captain's tone is clear.

"There was no reason to think—" Castor begins.

"Well, clearly there was."

There's an intensity in the captain's eyes that Jasyn is glad isn't aimed her way. Pollux bows his head, avoiding eye contact, while Castor glowers up at the captain.

Herakles's demeanour shifts from *telling off* to *commanding*:

"Call up the overseer records for the time of the course adjustment."

"Already have, Captain," says Castor. Conciliatory? Hurt? Annoyed? It's difficult to tell.

"And?"

At Castor's gesture, her flight-station data hazes up into the ether at the centre of the helm deck. The image crackles like a blizzard.

"Ready when you are, Castor."

"That's it," says Castor, the line of her mouth tight. A few of the experienced crew gasp and mutter amongst themselves. Kalais gives one long whistle to underscore that *this is not a good thing*. Even the captain's eyes widen as she stares at the hanging static.

"Ship wide, the recordings are gone," adds Castor, to be completely clear.

No-one says it, but Jasyn can guess at the meaning. *Someone did this.* Two shifts ago... when the Ice Princess was locked away in the quarantine chamber. *Someone* messed with the coordinates and deleted the evidence of their transgression. Someone in this room.

"Well, fuck," Doctor Orpheus mutters. Jasyn flinches. She hadn't noticed her there in the shadows, a few feet away.

"I don't suppose whoever did this is going to step forward and volunteer what the heavens they're up to and what we're all doing here?" asks Herakles, rubbing the back of her neck. The crew look to each other, the tension as cutting as Iolcian ice. "No? Thought not."

"Why would someone send us here?" asks the doctor, her eyes a mix of fascinated at the world beyond the windows, and annoyed at, well, whatever she's perpetually annoyed at.

"Maybe they didn't," suggests Kalais. "They changed our course but, this place isn't on the map. And the planet did grasp us from the skies."

It's perplexing and annoying that unreasonable Kalais who

makes little sense to Jasyn can in fact use reason. What does that say about how she treats Jasyn?

Jasyn tries not to think about that.

"How do we not know of this place?" Hylas scratches his stubbled chin. "I know we've been put on an unfamiliar route, but, galactically speaking, this is practically on the Iolcian doorstep."

"Perhaps no-one's yet lived to tell the tale." The fact that Kalais winks at Hylas is a reminder that she is the worst. Even if she might be right. The captain's warning glare is enough for Kalais to raise her arms in retreat. "What? I said *yet*?"

"When can we get back to the skies?" Doctor Orpheus's swagger-pacing is making Jasyn nervous. "We don't exactly have all the time under the Seven Suns."

"We need to figure out what reeled us in like a fish on the line in the first place," says the captain.

"If it returns on take-off, it'll rip us apart." Gus's tone is matter of fact and almost apologetic as she looks at the doctor.

In a split second, a range of indecipherable emotions play across the doctors face before she grunts — possible agreement? — and ceases her pacing. *Thank the heavens.*

"I can tell you the mechanics..." Everyone turns to Lynk as she sifts through her haze of data. "A concentrated burst of magnetism pulled us in. Whatever caused it is dormant now, but I have pinpointed the origin."

"If we are caught in some sort of tether," says the captain, "we need to figure out how to unhook. We go out there, find the source and solve it. The sooner we do that, the sooner we can return to our mission."

With a couple of goggle-data manoeuvres, Lynk casts the cartographic image of the jungle terrain to the centre of the deck for all to see. The cartography lacks details and has several blank spots, but still, it's impressive she can create a 3D map from what she's observed. It at least shows the location of the ship and a hot spot that must be the magnetism's origin.

"It could be a trap," says Kalais.

"*It could be*," agrees Herakles. "But if it is, we're already caught in it. And we're not going to figure out how to be free of it without investigating. We proceed with caution," she determines. "Kalais, Castor, Hylas." She pauses before adding: "Axe-boy. You're with me."

The speed with which Herakles heads for the stairs suggests those summoned are to follow. Now. Castor and Hylas fall in-step behind her, while Kalais takes her time, as if assessing whether she can be bothered. From the look on Peleus's face, he's either thrilled or terrified to be included.

As she approaches the stairwell, Herakles's gaze flits between Jasyn and Atalanta. Whatever she's observing, it tightens her jaw. Seems like she really doesn't like one or both of them. Which is why Jasyn is surprised when the captain casts a glance at her as she passes and says:

"And you."

23

EXPEDITION

JASYN

Jasyn follows the selected crew down into the belly of the ship. At each porthole, she attempts to peer out. The prospect of discovering somewhere new has been a source of intrigue throughout her life. Though now she's stepping closer to it, she's put in mind of a gull at a cliff edge about to take to the skies for the first time, not knowing if they'll soar or plummet.

"Orpheus, you're staying here," says Herakles as the doctor bustles up behind them with her medician case in tow.

The doctor slows, but doesn't stop.

"Every new world holds possible cures," she protests, and Jasyn can't help but be impressed at her drive to explore the unknown. It's a shame the doctor doesn't like her, because they have curiosity in common, at least. "You know that," adds the doctor. The quietness of the words have a certain gravity to them, a vulnerability, a desperation.

There's a flash of apology in the captain's eyes, but she holds a firm hand out, indicating the doctor is to go no further. Begrudgingly, Doctor Orpheus stops short, as if to touch the captain would be an unwelcome event.

"Once we've determined whether it's safe, you'll have your time," says the captain. "But not before."

From the clench of the doctor's jaw, it's clear she has something to say about it. But, perhaps from reluctant respect for the captain or for protocol, she merely grunts. As Herakles continues on, the doctor crosses her arms and rolls her eyes in silent disapproval.

"Don't think I can't sense that eye-roll," says the captain. "Careful doctor, or I'll have you thrown in the brig for insubordination."

For some reason, as she passes, Kalais throws a wink at the doctor. *Seriously, does she flirt with everyone?*

After a huff, the doctor swagger-storms away, mumbling "Fucking... captain," as she goes.

A tug at her sleeve has Jasyn turning.

Atalanta.

"You don't have to go out there," Atalanta signs with a nervous energy. "Or you could ask the captain if I can join you?" It's as if she knows asking Jasyn not to explore is asking the impossible.

Jasyn already knows how this will go. But they've always had an unspoken rule: that she will never silence Atalanta's words. If Atalanta wants something said, Jasyn will make sure of it, even when she thinks it unwise or fruitless.

"Captain? Um..."

Herakles stops and turns, training the entirety of her confident stare on Jasyn. It could be because the captain is in charge of this ship, that her reputation precedes her, or because she's built like some sort of statue inspired by myth, but all coherence dies in Jasyn's throat. The captain's eyes flit to Atalanta and the severity in them gentles, but only until her focus snaps back to Jasyn.

"Please, don't let me rush you," says the captain.

"It's um..." says Jasyn, mentally tripping over herself and inwardly cursing her own inability to function. "Just that... You've seen Atalanta's skill with a bow..." Herakles would have been arena-side when Atalanta took perfectly accurate aim at the Ice King. "...she'd like to join us. On planet."

Herakles keeps her expectant focus on Jasyn, which is unnerving. "Your request has been noted. And denied," she says, before carrying on along the corridor.

"But —"

The captain stops suddenly and Jasyn almost runs into the solid wall of her back. There's enough warning in the captain's tensed shoulders to have Jasyn rolling over and admitting defeat.

When the captain continues on, having made her silent point, Jasyn shrugs an apology to Atalanta. In truth, she'd much prefer to be out in the unknown with her. At least then she'd know someone's got her back. Though if the ship is the safer place to be, there's comfort in knowing Atalanta is within its walls.

"Be careful out there," Atalanta signs, as Jasyn follows the captain and the rest of the crew into the airlock tunnel. The words themselves might be redundant, but the feeling behind them is crystallised in her eyes.

Thanks to Herakles and a crank of door mechanisms, that look is stolen from view.

Like an unwelcome asteroid entering Jasyn's orbit, Kalais thrusts an astro-suit at her. *Deep breath.* She should be focusing on how to put the astro-suit on, not on her favourite person behind the airlock door. Then she'll at least have a chance of breathing on an unfamiliar world.

An unknown world! And she gets to explore it. Jasyn's mild panic about the unknown is usurped by excitement as she examines her astro-suit.

Her boots feature an abrasive grip across all sides that might even allow the climbing of a cliff face, should one be so inclined. *Hail*, she misses the mountains and trees of their home world. The only things to climb in the ship are stairs.

Like the other astro-suits, Jasyn's is formed of a dark grey mesh-armour with thin stripes of coloured detailing. Where her detailing is green, Herakles's is purple, not unlike her neon hair. Hylas's is red. Peleus looks about as sickly yellow as his stripes. And, Castor and Kalais complete the set with burnt orange and neon blue respectively.

The colours and luminosity must be designed to enable them to identify each other from afar, but Jasyn can't help feeling like she's part of Peleus's gladiator Trading-Shard collection, each of them with their own distinctive colour scheme.

Handing across Jasyn's astro-helmet, Kalais demonstrates how to make contact with the suit and helmet to enable features like location, comms, oxygen levels, and so on. The details appear in the invisi-visor, or illuminate on the left forearm sleeve. Kalais's manner is mundanely list-like and has the air of *great, I have to deal with you out there, too.*

When she passes Jasyn a short-sword in a scabbard, it's notably not *her* sword. Size-wise it's similar, about the length of her own forearm, but there'll be no ice-stunts emerging from this blade. Kalais sports a multi-round pellet rifle with a dagger affixed to the end. Hylas carries a holstered hand gun. True to her Games arena persona, Castor carries a spear.

As the captain hands Peleus his axe knives, he appears to momentarily forget his crush on the hero of the arena. The emotional sparkle in his eyes would suggest he's being reunited not with instruments of butchery, but with a long lost friend. Yeah, it doesn't take much to remind Jasyn why she and Peleus — despite being in the minority of Ice Lumpians in their age bracket — never became friends.

Just as Jasyn is considering how confrontational they'll all look wandering out there, armed to the teeth, Herakles buckles a scabbard and long-sword about her waist, and instructs all in the airlock chamber:

"Weapons stay holstered unless we're under threat. Is that clear?"

"Aye, Captain," reply Kalais, Castor and Hylas, with Jasyn and Peleus adding their agreement out of step.

"For those of you new to the skies..." Herakles directs her words at Jasyn and Peleus. "...your suits are armoured, but not indestructible. Make use of the in-built breathing apparatus."

Thermometer-like markings inside the helmet denote Jasyn's as fully charged. A series of data points summarise their current surroundings:

> Atmosphere: Breathable
> Toxicity: Nil
> Gravity: 1.01

A similar selection of data points illuminate on the screen nestled within the door of the exit-hatch:

> Atmosphere: Breathable.
> Toxicity: None detected. Visor filtration activated.
> Gravity: 0.5

"If the air out there's breathable, does that mean we can —?" begins Peleus, only for Herakles to pre-empt the rest:

"Helmets stay in place at all times. They do a lot more than keep us breathing."

The helmet fit is snug, with faces in full view behind the ether-mesh of the invisi-visors. Jasyn can't help but be impressed with the technology that keeps her oxygenated, filters out toxins, *and* lets her scratch her nose.

Something taps the back of Jasyn's helmet. She whips around to confront whoever's manhandling it. Kalais definitely looks guilty of something, and Jasyn doesn't appreciate her and Castor sharing a smirk. Instead of starting something, instead of annoying the captain more and having her regret including her, Jasyn returns eyes forward and buries a sigh.

It's time.

With a nod from Herakles, Castor hits the big blue button and a steam-like mist spurts into the chamber, frazzling against the visor forcefields of their helmet fronts.

"One last thing..." The captain draws a breath as if building to an epic speech. The natural topic would be new worlds, adventure and discovery, and Jasyn is more than ready to hear it. As the outer door opens to the unknown with a hiss, as they are about to embark on a journey of wonder, the inspirational words that emerge from the captain's mouth are:

"...for hail's sake, don't poke anything."

24

THE SNOW JUNGLE

JASYN

Launching forward and drifting in a shallow arc, Jasyn's legs swim through the air. How useful this skill would've been when she lived up in the mountains. The easy bounce of her steps has her smiling.

Her heart flutters in-line with whatever winged creature up in the canopy just took flight, because what surrounds them is nothing short of jaw-dropping.

Trees of a thousand varieties. Some sturdy, trunks as wide as ice-brick cottages. Others spindly, like over-sized river reeds. With root and branches blanketed in snow, all of them are taller than any tree she's seen before.

Where Iolcus is forbidding, with every wind shear wailing the possibility of death, this place, with its squeaks and squawks and pattering streams, is calm and full of life. Where Iolcus offers sharp and treacherous ice, with variations on white, blue and grey in its rock infested terrain, this place is gentler, more inviting, its snow more... well... *fluffy*. Rounded boulders peek from beneath the blanket of unblemished snow, along with the rich green of large leathery leaves. If there are sharp edges, they are hidden.

Abundant trees bear an array of colourful fruit — or what Jasyn guesses to be fruit. Some trees have multiple fruit-types on the same branches. Perfect and plentiful. Those are the words that bounce into Jasyn's thoughts. Of course, she shouldn't assume. The fruit could be as nutritionally redundant as the filament fruit of the Iolcian Glowing Woods.

Still, she can't imagine root rot taking hold here. Where Iolcus struggles to heave produce and greenery from the ground, this place is an oasis.

Not that the rest of the crew seem too impressed. Their discussion centres around the quickest path forward, following the partial map. Perhaps a world like this is nothing new to them.

If only Hera could see Jasyn now.

Before leaving the village, before crossing paths with the sky explorers, Hera had not only been the oldest friend Jasyn had ever made, but also the most adventurous. That is, according to her tales of her past travels.

Her parents would have a fit if they knew where Jasyn was. But Hera — she'd want details. Even Snowdrop, Jasyn's claw-goat, would stare up at her with her slightly crossed eyes and enjoy tales of adventure.

A full body gut punch of grief stops her in her tracks.

She forces a breath, reminding herself to focus on the here and now. While the mission-focused ground crew forge a path through the snow-jungle, Jasyn marvels at the unfamiliar vegetation. There's little foliage on the ground. At least, none that can be seen for the carpet of snow, thick enough that their footsteps don't make way for whatever lies beneath.

Already trailing at the back, she can't help but question what her role here is. True, she would never say no to an adventure, especially one that involves exploring unchartered territory. And she might wield an ice-sword with awesome and/or terrifying consequences (though that sword is currently locked out of her reach, for good reason). But no-one's been shy in letting her know she's a liability. So, why has she been invited to join them?

Herakles is... well, *Herakles. Captain of the Skies, Hero of the arena* and *Slayer of Monsters*. Of course she would lead this expedition.

With his linguistic abilities, Hylas is needed in case they cross paths with anyone or anything in need of translation.

Castor and Kalais carry themselves with athletic and street smart confidence, respectively. Castor has her proven combat abilities. Kalais wields the strength of someone who makes her trade in shovelling ice — not to mention the figurative claws of an alleycat who'd happily toy with you or kill you for its dinner. And both have previous experience amongst the stars.

Even Peleus is good with an axe.

The words the captain had uttered to the doctor pierce Jasyn's thoughts: *Once we've determined whether it's safe...* If those aboard are staying behind to keep them safe, what does that say about the rest of them?

That they're brave and ready to take on whatever the new world throws at them? Or that they're expendable?

Is that why Jasyn is here? To be a canary down an ice-mine?

No. That doesn't align with how Gus and even grumpy Doctor Orpheus had encouraged her on this journey. And Captain Herakles wouldn't have the reputation she does if she purposefully led her crew to their deaths. No matter how much of an asshole she's being.

But...

Jasyn was called upon to join this sky voyage to help them gain knowledge of her ice abilities. Perhaps that's all she is. A test subject. A source of information. Now that the doctor has her blood, and the Ice King's daughter is contained within the medical quarters prison, Jasyn isn't needed anymore.

Her cooled breath snags on her invisi-visor. She shivers as the hairs on her neck prickle. No-one grows up on Iolcus without a healthy sense of foreboding, and this place — as much as she welcomes the apparent perfection — seems too good to be true.

She whips around to confront the shadows—

A pair of eyes stare back.

She makes no move to run or scream or even communicate her discovery. Mostly, because the creature is cute. Fur-covered and bulbous, it's small enough to fit in Jasyn's palm. *Theoretically*, of course. Keeping in mind the captain's warning, and the general concept of common sense, Jasyn refuses to make the rookie error of poking it.

But that doesn't mean she can't look, does it?

The fur-blob has two short legs at its front and two long folded legs at its sides. Each foot ends in three toes with circular suckers connecting it to the branch, its perch. Its large eyes trained on Jasyn, each time it squeaks — its mouth almost the width of its own body — it bounces a little, propelling itself forward. The animal is either telling Jasyn to go away, or is as inquisitive as Jasyn herself.

She's seen something a little like this before in the knowledge banks of her family's Shard. A *frog*, she thinks it was called. Though she'd never encountered an image or description of one covered in fur. To her continued fascination, a series of ink-like stains take shape on the creature's fur, but before she can consider what it means, a voice snips at her through the comms:

"Hurry up, Frost-bite." *Ah, Kalais.* Famous for her patience. And another new nickname. *Joy.*

The multicoloured astro-suit stripes aid in locating the crew between shadows and massive trees. Jasyn is under no illusions.

In un-chartered territory, the best place to be is with those who have experience navigating the unknown.

As she must, she takes bouncing steps in pursuit of the ground crew, passing a shimmering stream coiling in crystal clear and glacial blue strands, like water formed of threads. A droplet repels against her invisi-visor, dividing it and sending it to drift and sparkle as a dozen miniature versions of its former self.

How can the crew just march — well, bounce-march — past all these natural wonders?

"If I have to tell you again..." warns Kalais. Jasyn can only assume she's using direct-comms communication for her ears only.

Jasyn strides to catch up, past branches iced with snow and clustered with deep purple tear-drop shaped flowers. Some formations are as large as her fists, others more the size of her head. As she passes, flowers that were mere buds unfurl their petals like a snow-hawk discovering its majestic wingspan. Unlike the wings of a snow-hawk, however, the petals are star-like in their arrangement.

"Look at that," she says, but to no response.

The rest of the crew, forging onward, apparently have no idea the petals are waking, angling, as though watching them. Jasyn's wonder turns to a shudder.

"Hey," she calls after them.

She scours through her memories of Kalais's astro-suit instructions. *If the helmet comms aren't working, press the thumb pad.* Jasyn does but nothing happens. She repeats, adding a "can anyone hear me?" for good measure. The suit makes a decisively negative sound (*merp!*). Either she's doing something wrong, there's something wrong with her suit, or something wrong with the person who instructed her.

She tries again, but with the same results.

"If you hold us up any more," scolds Kalais through the helmet comms. "We'll leave you as an offering to the planet to ensure our safe departure."

That's a joke, right?

Jasyn grumbles. Not that anyone can hear her right now. She tries gesturing up at the trees, but the crew are all too far and facing away from her.

She knows better than to press random buttons on a suit designed to keep her safe in a world of unknown parameters. Slightly worried she might get sacrificed, or be outnumbered by staring star-flowers that are somehow both creepy and majestic — she does what she can in strange gravity to catch up.

At the back of the pack, Jasyn shares aloud that the flowers are opening, that they seem to be watching them (and she knows that is probably ridiculous). But her visor must actually be swallowing her sounds.

Peleus is too distracted trying to not fall on his face to pay much attention. When he finally does look her way, he flinches as if she'd snuck up on him. She gestures more dramatically behind her, in the hope of drawing attention, but when she turns to the jungle, the flowers are gone. Or, rather, they're dormant, closed, and ostentatiously *not doing anything*.

"What's your problem?" asks Peleus. His tone and darting eyes hint he's not bothered about knowing *her problems* and more bothered about getting back to the ship in one piece and soon, thank you.

She hadn't imagined it, had she? Hail, if she did, it's a good job no-one was paying her any attention. She doesn't need a crew already suspicious of her to think she's a hailstone short of a storm.

Neon coloured stripes flash from behind a curtain of vines draped between trees. Jasyn pushes aside the vine-curtain enough for herself and Peleus to step through.

"This is where the magnetism originated," confirms Castor, inspecting the map displayed within her visor.

Jasyn's about to wave for Hylas's attention, to sign to him about her comms situation, but what towers before them has her need to communicate side-swiped by curiosity.

A mesh of moss, vines and snow powder shroud its details and trees have grown epic roots around its shape, and into it, piercing its metal shell. A sky ship of some sort, no bigger than the [C]ARGO ship's helm. Perhaps a raft? Or a vehicle designed for survey and exploration?

Whatever it's for, it won't be doing it again. With the main body of the ship wedged between a collection of sturdy trees, it's nothing more than a carcass, its hull cracked open like a broken skull. Its wings and tail are torn and crumpled.

How can a world with low gravity cause that? Unless the roots and vines have pulled it apart over time? Or magnetism reeled it in in more aggressively than they'd experienced?

"Looks like we're not the first ones here," says Kalais, unnecessarily in Jasyn's opinion. It's unfair that she has to listen to Kalais's voice when Kalais doesn't have to listen to hers.

Jasyn's halfway through opening her mouth to attempt to communicate again, when static scratches through the helmet comms. Judging by the others' rigid postures, that's not a good sign.

"Captain to flight deck, come in?"

But looping static is the brain-scouring response.

As Herakles tries again, Jasyn is distracted by the structure before her. Seams in the metal denote where doors are sealed in place by trunks and roots. But the fractured hull? She can fathom three methods of approach. Scaling the trees that cling to the vessel is one. Using the hanging vines like ropes is another. The third is a combination of the two.

She could have been in there already, if left to her own devices.

With an upward bounce, she tests the limited gravity. If she were to fall, she'd feel it, but it wouldn't be catastrophic. Not that she's going to fall, of course. It's just that Atalanta would kill her if she did something stupid. Well, she'd give her a look at the very least.

With the ground crew focused on attempting contact with their ship, Jasyn starts her climb.

25

LOOK OUT

JASYN

The thick vines are sturdy and easily carry her weight as her hands, encased in snug-fitting astro-gloves, find the right holds. She already appreciates the almost bristle-like grip of her boot edges, perfect for scaling the tree trunks.

Jasyn's limbs co-ordinating fluidly with her new surroundings, her inner-wings unfurling. Unlike her lurching muscles in the engine-chamber, out here, up here, every part of her is in alignment. It may be with the gentle hiss of an astro-suit air supply, but finally she can breathe. Her heart thumps with the freedom.

What a rush.

She's so fast, in fact (or perhaps *so un-noticed*), it's only when she's fifty feet up, almost at the break in the hull, that the crew hone in on what she's doing. Peleus calls for her to "be careful," which is well intentioned but redundant, because — *obviously*. Hylas mutters something like "Heavens above," with an undertone of awe Jasyn appreciates. Kalais hollers up: "Don't go falling, Snowflake." Castor mutters something about "fucking frostbite." Herakles simply mutters: "Well, we're here now. Let's get this over with," before making swift work of catching up to her.

With the hull-entrance only one reach away, Jasyn continues into the thick shadows of the crashed vessel.

If there are portholes, they've been enmeshed by jungle — inside, outside, or both. At least she knows enough of her suit functions to shine her helmet and cuff torches into the darkness. Her eyes refocus, deciphering the shapes in her torchlight.

The ancient jungle has forged its way in, cabled around consoles and noosed about every facet of the ship. Beyond the tangle, the sky ship technology is different from their Iolcian [C]ARGO ship. While the shell is unmistakably metal, its consoles and surfaces are a dark and shiny material she can't place. Something about the sheened surfaces makes her skin crawl. The ship's innards don't seem to match its exterior, but then, what does she know?

Leeches. That's what the strange glossy surfaces remind her of. When she'd braved the Glowing Wood lagoon one time, she'd got covered in them. Atalanta had never been afflicted. It was just Jasyn's luck. *Bleugh*.

Herakles hops through the broken shell of the ship, questioning whether Jasyn is "brave or stupid." Jasyn expects more of a telling off, or to get shoved through the gap in the hull, but instead the captain reels in whoever is climbing the vines behind her.

As she steps in to assist, Jasyn tries not to stare at the close-up of the captain's biceps straining her suit. She fails miserably. When the captain catches her, Jasyn blushes perfectly. The captain merely continues in her task, probably used to such reactions.

Jasyn's just about to muster words or gestures that indicate her failed comms status, when Castor tumbles in through the hull in uncharacteristic — purposeful? — clumsiness, getting a good grip on the captain's arms and leaning into her space (apparently for support). Castor's positively beaming, while the captain's back straightens and her jaw tightens.

"Thank you, Captain." Castor bats her eyelashes with the kind of sweetness that's liable to cause both stomach and tooth ache. Before the captain can respond, Castor strides in and observes their surroundings in a more official manner, determining:

"No lifeforms present." And: "What the hail kind of ship-tech is this?"

Jasyn keeps pulling at the other vine until Kalais summits, refusing both Jasyn and the captain's outstretched hands.

"Think you're trying to get the captain to burst a blood vessel, Snowflake," she says. Her mischievous smile dies and a wariness sharpens the engine-tech's eyes as she takes in her new surroundings.

"Kal?" asks Herakles, concern in her voice.

"It's a Wrecker ship," says Kalais in a breathless whisper.

The trio of seasoned crew bristle.

"A what?" is what Jasyn would ask, if anyone could hear her. She's about to ask anyway, so that maybe the captain — or someone — can notice her situation and do something. But Kalais's eyes flick to hers and, through a tense frown, she explains:

"Wrecker ships disguise themselves as harmless vessels. They lure in other ships by various means. Targeted magnetism is one trick. But I've never heard of that method working from such a distance. Once they latch on, there's no letting go. Not without a sacrifice."

A sacrifice? *What the hail does that mean?*

"No-one survives a Wrecker ship." Kalais continues. Her words — quiet like a secret — send a shiver down Jasyn's spine.

"Looks like the Wrecker ship didn't survive *something*," says Herakles, possibly as a statement of fact, or to lighten Kalais's mood. It's the last thing Jasyn expected of the unhinged engine-tech — seemingly frozen in place by her own disquiet — to be afraid of a broken ship.

"There'll be a magnetism release," says Kalais, snapping out of whatever is troubling her. She seems to know her way around the ship that apparently no-one survives.

"Watch the perimeter, Ice-monger," says Castor over her shoulder, as the trio of experienced crew huddle about what looks to be the main console.

For now, Jasyn does as she's told, positioning herself at the break in the hull. She peers down to where Hylas and Peleus stand guard, keeping an eye on everything at ground level. Peleus shifts on his feet like he's got fire-ants in his boots, while Hylas observes their surroundings in a much calmer manner.

Jasyn instinctively steps back as a crown-sized bud unfurls beside her head. It peers down at her as if it were part of the crew assessing the situation. Its ability to swivel and *observe her*, makes her stomach sink. Its white inner petals are red tipped with blue veins cabling within. Beautiful on the outside, a night-mare within. Its outer beauty, its brilliant purple, is somewhat overshadowed by this new perspective.

Another bud blossoms, its petals dripping red.

"Bloody hail," says Jasyn, though no-one can hear her.

With the captain and the two techs looking the other way, Jasyn pulls Kalais's sleeve, only to be shrugged away. More insis-tent, Jasyn points to the flower.

"Yes, very pretty. The grown-ups are trying to concentrate." Kalais shrugs her away again.

Enough.

Jasyn grasps the captain's arm and — to her surprise — Herakles doesn't greet her with a fist to the face. With a perturbed frown, she watches Jasyn's mouth move as no sounds emerge ("I know you can't hear me, but... *seriously...!*") and lets herself be lead to the hull-break.

The situation is much worse than Jasyn had thought. Instead of one bloody blue-veined star-flower, there are dozens of nightmare blooms.

In the canopy of lush leaves and hanging vines, the bulbous flowers swivel to glare at them like a thousand judgemental eyes.

Herakles's eyes open wider.

"Well, that's... unlikely to be good."

26

A THOUSAND EYES

JASYN

Competitive staring with judgmental bloody flowers is not what Jasyn had imagined for her first sky voyage. It's more interesting than washing up and ice-shovelling, sure... but what happens next will determine which she'd rather be doing.

"How's it going over there, Kal?" asks the captain without taking her eyes off the star-flowers as she retreats to the main console. Her grip on Jasyn's arm invites her to move with her.

"It's not working..." says Kalais, her voice more elevated than Jasyn's ever heard it.

Sure enough, each time Kalais disengages a particular console switch, a vine snakes across to reengage it.

What in the heavens? Something sluices in Jasyn's stomach. She's never known vegetation to do that. Kalais reaches again. This time, a creeper lashes about her wrist.

Castor grabs the rope of vegetation enough to loosen it with jerky movements. Kalais escapes its clutches, but now Castor is trapped, nonchalance being squeezed from her.

"This place has a mind of its own." Attempting to free Castor, Kalais gets more tangled.

Jasyn draws her short-sword, but Herakles is faster and, to be honest, Jasyn is glad because her blade-dexterity is much more impressive. As the blade cuts through, a sharp screech trips out from the cut cables of greenery and a bright yellow-green liquid spills out. One end of the vine rendered inert, the other end flails and slithers away.

Are plants meant to scream? Perhaps the vine's surface being split let out pressure and sound... Anyway, she's sure she's focusing on the wrong thing right now. With limbs freed, enough new vines have lashed across the console to shroud it from view.

"*Heavens above and below.* It's like..." begins Herakles.

"...it's using the ship." Kalais completes.

Why would a bunch of vines want to lure their ship?

A rumble percolates from the thickest shadows in the cavern of the ship, at the end furthest from the break in the hull. All heads, human and star-flower, swerve in its direction.

Jasyn's not sure if that tingle in her stomach is terror or excitement. She's sure it *should* be the former.

Another nerve frazzling sound. This one more like a growl. Vine curtains part, making way for the unmistakeable gait of a predator: a feline-esque creature, as large as any of them, slender but with strong shoulders, with calculating, luminous milk-white eyes and a face punctuated by pincers.

Fascinating, yes. But the pincers, *the extra jaw,* has serrated edges much like teeth, and something slick that might be sap or saliva.

Jasyn's heart rate steps up a notch. *Terror*. That tingle in her stomach is definitely terror.

"Thought you said there were no lifeforms...?" Kalais mutters to Castor, her finger poised on the trigger of her ice-pellet rifle.

"Not by bio-scan standards," Castor snaps, angling her spear in pre-emptive defence. "There's no heartbeat."

The creature's markings *move*, like clouds or ink blots through its thin sheen of fur, fluidly reshaping. Helmet torches shine against its skin, turning the thin layer of fur translucent, shedding light on its organic, green cabling within.

Placing herself between the creature and the crew, Herakles waves them back. "Move slowly," she says, never taking her eyes off the threat. "Watch where you're going. Don't strike unless absolutely necessary."

Jasyn would have thought she'd be more gung-ho, but that's something to think on another time.

As Jasyn concentrates on reining in her galloping heart and lowering down the exterior of the overgrown ship, she waits halfway, clutching the wall of moss, vines, branches and roots.

Scaling a mesh of greenery, which may or may not be *alive*, is challenging at the best of times, but Kalais lowers herself with one arm, using a vine wrapped about her leg to control her descent.

As if sensing why Jasyn has lingered, she gives a powerful eye-roll as she passes. *Sigh.* Jasyn should stop trying to help, her input clearly isn't welcome. Castor scales past both of them, while Herakles grasps the vine-ropes and lowers carefully without turning her back on the threat.

They each find the ground with a cushioned bounce as the warped feline leans out from the rip in the hull, watching over them.

Why isn't it taking chase? Does it simply want them gone? Out of its territory?

"Above and below," mutters Hylas, nudging at them to please turn to what he's staring at, which apparently includes a kaleidoscope of unfurling buds, the eyes of multi-coloured star-flowers, staring down at them from trunks and branches. The entire canopy.

A growing rumble shudders up the trunks and along branches until white flakes erupt, puffing out en masse from the bloody star-flowers. The flakes hang in the air like snow caught in a snowglobe, drifting in the low gravity as if they have all the time in the world.

"Stay where you are," Herakles instructs, no doubt trying to discourage any fear-induced flailing into the jungle. Probably by Peleus. Or, let's be honest, right now — Jasyn.

Peleus clutches his axe-knives, ready and terrified for battle. Hylas places his hand against the holster of his hand-gun.

Castor and Kalais are already weapons-drawn, and Herakles's claim on her sword is subtle but firm as the trio triangulate around the rest of them in a manoeuvre that seems second nature.

They might be a trio of arrogant assholes, but right now Jasyn is grateful for their defensive manoeuvre and tactical know-how.

Whatever the flakes are frazzle to nothing against their visor forcefields as the mist covers them. *Thank the heavens for invisi-visors!* Though their helmet torches do little to cut through the haze.

"Captain to Helm. Are you seeing this?" The only response is an ear-scouring crackle. "Helm? Do you receive?"

"Can I shoot something yet?" Kalais's rifle trains into the thickening mist. A shared glance — more of a grimace — has Jasyn wondering whether Kalais would in fact shoot her, given half a chance.

"Hold steady," commands Herakles. "If we try to move in the mist we'll lose each other."

Which is all very easy to say, but when the ground itself is starting to writhe, staying still is a challenge. Yes, there's definitely something moving on or *in* the forest floor. *Something* beneath and around all of them. If only they could see beyond the mist...

"Bio-scan's showing noth—" Castor falters.

The ground buckles. Stomach swoops. Any sense of balance upended, as they scatter as if they're atop an ice-lake shattering to fragments.

"What was—?" starts Hylas, only to be cut short. The luminous red of his suit-lines blur as his feet sweep from under him. He drifts to the ground with an "oof."

Peleus screams — "It's got me!" — as his axe slices through the mist and cuts through *something*—

Vibrating squeaks of the fur-frogs chirp through the air, near and far. Judging by the shrill cacophony, the bulbous creature has friends. A lot of them. There's a sharpness to the cries, an otherworldly harmonic pain, or anger.

Jasyn wades through the mist towards Peleus's terrified sounds.

"Does anyone have eyes on Jasyn?" Herakles is no more than a neon-purple striped silhouette in the mist, possibly facing the other direction.

"I'm right here," says Jasyn, to obviously no avail.

"Snowflake is having comms issues," says Kalais, from the direction of blue-neon stripes, becoming less and less visible in the congealing fog. "I've got eyes on."

Sure enough, a target dot arrives on Jasyn's chest. Jasyn loses her breath. *She wouldn't? Would she?* Blue blips of Kalais's rifle-fire chip through the mist, punctuated only by jungle screams and protest.

Jasyn checks her torso. No wounds. Kalais must have been aiming past her.

Relief is cut short by a sudden pressure at her leg. Something is lashing around Jasyn's ankle, slithering around her astro-boot. It coils up her body as swiftly as her terror, gripping just as tightly too.

Jasyn's not the only one fighting and failing, as the rainbow of silhouettes call out. Neon-lined arms and legs swipe at the mist, the ground, everything.

Herakles grunts, as if something has stopped her in her tracks.

Jasyn tries to use her short-sword, but whatever the thick dark green cables are, wrapping tighter around her, have off-shoots webbing and suckering about the hilt and scabbard, anchoring it and her in place.

— *Hail* —

The fear induced temperature in Jasyn's suit plummets.

No. No. No.

Were she out of her suit, her ice-abilities might help fight off whatever is attacking, but encased in attire designed to be a closed system, the only one receiving a dose of unwelcome frost is herself.

Thanks to the mesh restraining her, she can no longer move her legs. Nor her arms. Her torso can't turn. She's at the mercy of whatever has ahold of her. Her stomach discovers new depths. Which is apt...

...because the ground that was beneath her feet is now, somehow, up to her thighs. Now her shoulders. It's strong, racing faster than her heavy pulse, pulling her down, swallowing her deeper into the animated forest floor.

A creeper coils about her head, wrenching her helmet free with the kind of crunching-hiss that puts Jasyn in mind of a crushed windpipe. That'll be her oxygen supply, then.

She holds her breath—

As the snowfall drifts across her face and into her eyes, she expects the sharp bite of cold, the burn of snow on tender skin.

But the white flakes aren't cold. In fact, they make little sensory impact at all. Though the smell makes up for it.

Whatever it is assaults her nostrils, sharp and sour, coating her nasal passage and dripping down the back of her throat — *Urgh* — while ropes of vine slither across her skin, knotting about her midriff, reeling her down into ethereal, undulating darkness, so thick, so final, she's in no doubt she's being buried alive.

Her sense of smell must have been scrubbed out, because the stench is gone.

Jasyn blinks. It's dark, but her eyes adjust to decipher the network of roots and vines in her subterranean prison. At least the shadows aren't writhing anymore. She must have fallen unconscious when they squeezed too tight. Her surroundings are so still, she could be convinced it was all in her mind.

How long has she been here? Minutes? Hours? Her helmet is off, she recalls that much. It can't be wise to breathe unknown air, but her lungs insist. She awaits the adverse affects but the air is full and fresh, her lungs rejuvenated.

She tests her arms, legs, fingers and toes for functionality. There's no pain, just limited movement due to being knotted in place. Roots frame the lazy snowfall over-head. The blizzard has calmed and the star-flowers look no more threatening than, well... *flowers*.

At least the jungle no longer stares. There's no sign of the creatures. Other than being lodged in the ground, there's nothing that signals danger. Though it is difficult to ascertain these things when buried in soil and roots.

Something or someone yanks the back of her collar, expertly plucking her from the ground, freeing her from her restraints. She's not quite sure how they manage it, but the question is forgotten as soon as she drifts back to solid ground, landing on her feet, with a measure more grace than expected.

Finally, the fluttering in her stomach is the good kind. Because the face that greets her is familiar and welcome and everything to Jasyn: galactic eyes and a mischievous smile, framed by the glowing gold of astro-suit stripes...

"How did you —?" begins Jasyn. She would've thought it impossible, but *Atalanta has found her*.

"I'd find you even if you were lost half way across an unknown galaxy," signs Atalanta. "But it's much easier when astro-suits have trackers."

Trackers. Yes. That makes sense.

In a blur of luminous green and gold, Atalanta wraps her arms around Jasyn and squeezes tighter than any vine could as the momentum of the embrace knocks them off their feet.

Caught mid-air, hovering in low gravity, Jasyn could stay in this moment forever. She might not belong on the ship, according to most of its crew. She might not belong on Iolcus, according to its ruler and brainwashed citizens. But she belongs in Atalanta's arms.

The perfection of the moment is usurped by Atalanta's mouth finding hers in a head-to-toe tingling kiss. *Hail.* It's too long since they've been able to be close.

"Do I have to give another speech about contagion pathways?" With a sigh, Doctor Orpheus struts out of the thicket in her matte black astro-suit detailed with white. How she manages to *strut* in low gravity is really rather impressive.

Jasyn snaps out of her Atalanta-induced stupor. *Everyone else. Where are they?*

Atalanta must notice her panic because she's quick to sign: "Don't worry. They're okay. Vitals are good and locations are known."

A flash of blue sparks silently between the trees—

Why is she bounce-walking through the snow-jungle? How did she get here? The last she recalls, Atalanta was telling her everyone is okay, which is obviously the case since she can see them up ahead.

Herakles is leading the way, followed closely by Kalais and Castor. Peleus lumbers to catch up to them; either to be closer to his hero, or simply appreciating that these three are the ones with the power to keep him safe.

Atalanta is by Jasyn's side, and Doctor Orpheus, Tiphys and Hylas are trailing not far behind.

As if sensing their movement, star-flowers light up in the jungle darkness like street lanterns. Where the jungle had seemed threatening before, it now *seems* to be actively helping them find their way.

But why would their surroundings go to the trouble of capturing them, only to let them loose? Where did the creatures go? And how did she get precisely here?

The questions all have Jasyn's head in a bit of a spin.

"Where are we going?" she asks Atalanta. She's about to sign the words, too, but apparently her helmet has been re-affixed and her comms are working. *When did that happen?*

"Ah, there you are!" The voice, deep and confident, calls to them as a man tromps out from the copse of trees.

There's something familiar about him, nudging the corners of Jasyn's mind. But familiarity is impossible, isn't it? They're on a planet none of them have ever been to. A planet no-one knew existed. His outfit: midnight blue waistcoat, light grey long sleeves, dark breeches and boots. Herakles could be looking at her clothing double. But it's his beaming smile and the familiar sparkle in his eyes that gives Jasyn pause.

"Managed to untangle yourselves, I see," says the man with a mop of wavy dark hair. "I apologise. You got caught in our defences." He gestures to the jungle as if that explains everything. "Our comms aren't functional. Otherwise I'd have warned you."

The familiarity of his posture, his features, trickles through Jasyn's thoughts. *Water*. Something about him makes her think of water. Of *rushing*. Of *the sky*. Her thoughts churn as loud as a river—

Ice air... forward momentum... water rushing... an ice-billboard crackling through visual announcements... one image in particular... a silhouette: a soaring bird, pointing skyward? Aimed at spheres and twinkling stars. A person's silhouette, gazing up at the stars, an unflinching stance of heroic determination.

A god of the skies.

The memory of her childhood dream, her river-journey from the Ice City as a baby on an ice-raft, crashes into place. The man, the astronaut, with the glinting smile that encouraged a world to take to the skies, is before them.

"Agnius?" says Herakles with disbelief. She reaches out with open arms, as if greeting an old friend.

Agnius. Captain and Navigator of the SAVIOUR? The last captain and ship before them to leave the Iolcian skies.

"Dad?" The voice of Tiphys is small and shaky, filled with hope and disbelief.

On their journey to the Ice City, Tiphys had proudly claimed the man on the billboard to be his father. Jasyn had thought it a tall tale or wishful thinking, but when the man grins, it's as clear as snowflakes are unique that he has the essence of Tiphys in his features.

The crew step aside as father and son stare at each other, as if neither can believe the other is here. Tiphys's bottom lip quivers, while Agnius's eyes fill with tears.

"Tiphys?"

Tiphys makes full use of the runway left by the parted crew to race into his father's arms, laughing, crying, beaming: "I knew

I'd find you." His voice muffles in his father's shoulder. "I told them I would."

Jasyn swallows the lump in her throat. Tears crowd the corner of Atalanta's eyes, but when she catches Jasyn smiling at her she rolls her eyes at herself. Herakles and Hylas share a warm smile, while Kalais and Castor are busy inspecting their own boots (either immune to emotion, or trying to be). Even the doctor's grimace looks more strained than usual.

Electricity judders the air—

WHAT IS HAPPENING?

It would seem she's not just drifting through low gravity, but time, too, bouncing between one moment and the next, missing several in between.

Tiphys doesn't budge from his father's side, as if he fears he might look away and lose what he's only just found, as Agnius guides them along a route that avoids further natural defences. No reaching vines, no staring animals, no flowers spewing snow-dust, no being swallowed by the ground.

Jasyn's not complaining, but she'd love an explanation for, well… everything.

The crew line-up is different to before. Now that she thinks about it, Jasyn vaguely recalls Herakles instructing Kalais and Castor to return to the ship to send the rest of the crew to join them, and to stay behind to keep an eye on the Ice Princess. Jasyn gives a mental nod: that's who she'd choose to stay on the ship, too. Even a ferocious ice royal would think twice about messing with cruel Castor and scrappy, scathing Kalais. And, admittedly, Jasyn would welcome a break from their not-so-veiled threats.

"I suppose you'd all like to know where you are and what's

going on?" Agnius dazzles with a cheeky Tiphys-esque grin as — in the manner of a showman — he draws back a curtain of vines to unveil what lies beyond the thicket.

Eyes wide, jaws dropped, that's the appropriate response when the valley before them is filled with the impossible. Even Doctor Orpheus looks like she might be impressed as they all stare at the middle distance and the, well, *distant* distance where a jungle city sprawls, occupying the valley with towering trees entwined into high-rises.

An entire city grown from trees. An oasis of possibility.

Like magnets, Jasyn and Atalanta's hands drift together. Discovering new worlds is exactly what she's always wanted. To do so at Atalanta's side... she couldn't ask for more. It's all enough to make Jasyn lose her breath.

An electrical spark—

28

JUNGLE CITY

JASYN

"You might be feeling a little light headed," says Agnius as he leads them through the towering tree-entwined epic gateway to the city. It's the kind of entranceway that lets those who cross it know: this is a place where people don't just survive, they thrive.

"Oxygen here is more plentiful than on Iolcus. It takes some getting used to." Agnius pauses in what Jasyn guesses to be the city's main street.

Treetops spindle high. They sway, but never fall. An irregular sphere of water above the city, a lake in the formation of a raindrop, morphs mid-air.

"You'll feel a little off every now and then — you might miss a few things — but don't worry, it's temporary. You'll acclimatise."

That's when Jasyn sees it; the nose of a large, grey, marine mammal breaking the surface of the free-hanging water, before about-turning and swimming into the upward depths, kicking out its tail in its wake. It's like the *sea creatures* Tiphys has told her about, that live on Iolcus — or perhaps used to — under the ice and in the oceans. But she's too busy being awed by the sight to dwell on the on the history of it all.

Though Jasyn's grin is echoed by Atalanta's, there's something odd about this place, needling at her thoughts. And it's not just that it's composed mainly of interwoven trees.

It could be that she's never seen a city like this. It could be that the people emerging from the organically shaped buildings are all smiling. It shouldn't be unsettling, but she's never seen so many calm and happy faces. Children dart between the trunks and across the polished stone piazza, playing, laughing. It should be cause for celebration, not suspicion.

The reaction likely says more about her than them.

Jasyn must have absorbed something from Tiphys's many ramblings on the topic, because she knows that it was ten Iolcian sun-orbits ago that thirty-six crew took to the skies on the SAVIOUR. There won't have been children on the sky ship, so it can be assumed that they were born here. It seems the trees aren't the only ones to have established roots in this place.

When Agnius suggests everyone rest after their journey, or join him for a tour, for a bunch of supposedly brave explorers surprisingly few of the crew stick around. The majority follow a citizen to a tavern grown within the twining trunks of several trees. The rest — Herakles, Gus, Doctor Orpheus, Tiphys, Atalanta and Jasyn only — follow Agnius towards the greenest, most plentiful portion and apparent epicentre of the city, where a tangle of trees tower towards the skies.

No-one complains that Jasyn and Atalanta are hanging about, so Jasyn keeps quiet as she and Atalanta follow behind.

"We followed your path, your route for the Fleece," says Herakles to Agnius, both leading the way in a shoulders back, chest puffed, *captainly* fashion, "but I have to admit I thought finding you would be like locating a hailstone in the ice bucket of the stars."

"There's no version of events," agrees Gus, following alongside Doctor Orpheus, "where we'd have imagined finding you on the first leg of our journey."

Not to mention their co-ordinates were sabotaged... So...?

"How in the heavens are we here?" asks Doctor Orpheus, her brow contorting.

"I'll get to that, I promise." Agnius grins. "But first, welcome to my ship." He gestures at the towering mass of crisscrossing roots, branches and foliage.

Strange. The bark walls are flecked with gold. Only in Jasyn's dreams has she seen a tree of this type. It takes a moment to focus beyond the surface. Between the lattice of trunks and lush canopy, something glints. *Metal.* The kind of tarnished chrome the [C]ARGO ship boasts. Scuffed letters peek between the browns and green, enough to assume it reads: SAVIOUR.

Agnius grins over his shoulder as he leads them under the arches that are apparently the buckled legs of the grounded sky ship, scaffolded by the spiral mesh of trunks.

Beneath the ship, bundles of spindling branches, roots and vines stretch from the ship's open cargo hold, down into the ground, like some sort of organic wire-bundle.

"I'm no sky ship scientist," mumbles Doctor Orpheus, "but that thing's not flying again."

Gus nods her agreement.

"Our ship suffered damage on the return journey," says Agnius, leading them up a side ladder and into one of the ship leg's access hatches.

The return journey?

Jasyn focuses on each rung, until she regroups with the rest of them in the ship. Its airlock is notably left open, its door held in place by branches and roots enmeshed along the internal walls. The crew are moving on. Atalanta turns back and holds out her hand, inviting Jasyn to catch up.

"A cosmic storm knocked us off course," continues Agnius, leading them along the corridor that — apart from the bountiful plant-life — is similar to the wire bundles, pipes and grate floors of the [C]ARGO ship. "We were got by the magnetic grip of a Wrecker ship." He pauses. "Ever since, we've been trawling the skies remotely along my original co-ordinates, in the hope of an Iolcian ship following our path."

"You used the Wrecker's technology to steer us here from afar?" asks Gus. *So that explains their route being altered?* It hadn't been by someone on the ship.

"I hope you don't mind," says Agnius, with a winning smile. "Our comms have been down since the crash, otherwise I'd have given you warning. I might even have asked nicely."

"You said return journey?" asks Jasyn, fully expecting Herakles, Doctor Orpheus, or Gus to tell her to keep quiet, or even to question what she's still doing here. But the three of them simply look to Agnius as if they're glad the question has been asked. Even Agnius nods his approval.

"I could wax lyrical," he says, "about each step of the journey. I'm sure I could write a series of Shard fictions on the topic..." Agnius continues to lead the way through the corridors. Tiphys hangs on his every word. They all do. "...but for now, let's say obtaining the Fleece was a near-impossible task."

Near impossible?

The question is too big to give it voice.

"When we crash landed, we were surrounded by unfavourable conditions. The temperature freezing. The air poison. This world was weighted against us in a thousand ways."

Agnius turns down a corridor where metal doors are lashed open by solid branches, like a network of arteries and veins. Beyond the doors, golden light pulses like a solar heartbeat. The intensity makes it impossible to stare directly at the source, but in the haze around its orbit, it's clear that *this* is from where the vegetation stems.

"Our ship was spent, but the Fleece was anything but. When we crashed, the Fleece took root and this city grew. *This jungle.* It balanced resources. The ground turned plentiful. Air became breathable. It turned this husk of nothing into an oasis."

Jasyn tries to play it cool, as any ice-monger should... but... *all this from one item.* A mystical, little-understood item about which fantastical stories are told, but still!

"We now have first-hand proof that the Fleece changes the fabric of what surrounds it. We can turn its energy to crops, to water, to shelter. We co-exist with the creatures here. With sustenance plentiful, life is calm. The Fleece has solved all issues of balance and resources, as we hoped it would. Though one thing it does not do is create a functioning sky ship."

"The temperature isn't cold, but the snow remains?" asks Doctor Orpheus, inspecting the snow-powder decorating the portholes.

"The Fleece makes the impossible possible," says Agnius, clearly pleased with himself or the situation. Understandably so.

Something electric dances in Jasyn's vision—

29

RELAX

JASYN

How Jasyn is now in the tavern, she isn't sure…

If she thinks on it, she can vaguely recall talk of "leaving the planet with the Fleece in tow," but also that "this planet is a wonder and they should take time to enjoy it." Apparently, that means being in the tavern.

Seeking a clue to Atalanta's whereabouts, Jasyn scans the room. From her vantage point at the bar: Tiphys is bending his father's willing ear, probably about the adventures they've both been on to get here. The fawn is successfully inviting scraps from the tables stuffed with plentiful produce, colourful fruit. Even Gus is smiling, no doubt relieved and eager to get back to Iolcus and her family. Kalais and Castor must still be relegated to the ship and keeping an eye on the caged Ice Princess. (Best place for them.) And the rest of the [C]ARGO crew are drinking and dancing with the SAVIOUR crew and each other.

"You'd think," grumbles Doctor Orpheus, occupying a coiled-branch bar stool and staring into her mug of liquor as if it contains the secrets of the universe (and those secrets have personally offended her), "a sky ship crew on a mission to discover all the worlds under the Seven Suns would have more of an imagination when it comes to *enjoying* a new world."

Jasyn refrains from pointing out that the doctor is in here drinking, too.

"You're not dancing, Doctor?"

"It wouldn't be fair to show off my skills," she says, her mouth pursing above her cup. "I have excellent rhythm."

There's a suggestive raise to her brow — *Hail... Is Doctor Orpheus flirting with her?* The over-oxygenation or the liquor must be getting to either Jasyn, the doctor, or both. Or proximity to the Fleece really does make the impossible possible.

"Am I the only one thinking this all seems too good to be true?" the doctor grumbles. From her nod to the tavern in general, Jasyn assumes she means the situation of the Fleece rather than the tavern itself, or Jasyn's proximity. "All fallen into place too easily. And let's not forget we've got an Ice Princess with her own aspirations occupying my quarantine chamber."

Jasyn wants to tell the doctor to lighten up. What does it matter what the Ice Princess wants, when she's safely stowed away? Now they have the Fleece, saving Iolcus and Corinth is within reach. They took to the skies and found what they hoped to find — on their first unintentional pit stop, no less.

When put like that, it *does* all seem too good to be true... But Agnius had guided them: strings were pulled to get them here. It's logical. Not unbelievable. Nor impossible, clearly.

Speaking of the impossible...

Jasyn's heart lights up as the familiar, friendly face complete with half-moon glasses, greets her from across the tavern. She'd know that face anywhere. Encased in an armchair beside the oversized and welcoming fireplace, her back as crooked as an Iolcian mountain peak, is none other than Hera.

Jasyn swallows the automatic lump in her throat.

Hera had been a source of endless wonder for half her life,

rekindling daily Jasyn's longing to explore beyond their village, to experience Iolcus and beyond. What Jasyn wouldn't give to be able to tell her of the adventure she's on. That she's on a mission to save not just one world but two.

But this world or the after-effects of death must be getting to her, because Hera can't be here... Nor can Snowdrop the claw-goat be lounging at her feet. Nor can her parents — hail, *her parents* — be idly chatting at the fireside as if it's just another day in Ice Lump.

As relief, happiness and confusion clash in their own arena battle, Jasyn takes an automatic step towards them. In spite of logic, she hopes to hug them. And to ruffle Snowdrop's wiry fur.

A melodic whisper in a foreign tongue tickles her ears. She hesitates. Because, there, in the square of space between Jasyn's parents, Hera and Snowdrop, is Medea, her eyes flickering purple flames.

Given that Medea is surrounded in a haze not of this world, and no-one else in the tavern is responding to her presence, it can only be assumed the apparition is in Jasyn's mind.

There's a flustered urgency to Medea's scowl as she steps towards Jasyn—

The lights flicker—

✦

A HEARTY SLAP TO JASYN'S BACK JOLTS HER —

The tavern is little changed. But the armchairs by the fireplace are empty. Her parents, Hera and Snowdrop are gone. Medea, too.

Apart from an instinctive understanding that she's imagining things, Jasyn doesn't have time to settle on an emotion stemming from the sudden appearance and loss of those she cares about (and Medea), because Herakles is busy raising a tankard and merrily commanding that Jasyn "Drink" and "Have fun."

The captain is more relaxed than she was on the ship. Doctor Orpheus remains her usual sullen self, however, grumbling something about "you'll regret it," and "no-one listens to me."

Jasyn isn't fully listening. Her attention is entirely drawn beyond the dance floor to Atalanta, idly surveying the busy room. How she makes leaning on a tavern's stairway look both graceful and strong, Jasyn can only admire. It has her both jittery and calm. And when Atalanta's eyes lock with hers, the opposing sensations escalate by several notches.

Heaven's hail. Even from afar, those eyes sparkle like nebulae—

Sparks—

✦

AND THEN, SHE'S THERE...

She's not sure how, exactly... She doesn't remember navigating her way through the crowds to the foot of the stairway.

With Atalanta on the third rung, Jasyn can only look up at her and the light source behind her, halo-ing her in an otherworldly glow.

Jasyn is exactly where she wants to be. Within the orbit of Atalanta's warm and knowing smile. From afar or close, it hits the mark as the star-like glint in Atalanta's eyes confirms that *yes, she very much heard Jasyn's breath hitch.* Can she hear her knees weaken, too?

It's never made sense to Jasyn why knees go weak at moments like this, because now seems the worst moment to malfunction. Anyone would think she's experiencing the delightful torture of an unrequited crush. Right now, her heart and cheeks must rival the Fleece for their glow.

With hand outstretched, Atalanta invites Jasyn to follow, and within ten thunderous heartbeats and three suppressed breaths, Jasyn is being led up the winding staircase, the warmth of Atalanta's palm pressed against her own.

"Where are we going?" asks Jasyn. *Oh good, she's remembered what words are.*

Atalanta throws a smile over her shoulder, her eyes lit up with mischief and more. With her other hand, she signs: "You're the adventurous one. I thought you'd want to explore."

Jasyn's heartbeat climbs to the heavens.

Electricity —

✦

STAR-FLOWER LANTERNS ILLUMINATE TO GUIDE THEM (THESE ONES, thankfully, showcasing a delicate beauty, inside and out), as Atalanta leads the way across the threshold and into the empty cavern of a room. From its intricate canopy of branches domed into walls and ceiling, it must have been grown rather than built. Everything is lush, with soft edges.

The door clicks shut behind them, and tavern merriment and other people's existence fades away. Jasyn can hardly believe it. That she and Atalanta actually — *finally* — get to be alone together seems too good to be true.

They might only have been separated for a matter of days and nights on the ship, but given the recent chaos of their lives it may as well have been an eternity. She was starting to think the captain was trying to keep them apart.

"I may have put in some requests," signs Atalanta, as if that explains why the room is weaving into a new formation.

That she's gazing at the chamber in the manner Jasyn would

observe the shimmering night sky would suggest this is all perfectly normal and to be expected. Like a moving mosaic, branches, leaves and flower-lanterns shift and reform. The bark patterns of the inner walls morph from brown with gold flecks to the black and silver of the Iolcian Glowing Woods. Buds emerge from the smooth branches, unfurling into star-flowers with warm glowing bulbs at their centre, a rainbow constellation not far removed from filament fruits.

Jasyn can only look on in wonder and assume the evolution to be the result of the Fleece (and Atalanta's requests). She wants to know exactly what's happening and why (of course she does!), but such concerns pale in comparison to more immediate thrills.

As the newly formed filament trees weave into a dome above them in a recreation of Atalanta's Iolcian woodland den, Jasyn smiles and her heart dances.

It was in the Glowing Woods and Atalanta's den that they'd made their feelings for each other known. *Hail.* If only they could go back to that moment:

The den... bodies bathed in the light of filament fruits and fire... the new frontier of exploring each other for the first time... every touch a new adventure...

The memories blaze bright in Jasyn's thoughts. Her synapses glow like filaments and fire. It must be written across her face, because Atalanta closes the distance between them, catching Jasyn's mouth in a kiss so deep every atom in the universe aligns. With a *whoosh*, a fire pit forms at the den's centre, flame and heat crackling — *because that's a normal thing to happen...*

Jasyn turns to raise a quizzical eyebrow, only for Atalanta to guide her into a deeper kiss instead.

Filaments pulse, melding with the gold blush of the flames. It could be the effects of higher quality oxygen, but with the universe of colours rippling around them, she could be convinced that they're not within the walls of a tavern guest room on an oasis planet, but submerged in the rippling aurora of Atalanta's eyes.

Impossible, of course.

But then, so much of this world is.

Atalanta traces her fingers down Jasyn's bare torso as moonlight hazes in through the latticed window-branches.

Hang on... Jasyn doesn't recall removing her own clothes, nor having them removed... She gulps, her breath and heart rate scrambling for footing. *When did Atalanta undress?* Jasyn forgets how to *not stare.*

A quick glance over Atalanta's shoulder locates their intertwined clothes, drifting to the floor. Atalanta quirks a smile. Such stealth and dexterity.

Nerves ignite with pleasure, crystallising into snowflakes drifting mid-air. *Yeah, that's actually not unusual for her...* at least, not when Atalanta is within her thoughts, her reach.

Weightless. That's how Jasyn feels as Atalanta navigates Jasyn's touch to her desired location, and each unique crystalline pattern pulses to the thrum of Jasyn's heartbeat.

The cooled mist of her quickening breaths reflect and refract the light of the star-filaments and the fire-pit flames. In perfect synchronicity, snow and embers drift, pausing only when Atalanta's body stills — coiled tension promising release—

A perfect moment, frozen in time.

A synaptic crackle—

30

ASPIRATIONS

JASYN

As Atalanta nestles against her, the pulsing filament-starflowers are as gentle as sleeping breaths. Jasyn's not sure when they fell asleep. She's not sure on many details, in fact. She knows they spent the night together — that much is obvious — but the specifics are beyond her reach. That she and Atalanta can be together like this is thrilling, but if she could dwell a little more on the details of their intimate moments, she'd be much more content. But time and events are as elastic as her concentration.

And it's not the only thing that isn't sitting right...

It would be ungrateful to think it's all been too easy, wouldn't it? It is good the Fleece has already been found. It is good to discover it a shareable resource and that the journey hasn't cost lives. *It is good* that soon they will return to solve the ills of Iolcus and save Corinth. It would be wrong to invite more of a challenge...

But the idea of returning to Iolcus so soon... It's as though they've just started scaling the most mysterious mountain, its peaks masked by clouds, and already they have to return to mundane and solid ground. The adventure is over when it's only just begun.

"Hey," signs Atalanta, waking and tracing a fingertip over Jasyn's temple and down to her frown. "I know what you're thinking." She smiles. "There will be time to explore the universe once we've saved a planet or two."

"The universe?" If Jasyn's heart could literally glow, it would. The filament-star-flowers must have an inkling, because they glow for her.

"Why start small?" Atalanta shrugs. "With the Ice King removed from the throne, the skies can be open again. Soon we'll discover every adventure under the Seven Suns."

Jasyn sighs. That sounds like perfection, outdone only by Atalanta manoeuvring to straddle her hips.

The filaments glow even brighter, only to stutter—

It's the adventure she's always wanted. But, there's something tickling the edge of her thoughts. A missing part of the puzzle.

Wasn't part of the plan for her ice abilities to be understood by the time they return, so they can use that knowledge to defuse the Ice King? Perhaps even for her to understand her powers enough to better him, this time? The journey's been so short, they've had no time to scratch the surface of what she can do, never mind the how and why. If they return to Iolcus now, she's unlikely to be of much use against the tyrant who took her life with her own ice-sword once already.

The tavern-den door flies open—

Herakles occupies the doorway, her face set to serious, her stature impressive. "Quick," she says, casting a bow and arrows at Atalanta and the inert ice-sword at Jasyn.

Whether it's because her heart is thumping harder at the sudden turn in events, or because of the cushion of low gravity, Jasyn plucks the sword from the air in a manner only a potential hero might.

It blossoms to a sharp blue blade as it sparkles in the captain's eyes. Though whether the source of awe is Jasyn's ability to catch a sword, or her outright nakedness... either way, the captain averts her gaze after a moment of unmistakable appreciation.

"We need you," says the captain, clearing her throat. "The Ice Princess has escaped."

Sparks prickle at the periphery of vision and thoughts—

✦

STRIDING DOWN THE TAVERN STAIRWAY, JASYN DOESN'T RECALL getting dressed, exactly, but a quick assessment indicates she's fully clothed in her astro-suit. *Thank the heavens*. She adjusts the sword at her hip and Atalanta keeps pace, bow in hand, her quiver of arrows strapped across her shoulders.

In the tavern, [C]ARGO and SAVIOUR ship crew — a frenzy of faces — busy themselves getting weapon-ready. Castor and Pollux wield spears. (*Guess Castor's back, then...*) Zetes prepares an ice-pellet rifle. Even Hylas is checking the chamber of his hand gun. And Peleus clutches his axe-knives close, looking as though he wants the ground to swallow him.

Moments later, the astronauts fan out into the jungle-city piazza. The mix of mist and silence could be ethereal, otherworldly, beautiful, but in these circumstances serve only to be ominous as they wait.

Something unpleasant coils in Jasyn's stomach. What would someone like the Ice Princess, whose job it is to enact the will of the Ice King, who obliterates villages to steal their resources... what would she do with the Fleece?

Power for the sake of personal gain. Power for the sake of cruelty. Power for the sake of more of it. If the Fleece brings prosperity, whoever possesses it could conceivably control a world. Several worlds. All the worlds under the Seven Suns.

Is that why she stowed away and took to the skies with them? Not to sabotage the retrieval of the Fleece, but to take it for herself? Arguably, she could have waited until the Fleece was on board and en route to Iolcus, but perhaps she's simply taken her chance with Kalais and broken free... Perhaps she enjoys the theatre of it all, creating chaos in a world of perfection. Who knows how an ice royal's mind works.

Mutterings of discomfort and defiance reach out from the mist. The formidable silhouette of the Ice Princess struts under the city's tree-entwined gateway arch. Wielding her ice-sword in one hand, it sparks like a severed water-doused cable. With her other hand, she drags Kalais like a rag doll with an audible attitude problem.

Ice-formations, sharp and serrated, take shape in the Ice Princess's wake.

Of course she's here. Because what's worse than an ice royal with the power of ice? An ice royal with the power of ice *and* a Golden Fleece. She and the Ice Princess might originate from the same family tree, but Jasyn's leaf escaped the poisoned branches long ago.

A sour smile creeps across the Ice Princess's features as she shoves Kalais forward. The engine-tech stumbles in the low gravity, scrambling for the safety of the crew.

As her hand reaches for her brother, a lash of ice whips from the Ice Princess's sword. Blades of ice pierce Kalais's chest. There's no time to react. No time for shock and pain to cross Kalais's features before the life freezes from her eyes.

Gasps of horror shake the crowd. Jasyn is left breathless as her gut wretches. She might have flippantly wished Kalais ill, but seeing the nauseating reality of Kalais harmed... a bouquet of blood and ice... no-one deserves that.

Low gravity cushions Kalais into Zetes's arms. His feral cries are much like the sounds he's aimed at the ice-engine, only now dampened by grief.

Agnius steps protectively in front of his son.

The Ice Princess's grinning-grimace grows as her tyrant laughter echoes.

Jasyn's fingers twitch at the hilt of her ice-sword, but before anyone else can move, Captain Herakles steps forward as if she and the Ice Princess are contenders in The Games.

"You know..." the Ice Princess keeps her focus on Herakles but raises her voice as though putting on a show, "...in the arena, I always held back. It's not much fun for an audience if all the contenders die in one tournament, apparently."

She dips to contact the ground with the tip of her sword. Herakles only has time for one backward step before the ice meshes up her legs, encasing her lower half and freezing her in place.

The captain hacks at the ice, but the infection only spreads, every shard replacing with new layers, deformed and undulated like scar tissue, until even her sword-wielding arm is anchored and immovable.

Hail.

Castor and Pollux raise their spears, only for the Ice Princess to dip her sword to the ground again, catching the duo mid-motion with her flood of ice. Their last gasps hit the air in frozen plumes.

The sight punches the breath from Jasyn's lungs.

Zetes aims at the Ice Princess, only for a targeted blast of ice to scorch the rifle from his hands.

Hylas fires his hand gun, but with the swipe of her sword, a suddenly formed ice-shield absorbs each shot with a dying spark.

Atalanta raises her bow.

Fear crackles in Jasyn's veins—

She steps in front of Atalanta's un-released arrow, whipping her ice-sword from scabbard. Her weapon blooms ice-electric as she hazards to the middle of the street, entering the unofficial arena.

An echo of familiarity ricochets through her. There had been a moment in her own altercation with the Ice Princess in the Games arena when she'd thought she glimpsed a flash of humanity in her foe's eyes. It had been a trick, of course. It seems a ridiculous notion, now, seeing her strutting with the cruel self-importance of a royal brat.

It's a fact of the universe that the Ice Princess needs putting in her place. For Jasyn's parents. For Hera. For Snowdrop. For the fallen astronauts. And for every other individual she has harmed, or worse.

Navigating the frozen ground, conviction in place of confidence, Jasyn stands tall.

The Ice Princess's mouth cracks into a wicked grin and Jasyn hesitates. What if the crew are right to think her nothing more than a liability? Useless at best, an ice-creating nightmare at worst?

With the flick of her wrist, the Ice Princess casts sharp, elongated crystals through the air as she charges at Jasyn—

Electricity lashes—

31

WHAT IN THE HEAVENS—?

JASYN

The tapestry of lush green and pristine white, threaded together with a thousand lines of glacial blue, becomes a buoy in a sea of stars as the ship forges a course away from the snow-jungle world into the sparking synapses of space.

Wait... What?

What happened? Did she win?

Is Atalanta okay?

Jasyn's still alive, evidently. That's something. But she doesn't recall returning to the ship. If she thinks on it she can recall the vague shape of events — the death and destruction, the standing against an ice royal who's had a lifetime to ready for battle — but the details evade her. The bridge connecting her thoughts seems to be missing many crucial slats and the rope is fraying.

Why is she in this chamber? Even though she's never been in here, she knows it's the captain's quarters. Where the crew dwellings consist of narrow sleeping tubes and not much else, the bed here is quadruple the size of the bunks and the chamber is large enough to dance across, should anyone feel so inclined. But by far the most striking aspect is the floor-to-ceiling porthole framing the ever-changing canvas of the cosmos.

Atalanta joins her at the porthole and Jasyn's shoulders lower, her breathing calms. *She's okay.*

The captain's reflection joins them at the porthole, and a hearty slap to Jasyn's shoulder follows.

Hang on... The captain...? Not only is she alive, she's not showing any signs of having been encased in ice.

"Thanks to you," says Herakles, grinning, and something in Jasyn's chest glows at her tone, "the Ice Princess won't be bothering us anymore."

Seriously?!

First she and Atalanta finally get to be intimate at the tavern, and all she has are moments of clarity with significant gaps in between? Then she faces the Ice Princess and *wins*, and all she gets is a vague shape of events? *Unbelievable.*

"She's where she should be." Herakles doesn't say it, but Jasyn understands she means *in quarantine.* "We've increased security. This time, there won't be any mishaps."

For the first time in a while, the captain's muscles aren't bunched in her jaw, her shoulders. She looks... relaxed.

"Kalais, is she...?" Jasyn doesn't want to use the word *dead.* And, for that matter, how are Castor, Pollux and... everyone else?

"Doctor Orpheus is working her magic."

Jasyn nods, relieved. She might not like how some of the crew have treated her, but she doesn't wish them dead. Not in any lasting, meaningful way.

"And we're...?" She wonders how to find out what she and Atalanta are doing here without making it sound like she has the kind of memory issues that'll land her in the medical quarters.

"Ship life hasn't exactly given you two much time together..."

You mean you *haven't given us much time together?* Jasyn

refrains from adding, but the captain's bashful smile suggests she knows as much.

"...the least I can do is give you a break, try to make up for it, and offer my sleeping quarters for the return trip."

Jasyn and Atalanta share raised brows. *Seriously?*

She half expects the crew to jump out and start laughing, because this all seems too good to be true.

"But you're the captain," signs Atalanta and Jasyn translates.

"Yes. And I wouldn't be if you hadn't stopped the Ice Princess." The captain clears her throat. "You saved everyone. *Hail*, extend the logic, and you've technically saved Iolcus and Corinth too."

Heaven's above! Would it be too much to remember the particulars of these events? There's the general idea that these things happened, that she did something brave and good — and perhaps even demonstrated that standing up to the Ice King might be a possibility — but the details are like a pavement lost to frost.

She's not entirely comfortable taking the credit. But she can't deny it feels good to not be the ship's punching bag for a change.

"Make the most of it," says the captain with a nod to the bed in particular. "We'll be back on Iolcus soon enough."

Jasyn might have confronted an Ice Princess and won, but when the captain winks at her, Jasyn is more impressed with her ability to repress her own blush.

Showing herself out, the captain pauses just beyond the doorway and turns back to them, her amber eyes lit up and playful.

"If you two want me to show my appreciation—"

But Atalanta is already heel-kicking the door shut, her eyes only on Jasyn.

With a tug of Jasyn's shirt, Atalanta invites her into her orbit, slanting their mouths together in the most otherworldly way. Nimble fingers pull at fabric—

Framed space tremors branching light—

✦

THE ROAR OF APPLAUSE AND CHEERS FROM THE CREW. OLD FACES and new.

Apparently Jasyn and Atalanta are in the mess hall now...

There must be spirits in the cups because there's a celebratory atmosphere. She can only assume they're not cheering the recent adventures in the captain's quarters because... well, that would be weird.

Though what exactly did happen in the captain's quarters, Jasyn couldn't say exactly. She's sure whatever she and Atalanta achieved deserves a standing ovation, but she can't give details to the events. Not that she would give out such details, but replaying them in her own thoughts would be more than welcome.

She can only assume the crew are high on the fact that they're ahead of themselves in achieving their mission. *And that no-one is dead.*

Jasyn rubs her temples. Now that they're back on the ship, shouldn't those effects be over with?

A synaptic tremor—

✦

WHERE DID EVERYONE GO?

The ship is strangely quiet. Jasyn's eyes dart left and right, but find only an empty long-table, benches, chairs and shadows. Fear slithers in her gut, nausea threatening to take grip as she retreats, only to stumble.

What is happening?

In the doorway, a familiar tail flicks as a familiar claw-goat saunters into the corridor. *Snowdrop?*

She can only be in Jasyn's mind, but Jasyn pursues anyway. In the five paces it takes her to reach the door, Snowdrop is already turning into the next, accompanied by the flood of her own shadow, disconcertingly ten times her size.

Jasyn follows, but with each corridor Snowdrop is beyond her reach, and the further she goes, the more turnings — some of which Jasyn is sure don't make sense according to the layout of the ship — the colder the corridors become.

At a waterlogged distance, murmurs rumble, taunting voices chanting: "Kill. Kill. Kill." with an incurable venom, growing louder the deeper into the ship she goes. Jasyn knows that sound. Remembers it. The Iolcian crowds inviting her demise in The Games arena.

Her breath hits the air in clouds as the surfaces around her crackle with ice. A building snow-blizzard churns in the wind-tunnel of the corridor—

Am I doing this?

The voices quieten, but she has to tread carefully along the aggressive tunnel of ice.

Snowfall turns to sleet—

It chills her, and not just because a sky ship shouldn't be frozen, but because the ice is crackling in root rot formation, blooming outwards in fibrous infection.

Petrified faces of the crew — Castor, Kalais, Herakles — all stare dead-eyed from within the block-ice.

Sleet turns to hail, lashing at Jasyn every which way—

She stumbles and slips—

Only to land on something solid. She rolls over to push herself up, but Atalanta's iced complexion, her frozen eyes, stare lifelessly up at her.

Nausea burns her throat. Tears scorch her eyes, her cheeks.

Hail deforms, morphing to knives of ice, cutting her deeper than skin—

The ice closes in as though she and Atalanta are trapped within the wagon's blanket box.

No, this isn't what happened... It can't be happening...

A distant, inexplicable audience cry out in terror.

"...you're the monster," says a taunting, deep, familiar voice, as agony spikes within her every fibre.

Her ruptured lungs are heavy, full. Her tongue tastes metallic.

"Look at you..." the voice hisses by her ear. She can't see him, but the Ice King's breath clouds around her, worse than festering root rot. "Nothing but a little girl who can't control her ice."

Forced to stare into Atalanta's lifeless eyes, a chest-splitting pain cuts through Jasyn as distant crowds cheer her demise.

Electricity flares—

32

LOST

JASYN

Darkness reforms, melding to the shape of a ship corridor.

Jasyn hazards a breath. Her lungs aren't clogged, but her breaths stutter. Atalanta isn't beneath her. There's no ice, no imagined crowds. Only the green tinted corridor leading to the medical quarters.

Jasyn swipes at her hot tears. *What is going on?*

Doctor Orpheus will know what to do. Did she mean what she said about not doing anything to Jasyn's detriment? Is this all the result of atmospheric changes? Or will this turn her from celebrated hero (apparently), to a threat deserving of the quarantine chamber?

The music of a stringed instrument drifts...

Wrestling her own uncertain breaths, Jasyn pushes the door. It creaks open and there, centre stage, the dark-robed doctor plays her V-iolin to her audience of porthole-framed stars.

The snapshot would be majestic, awe inspiring, even, if not for the unsettling resonance of the minor key, enticing Jasyn's nerves to a fearful dance.

Electricity shivers—

✦

Torchlight gleams into Jasyn's eyes like a sweeping searchlight. The music has stopped, and beyond the light looms the concerned grimace of Doctor Orpheus. Jasyn doesn't recall interacting with her, or perching at the edge of a gurney.

"You want my advice?" asks the doctor.

Has she told her anything? Has she confessed the strange wanderings of her body and mind?

"If you're lost or you find yourself losing control... *Just fucking breathe.*"

Jasyn's laughter surprises them both. Of course Doctor Orpheus would make it sound so easy.

Despite her trademark gruffness, there's something about the doctor's presence that has Jasyn's shoulders relaxing. It doesn't make sense, really, because it's not so long ago that they were trading punches in these same medical quarters.

Still, for reasons she cannot decipher, when Doctor Orpheus gave her speech about how she could be trusted, something deep in Jasyn had decided to believe her.

It could be something to do with those eyes. They're stormy, yes, but honest, too. It could be something to do with wanting to unravel that storm and find calm in its wake. It could be something to do with the usually stand-off-ish doctor pressing her hips between Jasyn's knees and parting them gently—

Wait... *What?*

Unexpected heat coils within Jasyn as the doctor raises an eyebrow, perhaps in challenge, perhaps seeking permission. *Heaven's hail.* Jasyn's heart hammers. *Where did this come from?*

This is the last thing she expected from the ill-tempered doctor. It's surprising, confusing, and — when the doctor lowers her medi-mask and leans closer still, Jasyn has enough of her wits about her to turn away—

Because... *Atalanta!*

She has to find her and make sure she's okay.

The doctor's lips graze Jasyn's cheek, enough to feel her wry smile and her breath as she says in her slightly husky voice: "It looks like we'll be doing this dance awhile."

Sparks—

✦

WHAT IN THE HEAVENS —?

The starlight through the floor-to-ceiling porthole is enough to orientate her to being in the captain's quarters, and to the shape of someone under the covers next to her, stretching awake.

Don't be Doctor Orpheus... Jasyn pleads with the universe as her mystery bed-mate rolls over.

"Hey, you," signs Atalanta.

Oh, thank the heavens! You're okay. Jasyn lets out her breath, but her gut still twists at whatever just happened. With the frozen corridor, and with the doctor.

Atalanta is okay, so the events of the corridor and the medical quarters must have been a bad dream? A simmering disquiet shaped a lot like fear and guilt is taking hold all the same.

"Hey," signs Atalanta, tucking a fallen lock of hair behind Jasyn's ear and smoothing the furrow between her brows with her thumb. Familiar eyes filled with rippling galaxies invite Jasyn's inner compass to its calming Astro-pyxis.

Hail. Medea might have stopped flirting with her, but now the doctor? What in the Seven Heavens is going on?

"Dream or not, who can blame the doctor for being drawn in by you, hey?"

Jasyn's eyebrows salute the ceiling. She told her? She doesn't recall doing so... but she must have... Of course she'd tell her. Honesty is good. Sharing things with Atalanta is good.

The guilt unwinds and relief washes over her as she bathes in the warm glow of Atalanta's Transonics.

"You know," signs Atalanta, wriggling closer with a twinkle in her eyes that promises distraction, "I'm sure I can help soothe your thoughts..."

Jasyn's sure there's a smooth response she could come up with if given enough time, but really all that matters is Atalanta, skin lapped by the light of stars, leading the way to the frosted glass wash chamber, and — with a smouldering smile over her shoulder — inviting Jasyn to follow.

Jasyn should be dwelling on the discrepancies between her recollections and events. Or the strange behaviour of the doctor. Or her ice-abilities and how she's going to deal with the Ice King on their return, but... well, Atalanta is really rather distracting, and all other thoughts and worries slip away as the ice-melt steam envelops them.

Warm hands find their way to Jasyn's bare skin. *She really needs to start remembering when she gets naked...* but she'll worry about that later.

Atalanta's kisses burn a trail down her front, already fulfilling the promise of distraction, as the epic porthole drizzles starlight over them both.

Lyrical words in a familiar yet foreign tongue displace wisps of steam, forcing Jasyn's attention to the woman silhouetted by stars. Her purple-flame eyes flicker as she drapes her gaze over Jasyn's naked form. There's no hint of flirtation or appreciation, as there might have been in their earlier interactions. The woman who'd been playful previously is now drawn, exhausted and on edge.

"What are you doing...?" asks Jasyn, breathless from

Atalanta's activities. She and Medea really need to have a discussion about boundaries.

Jasyn's eyes flit down. Atalanta certainly hasn't noticed the interruption. On her knees, she pauses to sign — "I hope it's obvious" — as her lips quirk into a smile before returning to their previous mission.

Hail...

"I need you to listen to me," the lyrical words return in their translation.

Why would Jasyn listen to someone intent on forcing her to the cliff edge, to the cave of memories that she'd nix from existence if she could?

She tries to concentrate on Atalanta, not Medea. Because one of them is real and the other probably isn't. And it's not good manners to be so distracted.

Maybe if she closes her eyes, the interloper will go away.

"You refuse to listen, Jasyn of Iolcus." The words have a melodic weight to them, as the gravity-defying silhouette of Medea eclipses the celestial glow-worms called stars. "And your resistance will end us all."

What the hail is she talking about? Jasyn intends to let her frustration be known, to demand answers, but Medea continues before Jasyn's divided thoughts can navigate the situation.

"I have tried to explain, to show you," says the silken voice with needles in its fabric. "But either our languages do not adequately align, or you're as dense as a solar core."

Just ignore her and she'll go away.

Jasyn's heart races as Atalanta traces up her midriff, her torso, with mouth and tongue.

Amethyst eyes ripple molten with elemental fury as Jasyn's sword flourishes — impossibly — in the intruder's grasp.

The steaming ice-blade slides so quickly through Atalanta's back, through her chest—

A cascade of red spills across them both. Pain bristles and burns, as though the gaping wound is Jasyn's own heart, sliced in two.

Horror chokes the breath from Jasyn's throat, as the stars extinguish in Atalanta's eyes.

Everything in Jasyn breaks.

The kaleidoscopic purple of Medea's stare sears into her. Her usually lyrical voice clangs like smashed piano keys:

"Do I have your attention now?"

PART IV

THE SNOW JUNGLE II

ATALANTA

33

LEFT BEHIND

ATALANTA

S*ome time ago...*

The decontamination mist of the airlock chamber steals Jasyn from sight.

That the person who means more to her than anyone in any galaxy under the Seven Suns is wading into the unknown has Atalanta's insides rebelling.

She commandeers any porthole aimed in Jasyn's direction. In her desperation, her Transonic reach casts beyond the glass and metal of the portholes, tripping past the beacons of bodily activity that are the crew, to snag on a series of crest-like pulsing undulations beneath the snow.

What in the heavens—? Is something following them?

The sounds slip from her grasp. *Creaks* and *whooshes* wrestle with *squawks* and *cackles.* Try as she might — her panicked focus stumbling on ship-wall viscera, roaming vole-rats, the distractions of every indecipherable sound-emitting entity beyond the ship — she can't replicate her findings.

As the ground crew trail beyond the dark wall of jungle, Atalanta stumbles from the portholes. The startled fawn blinks up at her. He's either on a mission to be where she is, or to be a tripping hazard.

Atalanta scoops him up before darting up the stairwell, two rungs at a time, until she's at the helm, breathless and — judging from the wide eyes of Pollux and Tiphys — looking on the wrong side of unhinged.

"You... okay?" asks Pollux, occupying his flight-tech station, not much concern in his words.

Bundling the fawn into Tiphys's arms, Atalanta gestures to the massive helm windows: "There's something out there, following them. You need to check." Only blinking and blank stares respond. She signs — admittedly, a little more wildly — for them to look out the window. That's more easily understood. Tiphys scowls in concentration, while Pollux merely stares at her like she's a sky ship with several screws loose. Unwelcome, at best. Dangerous, at worst.

"You want to go out there, too?" asks Tiphys, his voice pitching high as he hazards a guess.

She's just started gesturing for someone to give her something to write with — receiving equally perplexed expressions (*Seriously? It's not that difficult!*) — when Doctor Orpheus's voice snakes through the comms, summoning her to medical.

Pollux makes too much of a show of nonchalantly leaning away from the medical summons button to not be guilty of pressing it.

Atalanta sighs, but maybe the doctor can help.

As fast as her legs will carry her, she weaves down into the midriff of the ship and the medical quarters. Doctor Orpheus looks up from studying the stats monitors, paying attention to the information on one cube-monitor in particular.

"Your stress is spiking..." she says, tapping the screen. The doctor's not wrong. Atalanta's heart rate is thundering, but she hardly needs a series of squiggles and a medical professional to tell her that.

Atalanta strides to the knee-to-head sized porthole framing a perfect view of the snow-jungle. The same direction the ground crew headed in. That the pristine white-blanket of the snow-covered terrain could be hiding all manner of monsters and mayhem, drips through Atalanta's veins like melted snow. She presses against the porthole like her life — or Jasyn's — depends on it, intent on locating the sounds and movements that might give her a clue.

On an open plain, her reach can stretch for miles. Through layers of ship metal, it's much diminished, like trying to see through clouded glass. No matter how hard she tries, she can only Transonically stumble as far as the jungle edge.

"YOU LOOK LIKE YOU'RE ABOUT TO BURST A BLOOD VESSEL."

The doctor's words shout in her Transonic reaching ears. She reels from the doctor who has — apparently — enough understanding and empathy to look something resembling apologetic. Albeit briefly.

"You see something?" Doctor Orpheus asks more quietly, peering out the portholes. She might be surly, but she's not stupid. "Hear something?"

Atalanta nods, staring at the tree-line. She signs that "there was a kind of undulation, behind them," but doesn't expect the doctor to understand a word. Now that not even a snowflake adjusts its position, she's wondering if she'd imagined it all. Her mind has been playing tricks on her lately. Who's to say this isn't more of the same?

She hopes it is her imagination. Looking like an overreacting fool is better than Jasyn being in the path of danger.

"Medical to Ground Crew," says the doctor, after pressing a series of buttons on her comms console.

"What's up, Orpheus?" The calm, confident voice of their captain.

"Thought I saw something..." says the doctor. Atalanta knows she's just humouring her, but she appreciates the support all the same. "Keep an eye on your tail."

"Received. I trust you to keep an eye on my—"

Doctor Orpheus cuts the transmission and huffs, rolling her eyes. Atalanta might be panicked about what's going on out there, but the captain's and doctor's strange and sporadic flirtation has her smiling a little. As far as she can tell, their gallant captain and grumpy doctor have made it their life's missions to wind each other up.

"Stupid fucking captain," Doctor Orpheus mutters, before returning her attention to Atalanta. The doctor tenses and Atalanta can sense they're about equally matched on the social awkwardness front.

"Generally speaking," says the doctor, nodding to the terrain outside, "our arrival on unfamiliar worlds is more likely to cause damage to its indigenous species than to us. Astro-suits filter out anything harmful. The bio-scans will alert them to anything living. Probability-wise, they'll be fine."

There's a layer to her tone that Atalanta can't quite decipher. Whether she's telling the truth or not, she's trying to comfort her. And that, Atalanta appreciates. If she wasn't so preoccupied by Jasyn's safety, she'd find a way to communicate *thank you for trying.* But instead, she just stares out at the wisps of snow powder shrouding the porthole as thickly as a decontamination mist.

"You can stay here awhile," says the doctor. *Huh.* She might be kinder than Atalanta thought. "The helm crew think you're a little... wild? If you loiter up there they'll probably have me fetch you. If you stay here, it'll save me the trip."

Okay. Maybe not that kind.

With her view outside obscured by the building white-out, Atalanta gravitates to the vitals monitors.

"The elevated heart rates are normal for heading into the unknown," the doctor explains. "Even Castor and Kalais, who pretend to be tough, are as likely as the rest to soil themselves. Apart from the captain. Her heart rate usually runs slow." *Does it?* That's not been Atalanta's experience. "She says she has the heart of an adventurer. I say it's questionable brain function." The doctor points to one screen in particular with a steady heartbeat. "Your Jasyn's almost as slow."

Phrased like that, Atalanta's not sure it's a compliment, but her quizzical eyebrow is overshadowed by the icy sensation trickling down her spine.

In her haste to ensure Jasyn is safe, Atalanta had entirely forgotten the presence of the Ice Princess.

Only now does she notice the steely-eyed woman watching her from behind the clear walls of the quarantine chamber. The bridge of her nose and her cheeks are bruised. The injury at her neck is an angry confusion of red and purple. No wonder she's giving Atalanta the kind of glower that could turn water to ice.

Thank the Seven Heavens for bar-reinforced prison-glass.

34

STATIC

ATALANTA

Sharp bleeps shout from the stats-monitors. Doctor Orpheus's attention snaps to them.

"What the actual fuck?" Her fingers hover above each screen in turn, hunting for something — a clue, perhaps?

The alarms drills into Atalanta's eardrums. She narrows the reach of her Transonics but leaves them open enough to evaluate what's going on.

Six elevated ground-crew heart rates. One scowling-more-than-usual doctor. Atalanta's own heart rate trips.

Warning lights flash on three, then a further two. Then Jasyn's monitor joins the shrill chaos, too.

Until — *swiftly* — one by one, all six ground crew monitors are so silent, so still, only terror rings in Atalanta's ears. She can normally tune out her own heartbeat, discounting it as a sort of baseline, but now it shudders through her as if someone were striking her chest.

"Medical to Captain. Update," says the doctor into her portable comms. Her tone is level. Either she's experienced in situations such as this, or her stoicism extends even to matters of life and death.

When only static responds, the doctor tries again: "Ground Crew. Update."

Nothing.

"Helm, what are you making of this?" Doctor Orpheus looks up as if addressing the heavens, but is more likely aiming her words at the overseer.

"We have the alert," says Pollux over the comms, his voice as even as the doctor's. *Hail. Are the crew a bunch of automatons?* "Comms are down. We're unable to establish contact."

"What about their visual feeds?"

"Transferring now," says Pollux.

The stats monitors split to display the astro-helmet feeds alongside corresponding vitals. The images are dark, dancing with an eerie static that grates at Atalanta's ears. But that's all there is.

The doctor's foot taps a steady rhythm, while her heartbeat kicks up a notch. "Fuck, fuck, fuck," she mutters. *Not an automaton, then.*

Atalanta's feet move of their own accord. She can't be still when Jasyn is out there. *Lost. Without breath.* She strides for the door, vaguely registering the doctor asking where the fuck she's going, but the drum of both their heartbeats drowns her out.

A quick stop at the weapons store.

Atalanta closes her eyes, retrieving the memory of the series of *clicks* and *clunks* of internal mechanisms that preceded weapons being locked away. Her hands shake as she manipulates the dial, ripples of sound giving shape to what lies within the cavity of the heavy-set door. As it opens, up at the helm an alert sounds. Pollux must be tracking her via the overseers because he's questioning how in the heavens Atalanta knows the lock combination.

She makes quick work of sourcing a bow and quiver of arrows from amongst the cobwebs. Her next stop is the airlock tunnel. It gasps shut behind her as she ignores the stream of questions over the comms, Pollux understandably demanding what she's doing in the airlock and that this isn't protocol. Or *something*. All she cares about is getting Jasyn back.

From the cavernous vault of the airlock tunnel, Atalanta selects an astro-suit and helmet. She's glad she listened in on the astro-suit run-down, because now she knows how to activate the right settings. She could probably have figured it out, but it's always best to hit the ground running.

When her helmet clicks snugly into position, aligned with the in-built breathing apparatus in the back cavity, the ether-mesh of the invisi-visor almost imperceptibly bridges the gap between one side of her helmet and the other. Details of suit parameters light up across her visor. Oxygen at 98%.

That'll do.

She loops her quiver across her chest. Doctor Orpheus's footsteps ring louder, forging a path through the ship. *Is she going to stop her?*

Pollux is busy warning something about Atalanta not being able to leave the ship without the helm's permission. His voice slaps her through the airlock comms, the helmet comms *and* skitters down from the helm all at once.

In response, Atalanta uses an arrow head to remove the fascia of the airlock release mechanisms. Ship exits have fail-safes. Of course they do. Otherwise anyone could just wander out. But Atalanta knows a thing or two about ship composition and how fail-safes can be tricked. Before the doctor can reach her, before Pollux has thought of a way to stop her, Atalanta has already split the override circuit and hit the release.

Decontamination mist rolls around her, obscuring her vision, testing her resolve. Mist frazzles against her invisi-visor. All she has to do now is find Jasyn before it's too late. If only she could silence the voice in her head, the shadow voice, signing that "*it already is.*"

Breathing deeper than she'd like on her 98% oxygen supplies, she struggles to catch her breath. The astro-helmet forces her focus within, reflecting her own sounds back at her like some cruel echo chamber.

Blood *whooshes* along the junctions of her veins. Gases *fizz* as they cross through membranes. Her breaths cross the boundary of her invisi-visor with a *flutter*. Eyelashes *clash* with every blink.

Hail. This is the worst time to discover the helmet doesn't function the way she expects. When she'd worn astro-suits in the past, their qualities had been much different; designed to fit her capabilities. It turns out an Iolcian astro-helmet is worse than being enclosed in a sky ship. Its composition even hinders her ability to reach beyond its shell.

It's too late to remove the helmet and adjust her Transonics. The doors will open any second.

At least the outer and airlock doors can't be opened while decon is in progress. Otherwise Doctor Orpheus and Gus — both framed by the airlock's inner porthole — would've orchestrated her containment by now.

Atalanta can't hear what they're saying. She needs to focus. But that's easier said than done when the audible inner workings of her own body are conspiring against her.

Gus could overwrite the system and open the airlock, but that would only lead to decompressing the ship and letting whatever's out there inside. No sky ship scientist would be stupid enough to do that.

"That girl will be the death of you," signs the silhouette at the edge of her vision. That the decon mist doesn't shift at the movements is a *tick* in the *she isn't real* column. But, real or not, the words hit their target.

Fear needles at her mind, like the fangs of swarming vole-rats. Charging headfirst into the unknown has never been a winning strategy in her life.

A steadying breath...

But she refuses to give herself a lifetime of regret by not doing *something*. Because Time, space and oxygen wait for no-one.

The decon mist clears. Bow clutched in hand, Atalanta takes her first step out into strange and untrustworthy terrain.

35

EYES OF THE JUNGLE

ATALANTA

As she surveys her surroundings for threats, all Atalanta can decipher is layers of leaves, hanging vines, clusters of vibrant fruit and flowers, and a carpet of snow leading her path into the jungle.

Whatever she'd witnessed pursuing Jasyn — or whatever she thinks she heard — it's not possible to *see* it.

"ATALANTA, CAN YOU HEAR ME?" The brusque voice of Doctor Orpheus cuts through her eardrum like a stalactite. The doctor must be watching her wince through the helmet overseer — or be aware of Atalanta's skillset — because the next words are much quieter.

"Look. I'm going to bypass the speech about you being a fucking idiot and get to the bit where I'm helpful. Okay?"

Atalanta presses her comms thumb contact twice.

"I take it it's two for yes?" says the doctor.

Atalanta presses again — *click-click*-yes.

Her helmet BLIPS — another ear aching sound — as her invisi-visor populates with simplistic topography and locator beacons that include the ship.

"Right. Listen," says the doctor. "The suits are all on the

network. You can access the information through your helmet visor. All you have to do is—"

Radio static scores Atalanta's skull. She tries backtracking, but finds no improvement. She breaks the connection, giving her ears some respite, though sounds still churn in her helmet in tandem with her crashing sea of thoughts.

Either she can return to the ship and lose valuable time, linger to figure out how the map-beacons work, or she can follow the tracks in the snow.

She forges on.

Heading deep into the strange jungle, she swivels every few steps to check her surroundings. Her own bodily machinations reflect back at her with a vengeance, setting her teeth on edge.

In uncharacteristic clumsiness her foot catches on a protruding root. She trips, *almost* gracefully thanks to low gravity, and as she falls a stress-filled gasp escapes her.

Panic stretches the moment—

The glint in Jasyn's eyes...

That charming, lopsided smile...

This isn't the first time she's feared losing her.

When they were twelve sun-orbits old, in the cave up in the Unforgiving Mountains, they'd strayed into the path of glinting claws and mighty teeth. But while teeth as sharp as arrow heads had occupied her thoughts, other more positive feelings had unfurled.

Hiding. Pressed into shadows...

Fingers intertwined with Jasyn's, warm and welcome...

Breaths caught—

She hadn't known what that meant, then.

The second time she thought she's lost Jasyn was mere hours after they'd almost lost their lives to the bear cave. Jasyn's family had uprooted and left her behind but she'd decided to follow, to join Jasyn in her new life, even though their friendship had been strained by grief.

The third; ten sun-orbits later, she'd discovered Jasyn's plan to leave the village in search of adventure. Atalanta had thought she was being left behind, *again*. Which had caused some understandable upset, argument and — thankfully — the joy of kissing, being kissed, and more.

Far too soon, adventure had been thrust upon them, and with their village being ripped apart by the Ice King's military, Jasyn had charged head first into rifle fire, tearing up the skies in the process. That had been the fourth time Atalanta had feared losing her.

The fifth; the Iolcian Games. Atalanta's soaring arrow — on course to hit its royal target — had been unceremoniously snatched from the air, and her own life had been forfeit. As she'd slipped down the long, dark path towards death, she'd witnessed the horror of the Ice King intent on wrenching Jasyn's life from her.

And yet, somehow, they still survived to take the skies.

Is today the day their luck runs out?

Oof!

She might only have a soft landing, but Atalanta's echoing breaths and stomping heartbeats crash her back to the world around her.

The twist of her trajectory has her staring up at the tree-framed skies, where stars twinkle even in the daylight. Sky glitter might be beautiful, but she'll never trust it.

She returns to her feet, her eyes trained on the jungle. Following the trail, her unease grows. The dangers are invisible, but she intuits them in the prickle of her neck hairs and the grip of nausea in her gut.

It could be the misfirings of stress, but it'd be foolish to dismiss the instinct. It's likely there are many *somethings* out here. Whatever caused chaos for Jasyn and the ground crew, for a start. But all Atalanta can hear is her own rebellious heartbeat.

Hail. If there's *someone* or *something* or *some things* following her, she needs to know. She needs to be out of this amplifying echo-chamber, or she'll drown in the undertow. Her failure risks Jasyn's life, too.

According to her helmet and suit, the air is breathable.

She's not happy about this, but...

She pushes her helmet back.

The sounds contained within it leap for freedom, unwinding like an ethereal, audible fog on a breeze. *What a relief.* The helmet clips against the nape of her neck — a pleasing design choice — as the sounds of this world envelop her, along with the odd mix of cool and humid air.

Her breaths are as laboured as a mountain-hike on the cusp of a panic attack, but at least she can locate the *caws* and *chirps* in the canopy, the gentle breeze *shuffling* the leaves...

She might not have experienced a forest as impressive, tall and lush as this, but she knows the sounds of trees. How they *creak* in the breeze, how they *groan* as they grow, how leaves *flutter*, and *whisper* even when still. These sounds are familiar, but louder, sharper, with stronger undercurrents. The murmur of vegetation here is more insistent.

Something stares...

A moon-faced creature, encased in grey and oddly green fur, dangles from a branch from its four gangly arms. About the size of the fawn, its bright white eyes stare.

A changeable pattern ripples across its fur, like algae on the surface of the Glowing Wood lagoon. Though startled by its presence, Atalanta senses no malice. Its movements are too slow. It appears only to want to stare, and occasionally blink. It even does that slowly.

She might be staring another being in the eyes, but the only heartbeat is her own. She listens more intently, but there's nothing. There's a *whoosh-whoosh* of internal activity, travelling in a similar manner to veins and arteries, but with no central 'engine' of heart or lungs or stomach to power it all.

Odd. But there's no time to get lost in the details.

She picks up her pace, following the footprint trail left by the crew until a light crunch of snow stops her in her tracks.

The movement in the snow stops, too.

Something is stalking her.

36

HUNTED

ATALANTA

Atalanta angles her Transonics, but receives only the *hum* and *creak* of growing trees. Left hand tensing about her bow, she peers over her shoulder. Lush undergrowth peeks out from thick snow. It's the dusting of falling flakes drifting from branches that gives shape to the feline form.

As powerful shoulders adjust, a network of green and yellow veins shimmer through the thin white fur and translucent skin. Its face punctuated by white irises, pincers protrude as an extra jaw. *No heartbeat.*

Though her own is making itself known.

The creature coils and springs. With low gravity grace, it arcs as it soars towards her—

Her breaths stutter.

Everything slows. The world around her. Her movements, too.

Her mind has turned before her body catches up and yet — by luck — she dodges the creature's mid-air snapping pincer-jaws.

"Be the hunter, not the prey," insist the uninvited silhouette.

In direct opposition to the instruction, Atalanta launches

from the animal, and the words. Or she tries. Running in low gravity is more like swimming through air.

On Iolcus, she could spring between trees and churn the turf with her racing feet. Here her every movement is in stomach-churning, water-logged slow motion.

Thankfully, the creature in pursuit is bound by the same constraints, albeit more gracefully so. Atalanta's under no illusion who has the upper hand: most certainly the predator with teeth and claws who understands this world and how to move through it.

But she has an instinct for which trunks to leap between, which to use to change her direction, enough to tie the creature's path in a knot.

More crunching leaves. Foliage disrupted. Somewhere in the thicket, two more creatures have joined the hunt.

Her stomach turns.

They're working together, flanks closing in.

The ground shudders. Trees quake.

To her left, something disturbs the shadows. Atalanta glances over her shoulder as a feline shape breaks from the thicket, arcing above her, claws unsheathed.

Atalanta's every nerve bristles—

It lands in front of her, and all she can do with her momentum is raise her bow as an obstruction.

Glinting jaws rip it from her grasp, but release immediately, spitting out the unintentional floss of the bow's string.

The bow sails in a shallow arc, landing with a gentle bounce in a clearing of pristine snow.

But there's nothing gentle about the creature's back legs bucking into her midriff. Its claws piercing the armour of her astro-suit, the full force of its paws shoving her shoulders.

She sails backwards and instinct takes over. She grasps its

thick-muscled shoulders, rippling yellow and green beneath semi-translucent fur.

As her back meets the ground, she uses the momentum to cast her attacker over her shoulder, flinging them aside.

It's the sort of wrestling challenge she'd ordinarily take in her stride, but her sparring partner isn't here for fun and games.

The feline snarls as it drips saliva in a mid-air twist.

While it reorientates, Atalanta launches for her bow, her legs performing a surprisingly controlled skid, puffing up snow powder. *Getting the hang of this now.* Her right arm reaches behind her for balance as her left whips out to reclaim her weapon.

From the shadows, a pincer-faced wild-cat prowls into her path. Atalanta tries a different direction, but another oversized feline leaps to block her. The third lingers behind her.

Atalanta's jaw tightens; her teeth grind.

Calculation in their eyes, power in their shoulders, threat in the glint of claws and teeth, the creatures prowl in an ever tightening triangular formation.

Is she a threat? Is she food?

If the former, putting down her weapon and making herself small, inconsequential, would be the way forward. If the latter, that'll only speed up her own painful death.

She doesn't want to hurt these creatures, but it may be the only way to emerge with her life intact.

If that's even a possibility...

"Don't be weak. Fight for your life." The unwelcome silhouette lingers in the shadows as Atalanta's eyes flit to her surroundings.

Trunks and branches surround the snow covered clearing, decorated by a multitude of flowers, some as large as fists, others the size of skulls. Atalanta feels vastly outnumbered. Which is ridiculous. *They're flowers.*

Still, they don't half seem to be watching her every move,

twitching almost in unison. When she moves left or right, they follow. Is this what gladiators in the Iolcian Games arena feel like?

Maybe she's suffering a lack of oxygen. She could do with a decent lung-full of air right now.

The strange movements of the flowers, the clearing, the creatures prowling the perimeter, all have her questioning whether she'd chosen to run here, or whether she's been lured.

The jungle shudders and the flowers spew a kind of snowfall. Is it a powder? Spores?

Atalanta reaches to reinstate her helmet, but a creature's claws are already digging into her shoulder blades, piercing through her suit and into her flesh.

Skies above. She grits her teeth as the momentum sends her to the ground.

She whips back for an arrow and rolls, lashing out and scoring down the predator's face, before sharp claws pin her.

Nausea ties her in knots.

The creature's screech, echoed in the prickling shudder of the ground, scrapes within her skull.

Back to the ground, arms pinned, she has no choice but to look up at snarling fangs and its injured face leaking a sap-like mix of translucent and green.

As the snowfall, spores, whatever it is, drift from the branches, Atalanta can do nothing to swipe at the strange white flakes. She can only accept it as they cover her face, flooding her vision with shadows...

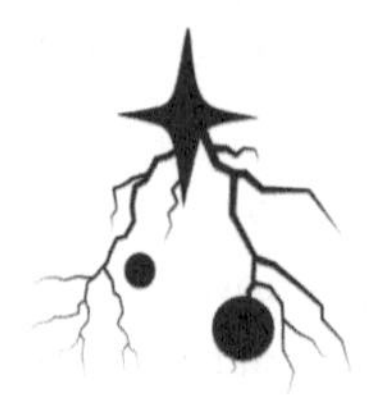

With each blink, colour seeps back into Atalanta's vision. The jungle is just as it was, but her shoulders and chest aren't compressed by claws intent on her demise.

She's not sure exactly what changed between this moment and the last, but she can draw a deep breath, now, and the strange felines are stalking away, tails swishing as if out for a stroll.

Was this just a game to them?

A thread of familiarity invites her attention to the terrain around her, to the dark and smooth volcanic stone. The clusters of rocks are dusted with snowfall or spores, but the network of lava-like circuitry-veins peek through.

How in the heavens—? How had she not noticed before? Okay, being threatened by a trio of clawed creatures and watched by a possibly-spore-spewing jungle can be a bit of a distraction. But... those rocks can't be what she thinks they are...

It's enough to claim her breath, caution and curiosity vying for attention, and to have her question statistical probabilities. Because *in what world* are Transonic rocks clustered in the undergrowth?

Well, according to Interplanetary Interpreter Hylas, that world is Arcadia.

Now that she's noticed them, the rocks are everywhere. Some formations are as large as boulders, others, mere gravel.

But there are more pressing things right now. The shrill flatline of the stats monitors pierces her thoughts. She needs to find Jasyn.

But which way to turn?

As if in answer to her question, flowers ignite like lanterns flanking the jungle path. Though she's suspicious of such displays of design and natural beauty, there are footprints in the snow. Crew footprints? An entire trail of them, leading her between the tree-pillars.

She follows the path as swiftly as she's able, weaving into the depths of the jungle with a keen eye and ear on everything around her. The further she hazards, the more the smooth, rounded lava-rocks form a pathway.

With each new illumination in the branches, each highlighting new tracks, it occurs to her that — *somehow* — the jungle is trying to help.

Glee and disbelief dance inside her. Fear, too. Just a healthy amount. Because since when do jungles guide travellers towards their desires?

If this place is what Atalanta suspects — if this is the world of her ancestors - she'd be a fool not to acknowledge that *something* caused her parents to risk their lives and sanity in escaping this world to take to the skies.

As much as her encounter with the jungle creatures has so far been unpleasant (and puzzling), Atalanta can't imagine them being enough of a reason to leave this oasis behind.

Which leads her to suspect there's something sinister about this world. Probably something Jasyn and the ground crew have already found for themselves.

Before Atalanta can lose herself in a thicket of panic, the path opens to a clearing.

Heavens above. She wants to believe what she's seeing. *More than anything.* Because the person up ahead, smiling in a lopsided fashion that targets Atalanta like an arrow of fuel in the fire-pit of her chest, is exactly the person she feared she'd lost...

Jasyn's smile lights up, letting her know: *All is well.*

In spite of unfamiliar gravitational circumstances, Jasyn strides to her, and there's nothing better than hearing Jasyn's heartbeat racing her own.

Atalanta trips over her own feet to get to her. When their arms wrap around each other, their momentum sends them spinning to the cushioned ground, fears dissipating in the strength of their embrace. The only worry Atalanta has in this moment is that she might never let Jasyn go.

As Jasyn leads Atalanta into the jungle village, she signs with a wince of sincere apology: "The terrain interferes with signals, apparently."

It takes Atalanta several moments to decipher the dwellings in the flower-lit forest. Dens nestle on the ground. Giant, leathery, overlapping leaves form roofs. Vine-rope ladders lead up to tent-like structures hanging from branches in chrysalis formations.

The ground crew. *Thank the heavens they're all alright.* They're being given a signed tour by the locals: adults and children, unfamiliar apart from their vibrant patchwork clothing and the Transonics behind their ears. Their language. *Her language.*

The locals snack on berries larger than any Iolcian fruit, while toying with bows and arrows composed of tree branches and natural fibres. Their dexterity matches Atalanta's own. A local signs to Hylas, and he explains to the rest of the crew that the bow and arrows are of their tradition, "an echo of a different time" and that wielding them is now "no more than sport".

Atalanta's shoulders lower a little at that. She's spent so many sun-orbits avoiding questions of her past, but now that she's here she's not minded to run. Perhaps she wants answers, after all.

Semi-translucent wild-cats sashay through the village without any passing local raising a bow, nor batting an eye. It would appear that the creatures who'd been so unwelcoming initially are no threat.

With a nudge, Jasyn guides Atalanta's attention to a lagoon — not unlike her own in the Glowing Woods, but hovering above the ground, with villagers diving in from all angles to cool off. The quiet, simple life. She could get used to a world like this.

"Looks like we found home," says Jasyn with a smile so warm, *so Jasyn*, that it lights up Atalanta's world.

Sparks—

38

HOME

ATALANTA

S*quawks* and *caws* and *hoots* and even the occasional *growling rumble* drift from the jungle.

How did she get here?

She vaguely recalls Jasyn grinning from ear to ear as they climbed the vine ladder to reach their leaf-created cocoon. With gravity being lower, she hadn't had to worry about what might happen should they miss a rung.

She vaguely recalls Jasyn explaining to her that their ship was reeled in not for nefarious reasons, but because of a gravitational quirk resulting from the positioning of the planet and its moons. Atalanta is certain Jasyn, the captain, chief engineer and doctor would love a diagram depicting the matter.

But it's all a bit hazy.

"You're getting the time-jumps," signs Jasyn before caressing a thumb over Atalanta's temple. "I asked about that." Of course she did. "It's caused by the same thing that interfered with our comms. Nothing serious."

Jasyn's smile is so sure, Atalanta nods her acceptance and presses Jasyn's affectionate palm closer to her cheek. *Hail.* Those grey eyes. She feared she'd never get to gaze into those eyes again.

The details of how she got up here might be riddled with gaps, but that she is here — that they are here, *together* in this treetop den — is a relief. From up here, they could be the only two people in this world. And she must admit, the view is breathtaking: Jasyn gazing out at the night sky, the moons and stars peeking between the canopy.

That there are no other hanging leaf-dens in the nearby branches satisfies Atalanta's hermit inclinations. Finally, the stress in her muscles and thoughts start to unwind.

The air is warm and sweet. The gentle blush of flower-lanterns hanging from branches glow between the lattice of vines and leaves, highlighting the intricate networks within each leaf.

With a gentle tug of her vest, Atalanta draws Jasyn's attention to within their cocoon. Jasyn's smile only widens as they shuffle closer.

Toying with Jasyn's fingertips, their hands entwine, and Atalanta can hardly fathom they get to spend time like this together.

But there are other things that have her brow furrowing. She reclaims her hand to sign: "It's almost unbelievable, isn't it? Landing on the world where I'm from."

Jasyn considers the question before answering with a wry smile: "Not impossible, clearly." There's a playful glint in her eyes. "Did you know you make shapes in your sleep?" She gets more mischievous then, pinning Atalanta gently but thoroughly in their nest of blankets.

Hail. Does she know how intoxicating this is? The sparkle in Jasyn's half-lidded eyes would suggest *yes, she does*.

"So many shapes..." signs Jasyn, sitting back on her knees, straddling her.

Atalanta tries to keep the obvious rise and fall of her chest to a sensible rhythm. A task made all the more difficult by Jasyn lifting her vest over her well-defined arms and shoulders; her half-naked form in the gentle nighttime glow is what dreams are made of. Atalanta bites her lip to keep her appreciative sigh to herself.

"So many words," Jasyn whispers, as she leans down to kiss Atalanta's jaw, her neck. "Jasyn... Heroic... Jasyn... So handsome... Jasyn... Charming..."

Her mouth pauses above Atalanta's and Atalanta forgets to breathe. She's missed Jasyn's confidence, waned under the tides of the ship and crew.

"Jasyn... So humble..." adds Atalanta, before flipping her with practiced ease and pinning her along the length of their bodies. *Hail. She could stay like this forever.*

With Jasyn's heart drumming an elevated rhythm, Atalanta sighs her contentment. For too many sun-orbits, she'd listened to Jasyn's quickstepping heart from afar. Right now, she gets to experience — gets to be the cause, even — of every hitched breath, every pull of oxygen into her lungs and her pulsing bloodstream.

She's in danger of getting lost in the details. But Jasyn brings her back to the moment, tucking stray hair behind her ear. She'd punch anyone else in the gut for being this close. But Jasyn... she can't get close enough. Especially when Jasyn gazes at her as if she engineered the stars and skies.

When their mouths meet, perhaps the rainbow of pulsing flower-lanterns in the branches around them is objectively *a bit much*, but this is a strange world, and who is she to say what is and isn't possible? She's sure the science-types on the crew would say there's no such thing as magic. But they're not feeling what she's feeling right now.

She doesn't want this to end.

"We could stay?" Jasyn says, softly, as she nuzzles Atalanta's neck and traces the waistband of her undershorts. Atalanta's senses swim.

Stay? Here? In a world that's calm, plentiful... A perfect life stretches out in her mind's eye; the promise of a lifetime with Jasyn, unhindered by risky sky adventures, free from the threat of arrogant ice royals, and the terrifying unknown.

Jasyn's words caress her hopes and dreams as her fingers caress beneath fabric. Atalanta bites her lip and tries not to be an archer with a wayward arrow, released too soon.

She has to be sure. It has to be what they both want. She's always feared Jasyn's hankering for adventure might have no reasonable limits.

"You don't want to explore all the worlds under the Seven Suns?" Atalanta's hands vibrate, unsteady as she tries to school her breathing and thoughts under Jasyn's touch.

"The sky is a dangerous place," signs Jasyn with one hand, moving against her in a sensuous, un-rushed rhythm. *Hail, multitasking is a skill!* "We could live a quiet life, here. Together." She has to whisper those words because *together* involves two hands to sign.

Jasyn's heart thrums steady and truthful, and her eyes sparkle in that way they do when she's embarking on the most thrilling of adventures.

Atalanta's inner arrow releases—

Electricity forks—

"ARE YOU COMING, OR NOT?" ASKS JASYN WITH A WRY SMILE.

It takes Atalanta a moment to process that they're no longer in the hanging leaf-hut, that they're fully clothed and standing on the jungle floor. *How did they get here?* The question is overshadowed by the thundering rumble in the sky.

Just visible between the giant leaves of the towering trees, the [C]ARGO ship trails thruster-steam on its upward soaring trajectory.

That's right, Atalanta reminds herself, the gaps in her memory filling in with each deep breath. The crew have left... or rather, *are leaving. Now.* To continue their mission for the Fleece. And now she and Jasyn get to stay here, to live their lives, together.

At that thought, her lungs open to the fresh air. A scuffling prompts her to turn. The fawn dances about in the low gravity as a wild-cat growls, stretching its pincers. Instead of panicking, Atalanta remembers a villager assuring her that no harm would come to the fawn from the creatures of the jungle. Not now that they know the newcomers are no threat.

The fawn boisterously head-butts the feline six times his size. The feline mirrors the fawn's playful dance and Atalanta can't help smiling. At least he has a friend now.

"Come on, Iceberg," calls Jasyn, playfully, drawing Atalanta's attention back to the middle distance of the jungle, where she grins.

That Jasyn's attention is trained entirely on her, and not at all on the soaring sky ship, has Atalanta's heart and happiness sailing skyward, too. She'd never imagined she might be more interesting to Jasyn than the skies.

"You're not going to catch me if you just stand there," says Jasyn with a mischievous glint in her eyes, before springboarding off the nearest tree and launching into the colourful and inviting jungle.

Oh, it's on!

Needing no encouragement, Atalanta sails through their low gravity surroundings in pursuit. A thousand varieties of flower-lanterns light up as they blaze past. Moon-faced creatures watch on, apparently not at all perturbed by Atalanta and Jasyn's presence.

Oversized felines gallop gracefully, briefly joining in the chase; this time — thankfully — with a whimsical air, before peeling away into the darkness, leaving Atalanta and Jasyn to forge their own path of flower-lantern light.

Vines act as ropes, allowing for sudden changes in direction, for mid-air acrobatics and climbing high. Racing along branches at height on Iolcus might have had Atalanta's stomach in knots, but with the security of lower gravity, she lets herself enjoy the thrill.

Venturing higher into the trees, clouds drift around them. Somehow this jungle combines the best traits of the Iolcian Glowing Woods and the Unforgiving Mountains. Perhaps this is what their days would have been if the Ice King and the Warden General's military hadn't intervened.

A well-timed leap from one branch to another—

Perhaps because Jasyn knows she's got no chance of outrunning her, or because she doesn't want to, she turns as Atalanta sails her way. The impact has Jasyn's back thudding against a tree trunk. She doesn't step aside or take off in a new direction. Instead, she wraps her arms around Atalanta, inviting her closer.

As Atalanta's hands rake through Jasyn's asymmetric hair, enjoying the gentle bristles of the shorter hair and the softness of the longer locks, she can't help but be thrilled that they're *together in the wilderness.*

"You caught me," whispers Jasyn—

An electric jolt—

⁺⁛

Atalanta stands tall, her shoulders set, strong and ready.

Ready for what?

The creak of her bow—

She blinks.

Mist shrouds everything as the crack of rifle fire punctuates with inconsolable cries, followed by the skull-scouring auditory-overwhelm of ice and stone obliterated by military blast—

She knows this moment.

She wishes she didn't.

The mist uncoils, only a little: enough to be confronted by the arrows angling from fallen soldiers. Life punctured from them.

Nausea grips Atalanta's stomach.

Why is Jasyn on the ground?

Why is she clawing away from her, terror in her eyes?

Atalanta's floundering senses catch up to the bow and arrow in her grip, trained at short range on her target — *Jasyn.*

This isn't what happened...

"*Be the hunter...*" says the hidden voice of shapes.

Electricity stutters—

39

HUNTER

ATALANTA

Atalanta stumbles, her breath and balance lost. She drops her arms to cast aside her weapon, but there's nothing there. Only her shaking hands.

What the hail—?

Her eyes refocus through the kaleidoscope of whites, browns and greens to find Jasyn assessing the potential grips at the base of a tree, as if everything is as it should be.

When Jasyn steps closer, arms open, Atalanta wants nothing more than to accept the embrace, but her muscles tense.

Only seconds ago she'd been about to release an arrow at her chest. Only moments ago Jasyn had stared at her with fear-widened eyes, features contorted.

Jasyn reaches for her, but Atalanta backs away.

"What just happened?" asks Atalanta, but Jasyn's easy smile lets her know there's nothing to worry about.

How can that be?

Something is off-kilter. Her thoughts haunted by her past is one thing. Pointing an arrow at Jasyn with deadly intent, and for it to be forgotten, is quite another.

But if your mind is playing tricks, how do you know if it's you or the world that's out of step?

Jasyn's open arms are inviting, but she can't risk it. She can't risk Jasyn. So she does what she's always been good at.

She runs.

Defying the state of gravity, Atalanta sprints faster and — impossibly — faster, as if she might outrun the situation, her confusion, and the sickness taking unwelcome residence inside her. Jasyn calls her name, but she refuses to turn.

She can't hunt Jasyn if she's running the other way, into the unchartered dark, can she?

The glowing flora that had lit her path previously fails to catch up. The world falls away, leaving her in inked darkness. She doesn't stop. She should be afraid of tripping on whatever's hidden in her path as she races into the void.

She slows.

The darkness seeps in, clogging her mind, her thoughts. Something smells terrible, like digestion or decay. Her skin sears as if aflame. A pop of released cranial pressure pulls a gasp from her. She can sense it, hear it, something branching within her head, exploring the pathways of her mind —

Is that ridiculous?

Has she lost her mind?

It's a new sensation, that's for sure.

A lone figure in the dark...

A single grey-stemmed navy flower emits an impossible glow. *Fever Root.* Indigenous to Iolcus. The medicine that saved Jasyn's parents.

Stomach knotted, every nerve bristling, Atalanta isn't certain whether to head towards it or run away.

It can't really be there. Logically, she knows that. But logic seems to be a difficult path to follow, lately.

White and grey floods the shadows, taking definition in

sharp peaks. The air bristles, too. She could almost be convinced she's back in the Iolcian mountains.

Eyes as familiar as her own level with her. A bow-shaped mouth purses. That, too, is a feature that could be her own.

But it's not her reflection, it's Mother.

As a child, Atalanta had never appreciated how similar their features were. After Mother's death, her image had only been reachable through her memories, any details too ephemeral to grasp onto. Even the after-effects of death have placed her in the shadows, just beyond visual reach.

But now, seeing the definition in her face, her eyes with multiple colours, the angles of her chin, it's like looking in a mirror.

"Be the hunter, not the prey," Mother signs, severity in her eyes. That is the wisdom she imparts and Atalanta remembers it well. She remembers *this moment*.

"What's happening?" signs Atalanta, but that mustn't be how this works, because Mother continues with the lesson from her past, demonstrating how to skewer an unsuspecting vole-rat from a hundred metres away with a bow created of recycled raft parts.

Thwack-squeak—

Bile taunts the back of Atalanta's throat, just as it had done in this moment when she was a child, because that was the first time she'd understood what her arrows were intended for. Until then, they'd been only a game, a way of honing her concentration and stretching her limbs.

She should have been impressed by the technically awesome feat of hitting such a tiny *moving* target. But the critter fights against the arrow until its snagging last breath. And that occupies Atalanta's stomach like a sharpened rock.

"It didn't want to die," she signs to Mother, as if going

through the motions of being her younger self. "Isn't that reason not to kill it?"

"Taking the life of another will sustain your own," Mother signs.

And that is how they survived in the mountain peaks. Mother taught her that the best life to take is that of a carnivore, because they hunt others. And, therefore the life that is taken is one that would also have taken. Even at the time, Atalanta hadn't been sure about the cosmic balance of that philosophy. While it seemed like it imbued their actions with a certain justice, she'd feared it — ultimately — made her deserving of her own arrows.

The scene from her past melts to shadows.

Darkness twists to light...

Jasyn at eight sun-orbits old takes shape in the distance, exploring the Iolcian peaks. Atalanta recalls seeing her like this for the first time. Mother had warned her not to get too close to the other creatures living in their orbit. Especially the three who looked a lot like them. ("They are Iolcian. They cannot be trusted.")

But Atalanta found them fascinating from afar. Their audible form of communication had been strange to her ears and over time she'd started to understand some of the words. While she'd technically kept her distance, she'd watched and listened enough to learn that the girl and the two older Iolcians were not hunters but foragers.

Curiosity drew her into the girl's orbit.

Where Atalanta had been taught to tread the same path each day, the girl had only smiled wider each time she found a new rocky outcrop, a new avenue between cliff faces, or a selection of grips in an oversized boulder.

The image drips to darkness.

An excursion through her memories, playing out like a strange, immersive glacier-house reel, is the last thing Atalanta expected, but at least she's not currently aiming any arrows at anyone.

In a furious, flame-like burst, Mother takes shape in the shadows. She'd been so angry when she found Atalanta had been following the girl. Mother had told her then, challenged her, instructed her:

"Be the hunter, not the prey. Don't be weak. Take them by your arrows."

Now, as then, Atalanta bristles at the order. She'd tried to explain how taking the life of something, *someone*, with facial expressions like their own just feels... wrong.

She'd refrained from sharing how the girl's smile lights up her world, because Mother was intent not to listen.

The mountain air whips around Atalanta as she watches the Iolcian girl stumble through the blizzard from afar. Now, as it was then, Atalanta's limbs are almost numb, as if her body and actions aren't her own.

Mother has kept her alive and safe for so many sun-orbits — in the skies and on solid ground. In all that time, Atalanta has never defied her. Never had a reason to.

Which is why she's creaking her arrow into her raised bow, her muscles tightening, ready.

Her target, in sight.

The arrow will penetrate her chest. Quick. Deadly.

But.

On this day, the girl — Jasyn — is upset. The churning skies are a clue, but so too are the tears she swipes from her cheeks. The blizzard seems to parallel her inner storm as she scours hidden nooks and different elevations.

Atalanta lowers her bow.

When the girl's grip slips mid-climb up a steep cliff face in forbidding conditions, Atalanta's chest tightens. That the girl might be dead, has her feeling... well, she hadn't understood it at the time, but looking back on the memory (*surprisingly literally*), she can now identify that feeling as loss.

Arrow raised, she approaches with care.

The girl opens her eyes, greeting Atalanta with a grimace (understandable), but also with a spark of curiosity and wonder in her grey eyes.

It was the first time Atalanta had seen the sparkle in Jasyn's eyes, and in that moment she knew (even if she couldn't explain it, then) that she'd chase that look forever — that look that told her she, Atalanta, was the most interesting discovery these mountains, this world, had to offer.

She lowers her arrow.

And that is how their friendship began. Because, one day, she decided not to kill her.

A synaptic electric shudder branches between the peaks—

40

EVOLVED

ATALANTA

Stumbling backwards, Atalanta covers her mouth. Her chest heaves. She'd chosen friendship with Jasyn, but it sickens her, gnaws at her insides like rodent teeth, to think she might have chosen a different path. That *one moment* could have made everything different.

The tapestry of the past undulates like the Glowing Wood lagoon at midnight. The multicoloured blush of filament fruits reflect in its surface like a painter's palette as the threads of memory reform into crisp air and branches, black and silver, sailing past.

She might not understand what in the heavens is going on, but she knows this moment.

The joy. The confusion. The elation. The fear.

Her feelings for Jasyn had evolved. Over their many sun-orbits of playing chase in the Unforgiving Mountains and the Glowing Woods, there was no reason why one day in particular should have been any different.

Like always, through a combination of well-placed arrow shots clipping at Jasyn's heels, and her in-built agility, Atalanta captures Jasyn before she reaches the woodland edge.

Landing on her, thighs pinning her in place, gasping for breath while face to face, it's then — as if for the first time — she notices Jasyn's mouth. Of course, ever since they've known each other, she's known Jasyn to have a mouth. But the odd impulse to place her own mouth against Jasyn's, well, that's new.

The realisation knocks her off her feet. Or, rather, Jasyn does.

The world upturns—

Jasyn flips her over and pins her down.

Adrenaline pumping has her elated and uncomfortable. Because what does it mean to chase Jasyn through the woods? Why does she enjoy getting ever closer? They already spend most of their time together, isn't that close enough? Why, when she wrestles her to the ground, does warmth surge in every part of her? She wants to be closer, even though she's already *on* her.

How deep is this lack of control?

She worries this enthusiasm stems from the predatory nature Mother had insisted was their way. While she's never had an urge to hurt Jasyn, she can't shake the fact that she had once been one arrow release from ending her.

To counterbalance her confusion, to escape the insidious thoughts, she leaps away and races at full pelt, apparently continuing their game of chase, when really she needs to chase her breath and hide, and figure out what *in the heavens* her body wants, and what it all meant.

Sparks—

✦

THE LAGOON OF THE PAST RIPPLES AND WHIPS INTO A WHIRLWIND of filament fruits blazing as bright as wagon headlamps as a more recent memory forms in the void.

"Why are you running from me?" Jasyn gasps, her stomping

heart rate rivalling the roar of the blizzard encircling them. Jasyn's inner storm painted outward.

The filaments pulse like the chaos in Atalanta's chest, but her tunnel vision stays on Jasyn.

"Me running from you?" Atalanta gestures. Her shoulders ache at the stretch of signing so loud. Because how can Jasyn be so obtuse to not know leaving her behind would hurt her?

"That is literally what is happening." Jasyn heaves in breaths and looks more confused than Atalanta has ever seen her.

"You're leaving me behind, again." Atalanta throws her words at Jasyn. "You left me in the mountains, and now you're leaving me here."

Atalanta might have pushed her away a little, or a lot, every now and then, but that was from fear... confusion... playing it safe... not that Jasyn knows any of that. She inwardly grumbles at herself. She'd pushed Jasyn away. She has no right to be angry that it worked.

Her instinct to run kicks in. It's a well worn furrow in her personality. But she can't because Jasyn's blizzard is blocking her path.

Unable to take the easy route, Atalanta's feet keep moving on the spot, her thoughts keep ticking.

In this moment, Jasyn has no idea of the source of her fears, of how and why they first met. Nor does she have any clue that Atalanta's feelings have evolved.

Yes, now and then Atalanta worries about her temperament and what it means for Jasyn. It creeps up on her like a vole-rat burrowed in the deep recesses of her mind. But in the last few sun-orbits she's started to figure out that it's not only when they play chase that her heart thrums. It's when Jasyn smiles, laughs, follows her curiosity, or simply breathes. Atalanta is — and always has been — captivated by it all. And more recently, everything Jasyn does seems to render her in need of a cooling dip in the Glowing Lagoon.

How can those feelings be anything but wondrous?

Right now, in the memory of the Glowing Wood, Atalanta doesn't fear hurting her, she fears losing her. She wants to reach out and smooth Jasyn's troubled brow. She wants to calm her storm, inside and out. But that's a difficult bridge to cross when you're the one causing the upheaval in the first place.

"I don't want to leave you, Atalanta." Jasyn raises her voice above the gusts. "I've wanted to ask you for so long. I'm afraid you'll say no. That you won't go with me."

"Not go with you? I left the mountains for you..." she signs, their eyes meeting as Atalanta's frustration emerges as tears.

The bulbs blaze through the encircling blanket of snow.

"But you retreated from me..." Jasyn's voice cracks as she says it, and it's like an arrow to Atalanta's heart. Because she *had* retreated. All those sun-orbits ago, trapped together in the blanket box of the wagon, Jasyn had leant in to kiss her, and Atalanta had been too dazed and grief-addled by the loss of Mother to know what to do. And she's been retreating from her at intervals ever since.

The blizzard howls.

"I needed time..." signs Atalanta.

By the time she'd started to understand her enthusiasm for Jasyn as a positive thing, she hadn't wanted to upset the balance.

If she could capture the look of hope in Jasyn's eyes and relive it forever, she would.

Jasyn's gaze drops to her lips.

The blizzard and blazing lights blur into insignificance as Atalanta does what she's wanted to for far too many sun-orbits.

One tug of Jasyn's cape is all it takes for their mouths to meet, for Atalanta to experience the enveloping warmth of this memory. Their hearts drum in time, shockwaves of sound rendering their embrace in perfect hi-definition.

Atalanta could get lost in this moment forever—

Sparks—

✦

JASYN'S GLEE FILLED EYES TURN PAINED AS SHE STUMBLES BACK.

Sickness sluices through Atalanta's veins.

Around them, the rainbow of filament fruits drip away. Blood is seeping into Jasyn's shirt from where the arrow has punched through the epicentre of her chest.

No. That's not what happened...

Atalanta had teased Jasyn by running away, inviting her to follow. They'd reunited in Atalanta's den...

But now, Atalanta holds the bow.

She can't have shot her, she's too close. But whatever is happening cares little for fact and logic.

Breaths snag her throat—

A sharp scratch at her ear, her chin. Vole-rats are nipping at her. She swipes them away.

She reaches for Jasyn, but Jasyn bats her away like she's as loathsome as the carnivorous rodents. Atalanta can only watch as Jasyn stumbles and crumbles to nothing, shadows folded in on themselves.

No, this isn't real, it can't be.

From the undulating darkness, the mass of *screeching* rodents gravitate to Atalanta like iron filings to a lode stone. She swipes at them, but they latch on with claws and teeth, threatening to burrow into her or bury her alive.

That fateful night in the Unforgiving Mountains, the creatures had sought her out. She'd been forced to choose whether to be the hunter or the prey. She'd escaped with her life, but carried the whisper of wounds on her body and mind ever since.

Atalanta whirls away from the creatures, losing them the faster she goes. A familiar and necessary tactic. But feelings and vole-rats are notoriously difficult to outrun...

A sudden electric storm lashes—

✦

HER STOMACH LURCHES AS THE GROUND FALLS AWAY, HER RACE into the dark abruptly anchored by an invisible tether line, tugging at her back.

She drifts. The sensation all too familiar.

No, she doesn't want to think about this, let alone be presented with an immersive re-enactment. But whatever is pulling the strings doesn't care for her comfort.

This is the sort of chaos that scores deep into one's thoughts. It's the same place death had taken her. The place buried in the unwelcome recesses of her memory.

Her breaths are unsteady as — one by one — pin-prick stars decorate the dark. Familiar sleek lines and lava-veined consoles take formation behind the rectangular slits of portholes.

The taut tether line connecting her to the raft, her home amongst the stars, slackens. Her stomach lurches anew—

Sloshing interrupts. Sounds that don't fit.

A mix of hot and cold slinks up her whole body, with no clue of its origin. As strange as this tour through her memories and fears might be, this latest sensation is more out of place...

Pain, sharp and burning, sears her right leg...

Her throat fills. She tries to breathe, but her lungs scream. Her chest lurches. Rushing water assaults her eyes.

As her mind scrambles to catch up, the canvas of outer space tears to ribbons of bright light...

41

EYES OPEN I

ATALANTA

Burning lungs splutter—

A frenzy of bubbles interrupt as Atalanta's eyes clear. The jungle canopy bites at the edges of her vision, framing the sky bleeding pink. Her face, her astro-suit, her body, are all soaked with whatever liquid she's being dragged through. Her back grazes the uneven ground, snagging on twigs and greenery.

Her lungs tighten. Satisfying breath evades her...

Is this her ongoing nightmare? Or is this something else?

A sharp pain in her right calf sets her nerves alight.

One look down the length of her body turns her stomach. An imposing cat-like creature has its bloodied pincer-jaws clamped about her leg and is the apparent captain of this unwelcome journey through the undergrowth.

Her injured leg throbs all the more at the knowledge. Her breaths are so strained, her chest so tight, she may as well still be under water. Her mind races, tripping over itself. But she forces no sudden movements and tells herself *not to panic*. Which is *easier said...*

She's thankful her spluttering hasn't drawn attention. Her heartbeat quicksteps, but doesn't echo back at her, which lets her know her astro-helmet isn't on. What she can see of her astro-suit is scuffed and scratched.

The rocks that line this impromptu path aren't Transonic rocks, and no lanterns light the way. She must be in another part of the jungle... Or...

*Nausea rises...*The cogs of her memories are out of alignment. What's real and what isn't is all a jumble. The last time she'd been on the ground in the presence of a feline like this... the last time she'd been in her astro-suit... she'd wrestled with the beasts and swiped one with her arrow.

There had been... snow? *Spores?* They'd covered her. They'd seeped into her eyes and... everything had been as she wanted it to be.

Until it all devolved into the fears and memories she's spent a lifetime trying to outrun.

The creature dragging her pauses for breath (or whatever an animal without a heart and lungs pauses for). Atalanta stays limp, peering through partially closed eyes.

A scar divides its face in exactly the place she'd struck, back when she'd been chased through the jungle.

How long has it been dragging her?

She bites down her panic. Her life may well depend on it.

If the wild-cat pinning her had been the last *real* moment, then... then she never found Jasyn. And the ship never left. Or, at least, it hadn't left when she thought it did, when she watched it take flight, only to be distracted by playing games.

How long has she been lost to the wilderness? Did the crew escape? Did Jasyn? Did they leave her behind?

That it was all some strange dream, some peculiar voyage through the pathways of her mind, makes more sense than it actually being *real.* Though it had *felt* real.

What if her mind is still playing tricks?

No. The depth of the pain branching from her leg lets her

know *this is real.* How it happened, she'll have to think on later, because her inbuilt sense for survival is screaming at her louder than her torn leg, and louder than any faulting sky ship.

A glance down at the state of her leg lets her know running may not be a possibility. From the little she's able to see, there are no broken bones, only skin mangled and blood leaking. Her roaming Transonics confirm the hive of healing activity warring with ruptured veins.

Don't vomit.

Adding to the bodily chaos is the last thing she needs.

She hazards a silent, difficult breath. If she can just get her helmet back on to stop the spores from reclaiming her, and so she can take a proper breath...

If she's lucky, the suit's perforations will be plugged by her own congealing blood. *(Every cloud...)*

A *fizz* of chemical reaction...

A careful visual inspection of her midriff, where a creature had previously claw-swiped her astro-suit, highlights the fabric's gel-like self-healing properties. *That's something.*

One of her arms already trails behind her head, so, with the kind of movement a dragged corpse might make, she checks her helmet. It's still clipped back. Sliding it into position, she reinstates the invisi-visor and returns to its unwelcome but necessary echo chamber.

Finally, she can fill her lungs with breath.

Heart *hammering*, breaths *clogging*, blood *whooshing*, her own internal machinations torture her ears.

Again, the feline pauses, flexing its muscular legs but keeping its paws firmly planted. That it doesn't loosen its fanged grip has her nerves sparking like a faulting circuit.

She tries to focus instead on the yellow-green vein-network beneath its dusting of white fuzz, the translucent skin glimmering in the sunlight. The flow of the algae-like substance connects through its unsheathed claws, down into the vein-cabled glow of green in the ground. Is the animal an extension of the ground, or vice versa?

Atalanta might be fascinated, if she weren't clamped in its mouth.

Finally, it spits her out. To rip her into a thousand pieces? To admire the view?

All you have to do, is outrun the predator with sharp claws and fangs and pincer-jaws, avoid any other hazards, and get back to the ship.

All with an injured leg.

The only way to find out if she can run is to try.

Not thrilled to bet her life on the functionality of her leg and a torn astro-suit, she considers her options. The item pushing into her back, that's her quiver of arrows. From the way it's digging into her, several arrows remain.

No bow, though.

With the creature's back still turned as it stretches, its vein-network pulsing, Atalanta springs from the ground with her good leg and launches into the race for her life—

42

LOSS OF LIFE

ATALANTA

Atalanta's racing heart returns to her in a thousand echoes as she chases her own breath with every searing step.

A cluster of snow-spores frazzle against her invisi-visor. Her leg might not be doing great, but at least the ether-mesh is doing its job.

Her usually nimble feet stumble between tree roots. Low gravity allows for swift progression, so long as she favours her other leg.

But she won't outrun a creature built for this world...

Without Transonic access to her surroundings, she's no idea whether its snapping at her heels, or hasn't even noticed she's gone. Looking back could cost valuable moments, and her life —

As much as she craves the wilderness, there's the caveat: *not if the wilderness is trying to kill her.* She splashes through drifting ropes of stream that not long ago cleared her eyes.

Her helmet *blips* as information populates her invisi-visor. Topography. A locator dot highlights the ship's position: exactly where it was before she'd ventured into the jungle.

Without slowing her pace, she signals the ship — *click-click*

— hoping someone will notice. She should be in range by now...

Click-click. She tries again.

Something grazes her ankle, tripping her.

"Don't be weak." "Fight to survive." "Be the hunter, not the prey." At this point, Atalanta's not sure whether the words are the uttering of Mother's haunting silhouette, or her own inner voice.

As she falls, cushioned by low gravity, she manoeuvres her body to face the jaws and pincers bearing down on her—

She angles an arrow with a solid shove—

White eyes widen. Jaws strain against the lodged arrow. Probably it's screeching, but thanks to the mismatch of Transonic and Iolcian helmet, the sounds don't reach her.

It raises a paw, claws unsheathed, and Atalanta swipes another arrow across its chest—

Green goo gushes from the wound—

Having chosen her life over theirs, the least she can do is look the creature in its eyes as it takes its last breath. She expects its chest to heave, to rise and fall one last time, but there's no theatrics. *No breaths.* The white light in the creature's eyes merely dulls. Extinguished.

The ground shudders, vibrating down to the marrow of her bones. Atalanta swallows bile. Dying might be the last thing she wants, but causing death is a close second.

As if seeking to make more of a spectacle, ground-level vines and creepers reach over the animal, dragging it into the writhing shadows.

A moon-eyed creature blinks down at her, hanging on its branch. Flowers shaped like birds of prey with multiple wings watch her from their branches.

Forging on, a thousand heartbeats and agonising footsteps later, the clearing highlighted by her visor map enters Atalanta's view.

If she didn't have the map to guide her, she wouldn't know

what she's looking at. The partial shine of chrome is barely visible between the web of vines straining over and across the ship like overzealous mooring ropes.

Amongst the criss-cross, the cargo hold is bound shut.

Heaven's hail, what happened?

Movement in the thicket—

Flashes of white—

More creatures with teeth and claws?

Atalanta doesn't wait to find out. She breaks from the treeline, out into the clearing. At the nearest leg of the ship, she propels herself upwards as quickly as her co-ordination and nerve-scorching injuries allow.

Vines help and hinder her progression. Some obscure the ladder, others act as rungs, and the worst grab at her, refusing to let go.

She arrow-stabs the dexterous greenery and slices at those blocking the hatch. Each broken vine shudders. As much as she wants to be free of her astro-helmet, if possibly sentient vegetation is screaming at her, she doesn't want that nightmare.

The vines tighten.

Something is scaling the tangle—

The blockade finally undone, Atalanta swipes her cuff at the hatch sensor and hopes.

An eternal second...

The hatch opens. She pulls herself in and swings the door closed.

The jaws of two snarling felines snap and salivate at the porthole as her shaking hands turn the locking wheel.

With an adrenaline-prickled exhale of exhaustion, she limps to the control panel and — with the strike of an obvious button — decon mist puffs into zero visibility around her as gravity-adjustment drags her down, her insides as heavy as an entire sky ship.

PART V

ABOARD

ATALANTA

43

DORMANT

ATALANTA

Atalanta stumbles out of the airlock and onto the triangular mesh metal of the floor. Ropes of vine and clumps of white cling to the ship's exterior, shrouding the portholes. The pink tint to the white substance, with light bleeding through it, gives the corridor an unwelcome bloody hue.

Her reverberating heartbeat drowning her in a deafening tinnitus, Atalanta prises open the nearest diagnostics terminal with the tip of an arrow and selects an on-screen update.

Atmosphere: Breathable
Toxicity: Nil
Gravity: 1.01

Thank the heavens.

With a swipe across the sensor, Atalanta dissolves her visor and pushes back her helmet. Being free allows her ears to rest, her Transonics to roam and — even though she'd had plenty of oxygen — her lungs to finally breathe. Though the relief is short lived.

Something isn't right here. There's a musty dampness in the cool air of the unkempt ship. A sharp and sour undercurrent of decay. *Hail.* She hopes the smell of death is nothing more than expired food or vole-rats.

Her Transonics stumble up through the ship's layers. No-one is responding to her arrival. A glance up at an overseer: the network is as dormant as the ship. But it's not just that there are no footsteps racing her way.

In their short time in the skies, she's learned the sounds of the crew and the vessel that houses them. Right now, the ship is out of alignment, somehow; quieter than it's ever been.

Though silence isn't ever really *silent*. There are fizzles of rodent heartbeats dotted about the ship, *bubbling* up in clusters like gas in a carbonated drink. But apart from them and the *creaking* metal and background *hum* of the oxygen filtration system that is — her lungs are thankful — still working, the ship is still. Even the *groans* of metal, the *grinding* cog teeth are not what they once were. It's as if the ship itself is in its death throes.

Of course, it could be her own terror and blood loss talking, the *whoosh-whoosh* of her heart straining to compensate.

Where is everyone?

Peeling through the ship's audible layers in search of human heartbeats is more of a challenge with her equilibrium disrupted by leaking blood. What should be contained within her body drips down her right leg. Some sinks into the fibres of her astro-suit, the rest escapes down the gaps in the metal grate floor, pulling her focus with it as the falling liquid disrupts the air.

Vertigo upends her, forcing her to cling to the wire bundles of the wall.

With a deep breath, she forces her focus to where she's slumped. Her own heartbeat trips over itself, demanding she get back out there and bring Jasyn to safety. Equally, it begs her to please take a minute.

Logic and lack of ability win out.

She won't get far unless she finds out what's happening, or if she doesn't piece herself back together first.

She yanks a redundant length of lighting-wire, cuts it with her arrow's point, and loops the cord just above the knee of her injured leg. Gritting her teeth against the crashing pain, she tightens it, stemming the blood flow.

It'll do, for now.

Okay. She misses the lack of gravity of the snow-jungle now, because the journey to the medical quarters feels too epic for the distance to be travelled. Every limb permeated with un-coordinated exhaustion, one nerve-bristling footstep at a time, she struggles through the labyrinth of the abandoned ship.

She's not far into her expedition before — *woosh-woosh-woosh... thrum-thrum-thrum...* She hadn't heard those sounds before, perhaps hidden by her fumbling auditory focus. Is it a struggling ship mechanism or a heartbeat? It's not her own, that's for sure. But with her swimming senses, she can hardly make sense of it.

Clunk-clunk... Clunk-clunk...

Footsteps that are neither her own nor human rattle through the carcass of the ship. Or through her mind. She hazards a shaky breath. If there's someone or something in here, is that better or worse than the ship being empty? Should she head towards or away from the sounds?

Her spiralling dizziness doesn't give her confidence in her ability to face whatever it is. Up and down are somewhat interchangeable right now. If they told her she had actually died back on Iolcus, or when the ship launched, or when they landed here, or at a thousand junctions in-between or since, and that this is all some eternal journey through nightmarish death, she wouldn't have much evidence to counter it.

But that really must be the blood loss talking.

"*That attitude will get you killed,"* warns Mother.

Laughter almost bubbles up in Atalanta, because of course Mother wouldn't see the irony of a probably hallucinated after-effect of death telling her it's stupid to *imagine* all that. Though, she might be right. If she gives into death, what is she fighting for?

Still, if she does encounter something predatory in these corridors, her chances against them won't be something to boast about.

Following the dim glow of green wires and wall-blips that promise to lead her to medical supplies, she lumbers out of the stairway. Ordinarily, she'd creep so silently the shadows might not suspect her presence, but currently only stumbling is possible.

Her irregular footsteps taunt her from several directions. She heaves in a couple of breaths. *Heavens. When did breathing get so hard?*

A burst decon pipe spews steam, sending her Transonics into overdrive. She wades into the enveloping mist as instinctive warning hisses within her.

She stops.

The unknown entity is *clunk-clunk-clunking* its way towards her, disguised by the mist. Her brain really isn't in gear, because she hadn't placed the *whatever-it-is* as being on this level.

It has a heavier footfall than the creatures she's encountered on this pristine but puzzling world, but that could be the result of the ship's gravity.

"Don't be weak," Mother signs.

Survival instinct overrides the urge to sink down and rest. She clutches an arrow, angled like a dagger, and stands, taller than her body will be able to maintain. She's made it this far...

The mist parts and the moment slows in reverse correlation to Atalanta's sprinting heart.

Its shoulders set and sturdy, the creature levels with her. It's immediately familiar and yet new to her eyes, its white fur no longer dappled with the grey spots of youth. Where once there had been only stubs that had promised antlers, now exists the branched epic crown that give it — *him* — a majestic and regal beauty.

Terror is replaced by jaw-dropping awe. Atalanta can hardly refer to him as a *fawn* anymore...

Feral fire enters the stag's eyes. His focus is on the arrow. His jaw drops, unleashing a bellow that ricochets off the metal walls and into the unforgiving echo chamber of Atalanta's Transonics.

He rears up, hooves paddling the air—

Antlers punch down in warning and the *clang-thud* reflects back from every surface possible.

Atalanta rolls aside, her leg screaming as she clashes with the wall. Better than being trampled to death by a terrified, if impressive, stag. But still.

To make clear that she means her old friend no harm, she throws her arrow aside and lowers her arms in a show of placation and apology. Time stretches and Atalanta can only hope he'll remember that she's friend and not foe as she gently signs: "It's me."

There's clear calculation in the fawn-turned-stag's eyes. Is he, too, asking *What under the Seven Suns is going on?* So many questions crowd Atalanta's thoughts. What happened here? How long has she been gone? Will her old friend recognise the person who who saved him from slaughter? The person who carried him in her shoulder sack, kept him fed and warm? Or will he see the person who threatened him with an arrow?

With each new breath splitting the mist, the fire in his eyes dampens and his breathing snorts back to a regular rhythm. But still he hesitates.

Atalanta risks extending her hand. His eyes ignite with suspicion and he retreats in a heavy clatter of hooves.

There was a time he would have met her hand and nuzzled against her. She closes her eyes but keeps her hand extended, holding her breath.

She's willing to wait until he's ready, but she's not sure her trembling body will hold out long enough.

Whether he can sense that, she isn't sure, but a fuzzy snout warms her fingertips.

Her eyes open to her friend's forehead pressing against her palm. The force behind the gesture has vastly increased since the last time they did this.

Atalanta lets herself breathe again.

In case she thought her friend too regal and imposing, he adds a snorting snuffle for good measure. It almost has her forgetting about the bloody perforation in her flesh, the chaos, and the confusion. In this moment of reconnection she's relieved to have a friend within her reach. Even if his increased stature makes no sense.

When Atalanta removes her hand, her blood smears on his snow-white forehead.

"You're right," she signs, "I should deal with my wounds."

Using her sturdy friend as a willing crutch, she limps the final stretch to the medical quarters. As they go, the stag nibbles at the moss-like growths protruding from the walls, where water pipes have leaked. Watching him lumber up or down stairs isn't the most graceful situation to witness. Though not as ungraceful as seeing him navigate through doors that are narrower than his antler-crown.

Still, after a bit of manoeuvring, he shows them into the chamber in question. When she was last here, there'd been stats monitors bleeping, alarms protesting, and the doctor's presence filling the room. Now, the lights are off and the vitals monitors are as inert as the rest of the ship.

She forces down her panic over how long it takes for a ship to deteriorate, for a fawn to grow to such heights, and where everyone is...

A wave of nausea threatens to floor her. Her heart rate hammers as if it's giving her a final countdown. She breathes as deep as she's able.

In search of anything useful, she opens and closes drawers. She misses when the only physical pain she had was the ache of an after-effect of death. *Simpler times.*

She's just about to grab a handful of gauze when a *woosh-w-woosh-woosh* takes shape under the *creaks* and *groans*. In her confusion, she must have mistaken it for the echoes of her own stumbling heartbeat.

She closes the latest drawer as silently as she's able. Because there's another heartbeat aboard the ship. And it's coming from from the quarantine chamber.

44

QUARANTINE

ATALANTA

The un-inked walls are scarred with scratches and smeared with darkened blood.

The inner chamber houses a narrow bed, lodged against the furthest wall. An ice-melt shower and hygiene facilities occupy one corner, with nothing to shield them from view. A runner machine, similar to those in the rec room, stands in front of a substantial porthole, clouded by pink-tinted snow-spores beyond.

The dwellings capture the concepts of 'optimistic road back to health' and 'worst case scenario' all in one.

But none of these details merit sustained focus, because it's the Ice Princess slumped unmoving against the porthole that has Atalanta limping closer.

Her face gaunt. Her eyes shut. Any sense of arrogance has been sapped from her. Her heartbeat is faint, only just clinging to the last threads of life. If Atalanta were more mentally dexterous herself, she might have located the heartbeat earlier.

She might be a monster, imprisoned, but the sad, broken figure of the Ice Princess strikes a chord of sympathy. No-one should die like this. Trapped and alone. Which is why Atalanta doesn't fully consider the consequences as she limps to the quarantine chamber's door.

Like many terrible ideas, it's the right thing to do.

Nearing the door, she stumbles on a pile of… what? Spanners, hammers, screwdrivers? Miscellaneous tools. *What are they doing in the middle of the floor?* Did someone try and fail to break in?

She squares up to the combination lock dial as best she can. Never having had reason to approach this chamber before, she's no idea what the combination might be. The reinforced glass isn't the kind that breaks under stress. The bloody blemishes — from fists hammered against the inner walls, judging by the blood-crusted knuckles of the inert princess — are evidence of that.

Atalanta traces the metal seams where the glass panels join, finding sturdy components with as much strength as the glass. With the right tools, she might be able to wrangle a way in. *If* she was firing on all cylinders.

She rolls her eyes at herself. She's not being the sharpest tool in the tool box, that's for sure. She doesn't need to deconstruct the chamber to gain entry. It's a mechanical lock: she just has to listen.

Instructing her laboured heartbeat to *please quieten down*, she hones in on the external door dial. It *click-click-clicks* past each number until the hammer within the mechanisms *clunks,* finding its groove. She repeats three further times before the inner workings shift and *crunch*. With a turn of the handle, the door slides open and Atalanta gains entry to the chamber's outer corridor.

With a careful eye on the unconscious Ice Princess, she repeats the exercise and the inner chamber door slides open. Nerves on a knife edge, an arrow clutched as a makeshift dagger, she hazards closer.

While the chamber itself is well-aired, the princess reeks of missed showers and despair. Her sleeves are dark, crusted with old blood.

Only now does Atalanta consider that she, herself, has lost a lot of the same, and is liable to make terrible decisions. *Like walking into a cage occupied by the Ice Princess.*

The stag lingers on the other side of the chamber glass, bright eyes watching. The Ice Princess might be on the doorstep of death, but if they've been here long enough for a fawn to turn into a stag, *how in the heavens did the Ice Princess manage to hold on all this time?*

Through her own fog, Atalanta seeks clues. There's a source of water — the ice-melt pipes and sink — and empty pouches of ration packs.

The Ice Princess's breaths stop.

Atalanta bends to her, grimacing through the pain lashing up her leg. But curiosity and good intentions die a death as the Ice Princess's eyes ignite with a sudden and deep inhalation.

Heartbeats collide as nerve jangling adrenaline kicks them both into overdrive. The feral terror in the Ice Princess's eyes has Atalanta raising her arrow-dagger.

The Ice Princess halts her stabbing strike and in that same motion musters enough energy to shove her backwards.

Somehow, Atalanta remains standing as the Ice Princess scrambles to her feet as gracelessly as an injured animal fighting to die in peace. The threat is undermined by the Ice Princess's backward collapse against the chamber wall.

The Ice Princess grasps Atalanta's wrist to keep the arrow from her and — in a sad echo of their first on-ship encounter — they grapple.

Where raw power had once occupied the princess's shoulders — born of a lifetime of combat training — her withered frame vibrates with exhaustion.

It wouldn't be a fair fight. Atalanta lets her loose and casts her arrow aside in a show of intent.

Through eyes battling to close, the Ice Princess stares at the fallen arrow, then at Atalanta. She's poised to bolt, or attempt to. She wouldn't get far without keeling over.

Neither of them would.

With the shaky uncertainty of someone powered only by adrenaline, the Ice Princess trains her wild and untrusting gaze on Atalanta, assessing her in a manner similar to the stag just minutes ago. Her wide eyes, piercing and glacial blue, drop to Atalanta's blood soaked leg.

Which is the last thing Atalanta observes, because — thanks to the universe's enthusiasm for irony, or just simple blood loss — instead of the Ice Princess folding to the ground, it is Atalanta who's pressed down by gravity and tunnel vision. It is Atalanta who collapses like a heavy sack of bones at the finely stitched, if scuffed, boots of the feral princess.

45

UNTETHERED

ATALANTA

Z

z Z

One by one, pinpricks of light pierce the darkness until the stars have you surrounded.

You've heard that at the moment of death your life flashes before your eyes. But something you're learning about dying — or almost dying, or dying briefly, as has been your experience so far — is that death has a habit of presenting you with unwelcome memories, perhaps even cursing you to spend eternity exploring them.

Which is likely why you're here, reliving the moment you first discovered you could be left behind. The tether line connecting you to the sky raft you call home slackens, and your stomach lurches. You press your comms, the series of clicks letting your parents know you're untethered, asking *What should I do?* But no-one responds.

Oxygen 32%.

Your parents warnings about the dangers of space prickle through your panicked thoughts. *"Time, oxygen and space wait for no-one."*

Perhaps there's a mechanical fault.

Perhaps it's a test?

Mother always focuses on the importance of physical and mental dexterity. It takes another breath to remind yourself that you know how to move through space. How to use your arrow, secured by twine looped about your waist, to propel yourself.

One arrow launch after another, you drift back towards the ship. Feeling a little foolish, even, for flustering. And when your feet finally touch the hull, you crouch and grip the railing.

A single misstep could see you drifting again, so you grasp your tether, retrieve its end and plug it into a ship-wall anchor.

It holds in place. Perhaps you'd merely used a faulty anchor. There are so many dotted across the ship's exterior, one was bound to fail at some point.

But your tether unplugs, apparently of its own accord. You try with another, but the result is the same. You peer in a porthole and Father's expression is exhausted, his eyes tear-filled and almost vacant.

It takes a few eternal seconds to wrap your understanding around the implication. It doesn't sink in until your attention falls to Mother, crumpled on the raft's floor, her temple blemished red.

Father refuses to look at either of you.

Nausea strangles your insides as your own tether threatens to tie in knots. Your heart hammers your ribs. Because you understand, now, that Father has succumbed to the uncertainties of the skies and chosen death for you, for Mother, and perhaps even himself.

When you'd been sent out to play a simple game of 'target practice' you'd been relieved to be outside the walls of the raft. You'd never considered what it might feel like to suffocate, suspended in the void.

Now that you're out here, the time-limit of your air canister counting down, the power of hindsight screams that your cocoon of family life had been unravelling. And you hadn't even noticed.

You hadn't thought much on what life for your parents looked like before you entered their world because... well, why would you? This journey to nowhere on your escape raft has been your whole life.

With bile souring your tongue, you wonder whether he intends to carry on. With you and Mother out of the equation, the air filtration won't be so taxed and rations will last longer.

Either he's made the ultimate decision for all of you, or prized his life above all else. You can't decide whether the sickness seeping through your veins is hatred or a strange sadness.

The haptics of your suit shudder you back to alertness.

05.00%

The image of Mother lying bloodied on the raft floor elbows into your thoughts. She didn't do that. He did. She hadn't wanted your lives to be forfeit. That fact fuels the fire of your rage. It grounds you, gives you strength.

Refusing to be discarded to the endless cavern of space, you knot your tether about an external grip. The tethers aren't made for such formations, and there's a risk it'll unravel, but 'a risk' is all you can take right now.

If your father won't let you in, you won't give him the mercy of dying beyond his sights.

00.42%

If you'd have thought about it before, you'd have considered suffocating in *the nothing* to be a quiet way to go. You'd have imagined drifting off to sleep and never waking.

But that is not what this is.

The vice grip about your lungs begs you to draw in a useful breath. You try, but there's nothing. The numbers flash, telling you what you already know:

0.00%

Invisible claws dig into your chest. Your body writhes within itself, attempting to jolt you to action. You wish you could obey, but wanting to survive isn't always enough.

The walls of space and time are closing in, stealing the pinprick stars from view.

Distantly, the airlock opens.

It's wishful thinking, or a trick of death, as it invites you into its arms. The distant tug of your tether being reeled in doesn't convince you otherwise. It's probably the final convulsion as your body is spent of breath.

An airlock hiss suggests there's hope. But, even if you're not dead, you've no way of knowing whether the person reeling you in is friend or foe.

46

PATCHED UP

ATALANTA

Eyes and lungs jolt open.

Muscles tense. Fists clench.

It takes a monumental moment to comprehend she's not adrift in outer space. Not being reeled aboard the sky raft of her past. Not dead or dying. Though she's not yet certain if what confronts her is better or worse.

The Ice Princess looks down at her, her royal posture buckled.

Atalanta's body kicks into action. Pain shoots through her, her shoulders and elbows protest, and her own feral cry echoes back at her as she tries and fails to launch at the woman.

What in the heavens...? Her wrists are anchored by restraints. She's atop a gurney in the medical quarters. *How did the Ice Princess get her up here?*

Her captor raises a hand in a manner not dissimilar to how Atalanta had raised a calming palm to the stag. And how she herself raised a hand to the Ice Princess.

"I put you in restraints only to stop you from strangling me when you woke," says the Ice Princess, quickly, her voice rasping as though it's been too long since she last spoke. Despite this, her tone is softer than Atalanta expects. "Looks like that might have been the right call."

The Ice Princess's face twitches. *Is she trying to smile, or laugh, or something?* Atalanta emphatically does not see what is funny. Perhaps if she wasn't the one cuffed in place, she might have more of a sense of humour.

Her captor's brow contorts. Is she cursing herself? Only now does Atalanta notice the other details of her face. Her pronounced facial scar, jagged like a series of overlapping arrow heads. It hadn't been noticeable when they'd sparred in the shadows of the cargo hold, nor when Atalanta had dragged her to the top deck. She can only assume the princess ordinarily conceals it and that whatever had taken place in the last *however long* either didn't call for such, or the materials were not available.

Atalanta's observation drifts down to the lightning shaped discolouration across her throat. The injury Jasyn had given her in the arena with the burn of her ice-sword. It had been angry and red raw the last time she'd seen it. Now, it's calmed.

"You've been unconscious for a few hours," says the Ice Princess, softly. "Probably a good thing you passed out. Your leg needed stitches."

Atalanta can only stare at her.

"Princesses must master needlework," says the Ice Princess in an affected voice, possibly echoing someone from her life. Or just being a bit weird. "So dull. But, I hate to admit, turns out it's quite useful in certain circumstances." Her eye twitches and she curses under her breath as she clamps a hand over the offending eye.

Was the Ice Princess always this... awkward? Or is this the result of being caged for however long?

Shaking her head, the Ice Princess laughs (at herself?). Atalanta narrows her eyes. She refuses to find the Ice Princess charming. Either she's a master manipulator, or it's the blood loss turning Atalanta strange.

Only now, processing the princess's words, does Atalanta, finally, let her suspicious stare stray to her own leg. It hurts, a lot, but the bandage pressing her wound dulls the sharpness to an ache.

The Ice Princess could have left her to die. Instead, she's looked after her? That might take a while to sink in...

"I had some help lifting you," says the Ice Princess, giving the stag's forehead a good scratch as he plods closer. With a washcloth, she wipes Atalanta's bloody handprint off his fur and — as if they're old friends — the stag nuzzles against the Ice Princess's touch.

The princess and the stag are... buddies? Is she really meant to believe *this* is the real world?

"I think he's relieved to see you," says the princess as the stag shuffles closer to Atalanta. "I've been pretty poor company this last..." she pauses as if trying to come up with a number, but settles on: "...while."

Atalanta can't stop staring. In the hours she's been lost to unconsciousness, the Ice Princess has seen to her wounds. She's also cleaned up her own bloodied knuckles, as well as washed and changed into engineering overalls. If not for her emaciated frame, she'd almost look like she belongs on this ship.

Atalanta lets her Transonics explore. Ordinarily she tries not to observe someone's inner workings, but these are extraordinary circumstances. The circulatory system before her is working hard, but more functional than before. The Ice Princess's stomach *churns* with digestion and the *fizz* of nutrient and energy absorption. She's not at death's door anymore, but it'll take a while to rebuild after the starvation damage.

"You don't need to worry about me." The Ice Princess's gentle eyes could almost convince her. *Don't be fooled.*

Atalanta pointedly glances to the cuffs holding her in place.

"The restraints are only loose." Sure enough, on closer inspection she is able to free her wrists by wriggling a bit. She struggles with one, but that's more an issue of her own ailing co-ordination.

The princess steps in to assist and Atalanta flinches. Of course she does. She's the Ice Princess. It's only the disappointment buckling the princess's features that has Atalanta questioning her response.

"Like I said," says the princess, taking the hint and stepping away, letting Atalanta find her own way out of the loose restraints, "I didn't want you killing me. It'd be a shame to get this far and then be strangled to death."

Atalanta can't argue with that.

With Atalanta's wrists freed, the princess doesn't leap away or put any distance between them. She simply sits, her shoulders and back buckled as though gravity still might win. Atalanta stares at her, but doesn't find an obvious or even subtle threat. It could be exhaustion, but she lets her suspicions melt a little.

"For how I reacted to you," the Ice Princess nods at the quarantine chamber, "I apologise. It's been a while since I've interacted with... anyone. And when we last met, if you recall, you tore several strips off me."

Atalanta can only raise a *What did you expect?* eyebrow in response.

The princess nods, as if she understands. "I'm aware of my reputation. I could tell you my noble reason for climbing aboard this ship — that all I wanted was to get the sword into safe hands — but I'm not sure you'd believe me. If I was in your position, I'd have wrestled me into submission, too."

As if on a covert mission to prove she's *not the worst person in the universe*, the Ice Princess reaches out to the stag, stroking his fur. "I don't expect you to trust me," she says, "but there are some things I want you to know. Whether you believe me or not..." She shrugs.

It's so strange to be looking at a face that has the essence of Jasyn, strange to think that the supposedly cruel, death-dealing Ice Princess is from the same genetic lineage as the woman Atalanta loves. Their chins have similar angles — although the princess's is thinner now — and the questioning brow is exactly Jasyn's. But their eyes are different. Jasyn's are more grey, more like a storm with silver lightning. The Ice Princess's — though mesmerising — are the pale blues and turquoise of a glacial lagoon.

Don't stare.

But the princess appears to be waiting for approval. *Since when do royals wait for approval?*

Atalanta gives a single nod.

"Despite what some of your crew think, I wasn't part of the attack that forced the ship to the skies. I snuck aboard because I wanted to ensure the Ice Sword — *Jasyn's sword* — was far from my family. When the ship took off unexpectedly, I was in the hold and... well, I guess I ran out of air." She rolls her eyes and smiles vaguely at herself as if acknowledging that's stupid.

Don't be charmed by her.

"When I came to, I saw you. I was trying to tell you that I didn't want to frighten you. I didn't realise my words weren't reaching you. I'm sorry I scared you." The princess pauses, perhaps to check Atalanta is following what she's saying. She almost looks embarrassed. Her heartbeat thrums steadily. If she's lying, she good at it.

The stag nudges the princess's hand, inviting further affection. Atalanta had thought him a good judge of character, but apparently he'll sidle up to anyone. *Traitor.* Atalanta narrows her eyes at him, but he's too busy wriggling to get a better scratch from the princess to notice. When the princess chuckles at his antics, stroking his neck and nose, it's difficult to imagine her capable of anything cruel.

"The food in the galley is gone, thanks to our *deer* friend," says the princess and Atalanta raises her brow, not at the stag's ability to chomp through any food source, but at the princess's attempt at a joke. "But the galley crates in the cargo hold are mostly still intact. If you're hungry?"

The princess places a bowl of something reconstituted within Atalanta's reach. The evidence of the princess's emaciated frame, the stag's increased stature, and the overall state of the vine-tethered ship, would suggest it's been many months since Atalanta last ate an actual meal. And yet, physically, there's no evidence of starvation. Only a hint of hunger.

"I promise I haven't poisoned it," says the princess with a strange sort of smile that Atalanta can't read. Is the joke that she *would* poison it? "Saying that out loud," she continues, her eye twitching a little, "I realise that's what someone who has poisoned it would say."

Heavens above. If this is the princess's actual personality: thoughtful, kind, apologetic, awkward? She's not at all what Atalanta thought. It could be a trick. Of course. But what's the point of that?

Unable to fathom a reason, and now growing hungrier by the second, Atalanta decides that someone intent on poisoning her would be unlikely to patch up her wounds first, so she accepts the bowl.

For several spoonfuls, the Ice Princess gives her space to eat and not feel too watched. But the urge to ask questions must be too much, because finally she asks:

"How did you know the combination?" She nods to the quarantine chamber. "I hoped our friend here," she pats the stag's head, "would help me out of my cage, but all he did was keep bringing me spanners and screwdrivers."

That explains the pile of tools. She buries her smile, because laughing with the Ice Princess isn't something she should be doing, is it? It's not an option that lingers long, because when she next looks up, the princess has tears in her eyes.

"Sorry," says the Ice Princess with a shaky breath. "It's just... I thought I was going to die. And the way I'm feeling, I'm not convinced that outcome is off the table. But you let me out. At least if I do die, now, it won't be in a cage." The princess looks right at Atalanta then and, as much as Atalanta wants to look away, the gratitude in those glacier-ravine eyes stops her. She's never known eyes that colour to look so warm. "Thank you."

After swiping her tears with her sleeve, the princess continues: "What the hail happened out there? Where is everybody?" The questions aren't casual. There's a hurried nature, a heaviness to them. It isn't mere curiosity. She cares.

Well, that makes two of them.

Atalanta has never excelled at trusting people. So, of course, to have any chance of doing something useful, of finding Jasyn and the crew, she has to trust the person known across Iolcus and the Seven Suns for her cruelty, her scheming, and for being a stone-cold killer.

47

OVERSEERS I

ATALANTA

If the ship had been in working order, they could have used the lift. Without it, the journey up through the ship is much slower. Atalanta tries not to push herself too much as she limps up the metal-grate stairway. To stand any chance of doing anything useful, she needs to remain conscious at the very least.

The princess must be of a similar mind, because they keep the same pace. Conquering the final rung of the stairs, the princess wheezes. Seeing someone ordinarily so strong become so weak tugs at Atalanta's sympathy.

With the vine-ropes tangled across the apex glass above the helm, the upper deck does a perfect impression of a ship abandoned to the perils of time.

Though Atalanta has become knowledgeable of the mechanical workings of this ship, her reach hasn't extended to the functioning of the helm consoles, which are decidedly less mechanical. She stares at the inert monitors, no idea where to start.

"The captain's terminal — the helm console — will access the overseers," says the princess between breaths. "We'll need to wake the ship first," she adds, swiping a series of motions at the console's edge.

There must be a sensor there because it lights up, the deck illuminates and the tinny voice of the [C]ARGO ship informs them:

"Ship status: waking."

Despite having been locked away for the majority of her time aboard, it would appear the princess is no stranger to this ship. Or, perhaps, ships in general?

Atalanta stares at her, but the royal's attention remains on the console.

It might be a trick of the princess's diminished stature, her withered frame and her brow rucked in concentration, but Atalanta can detect no threat, no malice, no scheming intent. She can't imagine her responsible for all the things an unhinged Ice Royal, Warden General of the Iolcian guard, is supposed to have done. Murdered her own sister for the power of Iolcian Ice. Levelled villages and stolen their lives and resources. Something about the cog of the Ice Princess's personality doesn't fit in the machine of her reputation.

She played fair in the arena battle against Jasyn, didn't she? It was her father, not her, who was set on Jasyn's demise. She wasn't cruel to Tiphys, either. She even gave the boy a fighting chance at redemption after he'd publicly humiliated her in the arena.

And, if Atalanta is honest, their scuffle in the cargo hold hadn't felt like an attack. She'd been far too easily victorious against the *ruthless Gladiator Princess.* Even if the gladiator in question had been suffering the effects of an impromptu take-off and reduced oxygen. If anyone had been attacking, it was Atalanta.

She even patched up Atalanta's wounds when she could've left her for dead. Perhaps she isn't the aggressor everyone assumes her to be. Take away her origins and any preconceptions, and the *Ice Princess* might even be someone Atalanta likes.

And it's difficult to hate a face that looks a little like Jasyn's...

"Are you okay?" The Ice Princess arches an empathetic eyebrow at her. Again, not the kind of thing Atalanta would have expected from a ruthless ice royal. Atalanta looks away. *Hail.* She'd been staring. Possibly even *gazing.*

The princess returns to studying the helm-screen. After some well chosen console options, she swipes across the screen and a constellation of images with timestamps from the overseer network illuminate in the helm-ether.

With a steadying breath, the princess selects the most recent recordings. They play out, zipping through where there was activity in the ship. The occasional vole-rat breaks from the walls and scurries along the corridors, but the main sources of activity are the princess in the quarantine chamber and the roaming stag. The princess in the ether isn't as gaunt, though she's still only a shadow of what she was. The stag's body and antlers are less developed. The pile of tools in front of the quarantine chamber isn't as high. There's no blood on the chamber's walls. That must have happened later.

The ship in the ether makes an announcement about non-essential protocols shutting down, at which point the ether images effervesce to nothing.

How long ago was this?

With a winding gesture, the princess scrolls the overseer-constellation backwards at pace through days and months. In that time, the only signs of life in the empty ship are frenetic movements of vole-rats, the stag exploring — raiding kitchen supplies, figuring out water taps, and visiting the princess as she paces her prison.

In all that time, the jungle of creepers and vines slither and vibrate across portholes. The stag ages backwards, his stature diminishing while the princess's physique grows stronger. Every now and then there's a burst of fruitless activity as the princess attempts to break apart the items of her cell and kick free of her confines.

Next to Atalanta, the princess's jaw is tight as she concentrates. Reliving what she's been through can't be easy, but she doesn't complain. Atalanta buries the urge to comfort her, which only makes herself bristle. She's never been one to reach out... It must be that pesky blood-loss again.

But then the princess buckles—

And Atalanta steps in, her arms wrapping around her before she's mentally caught up to what's happening—

By the time the princess is half-fallen, she's already reaching for something solid to grab onto.

Atalanta doesn't manage to prevent her fall, exactly — with her own leg igniting, sharp with pain — but as they fall together, she takes the heaviness out of their landing, ending up more or less in the Ice Princess's lap.

48

OVERSEERS II

ATALANTA

As her ice-blue eyes readjust, the princess flinches at Atalanta's proximity. There's a flash of assessment, questioning whether Atalanta is friend or foe. Atalanta can certainly relate.

"Sorry," says the princess, with a laboured and awkward laugh. "Usually when people are this close, they're trying to murder me."

Even if the princess could understand her signed language, Atalanta has no idea what to say to that. The princess forces another steadying breath. She's probably dizzy. Atalanta's experiencing her own bout of light-headedness, too. Something in her own chest tightens, a brief sensation as unsettling as being suffocated by a writhing mass of vole-rats. She forces her own steadying breath.

She hadn't expected to feel concern over the Ice Princess's welfare. She hadn't expected to feel sorry for her. Nor had she expected to want to wrap her in her arms and tell her she's safe now. She hadn't expected to be close enough to notice the flecks of green in her otherwise blue eyes.

The princess makes no move to put distance between them.

She does, however, raise a politely quirked eyebrow that would suggest perhaps Atalanta should remove herself from her lap.

Hail.

Atalanta scrambles to her feet, entirely lacking grace. She'd like to blame her injured leg for that, but really it's her unsettled thoughts toying with her equilibrium.

Still, she manages to stand enough that she can offer the princess a helping hand.

The princess stares at the hand a good few seconds before accepting. With slow, purposeful movements, Atalanta assists her back to her feet and guides her to rest in the captain's chair.

"I guess one meal, a shower and a change of clothes doesn't undo months of damage," says the princess, rolling her eyes at herself or the situation as she catches her breath. "Keep looking," she suggests, nodding Atalanta to the helm console and the overseer records drifting in the ether.

Using the same motions as the princess, Atalanta swirls her fingers against the track pad and watches as the images tumble backwards in time. Too far?

Atalanta stops.

The activity across the various overseer feeds suggests this is back when they were en route to this world. Her finger twitches against the track pad, which — inadvertently — hones in on the engine chamber feed, enlarging the images and adding sound.

There's no mistaking the frantic movements and moans, the dropped trousers and rucked shirts, the placement of hands and mouths. Kalais and Castor getting intimate, hidden in the shadows of the engine chamber. Well, not as hidden as they probably thought themselves.

Atalanta panics. *How does she get away from these images? And hail, those sounds?*

"At least someone was having some fun on this trip."

Atalanta can't help but smirk at the princess's deadpan delivery. She returns to the overseer and navigates back to the full constellation view and is relieved — *so relieved* — when the audio of Kalais and Castor *having fun* is muted.

She winds forward—

The airlock chamber. Jasyn with the rest of the ground crew. Herakles, Castor, Kalais, Hylas and Peleus, all kitted out in astro-gear, all about to head out on an ill-fated search for the source of magnetism. On the other side of the airlock porthole, Atalanta watches Jasyn go.

Forward—

The Medical quarters. Heartbeats flatline.

Forward—

The airlock. Atalanta shows herself out into the wilderness.

Medical. Doctor Orpheus commandeers the comms to tell Atalanta exactly how stupid she is and that she's going to help, only for their brief conversation to be drowned by static. "Fuck-fuck-fuck."

Forward—

Atalanta's monitor joins the flatline alerts.

"Heaven's hail," exclaims the princess in a tired, breathy manner.

Heaven's hail, indeed. Watching her own flatline play out, Atalanta gasps. *She was dead...? Or, at least, the ship thought she was...*

"Uh...doctor?" The voice of Pollux reaches out to the doctor through the medical comms. "The kid is showing himself out of the ship."

Sure enough, the airlock — the same one Atalanta used — is occupied by Tiphys making use of the override she'd left in place, showing himself out into the wilderness.

"Fuck," says the doctor.

Forward—

An airlock. Doctor Orpheus, armed with her medician case,

Zetes accompanying, armed with a rifle. Both are doused in decon mist.

Forward—

The helm deck. The remaining crew, Gus, Pollux and Lynk, cluster around the consoles as the comms crackle with screeching feedback. Tiphys's helmet-seer shows he's surrounded by whiteout. The view goes vertical, perhaps him falling over, or his helmet being wrenched off, and it's only a matter of seconds before his helmet-seer ripples only with static.

In the medical chamber, his stats monitor flatlines.

Forward—

Medical. Two more monitors flatline. Doctor Orpheus and Zetes?

"*Euryproktos,*" Gus mournfully cries out as she punches the drifting ether-image of the medical chamber with its flatline monitors.

Forward—

Medical. Gus loads armfuls of food pouches into the quarantine chamber hatch. The princess demands to know what's going on, but Gus is distracted and mutters only: "This is just in case. We'll be back. *We'll be back.*"

Forward—

Airlock. Gus, Pollux and Lynk, armed and kitted out in astrosuits: "The maps aren't working, but if we get close enough, the suit-to-suit link ups should work," just as they're doused in decontamination mist.

Forward—

Three more stats monitors flatline, leaving only the Ice Princess's beating.

Atalanta pauses the replay, letting silence settle. The princess lets out a long breath as she sits forward in the helm chair, her eyes sheened with tears or exhaustion. "What's out there? How did you escape it?"

Atalanta slicks her hands through her hair, snagging on the knots. She signs all she knows. "There were… spores? There was water. The latter washed away the former." *Is that what happened?* Her eyes cleared when she was dragged through the stream… Her signing is met with the princess's head tilt of incomprehension.

But Atalanta's focus drifts from the princess to the paused replay of the medical chamber. There, on the stats monitor, a single upward tick of a line, caught mid blip. Atalanta gestures for the replay to continue.

"Speed it up," the Ice Princess suggests.

Atalanta gestures for it to fast forward. Another blip on a different monitor. Then, nothing. After another bout of staring at the utter inactivity, another screen, another blip. All stats monitors — all apart from the princess's — follow the same pattern: a sea of nothing with an occasional wave. The faster the playback, the closer the blips, until they resemble…

Heartbeats.

Just impossibly spaced out? *Mind-bendingly slow*?

If Atalanta's leg weren't throbbing distractingly, she'd be pacing. How can she understand what all this means? How can she find out if Jasyn is still alive? And — just as Jasyn's lopsided grin teases her memories, just as Atalanta wants to scream: *How do I find you—?*

"I have an idea," says the princess, "Do you know where Jasyn's sword is?" Her raised hand and crumpled brow implore Atalanta to hear her out. "I know I'm a horrendous ice royal and everything, but if we have the sword, I think I can help."

49

COMPASS

ATALANTA

Letting the Ice Princess into the weapons store might not be the most sensible course of action, but if she was a threat, wouldn't she have done something *threatening* by now?

Either she knows exactly how to manipulate, or she's a decent human being. And Atalanta just has to hope it's the latter.

Mentally replaying the rhythm of clicks, she grasps the chunky metal lock of the weapons vault door and inputs the combination. She casts the lock aside and it lands with a *clunk*, which reverberates uncomfortably.

The door opens with a cry of metal on metal.

To get to where the sword is likely stored, Atalanta rips through layer upon layer of webs using an arrow. She tries not to think about how many spider eyes are watching as she destroys their life's work. The princess cringes with each torn web. *Who'd have thought?*

"There it is." The princess points to the bundle of purple and burgundy cloth. "Don't hold it by the hilt," she warns as Atalanta claims it from the shelf. "Just in case."

Just in case what? But the warning in the princess's tone has her obeying.

"When the owner of Iolcian Ice dies," explains the princess, shuffling closer, as Atalanta unwinds the cloth, "their link with their weapon is severed."

Atalanta doesn't like the words *dies* or *severed*. But she has an idea of what the princess is getting at. Though now they're behind the locked door, she fears the princess might just be here to claim the sword for herself.

"Don't panic," says the princess, with a playful glint in her eyes. "An individual can only align with one ice-weapon. I already have my sword. Well, I don't *have* it. It's probably here somewhere. My point is, I'm not out to steal Jasyn's. If I was, why would I have brought it here in the first place?"

Atalanta nods, appreciating the princess's ability to foresee her concerns. She's about to sign, to attempt to ask: *Why did you bring it to the ship?* She'd said she wanted the sword in safe hands. *Whose safe hands?*

"Look at the spirit measure," says the princess with bright eyes, pointing to the lump of glass inset within the handle where a blizzard-like haze storms within.

Atalanta might not be a sky ship scientist exactly, but she knows enough of Jasyn and her link with the sword to understand.

"She's alive." The princess underscores its meaning and Atalanta's heart could burst with the confirmation.

Instead, it's not Atalanta's heart bursting but her tears. Sobs shudder from her. She angles away, as if that might disguise her emotional display.

"Hey, it's okay," says the princess, reaching out a bandaged hand and squeezing Atalanta's shoulder. She expects to want to shirk away from it, but instead finds comfort in the contact. "We'll find her. We'll find them all."

Atalanta's sobs turn to vague laughter, then, because *in what world does the Ice Princess give comfort?* When did everything get so backwards?

"The suits have locators on them," says the princess as she wipes a clear space on the floor with the burgundy cloth. *What is she doing?* "But I don't know how to find that information — and poking random buttons on a sky ship is seldom a good idea..."

Is this meant to be encouraging? Atalanta sure hopes she's going somewhere with this. The princess knows how to access the overseer network but doesn't know how to locate the crew? Her knowledge of sky travel is inconsistent to say the least.

"There are many quirks of Iolcian Ice," says the princess, placing Jasyn's sword on the floor, resting it on its spirit measure. "One of which is that the hilt always — when free and able — points to its owner."

Sure enough, it turns like the needle of a compass.

The sword settles, its hilt pointing. That's where they'll find Jasyn? Atalanta stifles another relieved sob while the princess beams:

"All we need now is a plan."

From her knowing smile, it seems she already has one.

That lopsided grin. It jars that Atalanta recognises that same smile from Jasyn's face. Maybe that's why she trusts her.

The princess leads the way.

Or rather, she starts to, but slows once her stumbling body reminds her she isn't up to racing through the ship.

Side by side, they make the exhausting, limping journey from the weapons store in the ship's middle, to its cargo-filled underbelly. It's unclear which of them is leaning and which is the crutch, but they get there.

"Turns out a royal life of playing with geared machines and ice-engines, followed by lurking in a cargo hold on an unplanned take-off, might have been useful after all," says the princess, unveiling a tarp covered *something.*

There, affixed to the floor and walls by nets and ropes, is one of the ice-engine vehicles Atalanta had been drawn to early on their voyage, just before she and the Ice Princess stumbled into each other's paths for the first time.

"This is a tri-ice-cycle," the princess informs her with a glimmer of enthusiasm.

From its hefty wheels, Atalanta can imagine this will enable them to cover ground more quickly, but not how it'll deal with reduced gravity.

"It has inbuilt thrusters designed to assist its course in different gravitational and atmospheric environments," explains the princess, as if reading Atalanta's thoughts.

Atalanta runs her hands over its metal, noting the markings at the rear of its chassis suggesting it capable of carrying a crew-load of passengers. *Yes, this is the vehicle they need.*

Now all they need to figure out is how to prise the crew from the grip of this world. Atalanta offers a smile of her own, because she might have the missing components to make this plan work.

50

HILT

ATALANTA

It looks like they're really doing this.

At least this time Atalanta doesn't have to listen to her own echo-chamber of panic. Her Transonics are closed and silence surrounds her. Her heart rattles within her chest, but at least it's not amplified.

Astro-suits and helmets are in place, the latter strapped down with pipe-tape for good measure, decon canister packs are stowed within the tri-ice-cycle, and weapons are within reach. The compass of Jasyn's sword rests on the dash, safe under the canopy of metal and glass.

The princess secures herself to the driver's seat with a safety harness. As if on instinct, she gives Atalanta's a tug to ensure it's sturdy. When she notices Atalanta watching her, her concentrated features bloom to a lopsided smile.

It has Atalanta reaching out and smoothing down the tape affixing the princess's helmet before even thinking through what she's doing. *What* is *she doing?* She reclaims her hand, not sure if she can blame blood loss for the misjudged physical contact.

The princess offers a nod of thanks.

Atalanta clears her throat. If all goes to plan, she'll be seeing that smile on the face she wants to be gazing at.

After deep breaths, and a shared nod of agreement, *it's time.*

Atalanta strikes the button and decon mist fills the hold. Another button strike and the hold platform lowers. Or, at least, it starts to. What's happening is difficult to tell without being able to tune in, but Atalanta can guess well enough that it's snagging on vines.

As she hoped, the force of the platform mechanisms is enough to strain the moorings lashed across the exterior. Enough for her to lean out of the tri-ice-cycle's side-hatch and reach between the opened edges with a spear and slice through the green web.

Barricade cut, the platform drops so suddenly, Atalanta almost loses her footing, saved only by her safety harness and a helping hand from the princess.

There's no time to share her appreciation — though she's sure the princess reads the thanks in her startled eyes — as the grumbling vibration of the engine is already stepping up a gear. Closing the vehicle's side-hatch, Atalanta slips into position, back to back with the princess.

Another shuddering rev and they sail off the lowered hold platform to the powder-covered terrain beyond. Before the vines have a chance to reconnect, she scrolls through astro-helmet options and selects the one that closes the hold. The last thing they want is this world claiming the ship from within.

That this all occurs in a cocoon of silence does little to pave the way for calm. She'd much rather hear the battle of mechanisms vs vegetation to understand which is victorious. But removing her helmet would be more misguided than what they're already attempting.

At least it looks like the hold platform has closed and sealed, severing any greenery attempting to enter.

Atalanta keeps her eyes on the deceptive wilderness in their wake.

Hail and heavens. When they'd taken to the skies, Atalanta never considered she might be sailing into the wilderness, following the compass of a sword, with the Ice Princess forging their path.

She clutches a bow, claimed from the weapons store. Not that she can get to anything with the hatches shut, but it does settle her nerves a little.

For a jungle that seemed determined to devour her previously, the stillness that surrounds them feels filled with the threat of false security.

The universe of possibilities is notoriously hard to navigate, much like low-gravity on a speeding three wheeled vehicle. While the princess might have experience with two wheeled engines on Iolcus, a three wheeler in unfamiliar conditions, surrounded by a jungle that's likely out to get them, takes a bit of trial and error.

The low gravity gives their trajectory a certain uplift that has them soaring above ground just as often as contacting it. To her credit, the princess gets on with it, manoeuvring around obstacles, making quick work of weaving between trees, as though sewing a pattern, stitching her way through the jungle.

Princesses must master needlework. Atalanta chuckles to herself, hearing the affected voice the princess used earlier.

But she shouldn't be smiling at a time like this.

If they don't find Jasyn...

No. She can't think about that. The mere concept has her throat and chest constricting. She shoves the idea down.

If they can't find and rescue the crew, that'll be the end. Of this mission. Of their lives. No Fleece for Iolcus. For Corinth. No reuniting separated families. No righting the wrongs of a world infested by ice. No happily ever after for anyone. Well, apart for the Ice King, perhaps.

Atalanta can only hope the Ice Princess values her own survival over the triumph of her father.

The rumble against her back lets Atalanta know the princess is saying something. She cranes her neck to peer over their shoulders at the way ahead.

A wall of grey chaos and hail might startle any who haven't lived on Iolcus for most of their lives. Most wouldn't think of sailing full pelt towards it, but that's the way the hilt-compass is pointing, and weather-based chaos likely puts them on exactly the right track.

That the chances of their success are slim, sears like an over-heating therma-rock in Atalanta's stomach.

Because as much as it's a good thing to be on course to find Jasyn, the tone of the weather — the pelting hail vibrating the vehicle's hard exterior, the gusts rocking their trajectory — signals that Jasyn is suffering.

The princess's voice rumbles against her again and Atalanta tunes in to the fact that she's leaning against her, peering at the way ahead, her front pressed to the princess's shoulders.

With her Transonics closed, she can only guess at what she's saying. Probably "get off me" or "brace yourself," because in the next second they crash through the weather wall.

51

EYE OF THE STORM

ATALANTA

From every direction, ice-pellets hammer the vehicle's shell. Lashes of electricity hang in the grey air with no resolution, no fizzling out and finding new form.

It's an oddly synaptic arrangement and it takes a few moments to figure out that the strange inclement weather isn't *pelting them*, as such. More, they're *ploughing through it*. The hail isn't thrusting down from the sky, it's drifting.

It's as if the weather itself has slowed.

As they pass through the weather-wall, calm envelops them. Sunlight kisses the blanket of blossom carpeting the mossed ground. The whirlwind of hail surrounds the idyll like a swaying tower up to the skies.

The princess winds the engine down to light vibrations and the tri-ice-cycle halts. For a moment they take in their surroundings.

If an impossibly sluggish electric-hail-storm in a jungle weren't puzzling enough, the range of petals and shapes on show should be impossible. The snow has a shimmering field of diamonds quality, accentuating the vibrancy of the rainbow range of flowers. All with unique patterns. Some domed, some flat, others with artistic flare somewhere in between.

A place like this should not exist.

As much as Atalanta wants to linger in admiration for Jasyn's ability to change the atmosphere, they need to hurry. There's no doubt in Atalanta's mind that it's Jasyn's inner storm painting the perimeter. It may be a fortress wall keeping the world out, but it'll only be a matter of time before the jungle finds them... claims them...

Opening the hatch, Atalanta dismounts, keeping her eyes trained on *everything.* She pulls a decon pack onto her back and tightens the straps. The princess does the same, only to stumble to her knees.

Full of water, the pack is heavy. Manoeuvring the tri-ice-cycle must have sapped her reserves. Understandable. But far from ideal.

If Atalanta had any doubts about this being a good idea — and of course she has plenty — they're only accentuated now.

She steps in to help, but the princess waves her away, telling her with her eyes to *please carry on.* The exhausted princess grasps her decon pack's top handle to drag it across the ground instead.

That works too.

At the eye of the storm, at the epicentre of the whirlwind, flora overspill from the ground in a path-like formation. It's precisely where Jasyn's sword is pointing them, so it's the direction in which they tread.

Through her invisi-visor, there's a clear undulation in the air. An atmospheric discrepancy where hot and cold air meet. Here, at the centre, petals succumb to a creeping ice, turning the bright and lively blanket of curved and natural formations to something sharp and forbidding.

More ice is the last thing they need. No-one's eyes will be cleared if ice gets in the way.

"Here." The princess indicates where Jasyn's ice-sword swivels.

Atalanta digs the ground with her astro-gloved hands until sunlight catches on a boot. *She's here.* Atalanta's heart swells impossibly with relief, immediately usurped by panic as the jungle floor starts to wake, to writhe.

Green, brown, purple and all shades in between. The vines slither and reach for them, warning them off, or seeking to claim them, too.

There's no time to dig Jasyn out. The jungle won't let them.

With royal confidence, the princess swipes her own sword, sending a ripple through the air and freezing the rising vines in place.

Urgency twists within Atalanta as she soaks the ground with water from the repurposed decon canisters.

The mesh of snaking vines reaching under the hail-wall perimeter promises that if the jungle in the eye of the storm doesn't get them, the jungle surrounding them will.

The princess's next retaliation of ice has her buckling, her chest heaving.

Hail. With no movement from below, Atalanta's panic rises. Which will run out first? The water canisters? The princess's energy? Or their luck?

PART VI

ADRIFT

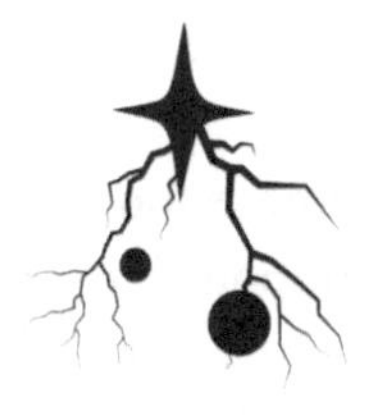

JASYN

Ship lights tremor, aching through the dark. A moment or a lifetime ago, the spark in Atalanta's eyes extinguished. Now, she hangs limp in Jasyn's arms.

Atalanta gone. Never seeing her smile again. Never playing chase. The flick-book of Jasyn's future cuts like paper in her heart and torments like ice in her bones. Air crushes from her lungs.

Ice crackles across the ship's walls and mid-air in synaptic formations as the fractures within her stretch. But she can't let herself collapse like a crumbling ice-shelf into the ocean. She needs to focus. To make it right. *To think.* They've battled death before. They can do it again. They must.

Jasyn swallows past her emotions, her vocal cords aligning to call for Doctor Orpheus — *she'll know what to do* — only to be interrupted by a jarring, silken and sinister echo rapping at the door of her mind, cutting through her frozen thoughts.

"Do I have your attention now?" asks the echo as Medea, bringer of death, towering over her.

With a single blink, Atalanta is gone. Disappeared. No longer in Jasyn's arms. It's as impossible as imagining her life without Atalanta in it.

Her lungs protest her inability to breathe as her disbelieving eyes scan the dark. Things might not make a whole lot of sense right now, but one thing is clear as she glowers at the woman inexplicably wielding her weapon:

You did this...

That Atalanta is no more is too devastating to coil her mind around. That Medea is responsible, that's something at which she can hurl her emotions.

Her focus crystallises as sharp as an Iolcian ice-sword as she launches at Medea with the kind of growl reserved for feral creatures and heartbroken lovers.

She's not sure what she expects. To collapse through the apparition, perhaps. For the menacing presence to retaliate in-line with the raw amethyst flames in her eyes.

She doesn't expect her forearm to pin the mysterious woman against some obstacle, invisible to Jasyn's eyes. It makes no more or less sense than everything else right now...

"What did you do?" Jasyn hisses, disbelief, hatred and terror twisting into an ice-devil within her. Though, oddly (for her) the impact of her inner turmoil on her shadow-drenched surroundings is minimal.

"Time is not on our side." Medea's words echo disjointedly, as though this escalation has her flustered too.

At this close range, there's a spark of uncertainty in her eyes. It's almost enough for Jasyn to retreat. Almost. Because then she thinks of Atalanta, and what this woman has done.

The ethereal stranger takes a ragged breath and forces out words lyrical but faltering. "This world has you in its grasp. It's taken root in your thoughts. Shaping them, building the world of your dreams. Keeping you compliant. You need to look past that now if we are to succeed. If you are to have any chance at survival."

Survival? How can she speak of survival after what she's done? Jasyn backtracks through the words... *This world... taken root in your thoughts. The world of your dreams.*

The pressure about Jasyn's lungs lets up a little, only to clamp tight again when she considers: *Is this a trick?* How can she trust the woman who haunts her nightmares with a blade?

"All is not as it seems, Jasyn of Iolcus. Consider the facts. You wanted her by your side, and so she came to you. You wanted to find the boy's father. You wanted the Fleece and found it. You wanted to matter, to prove yourself. You bested the Ice Princess. You gained respect aboard the ship. You desired *privacy*."

That last bit she says with a knowing sparkle in her eyes.

The pieces are starting to align. Perhaps it was all too *easy*... Perhaps...

And if it's not real, then...

"Atalanta. She's not...?" Jasyn loosens her grip on Medea, just a little.

"She's alive. Currently."

How can three words inspire both relief and fear?

"As long as you are on this world you are in danger. She is in danger. You all are. The sooner we complete our task here, the sooner you'll see her again. The sooner we can be free to continue our mission."

There are a lot of *we*'s and *our*'s and confusing sentences.

Medea's lyrical words embrace Jasyn's ears before her translation constricts her lungs: "Take me to the cave," she instructs, fire and ice warring in her eyes.

A fizzing sensation bursts within Jasyn's skull as the only cave she's liable to think of knifes its way into her consciousness.

Terror slicks through her like the deadliest of poisons. Her feet slip from under her as the roar from her past knocks her off her feet, quaking her insides, sending her sprawling face first to the cold and biting ground—

A meadow of burgundy and grey and a carpet of snow roll out around her. The cave entrance punctuates the way ahead, inexplicably inviting her closer.

This place. This moment. *Again.*

Jasyn grits her teeth. The universe is so unfair.

"Do *not* run from this," says Medea, her voice and eyes pleading and — for a moment — Jasyn forgets she's the same person who'd sliced Atalanta in two. (Real or not, that image is ingrained in her thoughts for all time.) "If you want to be back in the captain's quarters, having the time of your life, this world will give you that..." Medea searches the ground as though there isn't a territorial mountain bear on course to tear Jasyn to threads. "But it's only to keep you contained. You'll end up here, eventually. We reach for dreams, but our nightmares reach for us. This world will unravel you to your fears soon enough. And when it chooses this place for you, it will be too late."

Mountain air tainted with iron taunts her. Jasyn's palm, painful and hot, pulses with spilling blood, blemishing the snow, dented metal and bell-poppies stark red.

The sight and sensations pang with unwelcome familiarity.

When this had first happened, she'd been terrified by the dwindling possibility of survival. But now, experiencing the moment afresh, her focus hones in on the dented metal and scuffed paintwork beneath her; D-o-VE emblazoned on its surface:

An Iolcian life raft.

She'd never made the connection before that *that's* what this is. There isn't time to think on what it means—

Familiar terror sickens her gut as a blur of predator barrels towards her—

Fangs slick with saliva—

Its double row of claws *clack-clack-clacking* against rock, scratching at her sanity.

It's like she's right back there, up in the peaks, exploring where she shouldn't. And yet the feelings strangling her insides aren't just from her memory. They've been built upon. The shadows are darker, the beast's eyes brighter, its teeth sharper. Her guilt, stronger.

If she hadn't pushed the boundaries... if she hadn't gone where she shouldn't... Atalanta's mother wouldn't have died that day.

As much as Atalanta has told her she doesn't blame her, it's a fact that if Jasyn had been more careful, if she'd thought about the consequences, the direction of their lives could have been entirely different.

And yet Jasyn hasn't learned from her mistakes, has she? Because, here they are, in the stars, the last place Atalanta ever wanted to be, because Jasyn strayed where she shouldn't and pushed the boundaries again.

"If you keep running from this memory..." Medea crouches beside her, fear in her eyes, "...this voyage will be for nothing."

Nausea floods Jasyn and bile burns her throat. The components of her situation might be a tangled pile of thought-junk, but there's a vague shape to them now. Enough for her to know that *this* is why they're here.

This place. These memories. Her nightmare.

On the ship, Medea had told her she needed to find an artefact locked away in her thoughts.

"Why should I trust you?" Jasyn hisses.

"It will make your journey far easier if you do," says Medea matter of factly. "You can trust that I am invested in the outcome. I *know things*."

"Well, that makes one of us," says Jasyn, more flippantly than she feels.

The shadow of the bear floods over her as the air shifts with a swipe of massive paw—

✦

Panicked purple eyes fill Jasyn's vision, only to diffuse when they take in the cave around them. Relief passes across Medea's features, lit not by the cave but by whatever light source she has wherever she's from. *However that works.*

Jasyn's more rigid than the stalagmite against which she's pressed. But if she has to let this play out for Medea to find whatever it is she says they need, she'd better get this over and done with.

She just needs to breathe... And not freak out...

The dark grey cape of her memories blends her with her surroundings as she cradles her bleeding palm to her chest, now as she did then. Her shirt is in tatters, victim to mountain bear claws.

She might have skipped a few moments that lead to this point, but if Medea is seeking an artefact, Jasyn has an idea of where it might be found. Which Medea seems to understand, because she's hunting their surroundings as if there aren't two oversized beasts on the prowl.

Jasyn remembers that day, how — in her attempt to lose the creature — she'd unwittingly stumbled into its lair. *Its home.* She'd been the one trespassing. What happened was all her fault.

The darkness is so oppressive, seeping into her pores, her attempts at silent breaths so strained, it's like being buried in a pit of tar.

The rattle of bear-nostrils taunt her.

Jasyn squeezes her eyes shut. If this were a normal nightmare, she'd have woken herself by now through sweat and discomfort alone. She doesn't want to go any further along this path towards the event that uprooted Atalanta and fuelled the guilt that Jasyn had forever unbalanced their lives. The guilt that — like the sounds of bear claws scratching at her thoughts — Jasyn fears will always follow her.

A deep breath.

She does now what she had then. Channeling her fear into the need to hold onto something, anything, she grasps at the ground with her uninjured hand. There's something soft. Not fur or another beast, but fabric. It's in that moment she hones in on the shapes etched into the cavern wall.

Glow worms play the part of stars, while chipped grooves in the stone form a tree of fire with angular roots spanning into the artistically depicted ground as deep as the tree is tall. The image had ignited Jasyn's curiosity, in spite of the circumstances.

Her palm had happened across something cold, then. Or, perhaps, it was more purposeful than that. Something had drawn her to the cave. Is it too far fetched to think something had guided her there? Perhaps the only thread luring her there was her insatiable curiosity.

She finds it now, as she had then: the circular disc of metal, the golden-flecked clasp, similar in design to the wall-etching.

"Is this what you're looking for?" asks Jasyn in a whisper, not willing to risk mountain bears taking a new avenue in her nightmares.

As she had the first time around, she unclips and claims the item. That's when she'd added up the puzzle of her environment and figured out the nest she lingered within to be created not just of fabric, decorative metal and artistic depictions of trees composed of the elements, but of claw-tattered clothing and skeletal remains.

It was the moment Jasyn learned that not only are there other people who have braved the mountain, but that they didn't live to tell the tale.

Medea gravitates to her.

As much as Jasyn has no desire to be closer to her right now, at least this deviation can distract from her predetermined path of memory-events.

It can distract from young Atalanta startling her in the shadows, comforting her with her warmth and presence. It can distract from the both of them staring into the epic eyes of the beasts. And from what happens after: Atalanta's mother rescuing them and losing her life in the process.

But Atalanta doesn't reach for her in the shadows. She doesn't clamp her other hand over Jasyn's mouth to stop her crying out in fright.

Her shadow shape is there, still. The prowling mountain bears are mid-stride. The chaos of her memory, her nightmare, whatever this is, *has paused.*

Jasyn can only guess it has something to do with Medea diligently honing in on the nest of found items. The scraps of fabric, metal and bone. She leans closer to inspect the clasp.

Jasyn's about to object that if this is 'the artefact' this nightmare has all been about, Medea could have been clearer, because it's in amongst Jasyn's belongings back on the ship.

But the glint of triumph and relief in Medea's eyes is short lived. The item evades her grasp, as though she were trying to hold an image from a helm projection.

Her focus drifts past the clasp to another item in the nest of shadows.

"What's that?" asks Jasyn of the dull metal Medea cannot claim but appears desperate to inspect.

Had that been there when Jasyn had hidden in the cave? She'd been too distracted by the creatures haunting the shadows, Atalanta's safety, and the discovery of the clasp, to have noticed anything else within her reach.

The item has a complex sequence of patterns. Too complex to recall after one glance. Perhaps that's why the image is a little muddled. Jasyn must've seen the item briefly, but not lingered long enough for it to register.

Footsteps...

The familiar *crunch-crunch* of snow and leaves.

That can't be right…

The sounds emanate from somewhere below her feet.

A chilling liquid sensation slinks up around her neck. *What the—?* She checks her neck, but there's nothing there. So why does it feel damp?

"What's happening?" Jasyn whispers.

This sensation of cold and wet, that hadn't been a part of things… Now even her hair feels wet, and she loses her breath, choking, spluttering.

"No, not yet…" Medea's focus remains firmly on the mysterious artefact in the shadows, blurred, as if seen through a migraine.

The water, pouring invisibly, impossibly upwards, washes over Jasyn's eyes and laps into her ears and mouth, dissolving the cave, Medea, and the replay of her nightmares…

53

EYES OPEN II

JASYN

Slithering, untrustworthy shadows undulate around her. A fitting tapestry of confusion as water, *actual water now,* trickles *up* her face.

The air is thin. Her lungs heavy. Her wrist is grasped.

She expects Medea's glowing eyes, but the culprit isn't human. There's enough light drifting to decipher the vine lashed about her wrist, and that her palm is no longer injured.

Her feet are anchored and ropes of vine entangle her. Her skin crawls where creepers have burrowed under her astro-suit and suckered to her skin.

Apparently she's in her astro-suit now.

Upside down, says a voice of logic in her head. *You're upside down.* Her gut revolts at the smell of death — rot, decay — as her eyes adjust and a full-body skeleton stares empty-eyed back at her. It isn't the most unsettling thing she's seen, but it's up there in the list of *things she never wanted to see.*

Water burns her nostrils, biting her sinuses as she winces up at her feet, to the light beyond, just as something grasps her foot, hoisting her towards the light—

Sunlight bleeds into her vision. And so too do the chilling eyes of the Ice Princess.

What new nightmare is this?

With Jasyn's limbs squeezed against her body by coiled vines, she can only wriggle and curse as the Ice Princess claims her.

As she's plucked from the ground, Jasyn's focus trips to the chaos orbiting the jungle clearing in a churning wall of electric hailstorm.

Yep, that's about how she feels right now.

She thrashes as she's dragged closer to her enemy. But, her arms bound, she can do nothing as her attacker reaches behind her neck.

She grits her teeth, expecting her throat to strain against strangulation, but instead, a click and a hiss precedes her helmet adjusting into alignment. A *whoosh* and her breathing space decontaminates. Her lungs thank her for a deep and refreshing breath.

The Ice Princess's ice-sword glints, but before Jasyn can react to the blade sinking into her, her arms are freed with a single vine-searing slice.

Jasyn's sleeve snags on a dagger-sized thorn, tearing her astro-glove in two as she pins her attacker to the crunching carpet of ice-infected jungle flora.

Panic and anger ignite the chill of a thousand frosts in her veins—

But, palm hazing, poised just above her attacker's throat, she hesitates...

She's not been injured by the blade. In fact, the Ice Princess has freed her from her constraints.

Only now does her assailant's withered and weak state

resonate. Her over-angular facial features and the too-loose astro-suit suggest something has sapped the muscle and life-force from her.

If Jasyn had to ascribe a meaning to her features, it wouldn't be dark mischief and insatiable blood thirst, but exhaustion and panic. She doesn't look like she'll win a battle with a breeze, never mind an ice-monger with a vendetta.

Jasyn's jaw and stomach clench. The last time she'd seen the Ice Princess they'd battled in the jungle city piazza...

...but... no... that wasn't real...?

Electricity lashes between the trees, dancing confusion, like synapses seeking connection. Jasyn's thoughts are as knotted as the vines at the perimeter. *What is the Ice Princess doing? What has happened to—?*

Her thoughts are side-swiped as she's unceremoniously knocked to the ground in a manner more welcome than words can describe.

The weight of Atalanta upon her, gazing down at her with bright eyes.

Before Jasyn's thoughts have caught up, Atalanta is signing something ridiculous about the Ice Princess being a "friend" and "here to help."

Perhaps Jasyn's still stuck in the unreliable corridors of her mind. But in this moment, she doesn't care. She gets to be near Atalanta again. She gets to wrap her arms around her and pull her close. She can figure out the details later.

"Are you real?" signs Jasyn, keeping her ice-hazing palm away from Atalanta but running her other hand up her arms, her shoulders, her neck, trying to confirm.

"I hope so," signs Atalanta.

ATALANTA

JASYN'S IRISES ARE KALEIDOSCOPIC WITH CRYSTAL FORMATIONS, her veins alight with a white glow. She still has the same bruising to her jawline that she did *however long ago they landed here*, as if she'd been frozen by time itself.

The more she reaches for Atalanta, the more the crystals in her eyes and the ice in her veins dull, the haze at her palm dissipates, and the blizzard at the perimeter calms.

Ordinarily, Jasyn calming would be a good thing. But when it's her emotions forming the barrier that's keeping the jungle at bay, the situation's not so straight forward. They've enough reaching roots, creepers and vines to contend with within the clearing, never mind opening the floodgates to what's beyond.

Atalanta tugs Jasyn to her feet, beyond the reach of a root. Being pulled under would be the opposite of progress.

With a single touch of blade, the princess crystallises the vines reaching for them, before masterfully conjuring a wall of ice to keep them at bay. If Atalanta weren't so focused on Jasyn and getting her beyond harm's reach, she might be more impressed.

No sooner is the ice barricade formed than the animated flora set about dismantling it, finding their way over, under and through it.

Atalanta's thoughts race.

The water canisters are empty and they've only managed to clear the eyes of one person. Granted, if she had to choose just *one*, it would be Jasyn, but that isn't a good reason to abandon everyone else.

With a white hot flare pulsing at the veins in Jasyn's neck and within the silver of her eyes, Jasyn's baffled grimace is aimed either at the jungle or the princess. She looks like she's about to launch a physical attack on one or both.

"Hey," Atalanta signs, gently angling Jasyn's face to look at her. The sharpness in Jasyn's eyes softens. Invisi-visors frazzle as Atalanta places a gentle kiss against Jasyn's lips. Relief at finding Jasyn, at not running from her anymore, promises to tilt her world.

The ground shifts.

It could be the undergrowth reaching, threatening to pull them under. But no. It's the snow melting beneath their feet, turning to slush, seeping into the soil and down between roots.

Atalanta buries her smile. Jasyn's eyes, trained only on her, have exactly the heat they need right now.

"You want to melt some ice with me?" signs Atalanta.

✦

JASYN

ATALANTA'S MOUTH MEETS HERS AS THOUGH THEIR LIVES DEPEND on it. She's not entirely sure what in the Seven Heavens is going on, but all thoughts pale in comparison to Atalanta's lips on hers.

Is reality capable of a kiss like this?

There's an unpredictability in Atalanta's touch, and Jasyn's own hands fumble, too. The thrum of her racing heart has her dexterity waking, but her limbs still lack precision. Her body has been immobile for too long.

"Wow," says the unwelcome voice at the perimeter. *A crash back to reality if ever there was one.* The ice royal isn't staring at them, exactly, but the ground around them. Where a blanket of snow existed before, now lies only roots and soil.

"It's working," signs Atalanta, which is *a weird thing to say after a kiss...* but then, apparently she and Atalanta are embracing at the epicentre of melting ice, with the Ice Princess watching on, so *weird* certainly fits.

Before Jasyn can ask what *it's working* means, and why the Ice Princess looks like she's going to keel over while battling sentient greenery, the ground five feet from them bucks and a skeletal fist punches up between the lattice of roots and vines.

Jasyn instinctively wants to stamp it back down, but her body and mind aren't yet in alignment.

What other *horrific* events has this place got in store? At this point, an escalation of skeletons rising from the ground wouldn't surprise her.

On closer inspection, a black gloved hand clasps about the arm-bones as the skeleton is used as a grappling hook. A familiar item protrudes — *the doctor's medician case* — and Doctor Orpheus's unimpressed features emerge.

As her eyes focus on Jasyn and Atalanta — an assessing gaze that seems to take in their proximity — her scowl deepens and she mutters something about "fuck me," and "what fresh nightmare is this?" as she hoists herself from the ground. Without further fuss, she clicks her astro-helmet into place and takes a deep breath.

As Jasyn had thought it would be, the doctor's astro-suit is black, not unlike her gowns, with a sheen-mesh and glow-lines like the other astro-suits. It's blemished with inconsistent luminous markings, as if she's been rolling in glowing slime.

The doctor's nose crinkles, suggesting she's far from happy with the state of herself. That sets her to scowling even more, probably because her nose still sports the bruise of Jasyn's creation.

Ouch.

"kèpfos-katàratos-amathés..."

Her mind not caught up with much of anything, Jasyn can't

stop herself from staring at the gruff woman showcasing a stream of unfamiliar insults.

"I assume we're in some sort of imminent danger," the doctor brushes off bits of jungle from her astro-suit, "and standing there staring at me isn't the best use of your time?"

To the doctor's credit, she seems to be taking the strange surroundings — the lively jungle with strangling intent, and the presence of the Ice Princess — in her stride. There's probably not much she hasn't seen on her previous travels.

"This place is a fucking graveyard," says the doctor, snapping a finger bone from the skeleton arm she'd emerged with and placing it into a corked glass container, as if it's the most natural thing to do. "It's never wise to linger in graveyards."

"Yeah, I…" Jasyn mumbles, but her brain hasn't caught up enough to offer the doctor anything useful. Because the last time she saw the doctor (or thought she did), they were getting too close for comfort in the medical chambers.

Jasyn expects another tirade of swear words, but instead the doctor examines Jasyn's ripped sleeve, where the suit has automatically constricted about her forearm to keep the suit airtight. The doctor traces up her arm in a thorough and concentrated fashion, before turning Jasyn around and performing the same prodding, methodical inspection of her spine, neck and rounding to her other arm, placing her back where she'd started.

Jasyn is busy asking "What are you doing?" but something about the way her own voice echoes back at her reminds her that something isn't right…

"There's no sign of external tampering," says the doctor. Her focus on Jasyn's astro-helmet has their eyes meeting for long enough that they each look away. Her heart quick-stepping, Jasyn's glad not to be within reach of the doctor's stat monitors.

But it's worse, because—

"Scientifically fascinating. And oh so pretty," says Doctor Orpheus with a smirk, as she observes the colourful flora taking form at Jasyn's feet.

Hail. If only invisi-visors weren't so *invisi*, then she could hide her blazing cheeks.

Something changes in the doctor's demeanour, as if she's just told herself to stop messing around and get down to business: "Your comms aren't a malfunction, they're a helmet setting."

Kalais handing over her helmet with a surly smile elbows into Jasyn's thoughts.

The doctor opens her mouth, possibly to swear again, or to tell Jasyn what she needs to do to get her comms back, but Jasyn's doesn't discover which, because a growl whips their attention to the perimeter—

✦

ATALANTA

AT THE STARTLED CONFUSION ETCHED ON EVERYONE'S FACES, Atalanta turns. She expects to witness a threat of epic proportions, an impossible creature rising from the roots.

But it's not a creature...

Or rather, it's a beast who goes by the title *Captain* and the name *Herakles*, fighting free of the jungle floor fist and sword first like some mythical being bursting free from captivity.

With a vibrating stance and dropped jaw, the gladiator-skyship captain must be roaring or bellowing, giving this world a lesson on who's in charge as she severs several vines at once while *somehow* reinstating her astro-helmet in the same manoeuvre.

The captain might not know what's going on yet, her eyes

scanning every element of her surroundings, but she's not letting that stop her from being utterly untouchable.

Damn...

No wonder Peleus forgets how to form words when around her. No wonder Tiphys looks up to her. No wonder the hearts of several of her crew stumble and stutter in the woman's presence. Atalanta's not made of stone. She can see the attraction. If she didn't have eyes only for Jasyn, she might have to be fanning herself right now.

But, really, does the captain have to be such an animal? There's something to be said for quiet victories and controlled might. But try telling that to—

The captain's eyes connect with hers. Animalistic survival melts to relief and — as the captain looks past her to the princess — to something she can't decipher. Whatever the mix of emotions playing across the captain's buckled brow, there's vulnerability clear in her eyes.

JASYN

THE HERO OF THE ARENA LOOKS ASHEN IN THE PRESENCE OF THE Ice Princess. If only Jasyn could give a therma-stone for her thoughts.

"How about less staring and more saving your crew-mates?" The doctor skilfully aims her words at both Jasyn and the captain.

At least Jasyn isn't the only one who gets whipped with the doctor's barbed tongue.

The negative emotions threatening to break loose from the captain at the sight of the Ice Princess are usurped as she turns to battle the jungle that's snaking for them.

The screams and shudders of each vine Jasyn and the crew slice have Jasyn inwardly doing the same. Each vine recoils, only for new ones to take their place. A tiring and losing long-term strategy.

"Jasyn. Here," calls the voice she hates.

That breeze — That song — That whisper — A promise?

A sword sails towards her in a shallow arc. She flinches at its origin, but the sword is hilt first. And it's not just any sword. If the sensory interruption weren't enough, the glint of the snow-globe embedded within its hilt and the dull, blunt metal of the blade let her know: it's *her* ice-sword.

As Jasyn snatches it from the air, her palm meeting the hilt, the blade blooms ice-electric. A cooling balm washes through her veins, both calming her and setting her teeth on edge.

The sword's surface sparks. Smooth blade interrupted by sharp bursts.

Ice hazes at her fingertips.

She can sense Atalanta watching her, probably checking she isn't going to test the sword on the person who threw it. If the Ice Princess weren't looking so withered, she might.

Heavens. She has so many questions about how and why *The Ice Princess* is roaming free and being trusted to wield a weapon.

She may not have maniacally and murderously stolen the Fleece for her own gain. But still, it's difficult not to ruminate on her recent crimes... *even if they aren't real...*

"Try not to overthink it," says the Ice Princess with laboured breaths, obviously misunderstanding Jasyn's hesitation. "Use it like a sword and just, y'know, *try* not to freeze anyone to death." Her cocky grin tilts Jasyn towards anger. *How dare she tell me how to use my—*

With a simple sword gesture, the Ice Princess lifts water from the ground in a thousand droplets. With the flick of her wrist, the liquid turns to sharpened ice and catapults at the reaching vines, cutting through the web. She follows this with a lasso of water solidifying to ropes of ice that freeze any surface they hit.

Okay, then...

Even in her fading state, the Ice Princess's abilities are far superior and more controlled than anything Jasyn can *intentionally* manage.

Jasyn might have technically outmanoeuvred the Ice Princess in The Games arena back on Iolcus, but it's becoming clear that the princess took it easy on her. Or she was on the back foot only due to the shock of Jasyn unveiling the long lost ice-sword and her own existence.

Is it possible the Ice King's daughter, Warden General of the Iolcian Guard, hadn't unleashed her full abilities in the arena? Why? To prolong battles for Iolcian entertainment? To *not* steal the lives of the other competitors?

Well, that doesn't align with the arrogance Jasyn knows her to possess. The fierce reputation. Cool, uncaring, as slippery and deadly as an ice crater.

Jasyn swats at the vines reaching for her. A lash of ice strangles them, more out of luck than design. She gestures with her sword, attempting to create intentional lashes of ice, but all the sword does is fizzle a bit.

Great. Her capabilities have regressed, currently in the realm of stuttering live-wire.

Apparently, it's only when she's calm *or* out of control that she can conjure the kind of ice that has an impact. The kind of ice that would be useful right now.

But the ice-blade is serrated and sharp. She might be able to be of some use with that, at least.

Her world upends, just a little, as a boot kicks up from the ground, tripping her. Low gravity taunts her with a slow fall.

Before she face-plants, the captain grasps her collar and sets her back on solid ground, as if this all were no more than a rec room workout. Simultaneously and unceremoniously, Herakles grabs the offending boot, hoisting Castor into the air and landing her amongst the roots.

"What the actual f—?" Castor's reasonable question is cut short by a movement from above the frozen perimeter.

A pincer-panther arcs above the iced wall, sailing, snarling, its trajectory aimed at the back of Herakles's head.

But before Jasyn can do something useful, the creature's innards crystallise, freezing mid-air, its claws splayed out, aiming uselessly for a target it'll never reach.

Herakles whips around and swipes with her blade, smashing the part-frozen predator into a thousand green-goo covered shards.

Bleugh.

The electric whip of ice stems from the Ice Princess's blade. But there's no chance for gratitude or confusion, because the next moment the Ice Princess folds to the ground.

Herakles's knuckles whiten about her hilt as she strides for the fallen ice royal. But before she can reach her, the doctor steps into the captain's path and pushes her back, a sharp warning in her eyes.

Words are exchanged, but they're beyond Jasyn's reach. She can only guess the doctor's vow to guard life has her fighting the corner of even the Ice Princess.

Still gaining her bearings from her awkward landing, Castor glowers at the captain who's swiftly moved on. She shifts her negativity to the hand Jasyn offers before pointedly glaring between Jasyn and her ice-sword, as if Jasyn were carrying a decapitated head rather than an impressive weapon.

Reinstating her astro-helmet, Castor calls out, to no-one in particular (presumably as long as they're not Jasyn): "Where's Pollux? Where's my brother?"

There's plenty of space for Castor to avoid Jasyn, so the shoulder check that knocks her can only be purposeful.

Yep. Definitely back to reality now.

✦

ATALANTA

ATALANTA SUBCONSCIOUSLY STEPS TOWARDS THE FALLEN PRINCESS to ward off the vines with her blade. Relegated to the echo chamber of her astro-helmet, her heart thumps a crowding rhythm, like a stampede of stags.

If her Transonics weren't closed and confined within her helmet, she'd have stood a chance of listening in on the heated words Herakles and the doctor are exchanging. Whatever is said, the outcome is the doctor striding to the folded princess, her medician case in tow, and Herakles reluctantly turning her attention to the elbow nudging up through soil.

Thanks to Herakles, Peleus is plucked from the ground, wide-eyed, his arms flailing in the low-gravity air. Gripping his axe-knives, he looks half homicidal and half as though he's going to vomit.

Grasping him by the scruff, Herakles reinstates his unclipped helmet, only to receive an axe-swipe as thanks. Either he misjudges his low gravity trajectory or the captain has superior reflexes, because his blade merely paddles the air. Presumably his brain is tripping over itself to figure out what's going on.

The dull look in Herakles's eyes suggests she doesn't see him as a threat. In fact, her eyes are repeatedly returning to the princess rather than registering Peleus much at all.

Atalanta sword-hacks at the perimeter, battling determined greenery. Another turf undulation—

Rivalling the captain in her feral determination, Kalais claws out of the ground with all the energy and mania that must have won her all the skirmishes in her life.

Herakles strides in her direction, but by the time she's within her orbit, Kalais has already climbed to freedom and returned to the safety of her helmet. She snaps off a salute that's more "yeah, yeah, I'm fine" than an acknowledgement of the captain's status.

Atalanta pauses enough between swiping at vines to catch her breath and to notice the flash of *something* passing between the captain and engine-tech. Whatever the emotion is, it's charged. A simmering affection or hatred?

Hail. This crew has more buried emotions than this world has buried crew.

✦

JASYN

A MOMENTARY LULL IN THE JUNGLE'S MISSION TO ENCROACH ON the clearing—

"Listen up," announces Herakles, attracting everyone's attention with a map projecting from her helmet. It depicts pulsing dots, the colours corresponding to their suits and the suits of those still contained beneath the surface.

That the entire crew are clustered within twenty metres of each other, despite setting out at different times, is a puzzle they'll have to figure out later.

Right now, it's a relief.

"Pair up. Keep your eye on the perimeter," instructs the captain. "Let's get them free." With a thumb to her helmet sensors, she transfers the map to each of the invisi-visors.

Kalais reclaims her dagger-tipped pellet rifle from the animated undergrowth with the same abrasive attitude she'd hurled at Jasyn in the engine chamber.

Anger flares in Jasyn's chest like an army of fire ants.

While others tear at the ground in search of the rest of the crew, Jasyn marches up to Kalais.

"You want to pair up with me, Snowflake?" asks Kalais, looking her up and down in a wolfish manner as her finger covers the trigger. She's not aiming at Jasyn, exactly, but she's not far off.

"What did you do to my suit?" Jasyn demands.

"Sorry Snowflake. Can't hear you." Kalais shoulder-nudges past her, striding for the latest astronaut emerging from the undergrowth.

"Castor, I found your sibling," she calls out, pulling Pollux free.

"I found yours," replies Castor from across the clearing where a dazed Zetes scrambles to his feet.

Castor and Kalais swap, greeting their respective siblings. Castor swipes Pollux over the back of the head but her grin lets him know she's relieved.

Jasyn expects Kalais to punch Zetes on the arm, or something equally violent, but she wraps her arms around him. It's brief, but enough to let Jasyn know there's at least *something* human about her. Which is much less believable than anything she's witnessed on this planet so far.

Still, it has Jasyn retreating and focusing on more important matters. Spying Atalanta digging at an invisi-visor dot, Jasyn gravitates to her side—

✦

ATALANTA

A GREY GLOVED HAND WITH GLOWING CERULEAN DETAILING reaches up from the ground. With Jasyn's assistance, Atalanta unearths a moss covered Gus.

Floating spores frazzle and die against Gus's reinstated invisi-visor as confusion crowds her eyes. But, with just a sweeping observation of their surroundings, and a reluctant nod that seems to say *Of course that all wasn't real,* she seems to be up to speed.

She nods her thanks to Atalanta and Jasyn before striding for the tri-ice-cycle. Atalanta follows as Gus climbs into the driver's seat. A series of practiced motions across the console and the back wheels slide outwards, replaced by others hidden behind it, extending to form a trailer.

Yes. That's what she'd hoped for from the vehicle's chassis markings. Atalanta would love to pull this machine apart to piece it back together, to figure out how it works. Not now, obviously. She makes a mental note to pick Gus's brains about it later.

If they make it to later...

For now, Atalanta steps in to assist Doctor Orpheus in lifting the unconscious princess onto the trailer.

✦

JASYN

THAT ATALANTA IS SO CLOSE TO THE INFAMOUS ICE ROYAL HAS Jasyn's grip tightening about her hilt. She hadn't consciously tried to create the ice hazing about her blade, nor had she invited her veins to cable white through her forearm, visible even through her suit.

Liquid ice pulses within her grip, cooling and heating her all at once. It has her breath frazzling in a haze against her invisi-visor.

Judgmental green eyes watch her. Kalais doesn't seem to know whether to widen or narrow them at what she sees. Whatever her conclusion, it's interrupted—

Kalais launches past Jasyn to where Zetes wrestles a knot of serpentine vines. Each lashes about his limbs, pulling him towards the shadows of the jungle.

A smattering of well-aimed gunfire from Kalais is followed by expert slicing of bayonet blade. But thick vine-ropes prove difficult to cut.

Jasyn joins the fray, swatting and slicing.

With blades and bullets making little progress, Jasyn grasps the thickest of vines with her ice-hazed palm. The ice is quick to take, spilling the length of vine and rendering it immobile, brittle.

It splinters and obliterates.

The moment of victory is short lived as the spilling ice lashes across Zetes's limbs, his torso. Jasyn retreats, but her ice keeps climbing. When it reaches his uncovered neck, he cries out as the hazing ice scalds his skin.

Jasyn's storming heart rate pulses her vision. Everything is both fast and slow. Every new ice-fibre against his skin cuts in her consciousness, crystallising into regret. Her panic-fogged thoughts withhold any useful course of action.

She can melt ice. With Atalanta's help she's only just done it.

But right now, all she can do is stare in dumb horror as Zetes attempts to fight free not of the jungle, but of her ice.

It takes a moment and an age for the infection to stop and for Zetes's and Kalais to claw it away from his skin.

It's stopped, leaving an angry blemish in its place.

Jasyn's exhale of relief puffs a cloud of cooled air. Not exactly helping her image. She opens her mouth to say something...

anything... but her attempt is cut short by Kalais's forearm shoving her across the chest and sending her sailing backwards and skidding in the dirt.

"Keep your damn ice to your damn self." Kalais's bark is as sharp as the look in her eyes.

The captain bounds in with warning in her eyes. "Time to go," she calls, as she scoops Jasyn up by the scruff of her suit and returns her to her feet (again!).

Jasyn's not sure whether to feel patronised, useless, or grateful.

But at least Kalais is backing off, for now.

✦

ATALANTA

PANIC IS A MERE TWO HEARTBEATS FROM PROPELLING ATALANTA off the trailer and back into the clearing that's tangling with vines more than a store cupboard overrun with spider silk.

When she'd stepped in to help the doctor with the princess, Jasyn had left her side. And now, she's beyond Atalanta's sight.

But colourful dots on invisi-visor maps echo movement as the crew draw closer. Jasyn's green dot is on the move and heading her way. Atalanta refuses to feel relief until Jasyn is by her side again.

Peleus is the first to claw aboard, scrambling to the centre of the platform. His un-co-ordinated landing jostles the trailer and earns him a judgemental glare from Doctor Orpheus, who's in the middle of adjusting the anchoring-straps around the unconscious princess. The doctor's dexterity and confidence suggest *this is not her first adventure.*

Peleus shuffles behind Atalanta, either to hide from the

doctor, or to use Atalanta as a human shield against the jungle. Either way, *unsurprising*.

Searching for Jasyn, Atalanta's focus snags instead on Herakles as she hoists Tiphys from his ground-cocoon.

Whatever the boy encountered while buried in this world, the idea of leaving it has him scrapping and flailing. His contorted face suggests he's screaming but the captain keeps a firm grip on his suit, as if he might dart into the jungle at any moment. She kneels down to him and reinstates his helmet. Whatever she's saying, speaking to him at his eye level, it has his outburst subsiding. He even nods before she lets him loose, nudging him towards their escape vehicle.

Tiphys scrambles onto the trailer, boosted up by Kalais behind him. The boy swipes at his tears through his invisi-visor as he settles at the doctor's side.

At the captain's direction, Kalais and Zetes are next, followed by Castor and Pollux. Each board with the kind of grace that speaks of athleticism and experience. They unspool their astro-suit anchors and clip to the railings at opposing sides of the trailer, facing the jungle in defensive formation. Spears and ice-pellet rifles discourage encroaching threats.

When Jasyn emerges from the growing thicket, Atalanta remains as tense as a drawn bow string. *No.* She won't relax until they're back on the ship. Maybe not even then.

She outstretches her hand as Jasyn bounds up to the trailer edge, but Jasyn doesn't take her hand. In fact, she recoils from it.

Atalanta can hazard a guess that it's something to do with Jasyn holding her white-glowing sword aside as if it were a fire-torch. Logic tells her Jasyn is only trying to keep her safe, but the retreat still cuts like a blade through her chest.

Once aboard, Jasyn discards the sword. It lands on the trailer, its bloomed blade folded in on itself, rendered inert. The glow through Jasyn's forearm and even her astro-suit remains, however, ice coagulating at her fingertips.

Jasyn's widened eyes declare both panic and apology.

Three more invisi-visor dots linger beyond the trailer. Two far enough away to be obscured by the web of vines. The third is the captain.

Atalanta extends her hand. The captain's grasp is firm as she's hoisted aboard, but Atalanta over-compensates in the low gravity and pulls the captain off her feet, landing her solidly across her, straddling her on the bed of the trailer.

It's not the kind of proximity Atalanta would invite or ordinarily allow — even from a supposedly charming sky ship captain — but life and death do make for exceptional circumstances.

Besides, with her colouring cheeks and quirked dimples, the captain looks as surprised and uncomfortable as Atalanta feels.

It's probably because they're pressed together almost intimately, and that their hands are still pressed palm to palm, trapped by their bodies. And because it's all just, well, awkward.

With a visible gulp, Herakles pushes to her knees. She unspools a tether from Atalanta's astro-suit and clips it to the trailer's edge, before standing and observing the jungle clearing in the manner any plucky captain might. Her stance defiant, ready to face this world and any other that dares endanger her crew.

If that was the kind of heroics Atalanta was into, she'd be done for right now.

✦

JASYN

Watching Atalanta be straddled by the captain — albeit a result of circumstance and not intention, from what she can gather — isn't helping Jasyn's state of mind. *Hail.* She could really do without an overspill of inner chaos right now.

Even without the sword in her grasp, her forearm burns hot and cold, and ice still thickens at her palms.

A whisper... That whisper... Lyrical and inviting and — judging from its origin and the fact that no-one else is reacting to it — for her ears only. Is it strange to think the sword wants her to pick it up?

Yes. Definitely.

All the more reason not to.

She wishes she were hidden away. Wishes she could figure out her instability in peace, without risk of hurting anyone.

The trailer isn't exactly small, but the quantity of bodies crowding it puts Jasyn in mind of historical Shard images of sunken sea-ship crews clinging to too small a raft.

The suspicious glances of the flight-techs and engine-techs aren't helping. They're the kind of assessing once overs that label her 'liability'. It's making her skin itch, which only has her blood running colder.

The last time she'd felt this panicked, bewildered and lacking control, she'd terrified an entire Iolcian Games arena.

Glancing up from tending to the Ice Princess, Doctor Orpheus eyes Jasyn with her usual scowl. Though she looks more intrigued than disgusted or unsettled.

"Jasyn, fucking breathe," says the doctor, and Jasyn can't help but laugh. Because wasn't that the advice she'd given her before getting inappropriately close in the realm of her imaginings?

She only stops laughing when the doctor's stare, and everyone else's, suggests *yes, she is a little unhinged.*

Deep breaths.

"See what I mean," says Castor, "Ice-mongers are going to be the death of us." Her angered words swerve to the captain: "And what the actual *hail* is the Ice Princess doing here?"

At least on Castor's latter point, Jasyn mightily agrees.

The captain must think the question rhetorical, because she continues staring out at the mist shrouding the far end of the clearing. Speaking into her comms, she attempts to communicate with their lost crew but static remains the only response.

Herakles confers with Gus — something about a thruster needing realignment and that Gus needs "just a minute".

According to the two astro-dots on Jasyn's invisi-visor, two crew remain in the wilderness. A quick scan of who's present: Hylas and Lynk are yet to join their ranks.

"Are we leaving yet, or what?" calls Peleus, from the centre of the trailer.

"In times of crisis," the doctor raises her voice as she secures her medician case, "you can say something useful, you can even add some banter, *or you can shut the fuck up.*"

Well, that's Peleus told. Open mouthed, he looks to the rest of the crew.

"The doc has a point," Kalais agrees.

"Don't call me *doc,*" says Doctor Orpheus as she double checks the harness anchoring Tiphys.

Judging from Kalais's smirk, the doctor's grumbling is exactly why she calls her doc. At least Pollux offers Peleus a smile and a wink, which seems to divert Peleus's attention from spluttering annoyance to furiously blushing. *Interesting...*

Hylas and Lynk emerge from the mist, Lynk's arm clasped about Hylas's elbow as they stumble across uneven terrain.

That's when the trailer starts to vibrate and the jungle shivers. And yet, all is oddly quiet. An untrustworthy silence.

As if in answer to the unspoken question tensing the air, the trees at the clearing edge shudder, sending plumes of spores from the bulbous centre of the star-flowers. The whiteout sweeps across the clearing, faster than any blizzard, obscuring Hylas and Lynk. Mountaineers lost to an avalanche.

Spores frazzle against invisi-visors. Visibility reduced to almost zero.

The map dots are still visible, and Jasyn's muscles are already gearing up to leap off the trailer to assist — but a hand whips out, grasping her utility belt. She expects the culprit to be Atalanta, but her eyes connect instead with Doctor Orpheus, telling her both "no" and "wait".

Jasyn's about to protest — *What kind of doctor leaves her crew to perish?* — but Gus instructs them to "Hold tight". The next half-second has the trailer rumbling with the revs of the ice-engine and thrusters hissing as Gus kicks into gear and navigates them towards their missing crew-mates.

Silhouettes take form as the spores displace at Hylas and Lynk's movement. Hylas gestures in a manner that strongly suggests: *Turn around. Go the other way.*

Trailer occupants jostle against each other as Gus air-skids the vehicle to a stop ninety degrees to their new arrivals and the unseen threat.

Seamlessly, while Zetes and Castor remain in place, squinting into the whiteout with weapons ready, Kalais and Pollux unclip and hop down, wading into the mist to usher their crew-mates aboard.

Huh. Jasyn would have labelled Kalais as a *save your own skin and get out* type. She's further surprised when Kalais guides Lynk to a free space within the trailer, giving a running commentary of what she's doing as she anchors her for her safety.

Hylas follows and clips in.

Gus kicks the ignition, but it splutters. She tries again, but the engine only coughs.

"What is that?" asks Castor, staring at the moving wisps of

shadows within the fog. A formation of lights, like fireflies frozen mid-flight, blaze as they grow closer.

"Teeth" is the only words Hylas manages, while Lynk can only offer a startled sneeze. As if in answer, the panther-like creatures stalk out from the fog. White eyes blaze bright, claws glint, and serrated jaw-pincers flex about saliva-slickened teeth.

"Chief?" says Herakles with a hint of desperation, her focus never veering from the approaching threat.

"Aye, Captain," says Gus, kicking the engine's revs and setting them in motion with a satisfying mechanical roar that ricochets between the trees and Jasyn's nerves, as the advancing creatures roar in response.

✦

ATALANTA

KALAIS'S AND ZETES'S RIFLE FIRE KEEPS THE CREATURES FROM getting too close. Herakles's sword and Castor and Pollux's spears take care of any vegetation or predator that manages to break through.

That Jasyn is just lying atop the trailer, not getting stuck into the fray, has Atalanta worried. She's never been one to hang idly by, even in times of chaos. In fact, especially then.

The spurts of green goo that accompany the ruptured or skewered attackers has Atalanta's stomach threatening to unleash her own sickly goo.

She tamps it down.

But — with arrow after arrow to keep the creatures at bay — Atalanta's focus is on the jungle.

The snarling wild-cats slow. Tiring, perhaps.

The crew's efforts appear to be working, as the vehicle peels away, making a break for the tree line.

If there's one good thing in this situation, it's that none of the crew made it far from the ship, so the return journey isn't long. Even if it feels it.

Straightened backs, widened eyes and dropped jaws. The visible increase in crew tension signals the ship entering their view.

Their ship, as tall as a sky scraper, ensnared by vines is a startling sight. Atalanta's sure she lip-reads the word "fuck" from the doctor. Even Jasyn seems to wake from her stupor.

With the jungle noosed about the ship, merely instructing the hold ramp to lower won't do any good, so Atalanta angles her body, her bow, and trains her focus on where she needs her arrows to hit.

She releases and repeats, distracted only slightly by the captain's sudden focus on her, as though Atalanta has the power to hang the moon. *That look full of wonder isn't distracting at all...*

It's almost enough to make her miss. But not quite. After six arrows in quick succession, the platform is free.

An errant elbow from one of the crew sends her stumbling. Before she can consider whether the contact was purposeful, a sudden tug at her waist keeps her from confronting the fast-moving terrain beneath them.

She assumes it must be her tether doing its job, but when she glances back, it's the captain gripping her utility belt, hoisting her back to safety.

Unwieldy terrain jolts the trailer at an awkward angle, unbalancing even the captain, sending them falling to the platform. While it crosses Atalanta's mind that she really does have to stop ending up *under* the captain, the domino effect of falling crew has them tangled.

With a bump, the vehicle hits the base of the cargo ramp and arcs up towards the hold hatch.

Just get to the ship...

But the creatures of this world have other ideas. Before Atalanta can dig her way out from under the body pile, before she can align arrow in bow, an oversized feline has leapt across the trailer, glinting claws connecting with Kalais—

And no tether tightens to stop her—

As the vehicle shudders, reaching the summit of the ramp, lurching to a stop in the cargo hold, Atalanta's adrenaline sky rockets, shoving her every nerve onto a knife edge—

Because not only is Kalais being dragged away by a wild-cat, Jasyn has leapt from the trailer and is taking chase—

✦

JASYN

THIS IS A TERRIBLE IDEA—

By the time her brain has interjected, Jasyn's legs have already carried her across untrustworthy terrain.

Even from fifty metres away, Kalais's bloodied astro-suit highlights ripped flesh as the pincer-panther drags her by her lower leg. Kalais's response is the kind of feral violence Jasyn would expect from her.

Forty metres...

Kalais kicks herself free with a solid left boot to the creature's jaw. Perhaps she doesn't need help. She'll definitely find a way to give Jasyn a hard time about trying to rescue her, either way.

Hail, she hopes so, because at least then neither of them are dead.

Twenty metres...

Kalais's pellet-rifle would be useful right now, but it must've become snagged as she was stolen, because amongst the confusion of arm, leg and claw swipes, there's nothing but plucky mania in Kalais's possession.

Cries tear from her as jaws clamp about her right arm and twist her back to the ground. The agonised bellow and bone-crunch lurch Jasyn's stomach.

The edge of the jungle isn't far off.

It won't be long before the creature disappears with its prize.

Or the wall of fanged creatures will be upon them and they'll be ripped apart in a dozen different ways.

Or the jungle will bury them and they'll be forced to endure nightmares disguised as perfection.

This is a terrible idea...

She expects others to join her, but no-one does. And a glance back at the ship lets her know why.

✦

ATALANTA

THE CREW'S EFFORTS SERVE ONLY TO EXHAUST THEM AS EACH TIME the vines are cut, more lash across the platform, trapping them within the ship.

The vegetation seems to be on a mission to test resilience, as if knowing the crew can't keep this up forever.

Between the gaps, Atalanta raises her bow, her focus flitting past Jasyn to the sickening sight of Kalais being dragged towards the tree-line.

She aims for the creature, but the lack of gravity has Kalais repeatedly crossing her line of sight.

Is it better to kill her, or curse her to a terrible death?

It's the kind of existential and ethical question that makes Atalanta want to puke.

✦

JASYN

FOR BETTER OR FOR WORSE, IN THAT SPLIT SECOND WHERE instinct decided her course of action, Jasyn had claimed her ice-sword. And now it has her body buzzing, crackling ice-electric.

Kalais's thrashing has slowed her captor.

Jasyn strikes it on the haunches with the flat of her searing sword. Hindquarters scalded, it whips around, pincers and fangs dripping red.

It snarls and lunges—

Jasyn sidesteps and sword-swipes down its neck—

Its throat spurts green before the liquid crackles, freezing, solidifying the creature in place like some awful statue designed to celebrate the fighting of mythical monsters.

Jasyn's stomach lurches.

Sap-goo decorates her astro-suit and Kalais looks about as startled as the creature. The surprise and distrust in Kalais's eyes accuses Jasyn and her sword of being the real threat.

Jasyn would eye-roll at her, if white eyes weren't burning through the jungle shadows.

Jasyn pulls Kalais to her to her feet, avoiding her injured right arm. If the earlier crunch and cry weren't enough, the angle promises it's broken. A warble of pain and several curse words accompany as she encourages Kalais towards the ship.

It's only paces before Kalais's leg gives, folding her to the ground and dragging Jasyn with her. *There isn't time for this.* If they don't get back to the ship soon they're never *getting back anywhere* again.

"Lean on me," says Jasyn.

"What?" Kalais wheezes.

"Lean on me," Jasyn repeats, trying to haul Kalais to her feet as Kalais fights her at every step.

"I don't know what you're saying." Kalais cradles her fang punctured broken arm, her snarl more fierce than the predator's.

"And whose fault is that?" It needs saying, even if it can't be heard.

Jasyn manoeuvres to Kalais's side, guiding her uninjured arm around her neck and shouldering her weight. They stumble several paces, entirely out of step.

The sight of the sky ship restrained by vines, its hold platform lashed shut, makes Jasyn's stomach sink.

If even their ship can be dwarfed and trapped by this world, what chance do they have?

Kalais must catch her ankle, or lose her footing, because the next second sees them tripping, their legs tangling. The air cushions them, but the ground is less forgiving.

As their knees skitter on contact, each jolt tugs a cry from Kalais.

The ground is hard, like metal, not soft like soil, snow powder or vegetation. But there isn't time to dwell on that. What matters right now is their tumble has knocked Jasyn's sword from her grasp and beyond her reach.

Jasyn stretches as far as she can, but Kalais's body cages her, as her face and body contort with the aftershocks of pain.

Glinting white eyes close in—

Jasyn attempts to manoeuvre from under Kalais, but their limbs are caught in the vine-mesh. She reaches in vain for her sword, willing with every fibre of her being.

The hilt twitches.

The more she reaches, the more she wills it, the more the hilt moves. It's probably just wishful thinking, or the adrenaline shuddering her vision...

A scuffle snags her attention.

Jaws glint—

Her gut twists—

The ice-sword latches into her palm with force, as if an overactive magnet had drawn it there.

Well, that's new. And startling enough to distract Jasyn from doing anything useful.

A shadow descends—

Open jaws, pincers and fangs—

Thwack—

Knocked back, an arrow struck through its jaws, the screeching feline paws at its sap-leaking snout, failing to free itself of the arrow as it retreats.

Jasyn flashes a smile of thanks towards the ship, knowing Atalanta will see it. But, still, the ship is too far. Even without tripping, there's little chance they'll make it before the creatures of the jungle are upon them.

"We're going to need to work together," says Jasyn, untangling from Kalais and the ground.

"What?" demands Kalais, desperately. "Fuck. Fine, okay? You need to adjust your audio output."

Jasyn blinks at her.

"In the helmet settings."

Jasyn blinks again.

"Oh, heaven's hail, I'll do it." Kalais snarls as she grits her teeth, cradling her broken arm as she rolls into a sitting position. "Close your eyes and take a deep breath." With her left arm, she reaches behind Jasyn's neck for the helmet release but Jasyn's hand whips out to grasp her wrist. *You want me to trust you?*

"If you die, I die," says Kalais, as if she can read Jasyn's mind. "I'd say I'm pretty motivated to not mess this up."

The thicket edge is already glinting. Ordinarily she wouldn't trust Kalais as far as she can limp, but Kalais's desperation has Jasyn taking a deep breath and closing her eyes.

Kalais claims her helmet, and Jasyn tries not to think about how long a breath lasts, nor how even being able to communicate won't be enough to save them.

Kalais fiddling with the helmet is underscored by warbles and growls from the jungle. When a clunk that could be her helmet dropping resounds, Jasyn's eyes itch to open. A broken arm isn't going to make Kalais's task easier, is it? Or she could just be panicking, throwing the helmet away and making an ill-fated run for it, leaving her behind.

For all Jasyn knows, the creatures have already surrounded her. But she keeps her airways shut. No matter how much her lungs and nerves ache for breath.

Finally, the helmet pushed onto her head, a *whoosh* accompanies a series of *frazzles* as the decon kicks in and Jasyn gulps in air.

More eyes of the jungle are closing in, almost at the tree-line.

"Do what I say, okay?" says Jasyn, taking the lead.

Kalais scowls. "If *that's* your grand plan, I might as well just wear some garnish and wait for—"

A glance at the fast-approaching stampede turns Kalais a shade paler and she lets Jasyn assist her to her feet, her arm across her shoulder. But instead of running, Jasyn turns them to face the panthers.

Only fifty metres away...

"Why aren't we moving?" Kalais gasps between gritted teeth as the creatures break from the tree-line.

Jasyn wants to snap at her to just *Give her a minute*, but Kalais's panic is actually helping. Because she has an idea and — she hates to admit it — the Ice Princess is her inspiration. She'd used the tactic in The Games arena, and in Jasyn's dreams-turned-nightmares.

For it to work she either needs to be calm, or terrified. Calm isn't likely right now, so she lets her panic and Kalais's pulse through her — blood burning ice through her veins.

Soon the creatures will have them. Claws and fangs will tear at flesh. She lets that *certainty* permeate through her, sparking her bristling nerves.

Her cool breath hits the air in a plume. As the chaos flows through her veins, her grip tightens about her ice-sword and her blade ignites.

Kalais's arm tenses about Jasyn's shoulder as Jasyn swipes at the ground around them in a wide arc, igniting the air, spilling ice to cover the tangle of undergrowth, infilling until it's as flat as a frozen lake.

Jasyn lets out a hazy breath, hardly believing it worked.

"Well, shit," says Kalais. "I left my skates on Iolcus, Snowflake."

Jasyn rolls her eyes, because *of course* Kalais has to be a smart arse at a time like this.

"Now, don't claw me to death, okay?" says Jasyn as she lifts Kalais's legs to carry her. Though easier to achieve thanks to their gravity situation, it's a challenging manoeuvre with a reluctant passenger muttering curse words and how she could have "damn well rescued herself, thank you very much."

Despite her words, Kalais gives in and lets herself be carried as Jasyn runs up to the ice edge and bends to her knees, using the slick surface to skid at speed. *Growing up on an iced planet sure does result in certain skills.*

Lower gravity allow more of a glide, but the person in her arms and the creatures snapping at her heels ensure it's a challenge.

Paws thump the ice behind them. Claws scrape the surface.

A quick over-shoulder glance—

The creatures in pursuit scatter, slipping on the iced terrain.

The ice slick ends, depositing Jasyn and Kalais in an ungraceful heap. When Kalais growls up at her, Jasyn half expects her to launch an attack, but she only clutches at her injured arm. Tears crowd her eyes. *Hail*, Jasyn can only imagine the pain she's in.

A look ahead—

Their destination is only ten metres, but the cargo platform entryway is webbed with vines.

A glance back—

Their pursuers are adapting to the challenge, with vines snaking across the surface to give them the grip they need.

✦

ATALANTA

WEAPON WIELDING CREW CHIP AWAY AT THE EVER-THICKENING wall of vegetation.

Finally getting to use his axe-knives, even Peleus gives butchering the reaching jungle a good go.

Doctor Orpheus seems to be intent on her own side project, adding ingredients from the vials in her medician case into a decon spray pack. Gus is her assistant, closing vials that are no longer needed and returning them to the doctor's case.

But the hold is getting darker—

The wall is so thick now, each shot Atalanta lines up is rendered useless. She pauses only when something squeezes her shoulder—

She about-turns, claiming an arrow like a dagger, ready to drive it into her attacker, expecting it to be vegetation-based—

But her wrist is grasped and the apologetic features of the captain stare back, inviting her to back away from the hold platform. Everyone else has already done so.

Even these few seconds of distance have the matted mesh tightening, drowning them in shadows.

Atalanta swats the captain's hand away. "We're not leaving

them," she signs. Not that anyone can see her words in the dark. Not that the captain understands her anyway.

Fists at her sides, muscles straining, Atalanta steps up to Herakles, so close the captain can be in no doubt that she's launching a one-person rebellion.

Herakles nods for Atalanta to look at the doctor, who's brandishing the spray nozzle of the decon pack like a weapon as she approaches where the hold exit should be.

They're not abandoning the task? They're stepping back to let Doctor Orpheus through?

Atalanta joins the captain in backing away from the hold, as the doctor sprays the mysterious concoction across anything green and moving. At the contact, the vines squirm, leaves shrivel, surface tension buckles and colours blotch as they wilt, lifeless.

When the crew step forward and slice through them, no new vines take their place.

It should be a moment of triumph, of launching out to save Jasyn and Kalais, but the crew's united focus has veered to the deepest shadows of the hold.

All Atalanta can hear is her own heartbeat, but it's not difficult to read their startled expressions, and to understand that *there's something else lurking.*

JASYN

AT LEAST A DOZEN FANGED CREATURES ARE CLOSING IN—

Unwilling to be sent to her death with her back turned, Jasyn lets Kalais loose, gesturing for her to limp on. But Kalais can only fold to the ground.

"I'm not going on without you," says Kalais, her teeth gritted, attempting to bury her cries. “And I don’t mean that in a *we’re in this together* horseshit way. I mean I literally can’t stand. Obviously.”

“Did you know the collective term for panthers is a ‘claw’?” says Jasyn, rhetorically, as she squares up to the fast-approaching danger.

“I swear,” Kalais growls, “if those are the last words I hear, I'll kill you.”

Jasyn would laugh at her phrasing, if it all weren’t so dire.

She tests the weight of the sword in her hand, marvelling at how the blade’s surface fluctuates as though she were staring into a clouded sky composed of electricity or streaming water.

A deep breath.

“Stand back,” Herakles orders via helmet comms as a thumping of metal emanates from the ship. But Jasyn can’t be focusing on that because—

Two panthers are leaping—

The heaviness of finality thrums through her veins. Fear crystallises her focus. She sword-swipes the air in an arc and shards of ice burst out — *From her blade? From the air?* — pelting the creatures, piercing into them.

Wounded, the first wave retreat.

Five further creatures. The next wall of attack.

Tip of her sword to the ground, Jasyn flicks her wrist, crystallising into existence a bouquet of stalactites as tall as her, points angled in all directions.

“The fuck, Snowflake?”

Jasyn chooses to take Kalais’s words as awe and encouragement.

Attempting to stop, two creatures slip, bowling into the spikes, piercing them in a burst of yellow-green. *Heaven’s hail.* Talk about fuel for nightmares! She’d be impressed with her creation, if she weren’t so horrified by the results.

The next three felines score furrows in the ice and change direction, rounding the obstacle.

Jasyn's next attempt is too stuttering and scattered to be effective.

The creatures dart around the spindles of ice as though conquering an assault course.

And then Jasyn and Kalais are surrounded by glinting white eyes.

Hail.

Standing over Kalais, Jasyn might be adopting a defiant stance, but she fears it's not the confident threat she wishes it to be. But she's not giving up. She's not leaving Kalais to suffer an excruciating death.

She swipes at any who venture too close, injuring some, but there are more now. *Too many.* Ending one creature only results in more closing in.

Attempting to put some distance between them and the encroaching creatures, Jasyn grasps Kalais by the scruff of her astro-suit and drags her, accompanied by her vocal protests.

The rhythmic thumping grows louder, but its source is obscured by the pincer-panthers closing in around them. Kalais's sharp eyes meet hers. *What is that?* A bass beat counting down their demise?

"Get down," calls the voice of their captain over helmet comms, loud enough to punch Jasyn into action.

She drops to Kalais's side. Only now, her ability to sword-swipe is much reduced. What was the captain thinking?

On the ice, the felines gingerly approach. They're so close. The network of yellow and green beneath their fuzz-sheened translucent skin ripples.

A claw swipe sends Jasyn's sword clanging to the metal beneath the ground-mesh as the horde collectively block out the sky.

Encircled by doom, Jasyn and Kalais press closer together.

"Now would be a good moment for some sword-summoning, Snowflake."

Yes, it would... and's she's *trying*, but whatever she did before, she can't muster it...

She tries imagining the shape of events, but it's difficult to concentrate with so many pincers and fangs and claws and—

Kalais's hand squeezes Jasyn's forearm. Perhaps in fear or instinctive solidarity in their final moments. Either way, if this is the end, it's good to know Kalais is actually human.

Jaws closest to Jasyn snap, flinging saliva against her invisi-visor—

She grits her teeth, expecting pain to ignite—

But instead, Kalais's screaming-bellow vibrates through her. The creature has her broken arm in its mouth. Kalais must have blocked its bite with her own arm.

Spikes of ice bloom from Jasyn's palm, enough for her to claw-swipe the beast across the eyes. It spits out Kalais's arm and retreats into the crowd. Like floodwater, another fills the gap.

"Kalais..." Jasyn can hear the mix of disbelief, awe and gratitude in her own voice.

"Shut the fuck up, Snowflake," Kalais practically snarls, sweat beading on her brow.

The thumping rhythm stops—

Just as the weight of predators presses against them, threatening to drown them or pull them apart, the wall of bodies around them lurches... lifted... scattering as a solid animal ploughs through with a sprawling skid and a single flick of...

What the hail—?

Antlers?

A few felines try their luck against the new arrival, but even in their numbers they're no match for the towering beast with kicking hooves, swiping antlers, and a battle-worthy glint in his eyes.

The stag bellows, blasting the air with his almighty sound.

The pincer-panthers skitter back to the safety of their jungle. Jasyn would too, if it weren't for the incomer's strange familiarity. His fur as white as snow, his antlers — *heaven's hail, those antlers* — nature's crown and weapon. He might have lost the speckles of youth, he might not fit under Jasyn's arm anymore, but he's unmistakably the fawn... well, *the stag...*

How is this possible...? How long have they been gone from the ship?

"I'm hallucinating from the pain, right?" says Kalais, staring with wide eyes as the stag leans down to them, inviting them to climb on.

✦

ATALANTA

As hooves clatter up the platform, Jasyn and Kalais in tow, Atalanta keeps watch with arrow drawn. She wants nothing more than to wrap Jasyn in her arms and to check her *thoroughly* for injuries, but she refuses to lose vigilance now.

The last thing they need is for this world to find its way back into the ship.

Someone must hit the right button, because the platform closes and decon mist douses the entire hold. When it clears, the frazzled crew remove their helmets.

Atalanta joins them, sliding open her Transonics just enough to tune in to her surroundings.

Panicked heartbeats and breaths crowd the airwaves, but beneath the chaos, Jasyn's heartbeat thrums. Elevated. But *beating.*

She's looking right at her, so of course she knows Jasyn is alive, but with all that's happened, it takes this extra sensory layer for her to truly believe it.

"What the —?" Peleus trips on his words just as he trips over his own feet at the stag looming over him.

The fawn-turned-stag has proven himself intelligent enough to recognise Atalanta and to want to save Jasyn. Is it a stretch to think he recalls other events too? Does he remember his mother? And that her life was ended back on Iolcus by Peleus's blade?

There might have been a time when the stag was at Peleus's mercy, but now Peleus is at his. He raises a front hoof, ready to stomp—

Peleus clamps his eyes shut—

But instead, the stag splutters a cough in Peleus's face.

"You," Herakles points at Peleus. "Engine room. Do what Zetes tells you."

If Peleus has a problem being barked at, he keeps it to himself. Quaking just a little — either from the stag's stature, or the captain's — he finally has enough wherewithal to scramble away.

"Unless you're unconscious, or you have limbs hanging off," announces Herakles, "get to your stations."

Jasyn jumps down from the stag, holding a hand out for Kalais. Kalais growls, either at the concept of needing help, or her injuries. Understandable. A confusion of internal activity crowds the broken area of her arm and her injuries have tarnished the stag's fur red.

Kalais groans. "Gravity hurts. And not in a good way."

Herakles steps in to assist Jasyn in lowering Kalais from the stag.

"We need to get you to medical," says Herakles, more gently

than she'd spoken to the rest of the crew. Perhaps her injuries have allowed Kalais a dose of sympathy.

"Yeah, no shit, Captain," Kalais mutters.

With Jasyn and the captain looking after Kalais, Atalanta's thoughts swerve to the person no-one apart from the doctor seems to be looking out for.

Is the princess okay? That's a sentence she never imagined would occupy her thoughts. But then, she never thought she'd be on a snow-jungle planet battling vegetation with spores and creatures with sap for blood, either.

✦

JASYN

What happened here?

On their journey up through the ship, vines hang like curtains across portholes. There's a mossy aroma that gives the corridors a cave-like quality. Jasyn shudders. She's been trapped within enough cave walls lately.

The ship is tarnished, like it's been left to the elements. Either this place works fast, or they've been here longer than they think.

"I don't need your help." Kalais snarls as she nudges Jasyn and Herakles aside in the medical chamber to plonk herself on a gurney. Even Jasyn judders with the clumsy manoeuvre, so no wonder Kalais practically froths at the mouth at the aftershock.

"*Fuuuuuuck*," she cries, writhing.

Jasyn wishes there was something she could do. Something to take away the pain, to be useful, not just linger like an unwanted spectator.

A flash of cold prickles beneath her skin as Atalanta assists

Doctor Orpheus in lifting the unconscious Ice Princess onto a gurney. She buries her ice-cooled palm in her pocket.

With her jagged facial scar more pronounced, the Ice Princess looks more victim than aggressor, but Jasyn wouldn't put it past the Ice King's daughter to pretend to be something she's not. Nor would she put it past her to feign unconsciousness to bide her time and achieve the upper hand. She'd really rather the Ice Princess were a thousand measures in any direction.

The captain must be thinking along the same lines, because she's busy pacing between the gurneys with her arms crossed, biceps and neck straining, her focus flitting between Kalais, Atalanta, and the Ice Princess.

"Don't you have a ship to see to, captain?" says Doctor Orpheus, scouring over the Ice Princess's vitals and hooking her up to an elevated liquid pouch.

The doctor's nose is as bruised as it had been when Jasyn left the ship. And yet the Ice Princess looks like this place sucked the life from her. *In what world does any of this make sense?*

"We're good here," the doctor adds, sparing a moment of eye contact that seems to chase the captain away.

"Who'll strut at the helm if you're not there, Captain?" asks Kalais through gritted teeth, as Herakles makes her exit, and Jasyn can't tell if she's trying to be funny or taking the liberty of airing grievances. The pain is obviously making her delirious or bold.

The doctor adjusts the neighbouring gurney and instructs Atalanta to "Sit," and keep her "leg elevated."

Hail. Jasyn hadn't realised Atalanta was so injured. As she limps to the gurney, the darkened patches on Atalanta's lower leg highlight where her injury is. Adrenaline must have masked Atalanta's pain before, because as soon as she lies on the gurney, her features relax a little.

The ship fires up, coming to life in a frenetic, strobe-like fashion. Herakles must already be at the helm.

Doctor Orpheus settles on a chair that places her at eye level with Kalais. It takes only the slightest press of the doctor's medi-gloves to her bleeding, sickeningly angular arm for Kalais to thump her square on the jaw.

The momentum nearly knocks the doctor off her seat, but she recovers quickly. Though, Jasyn notes, Kalais doesn't get a returned right hook.

Doctor Orpheus must be reading Jasyn's mind, because — oddly — she's smirking at her, as if thinking *Yeah, I should have seen that coming.*

"*Mother of — Fuck,*" Kalais cries out. Looks like the doctor has a rival in the swears department.

To the doctor's credit, she continues as if there isn't a bump and bruise forming across her jaw. With the kind of calm Jasyn assumed her incapable of, the doctor waits for Kalais's wild eyes to settle on eye contact.

"Kalais. If you knock me out, I won't be able to reset your arm."

"You're not going anywhere near my arm." Kalais breathes unsteadily through her nostrils. "Can't you just heal me from within with your musical-crap magic or whatever?"

Doctor Orpheus almost smiles. "My musical-crap magic is a little more complicated than that."

"Well," counters Kalais, "just kill me and bring me back to life, if you want to be all dramatic about it."

Jasyn would laugh, if Kalais weren't vibrating with pain and didn't sound almost serious.

"The very definition of *overkill,*" says Doctor Orpheus, pulling a laugh from Kalais, followed by gritted teeth and a growl. "The sooner your arm's aligned, the sooner you can start healing."

"Can't you give her something for the pain?" asks Jasyn.

The doctor pauses, observing Kalais for the answer. Jasyn's sure there's something in this interaction she's not getting, as Kalais squeezes her eyes shut and shakes her head.

"Just do it."

Tears of rabid defiance stream down Kalais's cheeks. As she angles her injured arm to the doctor, she looks like she might pass out. For her sake, Jasyn wishes she would.

"Jasyn's going to hold your shoulders and other arm in place," says Doctor Orpheus, nodding to Jasyn.

"I don't need my hand held, doctor." Kalais spits the words.

Yes, what she said...

"But I would rather keep all my teeth," replies the doctor. "And now that we know your other arm is working..." She rubs her reddened jaw with the back of her hand.

How can she be making jokes—?

Kalais chuckles, then grimaces as the laughter shudders her. "Urgh, fuck you, doctor. Your humour literally hurts."

"It has been said."

Jasyn steps in to hold Kalais's shoulder, pressing her uninjured wrist at her side.

"Better not turn me into a snow-cone," Kalais quips.

Jasyn might be unsettled, her hands might be a little cold, but her instinctive reactions are holding in check. Freezing Kalais to death while she gets her arm reset would be... well, she doesn't want to think about that.

"Your hands are clammy for someone who deals in ice," says Kalais, more as an observation than a cutting remark.

Jasyn clears her throat, unsettled by invading the space of someone who's been so vocal about wanting to push her out an airlock. Someone who sabotaged her astro-suit. It's made more awkward by having to press her cheek against Kalais's, like they're in some awkward embrace.

"If it helps to think of it more like a choke-hold..." says the doctor, half-smiling.

"Don't get any ideas, Snowflake." Kalais wheezes, confirming for Jasyn that she absolutely isn't going to be a delight about this. "No kissing or killing me, okay?"

At least she's alive, Jasyn reminds herself. And Kalais *being a nightmare* is better than being dead. Probably.

No doubt it's the promise of more pain that has Kalais wheezing and turning her face into Jasyn's neck, breaths hot and sharp against her.

"So... You and Zetes look a lot alike?" Jasyn hedges.

Kalais scoffs. "If this is your attempt at small talk to distract me from—" Kalais's growling screams vibrate against Jasyn's neck as — with firm hands — the doctor adjusts her broken forearm.

Kalais slips her wrist free and Jasyn panics, tensing, before Kalais's fingers tighten against hers, clinging to her hand as if for dear life as her body arcs up from her sitting position.

Jasyn holds her tight until—

Something clicks. Bones crunching against each other, into position. Jasyn's stomach lurches as if the pain is her own. She keeps the pressure about Kalais's shoulders and tries not to think about how hard her fingers are being squeezed. Or that the person in her arms, holding her hand, is Kalais.

By the time Kalais looks back at her broken arm, by the time the tension uncoils from her shoulders, the doctor has her arm wrapped in bandages, kept steady with a splint.

"We're identical," Kal wheezes, and it takes Jasyn a moment to recall she'd started a conversation, "with a few modifications."

"You can let her go now," suggests Doctor Orpheus, when Jasyn and Kalais remain clutching each other. Though it's not clear which of them she's talking to, Jasyn doesn't appreciate the suggestion in the doctor's smirk.

Atalanta's death-stare from the neighbouring gurney suggests she appreciates it even less.

Kalais leans back against the gurney to catch her breath. That she doesn't let go of Jasyn's hand is something Jasyn decides to ignore in case that hand becomes a fist.

"The good news is," says the doctor, inspecting Kalais's other injuries, "your leg is merely lacerated. And, while you might be perfectly capable of it, there's no need to kick me."

Kalais chuckles, nodding her agreement. "Yeah, we'll see." Her words are lighter now. Relieved? Exhausted? Both?

It doesn't look like she's letting go.

Letting go...

It's a strange brain-burp to have right now, but...

Back in the crashed ship, Kalais had said something about Wrecker ships *not letting go. Not without sacrifice.* Her instincts have her orbiting the words. They're important, somehow...

Kalais's grip on Jasyn loosens as she finally passes out.

The room shudders, scattering Jasyn's thoughts. The ship creaks; the unsettling reverberation of metal under strain. The kind no-one wants rattling through a sky ship with a crew desperate to take flight.

"Warning. Warning," announces the voice of the ship. "Ship off axis."

ATALANTA

EVERY SINEW OF THE SHIP STRAINS, GASPS, LIKE A CREATURE having its throat squeezed. Winding simultaneously up and down through the ship, sidestepping the rattling echo of vole-rats — racing hearts sparkling, fizzing in vents — Atalanta's focus lands at the helm.

"Bloody hail. The vines are tilting us." Pollux's voice skitters around the hull as Castor adds: "A sideways launch won't do us any good."

The sturdy footsteps of the captain interrupt. A deep breath, and air rushes into Herakles's lungs, pulling Atalanta's focus with it, into her chest where a steady heartbeat thrums.

"We're anchored by magnetism and a multitude of vines. We need solutions. Chief?" says Herakles with a clear *how would you solve this?* tone.

"*Vines*. Starting with engines cold, there'll only be enough energy for one deterrent blast," says Gus. "We'll need to take to the skies swiftly after. As for the magnetism..."

"It's isolated," Lynk interjects. Atalanta guesses the vague crackle in the air around Lynk to be her scrolling through the analytical data orbiting her cosmic weather station. "The lure is trained solely on our ship. It's not strong, currently, but we've no guarantee it won't pluck us from the skies on launch."

Metal cries. The ship's outer shell strains. Captain and helm crew minds, too.

Jasyn stands, pulling Atalanta's focus back to the medical quarters. Her expression is one Atalanta knows well. Of pieces of a mental puzzle slotting together. And: *I'm taking matters into my own hands.* She mutters something about "sacrifice" before striding for the door, which is never going to be a calming turn of events...

"We need to give the planet something else to focus on," says Jasyn, obviously on some mission. *But what?*

Atalanta limps after her. Pain lashes up from her injured leg. Being preoccupied with rescuing Jasyn and matters of life and death had dulled the pain for a while. She's signing "what are you doing?" but Jasyn is too intent on forging down the stairs to see her question.

As Atalanta strains to keep up — made all the more difficult by the unsettling tilt of the corridor — her heart races. Her blood vessels — *whoosh-whoosh-whoosh* — contract, feeding her muscles, masking the ache in her leg, and spurring her on.

Her Transonic range skittering all over the place, she picks up Doctor Orpheus's voice snaking through the comms: "Medical to helm," and — much to Atalanta's surprise — relaying Jasyn's words as if they might be useful. Of course, Atalanta trusts Jasyn's judgement (mostly...) but she hadn't expected the same of the grumpy doctor.

"And what am I supposed to do with that information?" asks Herakles, but — *snap* — Gus clicks her fingers. "She's right." Whatever Gus and the captain have to say to each other then is lost to Atalanta while she assesses which way Jasyn went.

Down a level? More? To the cargo hold?

She aims at the top deck, only to find her auditory path interrupted by Gus's purposeful footsteps on a swift downward trajectory. The spiral stairs and her weakened state have her dizzy, landing her focus in the medical quarters where a bandage winds about Kalais's leg, fabric shifting against fabric.

A wave of vertigo teases her stomach.

Like a log being shunted along river rapids, her Transonic focus tilts into the comms wires, snaking from medical to the engine chamber, as the doctor makes the comms connection.

"Engine room, receiving" says the voice of Zetes, breath held as if what happens next has the power to make or break his world.

"Kal is okay," says the doctor. "Broken arm, but it hasn't dented her personality. Unfortunately."

Zetes lets his breath loose. "Thanks doc. I mean, doctor." His voice warbles before he clears his throat. The call disconnects and he returns to relaying ice into the furnace, his abdominal muscles lurching as if trying to contain tears.

"Jolt warning," announces the ship as Atalanta catches up to Jasyn at the hold airlock.

"Jolt warning? What does that—?" asks Jasyn, slowing, half a second before electricity lashes across the portholes, branching blue and white — vein-like — through each of the vines.

The thicket of vegetation retreats or falls away, flooding light through the portholes again.

"Axis correcting," announces the ship.

Thank the heavens.

"Engine room. Engage take-off sequence," says Herakles through the ship-wide comms.

Take off sequence? We're taking off already?

"Engine room," replies Zetes. "Confirm. Take-off sequence engaged."

"All crew, prepare for take-off," says Herakles, hurriedly.

"You two are with me," Gus asserts as she completes her final turn on the spiral stairs and overtakes them.

With a screech of metal against metal, Gus shows them into the airlock. In the eight echoing strides it takes to cover the length of the tunnel, a decon hiss accompanies as Gus affixes her helmet. The implication is clear: *get suited up.*

Such proximity to the outer shell of the ship has Atalanta's fears and pulse running riot. But time is of the essence. She slides her Transonics closed as she seals into her helmet.

Within moments the three of them are through the airlock chamber and in the cargo hold. Only when Gus unveils a vehicle, and Jasyn smiles, does Atalanta understand that *this* is the answer to *something else for the planet to focus on*.

Hail, she hopes this works.

✦

JASYN

Hail, Jasyn hopes this works.

The massive hunk of smooth, white painted metal has an air of familiarity about it. In the realm of her memories, in the mountain meadow all those sun-orbits ago, she'd injured her hand on scrap metal with the same D-0-V3 markings.

Does that mean the crashed ship and the astronauts who lost their lives to the Unforgiving Mountains were Iolcian? *What were they doing there?* It's not for dwelling on when your own sky ship is shuddering through launch prep and screeching in the same breath.

"Chief. If we don't go now —" The captain's voice crackles through the hold's comms.

"It's stuck," says Gus, unsuccessfully shoulder-shoving the vehicle against a warped portion of track. Jasyn and Atalanta step in to assist, lifting its guide-wheels over the broken section and lining it up with the hold platform.

"Flight-techs. Secure for take-off, confirm?" says the captain.

"Flight-tech. Confirm. Secure for take-off." Castor and Pollux, overlapping.

"Medical. Secure for take-off, confirm?"

"Medical. Confirm. Secure for take-off." Doctor Orpheus.

"Ship, ready," announces the detached voice of the ship. Its crackling and inconsistent tone makes the statement more like a question.

"Anchor up," says the captain.

The ship lurches, vibrating as though it might launch without warning.

"External eyes have us clear," says Gus hurriedly, as she inspects the overseer displays capturing a multitude of angles beneath the ship. Vines are reaching but are yet to make contact. If there are any creatures lurking, they're staying hidden.

Hydraulics hiss as Gus presses for the platform to lower. Atalanta raises her bow and arrow, aiming it at the space beyond the open platform, at the outer rim of the ship where readied thrusters percolate a blue mist.

With a shove from Gus and Jasyn, the raft slides along its track and out of the hold. The thud as the raft meets the ground isn't as satisfying as it might have been in higher gravity, but...

"It's working," says Lynk over the comms. "Magnetism is concentrating on the lure. Proximity wins out."

Jasyn's stomach rolls with relief, terror, excitement. She imagines Lynk's goggles streaming equations and fluid lines of magnetism pooling to the site of the discarded raft.

"Get that door closed, get out of the hold, and buckle in," instructs the captain, *as if that weren't an obvious course of immediate action.*

Gus strikes the platform-close button while Atalanta's weapon remains trained on the untrustworthy world beyond.

Jasyn turns to action the captain's redundant orders, only to be met with white eyes in a blur of motion from the shadows—

Claws pierce into her chest and an *oof* escapes her as she's propelled backwards—

A rush of air...

Falling...

Jasyn's arms swim as she sails backwards, tumbling out through the partially open platform, just as the sky ship leaves the ground—

✦

ATALANTA

TERROR HITS ATALANTA LIKE AN ARROW IN THE CHEST.

Her breath swept from her—

Her heart hammers—

They're lifting off—

The ground racing away—
Not thinking, only reacting—
She fires one arrow—
Reaches for the next—
Claims a cargo tether cable—
Affixes it to an arrow—
Aims and fires—

JASYN

JASYN'S BACK PRESSES TO THE GROUND AS CLAWS CUT DEEPER beneath her shoulders.

Thrusters roar with the rumbling, nerve-shredding power of a thousand mountain bears as nostril-burning fumes envelop her in a sudden white-out.

She grabs for the creature's sinuous neck, trying to push it away, but its skin-tearing grip binds them together.

Salivating jaws snap closer—

An arrow stabs through the creature's gnashing jaws, locking them in place.

Luminous green blood-sap bursts from its throat. The light extinguished from its eyes, it's claws retract and its body goes limp.

Jasyn shoves the creature aside, letting low gravity carry it as far as it likes.

Heaven's hail—

Her stomach drops in reverse correlation to the rising ship.

A second arrow pierces the ground a few feet from her. This one connected to rope, or netting, or something. There's no time to think.

She grabs it.

It tightens, plucking the arrow from the ground and Jasyn along with it.

A rush of air...

Soaring...

Looking down as she dangles above the fast retreating terrain might not be the most sensible course of action, but Jasyn lets herself absorb the thrill of it for a half second before she does what she does best.

She climbs.

✦

ATALANTA

DON'T THINK ABOUT LOSING HER... DON'T THINK ABOUT FALLING FROM a soaring sky ship... Don't imagine the ship being ripped apart... Don't vomit...

Atalanta manages only her last self-assigned instructions as she grips one end of the cable while Jasyn climbs the other. For a planet with relatively mild gravity, Jasyn is heavy cargo. Or perhaps it's more a matter of wind resistance.

Whatever it is, Atalanta's determined to fight it, one length of cable at a time.

Gus hooks a safety tether to Atalanta's belt loop and her own as she steps in to assist. They're soon joined by Doctor Orpheus in her black astro-gear. *Did Gus summon her? Was she sent here?* Whatever her origin, she assists in hoisting Jasyn back to the relative safety of the ship.

✦

JASYN

BICEPS, FOREARMS AND EVERY CORE MUSCLE IMAGINABLE BURN hotter than the Seven Suns. Her legs, like jelly. Her stomach, likely left behind. Jasyn summits into the cargo hold with the kind of groan reserved for athletes achieving the impossible, or astronauts defying death.

Several sets of arms grasp her, pulling her onto solid ground. Well, as solid as a hold can be when the ship is vibrating its way up into the skies, and when the thing she's landed on is Doctor Orpheus, whose breaths are as laboured as her own.

"*Euryproktos*, Jasyn." There's a strange glint in the doctor's eyes. "How many lives do you have?"

"This is only the first leg of our journey," adds Gus from the sidelines. "You should try to save a few."

Noted. Jasyn nods, breathless.

The platform hydraulics hiss shut and the voice of the ship confirms something about the door to oblivion being "locked."

Arms wrap around her so powerfully it takes a moment for her mind to catch up. She's not being swooped to the floor by a snow-jungle beast...

Not this time.

Because the arms promising to never let go, the eyes glinting with relief, the lips bypassing the ether-mesh of her invisi-visor and meeting her mouth in a desperate kiss... *all Atalanta.*

"Welcome," says the tired, crackling voice of the ship, probably more in relation to the hold door being closed than in reference to the kiss. But, still, Atalanta's kiss is more than welcome.

"*Myrton-Panoùgros-Kèpfos,*" Doctor Orpheus mutters as she wriggles out from the body pile. "For fuck's sake. Do you need a workshop titled *Don't Put Your Face On That.* Subtitle: *Fucking Contagion Pathways?*"

And, with that, the doctor strikes a green button on the wall labelled DECON and the white mist fills the hold.

Atalanta either doesn't hear the scolding or doesn't care,

because kissing is still happening. *Doctor Orpheus can be as miserable as she wants.*

Perhaps acknowledging that the both of them might need to breathe, or that the decon mist does taste kind of weird, Atalanta retreats, but stays within reach, holding Jasyn.

As the mist dissipates, the blue and orange smears on the doctor's matte black astro-suit lose their vibrancy. Her generally pissed off expression remains, however. Though, it morphs to stunned as — "Fuck me" — she stares out the in-floor platform porthole framing the fast-disappearing terrain. Her tone is enough to pull everyone's attention.

Where the ship had stood, where once there had been vines and snow (or spores, or whatever the stuff is), where the jungle-mesh now withers, there is chrome.

Dented metal, dilapidated paintwork. Vehicles shaped to take flight but broken to pieces, all jutting from the tangle of green and white.

The scraps put Jasyn in mind of the nest in the mountain bear cave. Evidence of those who didn't escape. Only on a much larger scale.

"It's a fucking sky ship graveyard," says Doctor Orpheus, always poetic.

PART VII

UNDERTOW

54

OUT OF REACH

ATALANTA

Clusters of vole-rats screech as they weave between hidden gaps, trying to outrun the ship's chaotic cries. The creatures aren't alone in roaming every pipe nook and wire-bundled cranny, as Atalanta Transonically scours every inch of the vessel, seeking weak points as the planet's upper atmosphere squeezes tight.

Half reclined on the gurney Doctor Orpheus has ushered her to, Atalanta's heart races. The stag nudges her palm with his muzzle, encouraging her to calm, but all she can think about is *Jasyn falling — Air rushing — Breath stolen—*

She doesn't recall deciding to pull arrow into bow. *It all happened so fast.* And yet, *so slow.* She remembers the noose tightening about her insides, but not making any decisions. Things just *happened.* And if they hadn't, Jasyn wouldn't be here. She'd be lost to that world, or worse.

If it hadn't been for the lower gravity, the fall alone would have killed her...

But she can't think about that... If she thinks about that she's going to decorate the ship with her stomach contents, again.

Hissing... Sizzling...

Down in the engine chamber, Jasyn's neck and forehead whisper with injury. The sites of activity must be surface burns where the vines contacted her skin. The sounds bristle Atalanta's own pain receptors.

The fibres of Jasyn's muscles expand and contract as her shoulders flex with each shovel of fuel-ice, and that has other parts of Atalanta reacting. Harnesses creak, tethering Jasyn and Zetes, preventing them from a grizzly end via the engine hatch as the ship bumps and tears through the skies.

With each shovel of fuel-ice, the amalgamation of sounds weaves through the ship like an overflowing nest of vipers. The fuel itself pulses through pipes, along junctions, winding through the arteries of the ship.

Occasional snags flair bright, but there's nothing catastrophic, nothing hindering their trajectory as the apex ploughs through the atmosphere with a roar like wildfire.

Atalanta forgets to breathe.

In an ideal world they would've taken time to check the ship's integrity and made necessary repairs, but — despite what they all had been temporarily tricked into thinking — an ideal world it was not.

At the helm, internal fibres adjust as the captain's impressive collection of muscles strain to steer the ship, her heart pulsing admirably — *inexplicably* — sure and steady. It's almost enough to convince Atalanta to calm, or to question the captain's sanity.

The ship rears, as if it's crested a wave, and the tension of apex metal and glass dissipates.

"Good news, folks," announces Herakles through the labyrinth of comms wires. "We're beyond gravitational and magnetic reach."

Letting out her breath, and hearing the entire crew do the

same, Atalanta could be convinced that even the ship itself is sighing relief.

In the engine chamber, a *clang* echoes, highlighting Jasyn as she downs her shovel and mops her brow. Her arms and shoulders pulse, protesting her recent bout of shovelling — and probably all that climbing, too.

"I CAN GIVE YOU SOMETHING FOR THE PAIN," says a voice, so loud and close, Atalanta winces as she reels in her Transonic reach to the medi-masked doctor inspecting her lacerated leg.

With a steadying breath, she reminds herself of her immediate surroundings: that her own wounds are whispering; that she's down to her vest and undershorts, that the stag is leaning against her for her comfort or his, that the doctor doesn't seem bothered by the encroaching antlers. And that Kalais occupies one of the recovery chambers at the edge of the room, struggling through her pain with laboured breaths and stifled groans.

Further breaths veer Atalanta's attention to the inked out tank of the quarantine chamber. The princess returned to her prison, "for her own safety," according to the doctor. Atalanta's heart aches — *literally aches* — at the knowledge that this is the last place the princess would want to be. The only saving grace is that the princess is currently too unconscious to know about it.

"Your wounds are clean. The stitching is neat," says the doctor as she gently lowers Atalanta's heel. "You did this?" she asks, apparently intrigued, as she makes quick but precise work of bandaging Atalanta's leg.

In answer, Atalanta nods to the quarantine chamber and the doctor's scowl returns. Perhaps, like Atalanta had previously, contending with the unbelievable notion that the Ice Princess isn't one of the worst people under the Seven Suns.

Doctor Orpheus nods as if she understands something, before she adds: "Her body needs time to heal, but she'll be okay."

The tension in Atalanta's shoulders loosens at the words.

"And you need the same. I'm assigning you rest in a recovery chamber. Your wind-down Rhythm will kick in shortly," she adds, inputting something on her own cuff, which Atalanta can only guess is updating the schedules.

Before Atalanta can object, or find a way to ask what this means for her seeing Jasyn, purposeful footsteps precede the door to the medical chambers bursting open.

There, the captain. Her ordinarily striking and stoic presence somewhat undermined by her staring, slack-jawed, at Atalanta in her underlayers.

"FUCK'S SAKE, HERAKLES." The doctor's exclamation is louder than Atalanta's Transonics appreciate.

The captain's jaw clenches as her gaze snags on Atalanta's bandages. The doctor looks between Atalanta and the captain.

"I mean… Fuck's sake, *Captain*," says the doctor, rolling her eyes, either at Herakles or herself.

But the captain keeps staring. Her mouth opens and closes. It's as if she's made of wires and metal and all aspects have malfunctioned. Atalanta has no clue what her facial features amount to. Worry? Fear? It's not the best reaction Atalanta's had to her semi-naked state.

The captain's eyes snap up to Atalanta's, but whatever language they're speaking, it's not one Atalanta understands.

The doctor closes in on where the captain is apparently rooted to the spot and speaks more quietly. Not that it does much use, with Atalanta's notable skillset.

"Barging in and staring at my half-clothed patients, Captain? Mighty oafish, don't you think?"

That seems to catch Herakles's attention. She clears her throat, her features buckling with... what? *Embarrassment?*

"Just because your captain-cuff means you *can* waltz into any chamber you like, doesn't mean you should."

"Of course." Herakles looks everywhere but at Atalanta, but the "sorry," she mutters seems aimed in her general direction.

"Everything is under control," says the doctor. "Perhaps you could come back when we're done here? Or at least when everyone is fully dressed?"

The captain's eyes ping between the doctor, the closed-door recovery chamber where Kalais resides, the quarantine chamber, and Atalanta before, preoccupied, she runs her hand through the hair at the base of her neck — *scratch, scratch,* the hairs rustle, and her biceps flex — about-turns and leaves.

Well, that was weird...

The doctor continues as if nothing strange just happened and says something about how Atalanta needs to stick to her prescribed Rhythm, to get rest, but Atalanta's focus slips to the engine chamber just as sweat slicks down Jasyn's neck.

Atalanta's inner furnace *flames* as she follows its journey into the fibres of Jasyn's vest. The roar of the engine rivals that of Jasyn's pulse and Atalanta's own.

"You're looking a little flushed," says the voice of the doctor, somehow both distant and far too close. But Zetes is saying something about the engine ticking over now and that Jasyn can take a break.

Good. Because there's something Atalanta needs more than rest.

It's possible Jasyn has the same idea, because her footsteps stride from the engine chamber and along the corridor, slowing only when they intersect with the captain's as Herakles demands: "Where do you think you're going? Get back to work."

If ever there was a tone designed to pick a fight...

Jasyn's heart thumps harder in response.

"Atalanta's in medical—" begins Jasyn.

"The correct response, the only response," says Herakles, her manner far removed from the calm authority she'd demonstrated when they'd first taken to the skies, "...is *Aye, Captain*."

Either Jasyn is the hailstone that buckled the cottage roof, or their captain is an asshole.

Jasyn's heart thumps faster still, her blood pulsing to her clenched fists. Her palms crackle with a light frost.

"The engines are ticking over..." Her vocal cords adjust as she tries to keep her voice steady. "There's no reason for me not to—"

Atalanta's stomach tightens, expelling her breath. It's difficult to calm, to tell herself that Jasyn is safe and still within reach when she isn't right in front of her. It's more difficult still when an overbearing sky ship captain is midway through asserting her unreasonable authority.

Atalanta can vaguely hear the doctor asking whether she has a problem, but there's a rushing in her ears. And it isn't the imagined air that whisked past Jasyn as she fell, it isn't her own breath chasing after her, but the *woosh* of her heartbeat telling her what she wants.

She hops down from the gurney, carefully but quickly. She doesn't bother dressing before stride-limping out of the medical quarters and ignores the doctor's comments about the imminent Rhythm schedule and the question: "Where the fuck are you going?"

It takes longer than she'd like to reach the corridor where Jasyn and the captain are virtually toe to toe, the captain making good use of her superior stature (she's only a couple of inches taller than Jasyn, but she has a way of carrying herself that makes her more imposing), and unleashing at Jasyn about how she needs to respect authority and "heavens above and below, why can't you just do what you're told?"

What is the captain's problem? She doesn't treat anyone else this way. She must really hate ice royals, even those who've never been near the throne.

If Herakles's tirade is anything to go by, there'll be punishment on the horizon for what Atalanta is about to do. But, given that they've all just cheated death, she's not willing to abide the heartless authority of a moody sky ship captain on a mission to keep her and Jasyn apart.

When she sees her, the captain's features immediately morph. The fire in her eyes melts to something that might be shame. *Interesting... Confusing...*

Whatever.

Atalanta cares little for what Herakles thinks. She only cares that when Jasyn turns and sees her, her face lights up. That instinctive reaction has fuel shovelling into Atalanta's inner ice-furnace. *She'd follow that smile beyond the Seven Suns.*

As Atalanta strides forward, she barely registers her cuff buzzing. Light and shadows pulse in a clash of Rhythms, but she has no intention of winding-down right now.

The captain must know what's good for her, or can see the flourishing fire in Atalanta's eyes, because she steps aside.

Jasyn's eyes wash over Atalanta as she approaches. She must be perplexed or worried by Atalanta appearing in only her vest, shorts and a bandage, because her brow buckles and she starts to ask:

"Are you o—?"

Atalanta threads her fingers into Jasyn's sweat dampened hair and loses her breath, pressing their foreheads together as she slips her arms around Jasyn and presses her close.

She's in your arms. You haven't lost her.

Her inner-engines *wurring*, Atalanta pauses to catch her breath and to seek the answer to the question in her eyes.

Jasyn answers with a searing kiss.

How could she ever run from this? *She would never hurt Jasyn.* The truth of it asserts itself in her every atom. How could she, when being close to her has her grounded, safe and warm?

More than warm, in fact.

Which is ironic, given the air turning to drifting ice-crystals around them, shimmering like a stuttering glitter-snowfall.

Knowing Jasyn, that reaction's a good sign. The silver dancing in her eyes as they retreat for breath, that's good, too.

Atalanta steals a glance at the captain. The shock in Herakles's eyes is perhaps to be expected. The blush blooming in her cheeks and that she's been rendered speechless is less so.

But Atalanta's not here to stare at the captain and assess her issues. The captain can do what she likes, but she's not going to stop Atalanta from showing Jasyn how she feels. If this moment is cut short by arbitrary ship rules and a captain on a power trip, they need to make it count.

Which is one reason why Atalanta invites Jasyn into an even deeper kiss. She's vaguely aware of the gentle *clink-clink-clink* of mid-air ice meeting, and how at odds the calming sound is with the pulsing of shadows and light. *Damn Rhythm.*

Doctor Orpheus must have followed her, because she's only a few feet away, muttering something about how she "should really get a sample." Atalanta can only guess she's referring to the mid-air ice.

A mid-kiss sideways glance lets Atalanta know the doctor is guiding the captain away. Given how much the captain had to say to Jasyn on the topics of insubordination and sticking to Rhythm schedules, it's strange she's rendered mute, now. It's strange they're not being threatened with the brig, or worse.

But Atalanta's body is too flooded with the idea of Jasyn, and it's only the two of them in the corridor now. It's an opportunity not to waste.

Atalanta presses Jasyn up against the wall. Jasyn's lopsided smile blooms. *Hail, that smile.* She had wanted to make sure Jasyn is okay, to hold her close, but now? Now — tugging at the clothing layers between them — she wants much more...

"You seeing this?" Castor's voice burbles down from the helm, more of an icy interruption than Jasyn's actual ice. "Bet Ice-monger thinks she's still dreaming."

Atalanta breaks from the breath-stealing kiss. Amongst the pulsing of clashing Rhythm lights, the overseer winks down at them from the top corner of the corridor.

Privacy... They need some privacy.

Atalanta steps back and Jasyn's frown suggests the distance is possibly the worst situation in this galaxy and the next. When Atalanta holds her hand out as if they're at some formal event and she's asking Jasyn to dance, Jasyn's smile returns. Their palms touch, and everything is right with the universe.

Atalanta leads her along the corridor. The Rhythm of shadows and light battling around them, they manage only a few dozen paces before Jasyn pulls Atalanta back to her and pins her against the nearest flat surface.

"Snowflake's got moves, I'll give her that," says the unwelcome voice of Castor, dripping down from the helm.

The bunks. They need to get to the bunks. But making the journey is a challenge when Jasyn's lips are on hers and her hands are on a voyage beneath her vest.

With a valiant effort that really should warrant her some sort of medal, Atalanta encourages Jasyn along the corridor and into the lift.

With the illusion of privacy, it's only a half second before they're all over each other again. When the doors open, not only are they not on the right floor, but the opening doors frame their audience.

Gus merely blinks, vaguely distracted from the ice-tablet that otherwise had her attention. Tiphys's jaw drops, his wide eyes eclipsed by Gus's palm. Lynk merely adjusts her goggles, aimed squarely at them:

"Oh my. That's one hail of a heat signature."

55

COCOON FOR TWO

JASYN

That there's no-one else in the crew quarters at this moment is a welcome stroke of luck. The lights pulse as insistently as Jasyn's entire body. Atalanta leads the way, shuffling into a lower bunk, discarding Jasyn's vest and inviting her into the narrow space with her.

Fitting two people into a bunk isn't impossible, and those odds are good enough. Jasyn had thought she wanted the comparative luxurious of the captain's quarters to have privacy and time with Atalanta, but squeezed together within a tubular bunk is pretty close to perfection.

In their illusion of the perfect life, before it all unravelled, it had only been a matter of hours since they were getting intimate together. In actuality — if Jasyn is understanding the situation — it's been months.

And Jasyn's body seems to know it.

Keen to be reminded what *real* feels like, she manoeuvres free from overalls and shorts — a challenge in a bunk definitely designed to only be occupied by one, but together they triumph.

In their fumbling, their straining against a too-low ceiling, they're unlikely to win any awards for being swift or smooth, but it's these moments that capture the kind of intimacy which, for Jasyn, has all the power of perfection.

Atalanta's shorts are a challenge, getting caught on the bandage about her lower leg. With their injuries fresh and painful, now probably isn't the time for such adventures, but there's a determination and longing in Atalanta's eyes that Jasyn cannot ignore.

Naked but for her bandages, the new map of Atalanta's skin has an aurora of bruises and blemishes that tighten about Jasyn's heart like a sentient vine. Placing a stilling hand to Atalanta's sternum only serves to remind her—

The steaming ice-blade in Atalanta's chest... Cascading red... Atalanta limp, the stars in her eyes extinguished...

Jasyn retreats, but only manages to clock the back of her head on the bunk ceiling and lose her breath.

It might have been a dream, a nightmare, but the feelings, they were real. They *are* real.

Jasyn balls her fists. She wants to lash out, to pace, to scream. Instead, she pushes at the too-close walls as if they're pressing inwards and imagines screaming into the star-studded depths of space. They almost died on that world. Atalanta *had* died. In Jasyn's mind, at least.

Tears emerge, burning hot and cold. The air turns thick and sharp, making inhalation difficult and exhalation visible.

Atalanta supports herself on one elbow as she tucks strands of Jasyn's hair behind her ear. *Hail.* Jasyn loves it when she does that.

"I thought I lost you," Jasyn whispers, rogue tears cooling a trail down her cheeks. *I thought I lost you. Again.*

"If you're going to keep looking so sad, Jasyn," signs Atalanta, concern etched on her face, "I'm going to put my clothes back on."

Atalanta's faux-serious expression has laughter bubbling in Jasyn's chest, melting the tension from her. When Atalanta traces a careful finger across Jasyn's chest, skirting around her injuries, Jasyn loses her breath, caught between desire and discomfort.

Being sent to the engine room so soon after clawing her way back onto the ship, she'd ignored her wounds. The claw-punctures fan out beneath her collar bones. They sting with a vengeance, which is probably a reason to get them seen to. But Atalanta is beneath her, and *that* is an altogether more welcome reality on which to focus.

Atalanta tilts Jasyn's chin and thumbs away her tears, pressing kisses in their place. With a choked breath, Jasyn wraps her arms around her, pressing her close until her heavy heartbeat thrums against her chest.

She *is* real. *This is real.*

With the power to melt the discontent from her thoughts and dull the sharp edges in her body and mind, Atalanta's kisses trail down Jasyn's jaw and neck, inviting her thoughts away from death and doubts and back to her, back to calm.

It doesn't take long for their kisses to heat, and — under dexterous touch — for stifled sounds of sorrow to replace with not-so-stifled gasps and moans.

Atalanta seems to make it her mission to increase Jasyn's volume as she presses their hips so close Jasyn's senses would shoot for the stars if she weren't already on a sky ship and sailing amongst them.

As they move together to the rise and fall of shadow and light, their breaths combine and Atalanta's eyes sparkle. At her quickened breaths and *that look* in her eyes, the tension within Jasyn builds.

As Atalanta's inner-bow releases, she arches and bucks and clutches Jasyn close, pulling her into a kiss, grasping both her body and breath. Fingers dig into Jasyn's back as if she'll never let go.

At Atalanta's pleasure, the filament fruit of Jasyn's heart, *and other parts of her anatomy*, blaze brighter than the Seven Suns.

It could be her imagination, or a minor glitch with the gravity consoles, but at exactly the right moment, Jasyn feels weightless. There's no doubt in any corner of her mind, in any fibre of her being, that she won't ever tire of this; that in Atalanta's arms is the perfect way to spend a life.

As they breathe themselves back to solid ground, the lighting simmers down. Their cuffs bleep in tandem, telling them to wind-down.

Wind-down, indeed.

The timing makes them both smirk. The captain must have decided to embrace the inevitable rather than forcing chaos. *Thank the heavens.*

So focused on the stars reflected in Atalanta's eyes, and her own building sensations, Jasyn hadn't noticed the gentle kisses of snowfall, drifting as though this bunk were their own personal snow-globe.

Hail. For once, is it too much to ask not to have her feelings suspended mid-air?

But her annoyance melts, its edges smooth, as Atalanta gazes at the interior weather with wonder. Affection, even. And when she catches a flake on her tongue and smiles, Jasyn can't help smiling, too.

56

REGROUP

ATALANTA

All eyes turn to Jasyn and Atalanta in the mess hall entrance, and conversation stops. With almost all the crew staring, Atalanta buries her urge to run by adjusting her tool belt.

Hylas kindly moves over to make space for her and Jasyn to sit together. The atmosphere should be more lively, but heartbeats and breaths are slowed with exhaustion or gloom. The busiest inner-activity is the buzz of healing flesh. With wounds blemishing each of the crew where vines and creepers had latched onto them, they're all varying degrees of broken and bruised.

The captain is too sombre, staring into her drink, to pay them attention. Though the stutter-step of her heartbeat when they'd both entered the room likely suggests the promise of punishment on the horizon.

Perhaps she and Jasyn will get thrown into the brig together. *Now there's an idea...*

Castor looks like she's gearing up to saying something cutting, but is interrupted by—

"No need to die of boredom, sky-critters. I'm back," Kalais

announces as she limps to the table, crutch under her armpit, her right arm in a cast and sling.

"Shouldn't you be resting?" Gus shuffles aside to give Kalais more space to manoeuvre onto the bench.

"And miss *this party*?"

Zetes grins and Castor agrees: "We're lost without you, Kal." Even Gus can't help quirking the corner of her mouth as she fills a bowl of porridge for her. Atalanta might have a few choice words to say about Kalais, but at least she's making the crew smile.

"The things you do to get out of shovelling ice," says Zetes. An almost undetectable waver in his vocal cords.

Doctor Orpheus enters the mess hall muttering something about how "apparently doctor's orders are considered optional by this crew." Her gaze remains lowered to her time-piece, without so much as accidental eye contact with any of the crew as she sits at the end of the table beside Jasyn.

The stag follows with an ungraceful and clattering attempt at navigating through the doorway. That his wounds from fighting off the snow-jungle on the crew's behalf have been swaddled in bandages, while some of the crew's injuries are still on show, might be a point for contention... but it only makes Atalanta warm a little to the grumpy doctor.

Having conquered the door frame, the stag lumbers over to Atalanta, nuzzling against her outstretched hand. It takes some concentrated ducking from Jasyn and the doctor not to get antler-swiped.

"What under the Seven Suns is the walking banquet doing in here?" Peleus puffs out his chest but his heart betrays his disquiet.

The stag responds with an antler-swipe against his side. Those antlers might not be made for sky ship doorways, but Peleus better watch out.

Peleus is quick to glare daggers as he grasps at his chest, likely forgetting his axe-knives are once again locked in the weapons hold. He casts a look at the captain, as if expecting her to exact revenge on his behalf.

"The *walking banquet* saved your crew mates," says Herakles, with sparkless eyes as she toys with her half-eaten porridge. "Anyone thinking of turning him into a meal would do well to remember that."

Peleus pouts as the doctor places a bowl of porridge on the floor for the stag who happily — messily — laps it up.

Atalanta's focus snags on Kalais, staring at Jasyn from the other end of the table. There isn't the simmering animosity in her eyes that was trained on Jasyn before. *Saving someone's life can do that*. But there's still something sharp she cannot place.

"I hear I missed you two putting on a good show," says Kalais, her glinting eyes and salacious grin pinging between Atalanta and Jasyn. "Having some fun with the Rhythm..." Kalais thrusts her hips, surly-smiling at her own crudeness.

"Kalais," Gus interjects with a dose of quiet warning.

Kalais scowls, either at Gus's chastisement or the painful realisation that thrusting with a broken arm and injured leg isn't clever.

The captain clears her throat and sits forward. "We have more important matters to discuss than the new recruits not being able to keep their hands to themselves." *(Atalanta regrets nothing.)* "We're all alive. In the circumstances, that's an achievement."

"Us being alive isn't much good if the people and planets we're here to save are obliterated before our return," interjects Kalais. The crew's answering silence acknowledges the truth in the comment.

Thumbing her mug, Herakles nods. "It's better to reach our destination via the scenic route than not at all."

"According to the ship, we've been planet-bound three months," adds Castor.

A glare from Herakles suggests that was not Castor's information to share, as whistles of disbelief and a smattering of exclamations respond — *"Heaven's hail," "Above and below,"* and from Doctor Orpheus: *"katàratos-embròntetos-euryproktos."*

Castor merely raises a defiant eyebrow at the captain. It's subtle, but enough to make clear that all is not well at the helm.

"Our delay is regrettable," continues the captain, "but we still have time."

"What happened out there?" asks Hylas.

For the next three scoops of porridge, Doctor Orpheus seems oblivious to the fact that the entire table has turned to her. On the fourth, she swallows and demands: "What?"

"I'm no sky ship scientist," says Herakles, "but I assume the crew would like your input on what happened to us."

"I am a sky ship scientist," says Gus, "and, *yes*."

With a sigh, Doctor Orpheus returns spoon to bowl. "Any injuries we each had going into the jungle," the doctor's eyes flit to Jasyn, pointedly, "didn't heal or worsen during our time on planet."

Sure enough, the doctor still has the bruise across the bridge of her nose, and Jasyn's jaw buzzes as it had before they'd landed on that world.

"For those of us who menstruate, there's no sign that we did. Monitored hormone levels suggest our bodies were suspended, cocooned from time. From my observations, and a dose of hypothesis..."

The doctor pauses to give gravity to the situation, or just to have a drink.

"The spores latched on and altered our bodies' rhythms," she continues, looking more into her mug than at the crew. She's no public speaker, that's for sure, and yet the entire crew hang on her every word. "We could've starved, dehydrated, suffocated, but the spores virtually shut us down. Trapped in our own imaginations, we were tricked into thinking we were living our best lives. Shaped by our wants, wishes, desires."

A flicker of sadness haunts the doctor's features before she overwrites it with her usual frown.

"A planet in symbiosis. The jungle used the Wrecker tech to snatch sky ships from the sky and keep a grip on prey. Vegetation and creatures working together to capture us and move us through the ground in a kind of peristalsis, storing us for sustenance, while we remained unaware, compliant, thinking everything was as we wanted it to be. Remarkable, really."

"A flytrap planet," says Jasyn, more to herself than anyone else.

Doctor Orpheus stares and it's impossible to tell whether she's impressed with Jasyn's observation or about to scold her for the interruption.

"So the marks on our skin are...?" interrupts Castor.

"Chemical burns," says the doctor, returning to her porridge. "We were lucky."

"Do Medicians believe in luck?" asks Tiphys, curious.

"They do if being left to our own devices would have meant stewing in dissolving juices."

Tiphys diverts his porridge spoon away from his mouth.

"The planet was starting to digest us," adds the doctor, matter of factly.

Stomachs lurch. Doctor Orpheus might be minded to eat, but half the crew push their bowls away. Even Peleus pauses, spoon halfway between bowl and mouth. Like the rest of the crew, itchy all of a sudden, Atalanta can't help but scratch around her patches of blotchy red skin.

"Who do we have to thank around here for saving our lives?"

says Hylas aloud and through sign, clearly on a mission to veer the conversation into more positive terrain.

The flight-techs and engine-techs shake their heads, muttering between them who saved or dug up who on-planet and in what order. Lynk and Tiphys join in, while Peleus tries to claim he was one of the first to emerge.

Herakles tilts a questioning chin at the doctor which, despite the cacophony of indecision, the whole table hone in on just as the doctor's telling gaze lands on Jasyn and Atalanta.

Jasyn offers Atalanta's hand a supportive squeeze under the table. Perhaps telling her she should take the credit. Herakles sits up a little straighter then, her heart stammering a little. Her lips form a thin smile, but she manages to sound genuine as she raises her mug:

"To the new recruits."

When others start to raise their mugs it isn't right, so Atalanta signs the truth:

"It was the princess."

Jasyn withdraws her hand from Atalanta's. Perhaps through shock or lingering exhaustion, she doesn't repeat Atalanta's words. Hylas gets there first, translating for the rest of the crew who their rescuer was.

"I was injured," explains Atalanta. "The princess saved my life."

Hylas shares her words and the crew mutter disbelief, the general consensus being that a blood thirsty ice royal doesn't play hero. Jasyn's sour grimace underscores the point, but Atalanta continues:

"Knowingly or not, we left her for dead. She could have left me for the same. She could have left us all to perish. She was physically weak, but she was brave. We sure as hail wouldn't be here without her."

A silence of collective confusion follows Hylas's translation.

Jasyn's brow is so furrowed, it's as though Atalanta has announced there's no such thing as gravity, or that Iolcus isn't covered in ice.

Herakles stands and the entire crew look to her. Her muscular physique lends her an almost battle-ready posture. Her heart is thumping as though gearing up for the same.

"I have to check on the helm," says Herakles, leaving an epic silence in her wake.

"What kind of magic was that stuff, doc?" asks Pollux, finally. Perhaps trying to change the subject, or genuinely interested. "In the cargo hold. Our blades couldn't keep up with the jungle, but whatever you threw at it—"

"Don't call me *doc*," Doctor Orpheus snaps without looking up from scooping frost-berry jam into her porridge. "And it's *not* magic," she sighs and takes several gulps of her drink, "it's Glyphosate."

At the table full of befuddled faces, Gus clarifies:

"Weed killer."

57

REALITY CHECK

JASYN

In what world under the Seven Suns is the Ice Princess a hero?

Jasyn grumbles to herself as — over the sloshing of water and suds — she listens in on the chatter in the mess hall framed by the galley hatch.

Peleus tells the group how his dream involved finding treasure and being rich and in charge of a whole world. He sounds pretty pleased with himself, until Tiphys announces he'd dreamt of finding his long lost father; an altogether more emotionally satisfying adventure. Gus shares that her inner landscape involved this trip to the skies — *ironically* — being a bad dream; that the good queen and king were still on the Iolcian throne, and that she was back on Iolcus with her family.

Jasyn bets Peleus wishes he could retract his overshare now he knows others dreamt of much more meaningful things.

"Yeah, well," announces the lazy voice of Kalais, "in my world I had a lot of *fun*. Really got my engines going, if you get my drift."

"Oh yeah?" Castor grins.

Tiphys just blushes. Peleus leans forward, a little too keen. Gus looks a little tense.

"You know what they say: work like a captain, play like a pirate." Kalais throws a wink Jasyn's way. It's so unexpected and over so quickly, Jasyn has to assume she imagined it.

For once, she's glad not to be included in the conversation. She doesn't exactly want to admit that in her imagined world she cast herself as the hero. That her mind had turned the Ice Princess into a monster of unrealistic proportions, and her defeat of the monster ingratiated her with the crew, validating her presence on this voyage. Nor that the captain gave up her quarters just so Jasyn and Atalanta could have time alone. And she's definitely not admitting to the imaginary captain making a pass at them, only for Jasyn's ego to be soothed by Atalanta only having eyes for her.

Atalanta taking centre stage in Jasyn's dreams is something she didn't need to travel the galaxy to discover. That she has a hero complex and is desperate to prove herself, she probably could have guessed.

But, seriously, in what world is the Ice Princess a hero? It has to be a misunderstanding. But how is it that Atalanta, who's ordinarily so suspicious of people, has been taken in by *her*? The same woman who's in charge of the Ice King's military. The military responsible for the attack on their village, and all the deaths that followed. One act of supposed bravery doesn't clear the slate of all that blood.

At least the ice royal is back in her cage, now.

Standing up to her imagined version of the Ice Princess had been its own kind of therapy, but it seems the main thing they've achieved so far, in escaping their own fictional adventures, is *not dying*. A low bar, but a crucial one.

And, maybe the discovery of a 'crucial artefact' that aids their journey? Maybe that makes what they've suffered and risked worth while? Without the evidence of the item in question, or a clue about what it does, or even proof that Medea and her mission aren't all in Jasyn's head... It's not exactly something she's minded to share right now.

On this voyage, she knew to expect the unexpected, but she didn't think she'd have to question what's real and what isn't.

Still, she might not have learned much about objective truths of the universe, but there is one crucial thing she has learned about herself. Namely, that on the subject of her ice-abilities, her reality falls short of her fiction.

In her dream world, she'd been in command of her sword, her ice. In the real world, she's a stuttering live-wire at risk of causing more harm than good. The interplay of her abilities and the planet may not have been hers to predict, given the unfamiliarity of the surroundings, but had she been more in-tune with her abilities, she might have been more in control.

And now, not only does she lack mastery, she's back doing the damn washing up. She sighs. Someone's got to do it, but does it always have to be her? She'd wanted for so long to take to the skies, to explore and discover, to be part of something bigger. Atalanta, who wanted none of this, is a crucial cog in the machine, while Jasyn is stuck *again* with her fingers pruning in the suds.

She stares at the water as it threads with ice.

"What's got your shorts in a twist?"

Jasyn's hands splash within the water as she turns. There in the doorway is Kalais, leant on her crutch, looking her up and down. Even with one arm in a sling and limping, she has the knack of seeming like she might murder her.

"I suppose you think you're tough stuff?" Kalais's indecipherable tone has Jasyn keeping watch in the same way she'd observe a predator on the prowl. She tries not to tense as Kalais joins her at the sink. "Rescuing me? Saving my life?"

This is definitely a trap...

A sheen of sweat occupies Kalais's brow. It reminds Jasyn of the doctor painfully manipulating her arm and the desperate squeeze of Kalais's body against hers. *Human*. She's only human.

She lets Kalais loiter a moment longer, before letting out her breath. She's had enough. If she can stand up to an Ice Princess, even in her imagination, she can stand up to an engine-tech with an attitude problem.

"Look, Kalais. I don't know what your problem is..." Or maybe she does... hadn't she proven herself a loose cannon in causing Zetes's neck to burn with ice? Perhaps that's what Kalais is here to punish her for... She'd apologised to him when they'd been in the engine chamber: "Just another war wound," he'd shrugged.

"About what happened to your brother, I know an apology doesn't undo the damage. I don't want to hurt anyone. I'm here to learn to be better. I get that you don't like me. That you think my ice is a hazard and I know I've yet to prove you wrong. You don't have to treat me with respect — I won't ask the impossible — but criminals are treated better than how you treat me. When I ask questions I'm not trying to be difficult, I'm trying to learn. When I'm in the same room as you I'm not trying to annoy you. All I want..." No, that's too much to ask. She rephrases. "...the *minimum* I want to achieve on this voyage is to be useful. You don't have to like me, but can you give me that? And maybe not mess with my comms or astro-suit in the process?"

"Okay," says Kalais.

What?

"That's it? *Okay*?" Jasyn searches Kalais's face for any sign of sarcasm or budding cruelty. *How is it as simple as that?*

Kalais shrugs, then grits her teeth. "Heaven's hail, you'd think I'd remember not to keep moving my shoulder." She growls at herself before attempting to look nonchalant. "I had this whole heart-tugging speech about how you saved my life and how it's made me reassess my actions and how I treat others..."

Jasyn studies her. "No you didn't..."

Kalais smirks. "No. I didn't. But it might have been pointed out to me that I can be a monumental asshole. Apparently, if you figuratively shit on people, you get called an asshole." Kalais quirks her mouth and rolls her eyes as if to say *Who knew?*

"A *monumental* asshole," Jasyn corrects, testing the waters.

Kalais's blank expression could veer in either direction. Jasyn is quietly relieved when Kalais chuckles.

"Are you here to tell me I have to get to work in the engine chamber?" asks Jasyn.

"Nah." Kalais's smile is sly. "Engine fuel is cumulative. We're good."

Cumulative? Jasyn hasn't forgotten asking whether they were going to run out of fuel if they kept feeding the engine, back when she'd been virtually held hostage in the engine chamber. Then, Kalais had simply said no. Guess she stomachs her enough now to explain things a little and not trick her into doing needless back and spirit-breaking tasks. *Progress?*

"I'll take your washing up shift," says Kalais. "Even things out."

"You mess with my comms, risking my life. I save your life, and you offer to take on the washing up? The washing up that you said was 'the only thing I could be trusted with'? The washing up that I've almost finished?"

Kalais mumbles something about Jasyn being "too damn sensitive" and then does something Jasyn has never witnessed her do in their conversations. Well, not conversations, exactly, as Kalais has so far only really barked orders and insults at her. Kalais *smiles*, cheekily, at her. "Sounds about right to me," she says, doubling down on that smile.

"You're being nice to me," says Jasyn, suspicious. "Are you

sure we're not still stuck on that planet and this is all wishful thinking?"

"Wishful thinking? If washing up is the limit of your imagination..." Kalais pauses, a spark of mischief in her eyes. "Unless saving my life is all part of your fantasy?"

The sudden flirtation in her tone catches Jasyn off guard. The plate in her hand almost slips. *Hail. That took a turn.* It doesn't help that Jasyn hadn't moved over enough and Kalais squaring up to the sink has them almost pressed together. Apparently, Kalais has the knack for holding a smouldering stare.

Double hail.

Being in her presence has evolved from worrying she's going to be pushed into the furnace, to worrying she's going to be pushed against—

"You've got a broken arm," interjects Doctor Orpheus as she passes her mug through the serving hatch. "No getting the cast or dressing wet."

Kalais's wry features and the way she looks Jasyn up and down suggests she's about to say something crude. Before she can, the doctor clarifies "*No washing up,*" and leaves.

Though not welcoming the doctor snatching away the offer of someone else doing the most boring task under the Seven Suns, Jasyn is relieved for the get-out clause and to have the tension broken.

"Doctor's orders." Kalais smirks, reinstating a distance between them but not losing the flirtatious edge. "But there's no getting out of engine duties, Snowflake," she says in a more matter of fact tone. "I'm on bed rest."

She throws her a wink before leaving.

What the hail? Did anyone else witness that display? Beyond the hatch, no-one's looking her way and there's a certain lack of energy amongst the group.

Gus stares intently into the bottom of her mug, as if it might contain berry tea and sadness. Tiphys is similarly sombre. Evidently, having your own version of a perfect life snatched away can result in bouts of gloom.

Chipper as ever, Lynk shares details of the epic thunderstorms she'd experienced in her deadly slumber, entertaining Castor and Zetes, at least. Peleus doesn't hide his boredom, but he at least keeps quiet.

"How do we know we're not all still trapped?" asks Tiphys, in a voice flatter than the Iolcian plains.

The crew fall silent and no-one responds. Because, *really*, how would they know? And that's more chilling than Kalais's flirtation.

58

THE LEAP

ATALANTA

Ship repairs and engine chamber duties have tired them both, not to mention the fact that their bodies are trying to recover from what the snow-jungle has put them through. At least for now their schedules have been allowed to remain in alignment. Which means — *thank the heavens* — being able to occupy a bunk together.

At least now Atalanta can breathe a sigh of contentment, enjoying the warmth of Jasyn pressed naked against her as she lazily traces the freckles decorating her collar bone.

"What was it like, in your invented world?" asks Jasyn, smiling under her touch.

Atalanta's contentment dissipates. Her eyes flick to the bunk hatch. Tired as she may be, she considers leaving the bunk and burying herself in ship tasks so that they might never have this conversation.

Jasyn must feel her tense, see her tense, *hail*, even hear her tense — Atalanta doesn't exactly disguise it.

"You look like you want to run," whispers Jasyn, concern etched in her features.

She's right. If they were in the Glowing Woods, or the village, she'd dart away and avoid this conversation, like she has for more than half their lives. But even if she tried to run right now, with an injured leg she wouldn't get far. And on a sky ship, where is there to hide?

But they'd promised to be better, hadn't they? Back on Iolcus they'd promised to communicate. And Atalanta's had enough of keeping Jasyn at a distance. But Jasyn needs to know the truth.

Atalanta readjusts her position. She tries to get comfortable, because for Jasyn to understand, she's going to have to go the scenic route.

"It was perfect," she signs. "At first. It was — or I imagined it was — the world my parents were from. You and I, we made our home there." *Hail, how she wishes that had been real.* Another steadying breath allows some mischief to peek through: "We did a lot of this." Atalanta gestures between their bodies.

Jasyn grins ear to ear. "I can't say that wasn't a theme in my imaginings, too." Jasyn leans forward to kiss her, but Atalanta places a stilling palm to her chest. It would be so easy to lose themselves in intimacy and never have this conversation.

But that's the coward's way out.

She wants to kiss Jasyn, she wants to smile, but other thoughts are getting in her way. Jasyn must have noticed Atalanta's shift in mood and is echoing it with her own, because the temperature has dropped enough for their breaths to clash.

Atalanta stretches her fingers and palms, ready to broach the subject she's avoided her whole life.

"There are things about me you don't know." She rolls her eyes at herself at sounding so *mysterious*. "There are so many things about myself I don't know. But I need you to understand why I kept you at arm's length for so long. And I need you to know why the skies terrify me."

Jasyn's light scowl suggests she's wondering how the two topics are related, but she nods for Atalanta to continue.

"You've spent your life looking to the stars. I've spent mine trying to escape them. For you, the stars are a source of endless wonder, the promise of adventure. For me..." *A deep and unsteady breath.* "...between the stars, that's where my home, my family, fell apart. It's where my parents' bond withered to oblivion. It's where I almost died." *For the first time.*

Atalanta can see the sorrow on her behalf, and the thousand questions too, in the shimmering silver of Jasyn's eyes. She proceeds to tell her about her childhood, growing up in the skies before she ever knew anything of a planet gripped by ice, nor a charming lopsided smile.

She tells her about when they'd run out of fuel, but not yet run out of food, and about when their water filtration system threatened the end and their navigation system had bowed out long ago. She tells Jasyn about her games with bow and arrows in space. How Father had chosen the abyss, or it had chosen him. And how it felt to be suspended amongst the stars, on the precipice of death, oxygen and time running out.

Giving her breath, Mother had welcomed her into her arms with blood on her hands and tears in her eyes. That she'd chosen Atalanta's life over Father's is a strange victory. And Atalanta will never know whether he untethered her as a backwards kindness so she'd die quickly instead of starving as rations ran out, or whether he was prolonging his life over theirs.

Irony had interjected, and it hadn't been long after that that they'd happened across the Ice Planet. Luck or design had grasped them from the skies. It was then Atalanta had learned the plummeting pull of gravity and the crushing push of atmospheric pressure. The sound of ripping metal. She'd learned through experience to fear the space between stars, and what happens when falling from it.

Telling Jasyn all of this, the discussion is so new to them, there are signed words Jasyn doesn't understand. There are so many words Atalanta wishes she didn't have to say. When a tear spills down her cheek, Jasyn catches it with her thumb and smooths it away, and Atalanta can't help but lean into the touch.

"At first I didn't tell you because I didn't know you," Atalanta signs. "When we first met in the mountains, we couldn't communicate well enough. Then, I wasn't sure what to share. You had a thousand questions but—"

"That doesn't sound like me," signs Jasyn with a playful nudge.

"I didn't know if I was strong enough to revisit the past I wanted to leave behind."

With her understanding nods, it's clear Jasyn is doing all she can to give Atalanta the space she needs to tell her story. Because none of this answers why she didn't tell Jasyn. Not really. Nor does it answer why she put distance between them for so long.

Another deep breath, another hand stretch.

"Mother taught me to never trust anyone. I wasn't meant to be your friend. I was meant to keep my distance. In the mountains I watched you from afar. I saw how you survived by foraging, never hurting creatures. I thought: *if you can do it…* When I told Mother, she got angry. She told me I'd never survive with an outlook like that. She always told me…"

Atalanta hesitates at the words that have haunted her her whole life. Even on her dying breath, she hadn't told Atalanta she loved her more than the stars, or that she'd see her again one day. She'd simply told her what she'd told her every day of her life in the Unforgiving Mountains: *"Be the hunter, not the prey."*

It gives her chills to repeat it for Jasyn now.

"To make a point, she tasked me with…" Her stomach twists. Bile threatens her throat. Jasyn's fingers thread through hers, giving her hand a comforting squeeze. Atalanta reclaims her shaking hand. Because this is something she can't sign one handed. And it's unlikely Jasyn will still want to hold her hand once she tells her: "...to prove I was *the hunter*, she tasked me with hunting you."

She grimaces, awaiting judgement. Only silence follows, and in Jasyn's expression she detects... confusion? *Affection?* She tries to listen for clues to Jasyn's disposition in her heartbeat, her breathing, but her own is clogging her thoughts.

"Okay," says Jasyn.

Atalanta scowls. "I'm telling you I was meant to *kill you* and you say *Okay*?"

"I mean, don't get me wrong, I'm not *thrilled*. But if you recall when we first met, you had an arrow pointed at my head. You made a strong first impression. You were tasked with hunting me? Well, unless you're playing the long game, I'd say you didn't exactly do a good job."

Atalanta lets that sink in. How can Jasyn be so... *understanding* of all this?

Arrow through chest...

Jasyn's eyes, vacant...

Atalanta recoils, but there's only so far she can go in a bunk and *heaven's hail,* with the movement, pain both sharp and dull radiates up from her leg, enough for her to cry out and tears to spill.

"Hey, hey, it's okay," soothes Jasyn. Reaching for her strewn aside vest, she dabs at Atalanta's cheeks. "Talk to me."

Atalanta lets the horror of what happened in the realm of her dreams and nightmares shudder through her.

"I knew your feelings for me..." Affection peeks through the cloud of Atalanta's worries. "They weren't just written on your face, they were written in the skies."

She loves that Jasyn blushes at that. "Yeah, I guess sunshine and blizzards aren't exactly subtle."

This is why it's taken her so long to share who she is. She swipes the new tears streaming hot against her cheeks. *She can't lose this.*

"My feelings for you scare me," Atalanta's hands shake at the confession. "In the mountains, I loved chasing you. In the Glowing Woods, even more so. It terrifies me that my... *enjoyment* might be linked to being a hunter. That the thrill I experienced would somehow bring you harm."

Father tried to kill her. Mother killed him and brought her up to be a hunter. If that's where she's come from, if that's what's been designated for her, can she be anything else?

"In my imagined world — my nightmare — I killed you with my arrows." Atalanta tenses, bracing for her world to crumble.

Jasyn opens and closes her mouth a few times. "Is that... everything?" she asks, carefully. Atalanta frowns and nods. *What else could there be?*

"Atalanta. Do you have any idea how amazing you are?" Jasyn eyes light up.

Amazing? What? "That's your takeaway from all this?"

"How can it not be? You made an impossible decision," signs Jasyn. "You went against the one person who'd been constant in your life. The person tasked with teaching you how to *be*. But you chose your own path. That makes you brave. Incredible. I know you'd never hurt me. I'm so lucky, so grateful — so honoured, proud, happy — that we're here, that you're my..." She pauses, as if searching for the word. "*...my protector*." The way she gestures the words, as if the title were official, makes Atalanta laugh. Which seems to make Jasyn smile. "And I'm yours."

Jasyn threads their fingers together and Atalanta breathes easier as she thumbs the triangular scar on Jasyn's palm. She'd always thought it looked like a simplistic depiction of a mountain in the clouds.

When Atalanta confides that she suspects taking to the skies has reopened old wounds, that she's been seeing the shadow shape of Mother, Jasyn asks:

"Is she here, now?"

Atalanta shakes her head.

"Good. Because, y'know..." Jasyn's gestures to their naked bodies, "...that would be super weird."

A laugh bursts from Atalanta's chest, and from Jasyn's too. *Heavens above and below,* laughing together is the most effective balm.

Atalanta snuggles her cheek against Jasyn's shoulder. Exhaustion knocks at the door of her body and mind, and as they settle into sleep, she welcomes the gentle thrum of their heartbeats and the breath in their lungs *whooshing* like a breeze between trees.

59

BREATHE

JASYN

Z
z Z

The nerve-splicing sensation of an ice-sword blooms sharp within your chest, only for you to witness it's not your chest the sword is splitting, but Atalanta's.

Instead of Medea looming over the both of you, it's the Ice King. The sounds of the Iolcian Games arena are distant, waterlogged, as his sour snarl taunts you and his words burn like acid in your ears:

"Just a little girl who can't control her ice."

Those are the words he'd said as he took your life with your own ice-sword. Doctor Orpheus might have healed the physical injuries, but those words had cut deeper than your flesh.

But when the sword is plucked from flesh, it's the Ice Princess standing over you both with a gloating grin.

Atalanta's body hangs limp, her eyes without the spark of life. You know this is a nightmare, you know it's not real. But the utter despair hammering through your veins and pulsing your vision, that isn't imagined.

You wrap your arms around Atalanta to shield her, even though it's too late, only to be surrounded by ice—

The arena has disappeared.

The sword is gone.

The ice royals, too.

You don't need to observe the details of this space to know you're in the wagon's blanket box. To sneak through the Ice City gates, to trick the heat detectors and gateway guards, you'd turned the container into an ice box. You'd been terrified that in doing so you'd steal Atalanta's life with your ice, and now she lies frozen beneath you—

✦

JASYN WAKES WITH A GASP, CLUNKING HER HEAD ON THE BUNK'S cold ceiling. Bulbous ice-formations have latticed across the curved ceiling and walls like an infection, and for a moment she can't figure out if she's still in her nightmare. The ghost of the dream lingers in the crystallised panic.

Her breath must be matching the temperature, or thereabouts, as hardly a haze emerges as she gasps, fast and shallow.

She flexes her hands, tingling, aching and rigid with ice. Sweat cools and burns her skin. Wearing nothing, the white light pulses the branching network of her veins.

Atalanta isn't here. *Thank the heavens.* If she had been, what would have happened? Would she have woken Jasyn? Calmed her? Or would Jasyn's nightmares have been realised?

The last thing she wants is to hurt her. Or anyone, for that matter.

Those who despised the idea of an ice-monger aboard a sky ship might have been right.

"Just fucking breathe," says the voice of Doctor Orpheus in her thoughts.

She tries. Attempting to rein in her racing pulse, she swipes at the sweat beaded to hail on her brow. The pellets pull at her skin, frozen within her pores. What a mess. It's clearer than a golden day that Jasyn's inner landscape is far from calm. And she doesn't miss the irony that she's the one with the ability to turn everything to ice, yet Atalanta's the one confessing fears of doing harm.

Should Jasyn have shared her own fears? That she's terrified all she does is drag Atalanta into the path of danger? Should she have told her that as much as Atalanta is afraid of hurting her, Jasyn fears she'll do the same?

It's not that she's actively keeping her fears from her, it's just there's a lot going on — with mountain bears, Medea, apparitions of lost friends and family — and last night she'd wanted to focus on Atalanta. She hadn't wanted to layer on more things to worry about.

"Just fucking breathe."

At the doctor's words — abrupt even in her imagination — the stomach-souring terror starts to dull and drip away. The white-pulsing of her veins calms and her steadying breaths start to reach out in plumes.

The ice around her melts and her fears turn to frustration. She has this epic power and all she can do is wet the damn bed.

Her cuff chimes with the green icon of a caduceus, summoning her to medical.

60

OVERSEER

ATALANTA

Electricity flows through the ship like blood through veins. Ship components *turn* and *click* and *whistle* and make every other sound they're supposed to. And some they're not supposed to. But the weight of *those* sounds isn't something to worry about. At least, not imminently.

Still, there's always something that needs attention. Jasyn might be on a mission to discover the magic of the skies, but Atalanta's mission is to ensure that they survive them, to ensure the invisible claws of space never get to dig in.

The captain had determined Atalanta's 'punishment' for going against the Rhythm as "cleaning all the windows and portholes on the ship, inside and out." When Atalanta had paled at the addition of "and out," the captain had backtracked so that only "inside" is required. Which makes Atalanta think perhaps the so-called punishment is more for show than actually to make her suffer.

The skies might not be throwing arrows at her right now — there are no more memories tapping at the porthole of her mind — and she might no longer be vomiting her guts out at the idea of being drowned in the ocean of space, but that doesn't mean she has any desire to be suspended in it.

Maybe in time she'll be able to conquer the second half of her 'punishment' without fearing being left to suffocate, but for now she's happy to be able to square up to each porthole and not shrink from what's on the other side.

The skies may be a place of death, but they're also where she first triumphed over it. It's where Mother chose her. It's also where she now gets to claim time with Jasyn (ship schedules and possibly irrational captain allowing). At least the ship and Atalanta's attitude are now heading in a more positive direction.

She reaches for the cleaning rag hanging on the stag's antlers. With each spray of cleaning fluid and each wipe of cloth, she welcomes the opportunity to check on the porthole components and confirm their integrity. Given that she'd been meaning to check over every inch of the ship, anyway, this isn't really a punishment at all.

She checks the apex of the main deck is holding strong, doubly reinforced by ice and glass offcuts engineered into place (the former thanks to Jasyn, the latter thanks to a team effort by Atalanta and Gus).

She wanders the ship's corridors, methodically adjusting and cleaning as she goes. *Where is Gus?* The clinking of a tool belt has Atalanta Transonically honing in on the medical quarters.

A solid knock at the medical chamber door ripples over the impressive, if brooding, form of the captain. After a crackle of intercom static, and electricity zipping along connections to un-hitch the lock, the door's hinges *screech* (Atalanta makes a mental note to sort that) as the captain steps inside. She must have taken on board that the medical chamber isn't a place to burst into.

"You wanted to discuss something?" The captain's voice contains gentle authority, perhaps with a dose of concern.

"She's being all mysterious about it," says Doctor Orpheus in a vaguely teasing tone.

"I recovered the deleted overseer records," says Gus and Atalanta abandons any consideration of leaving them to their privacy. She wants to know what happened to their ship. How they ended up so far off course and nearly lost their lives in the process.

Hang, on, wasn't the captain meant to be the one checking for deleted records? Something about the captain's demeanour must be suggesting the question, because Gus explains:

"You're both busy. Atalanta's doing a great job with the repairs. I had some time, so I put it to good use. The records were buried deep. Took some reconstructing."

"I assume you found something?" asks Herakles, as two sets of footsteps follow Gus to an ice-screen terminal.

"What are we watching, here?" asks Doctor Orpheus. Atalanta can only guess that Gus has transferred the details to the screen.

"Seems we're watching someone in a dark robe hiding in the shadows," says Herakles, "creeping up on Pollux at the helm."

"I mean, I can see that," says Doctor Orpheus. "But that's my gown."

"Yes," says Gus. "And that's them playing your V-iolin, sending Pollux to sleep. I had to mute it. The first time I listened it sent me to sleep."

"The fuck...? Someone on board knows how to play—"

"And that's them toying with the helm's co-ordinates," Herakles commentates. "And looking right into the overseer lens."

"*Es kórakas,*" says the doctor. Her heart rate accelerates. Gus's too. Herakles's, only a little.

A tense silence stretches between the three of them and Atalanta wishes she could see what they're observing. She pauses tightening a porthole nut to focus on listening in.

"The records were deleted by console commands. I didn't know you knew how to do that." It's difficult to decipher whether Gus is impressed or disappointed.

"I don't. *Aphòdeuma.* I don't know what the fuck this is about. I was asleep. When I woke, we were off course. I'm not going to say it isn't me. I'm not an idiot. Clear as a fucking frost-filled morning, *that's me*. But I don't know *how*. Or *why*. Fuck. You have to know I wouldn't do anything to endanger the mission, or anyone on this ship."

The doctor's vocal cords tighten. Atalanta wonders what emotion she's straining to keep in check.

"I do know," says Herakles.

The air in the room shifts a little as Gus nods.

"It's the only reason neither of us are using our outside voices on you right now," adds Herakles. "Well, me, my outside voice. Gus only has an indoor voice."

"It could be an extension of the planet's ability to reach out to trap us," says the doctor, "but I don't know... I feel like I'm the one reaching..." Judging from the footsteps, shifting air and the pulsing beacon of her circulatory system, Doctor Orpheus is busy pacing.

"What are you feeling?" asks Gus.

"*Frustrated*," replies Doctor Orpheus, pausing, her foot tapping a nervous rhythm, "that I can't explain it. *Freaked out.* About going to sleep ever again. *Worried.* That you'll think I did something to endanger the crew, the ship. *Fucking terrified.* That I'm not in control of my faculties. My actions nearly ended our journey, our lives. Not knowing how it happened, I can't guarantee it won't happen again. *Fuck.*"

"The situation isn't ideal..." says the captain, in what

Atalanta assumes must be a purposeful understatement. Her biceps contract as she scratches the back of her neck.

Doctor Orpheus grunts in agreement.

"We'll figure it out," adds Gus.

"What would you do if you were me?" asks Herakles.

"Getting me to your job for you, Captain?" Doctor Orpheus snarks before sighing. "I'd lock me up. Keep me under surveillance."

Herakles's footsteps pace for several moments before they stop, a sense of decision drifting through the airwaves.

"You'll stick to medical quarters day and night, only leaving for meals with the crew and exercise. It's probably best if, where possible, you keep to yourself. Would you agree with my assessment, Chief?" asks Herakles.

"Yes, Captain," replies Gus, and Atalanta can hear the slight smile in her voice.

So, that's business as usual, then? The tension in the doctor's muscles slackens with her relief.

"We'll have to keep track of your whereabouts, though," adds the captain.

"I'd think you're idiots if you didn't," the doctor agrees.

There must be some sort of non-verbal exchange, because Gus's footsteps head out of the chamber and the door *screeches* and *clunks* behind her.

"So... " begins the doctor. "You want to know why I volunteered to go through the overseer recordings? Because that makes me look fucking guilty, right?"

Air shifts at the captain's slight nod.

"Well... I know you know I'd been living on this ship while it was stored in the workshop," says the doctor. "And, well... Sound carries on an empty ship." She clears her throat. There's a smile in her voice as she says: "I assume you thought I wasn't in on a few occasions."

Now it's Herakles's turn to clear her throat, as her jaw and neck tighten.

"I had a suspicion that there were more deleted overseer records," says the doctor. "I thought Gus might get curious and unlock those, too. I didn't think you'd want her seeing you and your conquests in all your... glory. That's all."

Blood rushes to the captain's cheeks.

"Oh." As she clears her throat again, her jaw and neck relax a little. "That's actually very nice of you."

"Why'd you say it like that? *I am nice.*"

"Yeah, yeah," Herakles smirks. "You can just admit to wanting to see me in all my glory, you know?"

"*Exòloio, Herakles,*" the doctor snaps before her tone lightens: "Oh, that reminds me, I need to put together an anti-nausea medication for any of the ground-hoggers who aren't adjusting."

"Ha ha."

"No, I actually do need to do that."

"Do you think Gus unlocked the other logs?" Herakles's tension returns a little.

"I think she likely approached the logs chronologically, most recent first, found the one with me at the helm doing something *inexplicably stupid*, summoned you, then marched in here to give me a piece of her mind."

A creak suggests the doctor is leaning back in her desk chair.

"I don't suppose," the doctor continues, "you were ridiculous enough to bring anyone to the ship who might have been stupid enough to report its existence to the Iolcian guard? Because, you know, then you would kind of be responsible for the Ice King's military trying to mow us down."

Herakles tuts. "Nice try, Orpheus. I think we can safely say, given the mysterious helm-footage, that there's something going on with *you*, which is far more likely linked to our sabotage predicament."

Doctor Orpheus sighs. "Yeah. It just would have been great for it to have been your fault and not mine."

"We'll figure this out, Orpheus," says the captain, softly. "Though, ironically, I dare say you're the one best equipped to do so."

A *clunk-clunk* of metal. Loud. Close. It bungees Atalanta's focus back to her corridor where an unimpressed snorting snuffle gives the answer of *who* and *why*.

Clunk-clunk — the fawn-turned-stag isn't having the best luck with doorways today. He saunters over for Atalanta to give his muzzle a good scratch.

Transonically returning to the medical quarters—

Gurgle-gurgle-glug-glug...

The doctor must have switched on the ice-melt shower facility in the adjacent chamber, because the water escaping down the drain snatches Atalanta's focus into the piping network. The water's spiralling, labyrinthine journey through the ship lands her in the region of the cargo hold where it collects in a cleansing tank.

In the hold, Gus *ratchets* the mechanisms of the tri-ice-cycle, dealing with its bumps and bruises. Keeping her company, Lynk gives an extensive rundown on her thoughts regarding the jungle planet's weather and its effects on her allergies.

While Atalanta continues her component integrity checks and porthole cleaning, she idly listens to ship mechanisms ticking over. That the ship sounds broadly in order soothes her. She only hopes that the doctor isn't the human equivalent of a malfunctioning machine part and that the captain and chief engineer's trust isn't misplaced.

61

CURIOSITY

JASYN

Heart and lungs are working out of tandem. Oxygen evades her.

As Jasyn winds her way towards the medical chamber, she replays the doctor's words over and over — *"Just fucking breathe."* — trying to distract herself from the tightness in her chest and the ache of ice in her forearm. Sure, there's a chance the doctor is going to throw her in the quarantine chamber, but maybe that's what's best for everyone right now.

That whisper... That song...

The captain had insisted Jasyn's sword, along with all other sharp implements, be returned to the weapons hold.

Should she be worried that she can pinpoint where her sword is?

Wherever she is in the ship, whichever way she's facing, even with her eyes closed, she can point to where her sword rests. It's as though there's some tether strengthening between her and the sword. She can't explain it. She can sense the percolation of activity within the hilt. A parallel to her own unsettled state.

That she'd been able to invite the weapon to her palm when she and Kalais were threatened with claws and fangs is an eye opening development. Something to explore with the doctor, perhaps?

If only she could hold her sword now. It doesn't feel like the most well-balanced of instincts. What logic is there in being calmed by holding a blade?

Clack-clack-cl-clack-clack...

That unwelcome and familiar sound of claws against rock scratches into her mind. That hair prickling sensation of being watched. Jasyn sighs. As if panic and nightmares aren't enough, she still has to deal with after-effects of death, too?

Which are what, exactly? Echoes from the afterlife? Visitations from the dead? Manifestations of her own guilt? She might have been brave enough to set foot in the bear cave in her nightmares, but that doesn't mean she's unravelled the underlying issues haunting her mind.

She tries for a deep breath but manages only an unsatisfying one as she squares up to the green tinted door of the medical quarters. She rubs her sternum to soothe the tightness and winces when she snags against the claw wounds.

The unmistakeable sounds of an ice-melt shower emanate from the chamber. Without thinking, instead of knocking, she tries the door handle. The mechanisms *thunk* and the door opens.

Once inside, she locates the source of the ice-melt shower warring with rattling pipes in the closed door room behind the doctor's desk. A muffled chuckle from the doctor, as if in response to a joke, piques Jasyn's interest, distracting her from her panic.

Try as she might, she can't identify another voice. Despite being an actual grown-up, the idea of the doctor in the shower with someone makes Jasyn smirk. *Who's in there with her?*

As much as Jasyn would love to discover the answer to that

question, to find out who the doctor welcomes into her orbit, she doesn't want to startle — or be startled by — a naked doctor.

"Doctor Orpheus?" she calls out.

There's a pause, followed by the doctor's usual "Fuck" and various other sounds that are most likely swear words, warring with the sounds of the ice-melt, along with something about a "locked door" and then — louder — words instructing Jasyn to "under no circumstances touch a fucking thing."

Which is always the worst thing to say to someone whose default setting is *curious*. An unsupervised medical chamber is too much to pass up and snooping — no, *exploring* — almost always calms Jasyn's nerves.

Though the inked out black box of the quarantine chamber in the corner of the medical quarters, lodged like an ice-sword in her thoughts, does little to calm her.

She's not sure whether it'd be better or worse to see the Ice Princess through the walls. At least if she could see her she'd be sure she's actually in there, locked away, not roaming the ship and plotting... *whatever it is* a power hungry, untrustworthy Ice Princess plots.

Beneath a large porthole, peppered with stars, stands a grand piano. Though Jasyn's fingers itch to press the keys, the sounds would immediately give her away.

The lamp-lit doctor's desk is occupied by her medician case. It's so tempting to peek, to find out what's in there, but she's distracted mid-reach by the sweet scent of honey and the crackling of flames.

Jasyn turns. Purple eyes flicker, reflecting flames that aren't there. As if trained in the art of *bad timing*, the familiar figure of Medea lingers, but only for a stuttering moment, like a synaptic misfire or a faulting electrical current. *Good riddance.* She'd happily never set eyes on Medea again.

Jasyn continues her exploration. Vials within perspex

fronted shelves contain leaves with blemishes not unlike root rot. That the doctor is investigating such things piques Jasyn's interest further.

She reaches, only for eyes of purple flame to ignite right in front of her. Medea's dark robes take shape, but lack definition, as if to confirm she isn't entirely here, or that Jasyn *isn't entirely there*. Imagined or not, Jasyn instinctively steps away.

"What do you want?" she hisses, aware that the doctor will emerge from the neighbouring chamber any moment, and that her own list of physical, mental and emotional ailments is long enough without adding *apparition who lured them onto the planet that nearly killed them.*

"You are displeased with me," says the lyrical voice, more in alignment with the woman's mouth movements than ever before. "My intention wasn't to hurt you, Jasyn of Iol—"

"Stop saying the whole thing. Just call me Jasyn. Or don't call me anything. I don't want to see you. I don't want to talk to you. I want you out of my head."

"Jasyn," says the voice with a melodious undercurrent, as if testing out the shape of the word alone. "But if you don't talk to me, you won't get the answers to your questions."

Jasyn huffs, hardly taking in any details of the medical chambers, with this new distraction. "As if you'll answer my questions. Your only setting is *mysterious*."

"If you don't ask, then I cannot answer..."

Jasyn huffs again. Never mind locating an artefact, Medea's main mission must be to piss her off.

"You knew..." says Jasyn, the puzzle pieces falling not quite into place, but at least landing the right way up.

"I know many things, Jasyn of—" She stops herself with a wry smile. "I know many things, *Jasyn*. You'll have to be more specific."

There's something different... There's a lyrical undercurrent of

Medea's own language still there, but it's less pronounced and there's almost no delay in the translation.

"How can I understand you now?" asks Jasyn. "Your words..."

When Medea smiles, she looks nothing like a sword-wielding murderer and everything like someone pleased to receive a compliment on her creativity.

"I've finessed my conversion tincture."

Jasyn nods as if she understands, which she doesn't. Not really. She has far too many questions to pretend knowledge of anything.

"Seems mighty convenient. We land on a world that explores our minds when you wanted something hidden in mine?"

"I'm not sure on your definition of convenient," replies the lyrical voice. "It took some orchestration. Trudging into the dark recesses of a mindscape with an unwilling participant hasn't felt particularly *convenient* to me."

Jasyn's not sure what to say to that. She hadn't expected Medea, Guardian of the Golden Fleece, haunting presence in her dreams, nightmares, days and nights, and ongoing thorn in her side, to be facetious. But she hasn't denied her involvement.

Pipes shudder from the adjoining room. The doctor must have switched off the ice-melt. The air-blast stutters, accompanied by muffled swear words.

"You thought sending us to a planet where we'd be eaten alive was a good idea?" Jasyn hisses.

Any playfulness in Medea's demeanour dissipates. "I admit, things did not take place in the manner I expected. The risk was calculated. But in hindsight, I did not have all the details. I'd planned for a much swifter visit. I didn't appreciate how challenging it would be to bridge the gap between your imagination and memories."

"We were there for months."

"I am aware." The purple-fire in Medea's eyes disguises whether she's regretful or offering stern warning.

"Was risking all our lives worth it?"

"That is yet to be determined..."

Jasyn scoffs. *The audacity.*

"...but we found what we needed."

"What 'artefact' is so important? And, for that matter: how did you know you'd find it in my memories? What are the chances of the artefact and the person you need being in the same range of mountains on one tiny planet? The universe is too vast for it be coincidence."

Jasyn takes a breath. Her lungs aren't happy. Because the contents of *her mind* being the reason they'd somehow detoured to a mind-invading carnivorous planet is somewhat stressful.

"Coincidence is a fascinating phenomenon," says Medea with a smirk.

Jasyn's curiosity coils to frustration. She opens her mouth to express as much, but Medea interjects —

"But, no. This is not coincidence."

That day, up in the mountains, Jasyn had felt the pull of something. Something drawing her in, inviting her higher. In hindsight, she'd thought it her own misguided curiosity. But, now? Now she wonders whether her strings were being pulled, whether she'd been lured there for the sake of finding something.

"You made me go into the cave. Not just in my nightmares. You made me overstep in the mountains." Which would mean Medea is the reason Jasyn explored too far? Is it possible *she's the reason* Atalanta's mother was lost to the mountain bear's claws, and why they left the mountains in the first place?

Jasyn's not sure whether to be angry or, selfishly, relieved. She'd welcome the events of that day not being her fault. She'd welcome them never having happened in the first place. She'd like to know whether the anger she's aimed at herself all these sun-orbits should be aimed at Medea instead.

"Is it not better to be guilty of your actions, than not be in control of them?" asks Medea, her smile suggesting she's enjoying the philosophical diversion.

Never mind which one is better, which one is the truth?

"It is not possible to make you do anything, Jasyn." Medea adds, quickly. No doubt the mist hazing around Jasyn is communicating loud and clear her frustration. "An invitation is only that."

Well, that's an answer firmly in the grey, isn't it? Though she'd welcome the chance to shift the burden of blame off her shoulders, it's not the most pressing issue.

"How did the artefact end up in the mountains?" Jasyn reiterates her question.

"It will take time, and several perspectives, to explain..." Medea glances at the closed door of the adjoining chamber. The doctor's muffled swearing remind that there's a time-limit on this discussion. "...but it can be summed up as *Fleece technology seeks fleece technology*."

Jasyn splutters as her words emerge: "Fleece *technology*? You mean it's not magic?"

Not that Jasyn believes in magic — apart from maybe Iolcian Ice Swords and life-restoring V-iolins, at a push... but even then, she's sure there must be other explanations — but to hear the so-called Guardian of the Golden Fleece confirm it as technology... well... she's sure the curious doctor wishes she were part of this conversation.

Medea raises an eyebrow. A vaguely patronising eyebrow at that. "I suppose that depends on your definition of both." Her mouth twitches. At least one of them is finding this blood-from-a-stone discussion amusing.

"The artefact is Fleece technology..." explains Medea.

Jasyn rubs her temples. She'd had a Fleece artefact within her reach and she'd been distracted by a stupid broach? It's enough to give her a headache.

"So, Iolcus already has the Golden Fleece?"

"It has an artefact of Fleece technology. It's not the same."

Jasyn scratches her head. Is it possible for her brain to hurt?

"As I was saying," continues Medea, "The artefact is Fleece technology, and your sword is Fleece technology."

Jasyn's mouth goes dry. "My sword... is Fleece technology?" She tries to wrap her mind around the words, to examine them, absorb them.

"It is not coincidence the Iolcian raft landed in the mountains. In the same way your sword seeks you out, whispers to you, all Fleece technology has invisible tethers inviting them closer. The raft was already on a downward trajectory, your sword merely adjusted its course." Jasyn has so many questions. *What was the Iolcian raft doing with Fleece technology? Why was it on a downward trajectory? Why didn't the Ice King with his ice-weapon and the Ice Princess with her sword gravitate to her? Did they? Is that how they found the village?* But the question she lands on instead is:

"How did you know where to find it? The artefact."

"I am guardian of the Fleece," says Medea, as if that answers all questions. "It speaks to me," she clarifies as she inspects the exterior of the quarantine chamber. The inked surface reflects everything in the room, except her.

"Can my sword be used to undo the damage to Iolcus?" asks Jasyn.

"If only it were that simple. I know everyone is the hero in their own story, Jasyn, but this isn't all about you." The expression on Medea's face is playful, quite in contrast to Jasyn's mood. "You and your sword are only part of the puzzle."

"What puzzle is that? What is the artefact? What have we risked our lives for? *What have you risked our lives for?*"

"I've already told you. The artefact will help get you to my world. To the Golden planet. To the Golden Fleece."

"How?"

"This is quite the collection," says Medea, gazing into Doctor Orpheus's medician case.

Unable to resist such a statement, Jasyn gravitates to her side, asking "Why do I get the feeling we're just puppets and you're the one pulling the strings?" uncertain whether she intends the question to be rhetorical or not.

As she arrives within peering distance of the case, the door to the adjoining chamber opens, and Jasyn can't help be suspicious that Medea lured her there on purpose.

62

FINDING CALM

JASYN

Stood too close to the doctor's desk and medician case, there's no way Jasyn isn't suspected of snooping. She probably looks startled, apologetic and guilty all at once, combining into a sort of wince. The doctor wastes no time in casting a disapproving look her way and clicking her medician case pointedly shut.

Jasyn glances to where Medea had just been to find a much more usual occurrence of *no-one standing there*. The doctor follows the direction of her gaze, but says nothing as she dries her rat-tailed dark hair with a towel. She must have rushed the air-blast to cut short Jasyn's exploration.

With Doctor Orpheus silently observing her like it's some sort of psychological test, Jasyn's eyes betray her thoughts when her gaze flits to the closed door of the ice-melt chamber.

Who's in there?

But if the doctor knows what Jasyn is wondering, she doesn't satisfy her with an answer.

Jasyn guesses whoever is hiding in the adjoining room is doing so because they want privacy. And Jasyn can at least respect that. Even if she is dying to know who is having fun shower time with the grumpy doctor. Though, she should probably be thinking about more important topics.

"You summoned me?" says Jasyn, since the doctor's forte isn't conversation.

The doctor scowls, thoughtfully this time, as she approaches the cube-monitor that presumably displays Jasyn's stats.

"Your cuff must have detected something and sent an automatic alert," says Doctor Orpheus, inspecting the vitals terminal, her finger hovering above the streaming information. "I didn't hear it over the ice-melt."

I bet you didn't... Jasyn tries to turn her instinctively quirked eyebrow into a more natural expression, but thankfully the doctor isn't looking at her.

"Hence, why you could just *wander in*," the doctor adds, pointedly. "Heart rate spiked. Adrenaline. Increased perspiration. Body temperature all over the fucking place." She pauses before adding, more in Jasyn's direction: "Shortness of breath...?"

Jasyn nods. She'd been distracted from her stuttering breaths and erratic heart rate by Medea's presence, and curiosity about the doctor. The ghost of the episode lingers, but she's not struggling the way she had been. *That's something, at least.*

"Take a seat," says the doctor, indicating a gurney.

"I'm fine," says Jasyn, wheezing a little. "I just... had a bad dream."

"Didn't we all," grumbles the doctor. "You need a check up anyway, so you may as well sit. Take deep, slow breaths. In through your nose, out through your mouth."

"Yep, just fucking breathe," Jasyn mutters to herself. "I do know how to breathe," she snaps, only to receive an irony-acknowledging raised brow from the doctor. "Usually," Jasyn adds. "I'm fine."

"Who are you trying to convince?" asks Doctor Orpheus. *Smart ass.*

Only now, with the doctor wheeling her chair closer, does Jasyn notice that her clothes are not only *not black*, for once, but they're looser fitting. This is the doctor out of uniform. Jasyn hadn't meant to have a meltdown just as the doctor was winding-down and having some fun. There's no lighting clash. Perhaps the alert has overwritten the doctor's Rhythm. *It's not important.*

"Sorry," Jasyn wheezes. "Please don't push me out an airlock."

She expects the doctor to smirk or say something sarcastic. But she doesn't. Instead, she observes her thoughtfully.

"I know the crew — I know *I* — idly throw that threat around... But, it's a figure of speech, really. You don't need to worry about being thrown out an airlock. Not on this ship, at least."

Oh. That's a relief. Though, she's fairly certain Castor hadn't been idly throwing the threat around when aimed at the Ice Princess. And the body check she gave Jasyn had felt like a promise. But, at the doctor's comforting words, Jasyn's lungs loosen a little further.

As she rubs her sternum to soothe herself, she winces as she mistakenly presses the raw claw scratches.

"When you were knocked from the hold, you got scratched across here?" asks the doctor, indicating the band beneath her collar bones.

Jasyn nods.

"Can I take a look?" asks Doctor Orpheus.

"You want me half-naked again?"

Heaven's hail, what is wrong with her? There are several better ways she could have phrased that. The doctor gives her a strange look. Stranger than usual.

"There's no need for a full examination right now," says the doctor. "I'll need to monitor your healed injuries, but that can be for another time. And the samples I took from you have spoiled... so we'll need to do those. But, for now, just strip down to your vest." It's as if she's actively trying not to trigger Jasyn's panic, because she adds: "Uh... Please?" *Has she ever used that word before?* It sounds wrong coming out of her mouth.

While the doctor covers the lower half of her face with her medi-mask and pulls on a pair of black medi-gloves, Jasyn unbuttons her overalls and pulls her arms out of the sleeves.

The doctor leans closer to inspect the wounds. Each puncture has a series of tiny vein lines branching towards it. As the doctor's fingers near the wounds, she locks eyes with Jasyn, seeking permission.

"I'm aware I have a very punchable face," she says, the bruise on the arch of her nose peeking above her medi-mask. *Was that a joke?*

Jasyn nods her permission before adding, playfully:

"It's not your face that's punchable, doctor. It's your personality."

It's difficult to see the doctor's response behind her mask, but she does grumble and make a disapproving "hhmn" sound. The cold touch of her gloves highlights how warm and itchy Jasyn's skin is, and at the doctor's gentle press the wounds ooze yellow-green.

"Gross," says Jasyn, but she can't look away.

"Your body's doing its best to heal, but..." The doctor's expressive brow does all the talking. She doesn't seem disgusted by what she's seeing. If anything, she's fascinated. "...there's some infection. Obviously."

Decorated by the yellow-green pus, the doctor's gloves bloom luminous blue. She discards them in a decon-container and sources a new pair. She doesn't exactly say that she's cleaning the wounds, but it becomes clear that's what she's doing by the selection of items she sources from nearby drawers.

She tips a vial, spilling the liquid onto absorbent circular pads, placing one against each of the puncture wounds. Whatever's in that vial reacts like a cooling balm against Jasyn's skin. She has to bite her lip to stop from sighing with relief.

This proximity absolutely isn't making her think about that moment in her imagined world when she'd sought Doctor Orpheus out and the doctor had pushed her hips between her thighs. Absolutely not. What an inappropriate attraction that would be… Where in the heavens did the idea even come from?

Pus. Just think about the gross green pus.

Jasyn's heart beats hard enough that a cube-monitor bleeps.

She can sense the doctor scowling at her in concentration, or mild confusion, but Jasyn refuses to look at her.

"Anyway, even if someone on board wanted to throw you out an airlock," the doctor says, as if they hadn't moved on from that conversation, "the helm's permission is required to do so."

"Is that meant to make me feel better?" Castor at the very least would give such permission.

A silence settles between them.

To Jasyn's surprise, it's the doctor who breaks it:

"I can't believe you fell out of the ship." The way she says it, like she's poking fun at her, makes Jasyn smile.

"I didn't fall. I was shoved by a terrifying beast. And, yeah, I wouldn't recommend it." Or, given that there were — in the end — no long-term adverse consequences, thanks to Atalanta's quick thinking, maybe she would. *It was quite the rush…*

Jasyn shakes free of such dangerous thoughts.

"Thank you. For hoisting me back in. You risked your life…"

The doctor's scowl deepens. "Hold doors open on launch would have risked the whole ship. At the very least, food and drink supplies would have been lost. It was either cut you loose or reel you in."

"Well..." says Jasyn, letting that non-compliment sink in, "... thank you for not cutting me loose."

In her dream world, the doctor had been a voice of truth, trying to tell her something wasn't right. Of course, now that she thinks about it, it makes much more sense that her mind had been invaded by mind scavenging spores than Doctor Orpheus *flirting* with her.

"I should've known something was off in my dreamworld when you started being nice to me," says Jasyn, offering her best cheeky smile. She doesn't have to give any details.

The doctor's mask crinkles as if she's smiling back. "Sounds like a nightmare to me." She sits back, removing her gloves. "You're done," she says, gesturing to the clean wounds that look a lot healthier now.

Jasyn's panic has gone, leaving only a general disquiet at the idea that her inability to function happened in the first place.

She might blame her parents for not letting her in on the secret of her ice-connection, but the truth is her actions are her own (no matter how much she wants to blame the mysterious keeper of the Golden Fleece). If she wants to keep those around her safe, if she wants to be useful, helpful, someone who can change the trajectory of a world or two for the better, she'd better start shaping the possibilities.

"When do we start studying me?" asks Jasyn. "Wasn't that the idea? That you poke and prod me until we know stuff?"

She could have phrased it differently, couldn't she? Less of the poking and prodding... different words and she'd likely be blushing less now.

"Soon," says the doctor as she places a vial of pills within Jasyn's reach. "Before you have a rebellion about me trying to sedate you: these are painkillers mainly, with a mix of mild sedative. For you to decide if and when you need them."

That the doctor is trusting her to make her own decisions on this is as cooling as the balm on her wounds.

"They'll calm you. Help you sleep. And ease your cramps."

"Cramps?"

Doctor Orpheus reviews the vitals monitor and nods.

"Oh."

"And this," the doctor places a palm sized pillow-like object beside Jasyn, "is a heat pack. It'll help with abdominal discomfort and can be used to melt any rogue ice."

Jasyn almost smiles, touched that the doctor is being so thoughtful.

"The last thing we need," adds the doctor, matter of factly, "is you piercing a hole in the hull because you've got your period."

Jasyn opens her mouth to protest before clamping her mouth shut because — in this instance — *fair*.

63

BOW

ATALANTA

A quick auditory sweep of the ship lets Atalanta know there's no-one nearby, and there's only one person up at the helm, nowhere near the overseer console.

The way is clear.

She lets herself into the airlock tunnel to the cargo hold. And, though the monitor in the airlock suggests the pressure and oxygen levels are good, she takes a deep breath anyway, and makes quick work of delving into the hold's shadows.

After Jasyn had climbed her way back to the ship and the hold platform had been cranked shut, everyone had been too focused on the surprise of their survival and their climb to the skies to notice Atalanta tactically storing the bow and arrows she'd been using between two cargo crates. It'd only be a matter of time before someone finds the lingering weapons.

Relief washes through her as she reclaims the items. All she has to do now is navigate her way through the ship without anyone seeing her.

Being able to tune in to the audible location of each of the crew allows her to time her movements as though solving a three-dimensional puzzle.

When Castor approaches from one direction and Hylas from the other, Atalanta pretends with absolute perfection the task of rewiring a light-tube.

The act itself plunges her portion of the corridor into darkness, and in the thickest shadows at the corridor edge she temporarily stows the forbidden implements.

Castor and Hylas pass. The former with a suspicious grimace, the latter with a smile. Atalanta breathes a sigh of relief when Hylas takes the unspoken hint to let her get on with her job.

A few corridors turns later, she's where she needs to be. A shadow-filled dead end. A questionable ship-design choice, perhaps, but one she's grateful for. There's no dull buzz of an overseer here. It's the perfect place to hide, and to hide *things*.

She dextrously seeks out the grooves in the wall panelling and — with a screwdriver from her utility belt — she removes its fixings. A collection of found materials occupy the wall cavity. Anyone might think it belongs to some strange and misguided rodent intent on nesting in metal.

Tucked away in the corner of the dead end corridor, Atalanta lets herself calm at the weight of the bow, as she considers its composition. The bow she'd lost to The Games arena on Iolcus had been made of broken ship parts by her and Mother. Making a new bow now won't be the same, but she can at least improve upon this one, adding to it with parts scavenged during ship upkeep.

As she relaxes into the activity that's as familiar to her as breathing, her Transonics pull at the threads of sounds within the ship.

Vole-rats scuttle in the cavities between floors. In a recovery chamber, Kalais's muscles tense and her teeth grind as bone fibres knit and heal. In the quarantine chamber, the princess's breathing is deep and slow. *Good.* She's getting much needed, healing rest. In a lower deck corridor, Zetes gives Jasyn a lesson on which pipes along the walls relate to the engine and what to do if they become blocked.

The glow of a Transonic haunts the shadows at the edge of her vision. She doesn't bother turning. She knows it's Mother, and she knows by now that she's beyond her sight.

Atalanta can invent a thousand stories to explain why her parents left their home world and risked their lives in the skies. *Practicality*: perhaps their origin planet had nothing to offer and the skies promised a better life. *Necessity*: had they been fugitives with no other choice? *Romance*: their stations in life were too different, or forbidden, and only in taking to the skies could they be together. The power of their love made them shoot for the stars.

But no matter what made them choose their skyward journey, it's an inescapable fact that their relationship hadn't survived.

Had her parents been happy when they took to the skies together? Was it the journey that drove them apart? If Atalanta thought the apparition in her orbit was something more than a manifestation of her own emotional wounds, she might ask.

"The skies bring impossible decisions," signs Mother. "Do you really think you can weather this journey?"

Sifting through her collection of found parts, Atalanta's in half a mind to tell Mother to talk to Lynk if she's so fascinated by the weather.

"She won't stop until she's explored everything the universe has to offer," Mother continues. "Perhaps not even then."

Atalanta's jaw clenches, refusing to engage.

"Arrows aiming at different targets don't end up in the same place."

"You're wrong," signs Atalanta, snapping like a fumbled bow string. "Even death and dreams can't keep us apart."

She whips around to address Mother — or whatever the technical term is for grief-personified resulting from a death-experience — but only a burning glow in the shadows lingers. Perhaps Mother doesn't particularly appreciate being shouted at. Perhaps she was never really there in the first place.

Atalanta sighs, smoothing the shaped metal of the bow, adjusting the grip and seeking comfort in the grooves of its detailing against her thumb. *What does Mother know?* She'd had Atalanta convinced Atalanta was a hunter, tried to shape her into the image of herself.

Telling her imagined mother where to stick her arrows won't magically smooth away fears. She and Jasyn may be on the same journey, even the same Rhythm, now, but what if they're on different trajectories?

A heartbeat and footsteps approach.

The stag seems to have developed the ability to hone in on her, wherever she is in the ship. His antlers only just fit the width of the corridor, which makes his ability to manoeuvre a challenge, but he manages.

He settles onto his rump, fascinated by the manipulation of metal, Atalanta's selection of tools, and occasional use of a blow torch. His sparkling eyes, black like marbles, watch, unblinking, until he grows tired and rests his heavy head on the floor. Atalanta hangs a couple of tools and materials on his antlers, which earns her a snort that she interprets as *happy to be included.*

Atalanta smiles. Perhaps she didn't need to embellish a bow to lift her spirits, perhaps she only needed some time with her buddy.

Another heartbeat... She'd assumed they'd veer off in another direction, because why would anyone venture this way?

Atalanta tucks her bow and arrows into the shadows and turns her attention to the wiring buckled to the wall. She trains her torch on it. 'Inspecting it.' So long as no-one sweeps a torch downwards, her contraband should remain undiscovered.

As if she's *just looking up from a routine inspection,* Atalanta turns to the captain. For someone so solidly built, she moves with relative silence through the ship when she chooses.

Atalanta expects surprise on Herakles's face, a question of *What are you doing here?* but her expression isn't surprise. It's gentle, apologetic almost, but — like an arrow to her own foot — Atalanta deciphers it as *You've been caught.*

64

CAUGHT

ATALANTA

Atalanta squints up at the ceiling, searching, but finds nothing.

"No, you're right," says the captain. Her voice is almost a whisper. Does she know talking near Atalanta is more comfortable at lower volume? "There's no overseer in this corridor."

The stag deigns to lift his head. The captain half-waves at him, but he merely blinks at her and returns to his nap. With a light grimace, Herakles balls her hand into a fist, as if embarrassed that she doesn't know how to interact with the animal. Or, perhaps, this situation. *Whatever this situation is...*

The captain stuffs her hands in her pockets, looking anything but relaxed.

"When the hold airlock opens, it triggers a silent alert at the helm," she explains. "It's the same for any airlock. This ship might currently be lacking in various ways, but it still has a safety feature or two up its sleeve. And that," Herakles nods at the cuff about Atalanta's wrist, "lets me know the location of everyone on this ship." Her smile is halfway between an apology and a grimace. "I know it all seems a bit military-state, but it's intended for everyone's safety."

Atalanta stares at her, uncertain what to make of all this.

"I know you only know me as an arena oaf, but *I can count.* And I don't tend to lose track of how many weapons there are in the store." Herakles scratches the back of her neck. The fine short hair rasps against her fingertips. Her breaths are shorter than they should be. Her heart a little too loud. Her nervous swallow, too, has Atalanta wondering what it is about her that puts the captain on edge. *Does she think she's a danger to the ship?* Probably. Hiding weapons isn't the best method of suggesting otherwise. Though she's not exactly treating her like a criminal.

"Can I see?" asks Herakles, holding out her hand and nodding to the shadows where the bow and arrows rest. If she thinks Atalanta a threat, this could be a simple ploy to get the weapons from her, but there's something about the captain's demeanour that invites her trust. Trusting her *to do* or *not do* what, she isn't sure.

Atalanta reaches across the stag's antlers and hands over the work-in-progress bow.

The captain keeps her distance, either from Atalanta, the stag, or both. Her focus on the bow, studying its details, its chiselled patterns, suggests she genuinely does want a closer look and isn't merely trying to remove it from her possession.

Atalanta's gaze snags on Herakles's forearm tattoos. The circuitry-like ink-lines wrap around each wrist before veering off at angles that make the designs look map-like.

"You're modifying this with found parts?" Herakles asks, snapping Atalanta's eyes back up to her face, as the captain tests the weight of the bow, bright eyed and... impressed?

Wary, Atalanta offers a slight nod.

"I trust the ship won't fall apart as a result?"

The sparkle in the captain's eyes is kind enough, her smile playful, but when their eyes connect she retreats. She returns the bow to her. Atalanta gingerly takes it, maintaining her suspicious but trying-to-be-neutral expression, uncertain what to make of this new and confusing dynamic.

She half expects the captain to launch at her, or put her in a headlock. She is the great Herakles, after all; her reputation for winning scuffles far exceeds Atalanta's own. And, Atalanta cannot forget, she's heard how the captain interrogated the princess. Nor can she forget how she antagonised Jasyn. The captain might seem immensely approachable right now, but she's not all about keeping the peace.

Atalanta shouldn't let herself be fooled, but she's struggling to place the captain's awkwardness; struggling to understand why the captain's heartbeat is hammering, why her stomach is churning, and why she's... *blushing?*

Herakles, Captain of the Skies, Hero of the Arena, Slayer of Monsters... is *blushing.*

In fact, as Herakles clears her throat and inspects her own boots, she returns her hands to her pockets and looks almost bashful. How in the heavens had Atalanta not seen it before? The captain's behaviour. It's not that far removed from how Atalanta and Jasyn were with each other before they finally admitted their feelings. The captain... has a crush on her?

Impossible, surely... They don't even know each other.

Herakles nods to the bow: "I guess it would be too obvious to say 'don't let anyone else know that's here'... so, I won't." She smiles, with an edge of nervousness.

What the hail is going on? This strange, one-sided camaraderie. Why isn't she berating her for harbouring a weapon?

The silence is getting loud.

Once it stretches too far, Herakles adds: "I mean... you don't have to say *thank you*, or anything." Cheekiness seems to overtake her nerves. That dimpled, charming smile is confusing.

If Atalanta were to believe that Herakles has a crush, this could be perceived as flirting.

Atalanta takes a moment to align with this information... and the fact that she doesn't hate it...? Though she probably should, because this is the same person who interrogated the princess and terrorised Jasyn.

But Atalanta can admit (if only to herself), she likes this playful side of Herakles. And she appreciates her weaponry not being claimed. So she signs, "Thank you," albeit in a slow manner so someone who doesn't know her language might understand. Though, in signing so slow, someone who knows her language might think she's being sarcastic.

As the captain rasps a nervous hand through her sculpted blue-purple hair, the time Atalanta vomited on that hair-do nudges into her thoughts. With the benefit of distance and hindsight, and now that her mind and body are more in tune with her surroundings, the memory is almost a little amusing. It must be making her smile because Herakles asks:

"What's so funny?"

Atalanta shrugs. She gestures between them, not quite signing, but expressing the general concept of: "Sorry I puked on you."

Herakles smirks, breaking down the wall of tension that bit further.

"It happens more often than you'd think," she says, looking much more relaxed when she smiles. But only a few moments pass and the tension returns, straining her features.

"Look. I wanted to apologise for my behaviour." Herakles speaks fast, as if she might lose her nerve. "Keeping you and Jasyn separate..." *So she hadn't imagined that...* "It won't happen again." There's a softness, a vulnerability in her eyes that makes Atalanta believe her. "You'll be on the same Rhythm when possible." Herakles rubs her forehead, betraying her stress. "Though if there are some discrepancies, please don't have a rebellion about it."

Herakles takes a deep breath.

"There's no excuse for my behaviour. We're on a mission to dethrone a ruthless dictator. Not for me to become one." She nods decisively. And, as if she can sense Atalanta is about to suggest it, she adds: "I'll apologise to Jasyn, too, of course."

She braves eye contact with Atalanta then, and it's impossible to decipher the combination of emotions running through the captain's thoughts. Gratitude? Panic? A little sadness?

"I also wanted to say thank you. For saving..." Herakles lets out a wry chuckle. "...well, everyone."

That's why she's here? To apologise and to thank her?

When Herakles doesn't add anything further, Atalanta signs, ignoring the practicality of being understood: "The skies don't care if we live or die. What else can we do but save each other? You should thank the princess too."

Herakles nods. "You're right. And I will."

Wait. She understood? She speaks her language.

What the actual hail?

The captain's eyes widen as if she's just given away an important secret.

"You know my language?" signs Atalanta, stepping closer without realising it. Though she can't go any further with a wall of sleeping stag in the way.

"I need to... get back to the helm," says Herakles, backing away, her heart hammering, her stomach protesting, her fingers rasping through the hair at her neck, her bicep curling with the gesture. "Captain things to do," she adds, before about-turning and leaving Atalanta barricaded, baffled and figuratively windswept, too.

65

KEY CHANGE

JASYN

In the same breath as acknowledging her 'brusque' treatment of Jasyn and noting appreciation for Jasyn's part in bringing the crew to safety — and for saving Kalais, specifically — Herakles had assigned Jasyn a dozen doses of washing up and floor scrubbing as her punishment for going against a direct order and the Rhythm of the ship.

While the encounter didn't exactly have Jasyn believing she'd been apologised to or thanked, at least her punishment isn't over the top. She gets to spend her waking hours and shift patterns in the company of the rest of the crew, so she no longer imagines she's wandering aboard a ghost ship.

She's still relegated to washing up duty, but whatever. It's progress.

A crackle of static across the comms precedes soft string music. Starting quiet, the music grows, each new note soothing, like a balm.

"What is that?" Jasyn asks Hylas as he deposits his cup beside the sink.

"You don't recognise the music?" he says. "From what I hear, you got an in-person show."

Does he mean the V-iolin music that brought her, Atalanta and Tiphys back to life?

"Seriously, get Orpheus drunk," continues Hylas, "and she'll talk about the healing powers of music as enthusiastically as Lynk talks about the weather."

Jasyn's brow salutes the ceiling. She's not sure she can imagine the doctor drunk, nor maintaining an enthusiastic conversation. Though it probably makes sense for someone who literally uses music to heal to believe in its powers. And there's no denying the music drifting from the comms speakers is restorative. The ache in her cheek where the doctor had walloped her dulls a little. So too does the lingering discomfort around the perforations below her collarbones.

"In the case of Doctor Orpheus, the restoration is literal," confirms Hylas, the vine-cut on his cheek calming and starting to close.

A quick scan across the crew in the mess hall confirms they're all basking in the V-iolin's positive effects. Cuts are healing, burns calming, bruises are fading.

That's one way to do it.

Though the relief crossing Kalais's face is partial, only. Out of all present, she has the most healing to do. The fact that the seasoned crew don't react as if they're witnessing something *extraordinary*, suggests that this is business as usual. Tiphys has a glint of "wow" in his eyes, even if it is tamped down a little by gloom.

Couldn't the doctor have done this when Jasyn visited her in the medical quarters? And, why, if this is within her skillset, didn't the doctor heal their punched-face injuries sooner?

There must be some logic to the delay. Perhaps all wounds need to be cleaned before being healed with... what... music? *Magic*? Perhaps she'd needed to reach out to the whole crew at once? She's sure the doctor won't be interested in explaining it to her, but Jasyn makes a mental note to ask her all the same.

The music morphs to something less soothing. With bass pumping, and several instruments weaving together, it can only be pre-recorded. It might not be *magic*, but it has Jasyn's inner metronome ticking and her foot tapping.

"She does this sometimes," Hylas raises his voice over the rising volume, "The doctor. She encourages us all to let loose. Says it helps us let off steam. To reset."

Jasyn's not sure *letting loose* is something she should be doing. From behind the galley hatch, she watches as the crew, who've been subdued since their encounter with the snow-jungle, start smiling, raising their hands in the air and getting to their feet. The mood dials up from sombre to playful.

"Yes, Orpheus," calls Castor, saluting the comms speakers as she flicks her loosened waves of silver hair over her shoulder and starts to bop to the music as if it were the most natural thing to do.

Zetes joins her, rare enthusiasm in his smile as he cheers Castor on. Their downright goofy wriggling about isn't what she expects from the athletic crew. If she'd seen Castor's dancing before, she might not have been so intimidated.

It's making everyone smile, Jasyn included. Lynk beams. Tiphys starts clapping, his default grin and eye-sparkle restored.

With her arm in a cast and her leg bandaged, Kalais makes do with remaining seated, but she swivels on the bench beside Gus to observe, grinning at the display.

The lights dim a little, then further, sliding suddenly between dark and dim, as if the mess hall is some sort of dance-den. Jasyn's never been to one, but she's heard about them: places where people go to move to music. The doctor — or someone — must be having some fun with the ship's Rhythm settings right now.

Jasyn can't help smirking as Castor exaggeratedly dances in Kal's direction, making a show of swaying her hips and shaking her behind. Kalais stares with a grin half lecherous and half amused.

With music thumping, infectious laughter, and smiles, Jasyn might even forget that Kalais and Castor in particular have made her time in the skies an assault course impossible to navigate.

Expertly avoiding her injuries, Castor straddles Kalais. Kalais responds with the kind of stomach rolling dance moves only a confident athlete can manage. Jasyn raises an eyebrow to herself: *okay, maybe Kalais has got some moves...*

As Castor and Kalais's proximity becomes suggestive, Zetes covers his eyes and vocally complains about witnessing his sibling doing *that*. At a more exuberant move, Kalais winces and grips her arm.

"I'm in recovery, here." Kalais laughs and playfully pushes Castor away.

Castor takes the hint and dances over to Zetes, leaving Kalais with Gus, both watching with quiet smiles as Zetes accepts Castor's invitation. Thankfully, the dancers' aim isn't to get intimate, but to energise and lift the mood.

Hylas might still be seated, but nods and laughs along with their antics. Lynk, always smiling, taps her feet until Zetes invites her to dance. Hail, they look cute together, dancing with dopey grins.

If the doctor's plan is to uptick the crew's positivity, it seems to be working. Even with her hands in the suds, Jasyn can't help smiling.

"Ice-monger," says Castor, gliding across to the galley hatch and challenging Jasyn's smile. Jasyn hates that term. It's never used with positive intent. She holds her breath, awaiting whatever negativity Castor is about to unleash.

"Why aren't you finding your girl and dancing?" As soon as Castor says the words, she sashays back over to the cluster of crew letting loose.

The exchange is so brief and bizarrely encouraging, Jasyn wonders whether it actually happened. It could be an olive branch, or a ploy to get rid of her. Either way, it sure beats being shoulder checked in a corridor.

And it's a good question: *Why isn't she dancing with Atalanta right now?*

66

EYE OF THE UNIVERSE

JASYN

A quick peek into the rec chamber and Jasyn discovers Pollux and Peleus engaged in a music-backed game of bounce-ball. Pollux is far more co-ordinated with his manoeuvres, but Peleus isn't being sore about it. Jasyn can't help smiling. She's never seen Peleus being a *good sport* before.

Continuing her search, journeying upwards through the ship, a quick visual sweep of the top deck confirms: no Atalanta. There's only the captain slumped within the helm chair, apparently immune to the good mood that's taken hold elsewhere in the ship. With the music pumping over the comms, she hasn't noticed Jasyn's presence.

Ordinarily, if she crosses paths with someone so glum, she'd ask them if they're okay and do whatever is in her power to cheer them up, but her recent run ins with the captain make her think she's liable to do more harm than good. She decides not to interrupt her solitude and retreats.

Each new corridor Jasyn tries is without reward. The sleeping quarters are empty, with all bunks marked 'vacant'. The engine chamber is empty too, all mechanisms ticking over as they should. Well, *she assumes*, since there are no alert lights pulsing or alarms blaring.

With the medical chambers door ajar, Jasyn doesn't knock. Over the music, the hinges don't even screech. Though, perhaps that has something to do with an archer who wields a toolbelt and has oil within her artillery.

The doctor mustn't have heard Jasyn enter, because she doesn't look up. With the rest of the crew — bar Herakles — jovial and celebrating thanks to the music, it looks like Doctor Orpheus isn't taking a dose of her own medicine. Her face is sallow, with dark circles under her eyes. Perhaps it's the lighting? She adjusts something that looks like an adapted telescope. But the studious scowl of the doctor only claims Jasyn's focus for a second—

What scores into her awareness isn't the fact that there's a stag jiggling about and rearing his head to the music, nor that Atalanta — in the outer-corridor of the the un-inked quarantine chamber, with her back to the medical quarters — has her Transonics closed. What burns Jasyn's nerves to ash is that Atalanta is palm to palm with the Ice Princess, only a layer of reinforced glass between them.

She might not be able to see Atalanta's expression, but there's a twinkle in the Ice Princess's eyes. Tears? Affection? Trickery? Jasyn's not sure which is worse.

Nausea grips her gut.

The doctor looks up, registering Jasyn's presence and the shared gesture in the quarantine chamber.

There must be a rational explanation, but Jasyn's rational brain has been overruled by something feral that already has her stumbling out of the medical quarters, bursting through the door as if she has the power to break the metal.

The motion only serves to wrench her wrist as a burst of ice webs across the surface. She doesn't stop. She doesn't want what she just saw to catch up to her.

Nor does she want to be *this person*. Dramatic. Uncontrolled. Unable to communicate and see sense. But if she stops, she'll have to consider what to do and what her sporadic abilities have to say.

She trusts Atalanta. Implicitly. But she does not trust the Ice Princess. Nor does she trust her own overspill of emotions.

Just keep moving.

Light fittings tremor as she strides past. The corridor cools. Her breaths are sharp in her chest. She stumbles, catching herself with her palm to the wall.

Ice spills from the contact, sending her feet slipping—

Heaven's hail. This is the last thing she needs!

The ship shudders and Jasyn's stomach constricts. A shadow drapes over her and she's minded to give whatever nightmare, after-effect or apparition might be there to torment her a piece of her mind.

The mumbled "fuck" is Jasyn's first clue.

She turns, just in time, to decipher the doctor's silhouette skidding towards her. Obviously she wasn't expecting a corridor flooded with ice.

Doctor Orpheus pinballs towards her. Jasyn reaches out, and they grasp at each other, trying not to fall.

But the ship and universe have other ideas.

The ship shunts, tilting on its axis, thudding the two of them against the wall, limbs tangling. As if it isn't enough for Jasyn's emotions to be turned on their head right now, the ship's gravity is on a mission to achieve the same.

Is she doing this? Is her own lack of control tearing at the ship?

Doctor Orpheus doesn't loosen her grip on Jasyn's shoulder

and shirt. She must understand the terror and question in Jasyn's eyes, because the doctor tells her:

"This isn't you."

The corridor shudders like a rock-filled wheel barrow forced along uneven terrain. It's not the sort of motion Jasyn expects in the middle of space. On landing, perhaps, but outside there should be *nothing*.

But beyond the portholes, churning storm clouds surround the ship. Fear flickers across the doctor's face as if she knows something Jasyn doesn't.

Over her heart thundering in her ears, the voice of the captain crackles across the comms: "Ship wide. Strap in."

Atalanta... What about Atalanta? Jasyn might be confused and flustered by whatever the hail she just saw in the medical quarters, but that pales in importance to Atalanta's safety.

Jasyn's attempts to retrace her steps only have her tripping on Doctor Orpheus, and skidding on her own ice.

"Don't be an idiot." The doctor grabs her by the collar and unspools strips of webbing from the wall, handing one to Jasyn and looping the other across her own chest. "She has more of a chance *not dying* in quarantine, than you do in trying to get there."

The ship groans in-line with Jasyn's mighty protestations on the matter. Doctor Orpheus is right. There's nothing Jasyn can do right now but hope that Atalanta's okay. *Hope* she reached for a tether in time.

While the doctor is already securely affixed, Jasyn's ice-crusted hand renders her dexterity next to useless as she scrabbles to push the latch plate into its buckle.

The ship shakes her insides. A promise of chaos.

Without hesitation, the doctor unhitches from her fastenings and slides to Jasyn to secure her buckle.

Everything flips—

The doctor slips, but Jasyn lurches forward to catch her. Her shoulder wrenches, but the doctor's got a good grip on her arm.

The corridor looms like a death-slide beneath them.

The next bout of ship movement sends the doctor's body lifting—

For the sake of life preservation and nothing more, Jasyn wraps her arms around Doctor Orpheus, pulling her close as the universe vibrates around them.

The ship bucks and every organ in Jasyn's body lurches. And yet, the doctor reaches for her own webbing.

"What are you doing?" Given the quantity of grimaces the doctor's thrown her way in the short time they've known each other, it's not a surprise that she'd rather risk her life than risk dying in Jasyn's arms. "I've got you. Just hold on."

The doctor grumbles but she grabs Jasyn's safety-webbing, pulling herself closer than the two of them have ever been, even in Jasyn's misguided dreams.

Jasyn angles her face to try to reduce the unwanted proximity. Given this is in the interest of keeping her alive, if the doctor could please tone down her obvious disgust, it would be appreciated.

"How is there turbulence in space?" Jasyn raises her voice above the protestations of the ship.

"This isn't turbulence, exactly..." says Doctor Orpheus, craning her neck to observe the portholes. A mix of panic and awe occupies her features. "All we can do is ride the waves."

Whatever that means.

Strings of light surround the ship as it sails. The chaotic swirl is like water down a plughole. Churning blues and whites and greys put Jasyn in mind of the ice-slush at a river's edge. Pinks and yellows... *What is this?* The digestive tract of the universe? No. *Sailing along its stormy river* is a much more welcome image.

"Sometimes the universe blinks," says Doctor Orpheus, finally, as if that explains anything.

Ship alarms kick in, as if blood pressure and panicking need any more fuel.

"Wouldn't alarms be more useful *before* a crisis?" asks Jasyn, rhetorically, and — to her surprise — the doctor laughs. Perhaps with an edge of terror-fuelled delirium, but a laugh all the same. The sound rumbles through Jasyn's chest. It's so unlike anything she's heard from the doctor before, Jasyn almost forgets the woman's default setting is a scowl.

"Not every vessel makes it through an Eye of the Universe." The doctor's breath whispers at Jasyn's ear. "If a vessel is too large for the eye, it loops back and crashes into itself."

Is this her idea of calming words?

With the chaos around them, Jasyn's ice should be tripping all over the place. Oddly, the facts, though terrifying, are intriguing enough to have her distracted. Yes. The doctor's *words*. She's definitely not distracted by being pressed so close...

Jasyn gulps.

It's the chaos, the threat of death, and definitely not the doctor's gruff, gravelly voice making her heart hammer.

The juddering stops so suddenly, she gasps.

Beyond the portholes the colourful strings of light unspool and fade to an almost star-free expanse. The darkness is so thick, it's not unlike being buried alive. The debris of unfamiliar ships, the vessels that must have failed their voyage through the Eye, litter as far as the ship's light can reach.

Metal carcasses clunk against the ship's shell as the [C]ARGO ship wades through. The ship groans at each encounter, and yet Jasyn's attention is more drawn to the doctor than anything beyond the portholes.

Jasyn's pulse is thrumming. Her palms are slick with melted ice. The doctor's eyes are wide and wild, detouring to stare at

Jasyn's mouth. Her breath catches in tandem with Jasyn's stuttering gasps—

It's just a misfiring of synapses and sensations from the all encompassing terror. The intense look in the doctor's eyes as she thumbs Jasyn's jaw, her lips... Jasyn's hold tightening, pulling her that little bit closer... that must be her imagination...

The warmth of her mouth, the kiss: gentle and questioning, evolving to curious and dizzying, sending excitement skittering down Jasyn's spine and igniting an impromptu snowfall... that can only be real, can't it?

Heaven's hail. Jasyn's not sure who moans — her, the doctor, or the ship — but it's enough to startle them apart. As apart as they can manage when they're tangled together in safety-webbing.

They stare at each other, chasing their breaths. Jasyn's snowfall hangs in the air, as if it too is trying to figure out *What next?*

The captain's voice booms over the comms:

"Well, that was something!" *A fortifying breath.* "Welcome, everyone, to the Elysian Expanse."

The doctor's startled brow morphs to thunderous.

"Oh, fuck."

END BOOK II.

The adventure continues in...

JASYN AND THE ASTRONAUTS

III.

TWO FACED PLANET

But before you sail on to the next adventure...

SIGN UP FOR FREE STUFF AND UPDATES!

If you'd like to hear more about my writing adventures (behind-the-scenes insights, new release announcements, special offers, and bonus materials) and would like **a free e-book of *Theseus and The Sky Labyrinth*** (due 2024):

SIGN UP at:

gwenhyver.com/theseus-sign-up

Set in the same universe as *Jasyn and The Astronauts*, *Theseus and the Sky Labyrinth* is a sapphic, swords & sorcery reimagining of the myth of Theseus, Ariadne, and the Minotaur.

Join Theseus as she explores the Sky Labyrinth — an architectural wonder, a prison, a death trap — on the hunt for the minotaur. In the maze of masks and monsters, can she be the hero Princess Ariadne needs her to be?

REVIEWS WELCOME!

Hello! Gwenhyver here. I hope you enjoyed *The Sea of Stars!*

If you feel compelled to share some spoiler-free thoughts about your experience, I'd really appreciate it if you'd leave a review wherever you bought the book. Your review will help encourage others to join the JASYN adventure!

Thank you!

ALSO BY GWENHYVER

<u>THE SERIES</u>

Book 1

Under The Ice Skies

Book 2

The Sea of Stars

Book 3

Two Faced Planet

(Due 2024)

Book 4

The Ice Princess

(Due 2024)

Book 5

The Sky Circus

(Due TBD)

For updates on these books, the series beyond, and more,

sign up to my mailing list at gwenhyver.com

ABOUT THE AUTHOR

Gwenhyver writes stories with fantastical elements and queer characters. Or is that fantastical characters and queer elements...? She lives in a village on Dartmoor, England, with her wonderful wife. When she's not happily hermit-ing in her writing den, she's likely roaming the moors or exploring cycle trails wearing too much hi-vis. *Jasyn and the Astronauts* is her debut novel series.

www.gwenhyver.com

instagram.com/gwenhyver
twitter.com/gwenhyver
facebook.com/gwenhyver.author
tiktok.com/@gwenhyver.writes

ACKNOWLEDGMENTS

First thanks go to you, the reader, for picking up this book and *even* reading the acknowledgments!

Jen — my best friend and Super Spouse — you are consistently awesome. Once again you kindly trudged through the early drafts. Thank you for your encouragement and support (and the ability to listen to me prattle on about story details, often without preamble!) My favourite feedback from you on an early draft: "Why is there so much washing up in this book?" And, more generally: "Does this bit make sense?" All comments entirely valid, and thanks to you there is significantly less washing up, and hopefully it all makes sense! :-)

Kit Mallory — It's always a delight to receive your feedback, and I am so grateful for the time you put into being so thorough with your comments (and, of course, letting me know which characters you find hot!). Your moral support and always astute observations are appreciated, as is the documenting of your own emotional journey as you read through the manuscript. Also, I am endlessly amused by your enthusiasm for Herakles's waistcoat!

Thank you to everyone who made the release of the first book a lot of fun. Everyone who posted or reposted about the book, readers who reviewed the book, and those who reached out to me, I appreciate you. While I write these books because I enjoy the characters and worlds, they're intended for others to enjoy. To know the books are finding readers who are enjoying them, that's just amazing to me.

Alyssa Winans has done another awesome job on the cover art. It's been difficult to stop staring at Alyssa's art long enough to actually write and edit books, but I've given it a good go :-)

I'm already looking forward to sharing book 3! I hope you'll join me for the next adventure!

JASYN AND THE ASTRONAUTS

Book 2: The Sea of Stars

First edition November 2023

Published by Sky Dog Books

ISBN (eBook): 978-1-916644-04-5

ISBN (Print): 978-1-916644-05-2

Cover illustration © Alyssa Winans

Story inspired by the myth of Jason and The Golden Fleece.

Made in United States
Troutdale, OR
03/13/2024

Seaside Sunshine - Book Six

Boardwalk Breezes - Fall 2025

KAY'S BOOKS

Find more information on all my books at
kaycorrell.com
Buy direct from Kay's Shop at
shop.kaycorrell.com

COMFORT CROSSING ~ THE SERIES

The Shop on Main - Book One
The Memory Box - Book Two
The Christmas Cottage - A Holiday Novella (Book 2.5)
The Letter - Book Three
The Christmas Scarf - A Holiday Novella (Book 3.5)
The Magnolia Cafe - Book Four
The Unexpected Wedding - Book Five

The Wedding in the Grove - (a crossover short story between series - with Josephine and Paul from The Letter.)

LIGHTHOUSE POINT ~ THE SERIES
Wish Upon a Shell - Book One
Wedding on the Beach - Book Two
Love at the Lighthouse - Book Three
Cottage near the Point - Book Four
Return to the Island - Book Five
Bungalow by the Bay - Book Six
Christmas Comes to Lighthouse Point - Book Seven

CHARMING INN ~ Return to Lighthouse Point
One Simple Wish - Book One
Two of a Kind - Book Two
Three Little Things - Book Three
Four Short Weeks - Book Four
Five Years or So - Book Five
Six Hours Away - Book Six
Charming Christmas - Book Seven

SWEET RIVER ~ THE SERIES
A Dream to Believe in - Book One
A Memory to Cherish - Book Two

A Song to Remember - Book Three

A Time to Forgive - Book Four

A Summer of Secrets - Book Five

A Moment in the Moonlight - Book Six

MOONBEAM BAY ~ THE SERIES

The Parker Women - Book One

The Parker Cafe - Book Two

A Heather Parker Original - Book Three

The Parker Family Secret - Book Four

Grace Parker's Peach Pie - Book Five

The Perks of Being a Parker - Book Six

BLUE HERON COTTAGES ~ THE SERIES

Memories of the Beach - Book One

Walks along the Shore - Book Two

Bookshop near the Coast - Book Three

Restaurant on the Wharf - Book Four

Lilacs by the Sea - Book Five

Flower Shop on Magnolia - Book Six

Christmas by the Bay - Book Seven

Sea Glass from the Past - Book Eight

MAGNOLIA KEY ~ THE SERIES

Saltwater Sunrise - Book One

Encore Echoes - Book Two

Coastal Candlelight - Book Three
Tidal Treasures - Book Four
Bayside Beginnings - Book Five
Seaside Sunshine - Book Six
Boardwalk Breezes - Book Seven

CHRISTMAS SEASHELLS AND SNOWFLAKES
Seaside Christmas Wishes

WIND CHIME BEACH ~ A stand-alone novel

INDIGO BAY ~
Sweet Days by the Bay - Kay's Complete Collection of stories in the Indigo Bay series

Sign up for my newsletter at my website *kaycorrell.com* to make sure you don't miss any new releases or sales.

CHAPTER 1

Darlene hummed softly as she wiped down the kitchen counters at Bayside B&B. The morning sun streamed through the windows, casting a warm, welcoming glow over the well-worn surface. She paused for a moment, breathing in the lingering scent of freshly brewed coffee and blueberry muffins. Today, like all the others, had begun with the clink of dishes, the smell of bacon, and the contented murmurs of her well-fed guests.

The breakfast rush had come and gone, leaving behind a satisfying mess that she took pleasure in tidying up. There was something so comforting about her daily routine, a rhythm she'd perfected over the years of running the B&B.

She moved with practiced ease, gathering dishes and loading the dishwasher, her hands knowing instinctively where everything belonged.

She reached for the broom to sweep the floors when the back door burst open. Felicity rushed in, her cheeks flushed and her eyes wide with excitement.

"Gran!" Her granddaughter bent over, catching her breath, before continuing. "You won't believe what I just heard!"

She set the broom aside. "What's got you so worked up?"

Felicity leaned against the counter, her words tumbling out in a rush. "Brent and I were at Coastal Coffee, and we saw Beverly. She told us about this new fancy inn opening up in town."

"A new inn?" She raised an eyebrow, her interest aroused. "Where are they putting it?"

"It's those two old Jackson family homes. You know them. They're side by side right on the beach," Felicity explained. "They've redesigned them completely. Beverly says they're turning it into some kind of upscale place with deluxe suites and fancy bathrooms. Can you believe it? Whirlpool tubs and everything!"

She felt a small twinge of concern. Competition was always a bit nerve-wracking, especially when it sounded so lavish. But she pushed the feeling aside, reminding herself that Bayside had its own charm.

"Well, isn't that something?" she said, keeping her voice neutral. "I'm sure it'll be quite the talk of the town."

Felicity nodded. "Oh, it already is. But that's not all, Gran. They're putting in a wine bar in the lobby! For guests and visitors alike."

Her eyes widened slightly. "A wine bar? My, my. They're certainly aiming for a different crowd than we usually get here at Bayside."

Felicity paced the kitchen, her forehead creased. "It sounds pretty fancy, doesn't it? I mean, whirlpool tubs and a wine bar?" She frowned. "That's not exactly the cozy, homey feel we have here."

Darlene smiled slightly at her granddaughter's protective tone. "You're right about that, dear. We offer something different here. A home away from home."

Felicity stopped pacing and looked at her. "Aren't you worried, Gran? I mean, this new place sounds like it could be some serious competition."

She took a deep breath, considering her words carefully. "Well, I'd be lying if I said it didn't give me pause. But there's room for all sorts in this town. Some folks might want all that fancy stuff, but others? They'll still want a place that feels like coming home." At least she hoped they would.

She walked over to Felicity and patted her arm gently. "We've weathered changes before, and we'll do it again. Bayside has its own special charm, and that's not something you can replicate with whirlpool tubs or wine bars."

Felicity's shoulders relaxed a bit. "You're right, of course. I just got all worked up when Beverly was talking about it. She seemed so excited."

She chuckled. "Oh, I'm sure she was. Beverly always hears every bit of gossip first. Comes with owning the coffee shop, I guess. Speaking of which, how was Coastal Coffee this morning? Did you and Brent enjoy yourselves?"

"We did," Felicity said, her cheeks coloring slightly. "The pastries were delicious as always. Beverly says they come over on the first ferry from The Sweet Shoppe on Belle Island. Brent couldn't stop raving about them."

She noticed the blush but decided not to

comment on it. Instead, she picked up the broom again. "Well, I'm glad you two had a nice time."

"If you don't need me, Brent and I are headed to the mainland. Can I pick up anything for you?"

"No, I think I'm good. Thanks."

As Felicity hurried out of the kitchen, Darlene began sweeping the floor in long, efficient swipes. Her thoughts drifted to the new inn. Change was always a bit unsettling, but she had faith in Bayside and the community that had supported it for so long. She supposed the island was up for a lot of changes when and if the bridge ever got finished. They'd have a lot more day traffic and visitors if people could just pop over instead of dealing with the ferry.

As she put the broom away in the closet, her thoughts shifted from the new inn to Felicity. Her granddaughter's arrival this summer had initially thrown her routine into a pleasant chaos. Felicity, usually so self-sufficient, had needed a place to land, to regroup after a difficult school year of teaching. Darlene had welcomed her with open arms, happy to have her help and her company.

Now, though, a different kind of shift had

taken place. Felicity still helped with many of the breakfasts, the guest check-ins, and the endless laundry that the B&B generated. But her focus had drifted. Toward Brent. Her granddaughter had blossomed over the summer, shedding the weariness she'd arrived with and rediscovering her spark. She smiled to herself, remembering the shy glances and tentative smiles that had passed between Felicity and Brent in the early days of their courtship.

Now, the two were practically inseparable. She'd grown accustomed to seeing them stroll hand in hand out in the garden or share quiet moments on the porch swing. It warmed her heart to see Felicity so happy, even if it meant their time together had become less frequent.

She dried her hands on a dish towel and gazed out the window at the clear blue sky. The day was perfect for exploring, and she had no doubt that Felicity and Brent would enjoy their trip to the mainland. A part of her missed the constant companionship, the way Felicity had relied on her in those first weeks of summer. But seeing the confidence and happiness radiating from her granddaughter now was worth any small pangs of loneliness. Besides, she was used to running the B&B on her own.

She laughed softly to herself. It was the natural order of things, wasn't it? You raise them, watch them grow, and then let them fly. But the B&B kept her busy enough, and she had her friends in town, of course. There was no need to feel sorry for herself. She wasn't one for melancholy, anyway. Life at Bayside had taught her to embrace the ebb and flow of life.

She opened the refrigerator and took stock of what she'd need for tomorrow's breakfast. As she jotted down a grocery list, she found herself looking forward to this evening when Felicity would surely pop in, full of stories about her day with Brent.

With a contented sigh, she finished her list and tucked it into her pocket. With the kitchen now spotless, she untied her apron and hung it on the hook behind the door. She poured herself a fresh cup of coffee and headed for the porch, ready to enjoy a moment of quiet before tackling the rest of her chores.

Yes, things would work out however they were meant to be. With the new inn and with Felicity and her new beau.

CHAPTER 2

Mark Donovan stood at the foot of the steps leading up to Bayside B&B, his weathered leather suitcase clutched in one hand. He really should get a new suitcase with those fancy spinning wheels. But he hadn't found the energy to order one before this trip.

The salt-tinged breeze ruffled his silver hair, carrying with it the distant cry of seagulls and the rhythmic lapping of waves against the shore. He took a deep breath, hoping the fresh coastal air might clear the fog that had settled over his mind these past few years.

With his ever-present weary sigh, he began his ascent. Each step felt heavier than the last, as if his writer's block had transformed into a physical weight that dragged him down. The once-prolific author who had captivated readers with his stories now struggled to string together a simple thought, a basic sentence.

As he reached the porch, he paused to take in the quaint charm of the B&B. Weathered shingles, window boxes bursting with cheerful flowers, and welcoming rocking chairs all spoke of a simpler time. It was a far cry from his sleek, modern apartment in Portland, where every corner echoed with memories and reminded him of his creative drought.

His gaze lingered on the doorknob. He hesitated, his hand hovering inches from it. Was he really ready for this? Ready to face new people, new conversations, new expectations? The thought of introducing himself as Mark Donovan made his stomach churn. Would anyone recognize him? How long before they asked about his next book? How long before the disappointment set in when they realized he was just a shell of the writer he once was?

He shook his head, trying to dislodge the doubts that clung to him. This was supposed to be a fresh start, a chance to rediscover his passion for writing. Yet here he was, paralyzed on the doorstep, the grief and frustration of the past three years threatening to overwhelm him once again.

With another look at the welcoming sign that simply said "come in," he took a deep breath and turned the doorknob.

The door swung open, revealing a warm, inviting interior. He squared his shoulders, summoning what little energy he had left to greet his host. He may have lost his creative spark, but he hadn't forgotten his manners. As he stepped over the threshold, he dared to hope that this change of scenery might be the key to unlocking the stories trapped inside him.

As he stepped into the B&B, the scent of freshly baked cookies wafted through the air, mingling with the faint hint of lemon-scented cleaner. The entryway opened into a cozy living room, where a silver-haired woman set down her knitting and rose from her armchair, a warm smile spreading across her face.

"You must be Mr. Donovan. Welcome to Bayside," she said, her voice rich with enthusiasm and warmth. "I'm Darlene Bond. We're so pleased to have you stay with us."

She approached him, arm outstretched. He hesitated for a split second before taking her hand in his. The moment their palms touched, a jolt of surprise coursed through him. How long had it been since he'd had such simple human contact? The warmth of her skin against his felt almost foreign, yet strangely comforting.

"Thank you, Mrs. Bond," he managed, his voice a bit rougher than he'd intended. "It's a pleasure to be here."

Darlene's grip was firm and reassuring, and he found himself reluctant to let go. When she finally released his hand, he felt an odd sense of loss.

"Oh, please, call me Darlene," she insisted, her eyes twinkling. "We don't stand on ceremony here at Bayside. Now, let me show you to your room. I'm sure you'd like to get settled in after your trip."

He nodded, grateful for her easy manner. He followed her up a narrow staircase, noting the family photos that lined the walls. Happy faces beamed down at him, reminding him of a time when his own home had been filled with such warmth.

"Here we are," Darlene announced, pushing open a door at the end of the hallway. "I've put you in one of our best rooms. It has a lovely view of the bay."

He stepped inside and took in the quaint

decor. A patchwork quilt adorned the bed, and lace curtains framed a large window that indeed offered a stunning view of the water.

"It's perfect," he said, surprised to find he meant it. The room radiated a sense of peace he hadn't felt in years.

"Wonderful," Darlene beamed. "Feel free to explore the grounds or relax on the porch. Breakfast is between about seven and ten. And if you need anything at all, just ask."

As she turned to leave, he felt a sudden urge to prolong the conversation. "Mrs. Bond—Darlene," he corrected himself, "I just wanted to say thank you for the warm welcome."

She paused in the doorway, her expression softening. "You're very welcome, Mr. Donovan. We're glad to have you here."

With that, she left, closing the door gently behind her. He stood in the middle of the room, suitcase still in hand, his laptop case slung over his shoulder, feeling oddly bereft. The silence that had been his constant companion for the past three years suddenly felt oppressive.

He set down his luggage and moved to the French doors, throwing them open and stepping onto the small balcony. He gazed out at the bay. The water sparkled in the afternoon sun, and a handful of sailboats dotted the horizon. It was a scene that once would have inspired pages of prose. Now, he only felt a dull ache where his creativity used to reside.

But as he watched a seagull swoop low over the water, he felt something stir within him. It wasn't quite inspiration, not yet. But it was a flicker of… of something. Interest, perhaps. Or maybe just a momentary respite from the grief that had become his constant companion.

He took a deep breath, inhaling the salty air. Maybe, just maybe, coming here hadn't been a mistake after all.

Maybe.

Darlene returned to the living room, settled into her favorite chair, and picked up her knitting. Soon she was back into the flow, her needles clicking a steady rhythm as she shaped the heel of a Christmas sock for Felicity. Yes, the holidays were a ways off, but it always paid to get a jumpstart on holiday knitting.

Her fingers moved deftly as she knitted, her mind drifting to their newest guest. Mr. Donovan's arrival had aroused feelings of curiosity and concern. She'd noticed the weariness etched on his face and the slump of his shoulders as he'd carried his bag up the stairs.

There was a certain sadness in his eyes that reminded her of Felicity when she'd first arrived at the B&B this summer, burned out and in need of a reprieve. But Mr. Donovan's exhaustion seemed to run even deeper, as if he carried an invisible weight.

She paused her knitting, her gaze drifting to the window. He'd barely said two words during check-in, his responses polite but clipped. In her years of running the B&B, she'd encountered all types of guests, but there was something different about Mr. Donovan. He seemed to be holding something back, guarding a deep sadness or secret.

She shook her head, chastising herself and reminding herself not to get too invested. He was just another guest, after all. It wasn't her place to pry into his personal life or try to solve whatever troubles he might be facing.

Still, she couldn't help wondering what brought him to Bayside. Was he running from something? Searching for inspiration? Or simply in need of a change of scenery?

She resumed her knitting as the gentle click of her needles filled the room. She'd seen many lost souls pass through the B&B over the years, each one carrying their own burdens. Some found what they were looking for during their stay, while others left just as lost as when they arrived.

She hoped, for Mr. Donovan's sake, he'd find some peace here at Bayside. But she knew better than to interfere. Her job was to provide a comfortable, welcoming space for her guests, not to solve their problems.

As she finished another row of stitches, she made a mental note to ensure Mr. Donovan had everything he needed for a comfortable stay. She'd keep an eye out, as she always did, but she'd respect his privacy. Sometimes, all a person needed was a quiet place to sort through their thoughts.

CHAPTER 3

Eleanor adjusted her grip on Winston's leash as they made their way down the street. Her cavalier dog moved slower these days, but their daily walks remained a treasured routine. A routine they both could count on. And she firmly believed routines were important.

She glanced down at Winston, his tail wagging as he sniffed along the sidewalk. "You're taking your sweet time today, aren't you?"

Winston looked up at her with those soulful eyes she'd grown to love over the years.

The familiar streets of Magnolia Key spread before them, and she considered her route. She rarely varied from walking the exact same streets. Though, Jonah had mentioned his new place on Wisteria Street when he'd called last night and said today was moving day for him. It wasn't far from her house—just a few blocks over. That wouldn't vary their routine that much.

Should she just stop by? Although, she didn't like surprises. Didn't like people dropping in without calling first. She paused at the corner, uncertain.

"What do you say, Winston? Should we see how Jonah's settling in?"

The dog's steady pace answered for them both as he tugged on her leash. They turned the corner and made their way toward Wisteria Street.

When they got to the street, she spotted the moving trailer right away. Jonah stood at the back, swinging boxes out and stacking them on the drive. His silver hair caught the afternoon light as he worked, and she allowed herself a brief study of him. He'd aged some, but in that way that some men had of just getting more handsome. His broad shoulders stretched the simple shirt he had on.

Winston's tail picked up speed, wagging excitedly back and forth at the sight of someone he knew. She let him set their pace as they approached.

Jonah turned at the sound of their footsteps, and his whole face brightened with a warm smile. "Well, hello, Ellie. And Winston, good to see you too, fella." He leaned down and patted Winston's head.

"Winston and I were just taking our walk and saw your trailer. Are you getting all moved in?"

Jonah laughed. "Not really. How can one man have so many boxes? Do I really need all this?" He motioned toward the stack of boxes.

She didn't think one measly trailer was really classified as too many possessions. She thought of her own home filled with furniture, paintings, rugs—every room brimming with items.

He stepped back. "Would you like to come inside? See the place? I still have lots of work to do on it, but it has good bones."

She frowned. "Shouldn't your landlord be taking care of all of that?"

His forehead creased. "No, I'm not renting. I bought the place."

"You what?"

"I bought it. Got a good deal on it since it needs work."

"But buying a house here—even though I know you said you were moving here…" She paused. "I guess I thought you meant you'd rent for a bit. Not make a permanent move like this. Before we…" She let the thought trail off. Before they even knew what was going on between them now, all these years later.

He stared at her for a moment. "I'm not giving up a second chance with you, Ellie." He nodded toward the house. "Now, would you like to see it?"

"We could come in for a few moments, couldn't we, Winston?" The dog wagged his tail in agreement.

Jonah grabbed some boxes and led the way up the stairs. She stepped through the doorway, and Winston padded along beside her. The living room stretched before them, bathed in afternoon sunlight that streamed through tall windows. Boxes were scattered around the room, some already opened with their contents spilling out on the floor.

She ran her gaze around the room. The walls were painted a faded yellow color that had seen better days. The hardwood floors creaked under her feet as she moved further into the room, showing their age, but still solid. Built-in bookshelves lined one wall, their craftsmanship speaking to an earlier era when things were made to last. She'd always loved these older homes. They had character and history. Stories within their walls. Winston's nails clicked against the floor as he meandered off to investigate a corner.

"The realtor said these floors are original to the house," Jonah said as he set down the boxes he'd carted inside. "I've got plans for this place. The kitchen needs updating, and I'd like to replace these old windows. Maybe add a deck out back for morning coffee." He shoved some boxes out of the way. "And of course, paint the place. Refinish the floors. Lots of work."

When she turned back to face him, his expression was cautious as if he was waiting for her verdict. "Well?" he asked.

She looked around once more, seeing past the current state to what it could become. "It needs work," she said, watching his face fall slightly before she continued, "but I can see why you bought it. These old houses, they're worth saving."

The tension in his shoulders eased. "I

thought maybe you'd think I was crazy, buying a place that needs so much renovation."

"Oh, I still think you're crazy," she said, but she smiled as she said it. "But it's a good kind of crazy."

Winston had made his way back to them and sat at her feet, looking up expectantly. She reached down to scratch behind his ears.

"I apologize for the mess," he said as he walked over and cleared some boxes from the couch. "I haven't quite found homes for everything yet."

"You certainly have plenty to unpack." She settled onto the worn but comfortable couch and Winston curled up at her feet.

"More than I realized," he admitted. He sank into the armchair across from her. "But there's no reason to hurry." He shrugged. "Except for living in this chaos."

She rested against the back of the couch. It felt oddly familiar being with him. Yet different too. They weren't the same people they'd been all those years ago. She looked over at him. "I think it has a lot of potential. I do. I just didn't realize you were going to *buy* a place here."

"You're worried. I can see it in your eyes,"

he said softly. "Talk to me. What are you worried about?"

She met his eyes for a moment. "People will talk. They already are."

"Let them." He leaned forward in his chair. "We're not kids anymore. We know who we are and what we want."

But did they? The question nagged at her as she absentmindedly stroked Winston's head. They'd both lived full lives in the years they'd been apart. He couldn't expect everything to fall back into place like no time had passed.

"I—" She glanced around the room. "It's just a lot of work." And she wasn't just talking about his house.

"Ellie." He leaned forward, his voice gentle. "I'm not going anywhere. I chose this place, this island, because it's where I want to be. The work doesn't scare me. Nothing about being here scares me—except maybe the thought of you walking away again."

She wanted to reassure him, to tell him that she wasn't going anywhere either. But the words stuck in her throat. It had been so long since they'd been together, really together. They'd both changed, grown, and lived separate lives.

Could they really pick up where they'd left off all those years ago?

Winston looked up at her, his brown eyes seeming to sense her unease. She reached down and stroked his head, finding comfort in his always-there-for-her presence.

Jonah watched her, his expression a mix of hope and uncertainty. She could see the questions in his eyes, the same ones that swirled in her own mind. What if they'd changed too much? What if they couldn't find their way back to each other?

She tapped her fingers on the arm of the couch, searching for words. "Jonah, I…" She trailed off.

"Ellie, I know it's been a long time. I know we can't just pick up where we left off. But I'm here now, and I want to try. I want to see where this goes."

"I want that too," she said softly. "I just… I don't know how to do this. It's been so many years. And I've lived all on my own for so long and… I just need time," she said quietly. "Time to adjust to all this."

"Then we'll take things slowly," he continued. "But I'd like the chance to get to know who you are now. For you to get the chance to know the man I've become." He reached out and took her hand, his fingers warm and solid against her own. "We'll figure it out together. One step at a time."

She nodded, feeling a flicker of hope in her chest. Maybe they could do this. Maybe they could find their way back to each other.

He squeezed her hand. "I'm not leaving you again. Not disappearing like last time. I'm here until we figure out what this is. What this can be."

Winston's tail thumped against the floor, as if in agreement. She smiled down at him, then back up at Jonah. "One step at a time," she repeated. "I think we can do that." She rose, taking back her hand. "I should leave you to your unpacking."

He led her to the door and stepped out onto his front porch. He smiled at her. "I'm glad you stopped by. Drop by anytime."

She climbed down the stairs and turned back to him, searching his face. A battle raged within her. She hesitated, then plunged on. "Would you like to come to dinner tomorrow night?"

"At your house? I'd love to." He nodded

eagerly. "So I guess you learned to cook in the years I've been gone."

She laughed softly. "No, not really. But I'll ask my cook to make us something nice."

He tried to hide his grin with little success. "Well, it still sounds nice."

"I'll see you at six." With that, she headed down the sidewalk with Winston trotting slowly at her side. She glanced back once and saw he was still standing outside on this porch, watching her. Just like he used to when they were young and she'd hurry off to return home before her father knew she was gone.

When they got home, Eleanor hung Winston's leash on the hook by the door. The familiar jingle of his tags and his nails clicking against the hardwood floors broke the silence as he trotted off to the kitchen and headed straight for his water bowl.

She wandered into the living room, her footsteps echoing in the empty house. The silence settled around her, a reminder of the solitude that she had grown accustomed to in recent years. She paused by the bookcase, her gaze drawn to the framed photographs that chronicled—or ridiculed—her life.

There was a picture of her and Theodore on their wedding day. Her expression held the expected smile even if her eyes showed a hint of sadness. Another showed Cliff as a baby, cradled in his father's arms, his tiny face scrunched up in sleep. Ah, Cliff, the son who now wanted to ruin the quaint look of the island with a multi-storied building at the end of the boardwalk. Eleanor's fingers traced the edges of the frames, wondering what life she thought she'd be living when she decided to marry Theodore. But she'd made her choice and did what her father expected of her. A Whitmore always did what was expected.

She moved to the window, looking out at the quiet street. The sun was beginning to set, its warm beams painting a soft layer of light over the neighborhood. She watched as a young couple walked by, hand in hand, their laughter carrying on the gentle breeze. For a moment, she was transported back to a time when she and Jonah had been that couple, lost in each other's company. Though, they had always hidden in the shadows, never allowing anyone to see them.

The sound of Winston's bark pulled her from her reverie. She turned to see him standing in the doorway, his tail wagging expectantly. "All right." She smiled indulgently, moving toward the kitchen. "I suppose it's time for your dinner."

As she filled Winston's bowl, a twinge of loneliness crept over her. The house felt too big sometimes for just her and Winston. But then, she couldn't imagine doing that downsize thing that older people were always talking about. This house was her home. Every corner held memories of the life she'd built here. Even if that life wasn't exactly as she'd hoped.

Pushing her thoughts aside, she walked back into the front room, her steps measured and precise. She moved to the bar cart in the corner, its polished brass gleaming. The wine bottles stood in neat rows—a collection she'd curated over the years. Her hand hesitated over several before selecting one of her favorite Cabernet Sauvignons.

The crystal wineglass clinked softly as she set it down, the deep red liquid catching the light as she poured. She took a small sip and let the rich flavor settle on her tongue. Theodore had never approved of women drinking alone, but

Theodore wasn't here anymore. No one was here to tell her what to do. Not Theodore. Not her father. No one could tell her how to live her life. And that freedom was welcome, almost enough to overcome the emptiness of the house.

Winston entered the room, gave her a lazy glance, and wandered over to settle in his bed. She walked over and sat on her favorite chair, her thoughts drifting to dinner tomorrow. She'd need to speak with her cook about the menu. Maybe a nice beef tenderloin. But perhaps that was too formal? She took another sip of wine, frustrated by her own indecision. When had she become this person who second-guessed everything?

She smoothed her hand over her skirt, a nervous gesture she thought she'd left behind decades ago. Just like that flutter in her heart when she saw Jonah earlier today. She'd felt like a young girl again for a brief moment, standing there on his front porch.

Foolish, really. She was far too old for such schoolgirl reactions. But there it was—that same skip in her heartbeat she'd felt the first time Jonah Burton smiled at her. Back then, she'd told herself it was just a passing fancy. Her father had already arranged her marriage to

Theodore Griffin, after all. The Whitmores and Griffins had been planning that union since she was in pigtails.

But Jonah's smile still had the same effect on her, even after all these years. Even after everything that had happened between them. Even after she'd chosen duty over love.

She took another sip of wine. For now, she allowed herself this moment of remembering—of feeling. The house was quiet except for Winston's soft snoring from his bed in the corner, and in that silence, she could admit to herself that some things never changed. No matter how much time passed, no matter how many carefully constructed walls she built around her heart, Jonah Burton still made it flutter.

CHAPTER 4

The next afternoon, Darlene stepped onto the porch carrying a batch of her famous chocolate chip oatmeal cookies, their edges perfectly baked to a golden brown. She offered some to a young couple nestled together on a loveseat with books resting on their laps. At the far end of the porch, Mr. Donovan sat hunched over a notebook, his pen tapping against the page.

She approached him slowly, not wanting to startle him. His brow creased in concentration, and he seemed lost in whatever world lived inside those pages. "Mr. Donovan, these just came out of the oven, if you'd care for one."

His gaze drifted up slowly, like someone swimming up from the depths of the sea. "Oh, thank you, Darlene. That's very kind of you." He reached for a cookie and the corners of his mouth tilted up in a small smile.

Darlene hesitated. "Care to take a break? Do you mind if I join you for a bit?"

"Not at all." He gestured toward the empty chair, his shoulders relaxing just a touch. "I could use the company."

She settled into the chair beside him. "You look a bit perplexed, Mr. Donovan. Something troubling you?"

He sighed, setting down his pen. "Please, call me Mark."

"Okay, Mark it is." She nodded and took one of the cookies off the tray.

"And yes, I'm a bit frustrated. I came here hoping to find inspiration, but it seems my muse has abandoned me."

"You're working on…?" She eyed the blank page in his open notebook and the crumpled pages beside him on the chair. The late afternoon sun cast shadows across the pristine white paper, making the emptiness seem even more vivid.

"A new book. Or I'm supposed to be working on it. I just can't… find the words." He drummed against the notebook's blank pages, a quiet movement filled with frustration.

Recognition dawned on her. *That* Mark Donovan. The highly successful mystery author. She hadn't seen a new book of his out in a while. How long had this writer's block been going on? His last novel—what was it called?—had been a bestseller about three or four years ago.

He looked out at the bay for a moment before turning back to her with a hint of vulnerability in his eyes. "Worst case of writer's block ever. I feel like the words are there, but they're stuck deep inside me, refusing to come out on the page. I thought that maybe coming here would help me find my way back to writing. But instead, it feels like I'm lost, spinning in circles."

"Sometimes the best thing we can do is to be patient with ourselves. Inspiration will come when it's ready."

He laughed, but there was little humor in it. "I wish I had your optimism. I feel like I've been waiting for inspiration for—well, a long time—ever since..." He trailed off, his gaze drifting to the horizon.

She sensed there was more to his story, but

she didn't pry. He could tell her in his own time, or keep his secrets.

"So," she said, "what story are you hoping to tell?"

His eyes widened in surprise, as if he hadn't expected the question. "I…" He shrugged. "I'm not sure yet. I think I've lost sight of it."

His hand drifted back to his pen, fidgeting with it. Frustration showed in every movement, in the tension across his shoulders.

"You know what I do when I'm stuck on a problem?" She adjusted her position in the chair, letting the sea breeze cool her face. "I bake. Or garden. Or take a walk along the shore. Anything but focus on the problem itself."

"But I have deadlines." He frowned. "My publisher—"

"Will still be there whether you write today or not." She gestured toward the water, where sailboats dotted the horizon. "This island has a way of helping people find what they need, but only if they let it."

He raised an eyebrow. "You sound like you're speaking from experience."

"Oh, I've seen it happen more times than I can count. People come here wound up tight as a spring, and after a few days, they remember how to breathe again."

"I suppose." He set his notebook aside. "It's just that writing used to be as natural as breathing. Now every word feels forced."

"Then don't force it. Take some time to explore. Take a walk. Visit the lighthouse. Grab dinner at Sharky's. Try the fried grouper and make sure you get a side of hushpuppies. Sit and watch the sunset from the beach." She leaned forward. "The words will come back when they're ready. But first, you need to give yourself permission to just… be."

His shoulders relaxed and for the first time since his arrival, she saw a glimmer of relief in his eyes.

"The island has its own rhythm," she continued. "Slower, steadier than life on the mainland. There's no rush here."

He studied his cookie for a moment before taking another bite. He smiled at her. "This is delicious."

"Family recipe. Been making them for years." She paused, letting him enjoy the moment. "See? Sometimes the simplest pleasures are the best medicine."

"You might be right." He brushed the

crumbs from his hands and looked out at the water again. "Maybe I have been pushing too hard."

"The best stories come from living, not from staring at blank pages. Give yourself time to experience the island. The rest will follow." She rose. "Well, I'll leave you to it. Or you could just sit here and watch the boats pass by. It's very relaxing."

He nodded slowly. "Thanks for… the wise words. Maybe I will just sit back and enjoy my time here for a bit. Maybe that's what I need."

"Anytime." She offered him the tray of cookies, and he took another one, smiling. She went back inside, hoping her words had helped him. He did look a tiny bit more at ease after they talked. But not enough to totally erase the haunted look in his eyes. The island would have to do its magic to help with that.

Mark settled deeper into the cushioned patio chair as Darlene went back inside. He turned his gaze to the garden, where brightly colored flowers swayed in the afternoon breeze. The second cookie he'd taken from Darlene sat untouched on the small table beside him, chocolate chips peeking out from the golden-brown surface.

The familiar scent of fresh-baked cookies stirred memories he usually kept locked away. Sarah had been the baker in their family, filling their home with the enticing scent of baked goods every Sunday afternoon. Even now, he could picture her hands dusted with flour, her reading glasses perched on the end of her nose as she studied her mother's recipe cards. The ache in his chest, unrelenting these days, squeezed a little tighter.

Two years, four months, and twelve days since Sarah had gone. He really should stop counting…

The same amount of time since he'd written anything worth keeping. His agent called weekly now, asking about progress on the new novel. She said his publisher was getting nervous. That his advance might have to be paid back. There was talk of dropping him entirely from their stable of authors. At this point, did he really care? Did he have any stories left inside him?

But there was no progress to report no matter how often his agent called.

His fingers traced the worn edges of his

notebook. Sarah had given it to him on their last Christmas together. "For your next bestseller," she'd said, her eyes bright with the certainty that he'd fill those pages with another best-selling mystery.

The notebook remained blank. Every time he opened it, he remembered her sitting across from him at their breakfast nook, reading his latest chapters with a red pen in hand. She'd been his first reader, his best critic, his partner in crafting stories that had kept millions of readers awake late into the night.

"Did you see that ending coming?" he'd ask her.

"Not until about page two hundred," she'd reply with a smile. "That's where you left that tiny clue about the muddy shoes."

Now his characters felt like strangers. Their voices no longer whispered to him late at night. Their stories no longer unfolded like movies playing slowly in his mind until he captured them on paper.

He'd told Darlene it was writer's block, but that wasn't the whole truth. How could he explain that writing meant stepping back into a world he'd shared with Sarah? Every plot twist he thought of reminded him of their discussions over coffee. Every character description brought back memories of her thoughtful suggestions.

The porch's peaceful atmosphere wrapped around him, but peace wasn't what he needed. Peace meant quiet, and quiet meant memories. The memories he'd come here to escape. But they followed him everywhere, even to this small island and this quaint bed-and-breakfast.

His agent had suggested Magnolia Key. "Get away from the city," she'd said. "Find somewhere quiet to write."

But she didn't understand. The words weren't simply stuck—they were gone, buried in the same cemetery where he'd laid his heart to rest beside Sarah's grave. The grave he visited weekly with fresh flowers to set by her headstone.

The breeze off the bay carried the salt-tinged air across the garden. A wind chime tinkled softly, its melody reminding him of the one that had hung on their back porch. Sarah had loved wind chimes. He took it down after she died, unable to bear hearing it any longer.

Mark clipped his pen to the notebook and shut it softly. Maybe Darlene saw him as just another writer struggling with a creative dry spell. It was easier that way. Easier than explaining how the simple act of putting words on paper now felt like betrayal—like trying to build a new life.

When the only life he wanted was the one he could never have back.

He knew that coming to the island was a desperate attempt to escape his grief, to find some semblance of inspiration amid the beauty. But now, as he sat there, he wondered if it had been a mistake. Could he really rediscover his passion for writing, for life itself, when everything seemed so gray, so bleak?

But maybe he should take Darlene's advice. Explore the island for a bit. Not try to force the words. But could he give himself permission to do as Darlene said?

To just… be?

CHAPTER 5

Eleanor walked over to the front window for the fourth—maybe fifth—time in the last ten minutes, scanning the street for any sign of Jonah. Not that he was late. She'd just been dressed and waiting for him for over an hour. She'd changed outfits twice, unsure of herself. Which annoyed her no end because she was never uncertain about anything. At least she hadn't been until Jonah's return.

She turned from the window and headed to the kitchen. Warmth radiated from the oven where Mrs. Paterson's masterpiece of the day waited—chicken infused with fresh rosemary, tender green beans, and homemade rolls. A peach pie sat on the counter, its lattice crust a perfect golden hue. The sweet scent of peaches and cinnamon filled the room.

The kitchen felt different without her cook's bustling movements. The house stood quiet now that she'd dismissed Mrs. Paterson for the evening. The privacy would allow her and Jonah to speak freely, without the sound of staff in nearby rooms or the gentle clink of dishes being washed. Although Mrs. Paterson, her cook of twenty years, had perfected the art of invisibility as she did her work, Eleanor preferred she and Jonah had the house to themselves tonight. While she trusted Mrs. Paterson's discretion—she'd never hired anyone who didn't understand the value of silence—she felt tonight's conversation required privacy, the kind only an empty house could provide.

Now, if she could only manage to plate up their meals with as much finesse as Mrs. Paterson…

Reassured that everything was ready for their dinner, she headed back to the front room. Winston's tail thumped against the floor as she crossed over to the window yet again. She peeked outside and spotted Jonah walking up the sidewalk to her front door. As she hurried to the door, the mirror in the entryway caught her eye. The silver-haired woman staring back at her seemed a stranger. So different from the young girl who had been so eager to meet up with Jonah in their youth. At the door, she smoothed her dress and waited for him to knock. And waited some more. Seconds stretched to minutes. She frowned and finally opened the door.

Jonah stood there, his hands in his pockets and a sheepish look on his face. The corners of his mouth lifted in that familiar half-smile she remembered so well. "I was just thinking how strange this was. That I could just walk up to your front door and knock. Your father never would have allowed that."

"No, he wouldn't." She nodded. "But then, he's long been resting in his grave."

Jonah still stood outside on the porch.

"Well, come in, come in." No use letting the whole town see him standing out there on her porch.

She closed the door behind him, her heart beating faster than it had any right to at her age. The familiar scent of his aftershave brought back memories she'd kept packed away for decades. The same crisp, clean scent.

He stood close to her, yet not too close. A

small smile crept across his features. "You know, the house looks almost exactly like I remember it. Well, the front of it. It wasn't like I was allowed inside all those years ago. But sometimes, late at night, I'd sneak over and look at your house, wondering which room was yours, if it was one with the light on."

"My room was on the back of the house, overlooking the gardens. It still is. I moved back into it after Theodore passed away. I much prefer it to the master suite." She wasn't sure why she told him all that. "Anyway, some things don't need changing. Just fresh paint on the front of the house and keeping up with the garden is all that's needed." Though plenty had changed, whether they wanted to acknowledge it or not.

Winston padded over to investigate their guest, his tail wagging in a slow, dignified manner. Jonah bent down to scratch behind the dog's ears.

"Shall we have a drink before dinner?" She gestured toward the front room. "And Mrs. Paterson left everything ready in the kitchen when we're ready to eat."

"I drink sounds nice." He followed her into

the front room, his footsteps echoing on the hardwood floors.

"Wine? Scotch?" She paused. "Or we might have some beer in the fridge." She did keep some beer for the few times her son, Cliff, stopped by.

"Red wine is fine."

She poured them each a glass and turned to see that Jonah had settled into one of the wingback chairs. Theodore's old chair, she realized with a start. She walked over and extended the wine, ensuring their fingers wouldn't brush during the exchange. She took her seat in her favorite chair, across from him.

Silence stretched between them, broken only by Winston's soft snuffling as he made himself comfortable on his bed in the corner. She took a sip of her wine, letting the liquid steel her nerves.

"You know, I thought about calling to cancel," he said quietly. "I know you want to take things slowly and you're a bit unsure of things."

"You were going to cancel?" Her hand tightened on her glass. "But what made you decide to come?"

"Because I've spent too many years *not* showing up at your door."

She didn't know what to say to that. She knew she'd hurt him when she chose Theodore. When she hadn't been brave enough to choose him. And it had been clear that her father would never approve of Jonah, not for his daughter.

"But that's in the past, Ellie. All of it. We have now and we have the future. To make of it what we want." He smiled at her. "But now, let's talk about something else, not rehash the past."

"That sounds like an excellent idea." Relief washed through her. The past was full of painful memories. Just normal, everyday conversation sounded like a lovely idea.

He took a sip of his wine. "Nice. Good round flavor with a hint of spice and maybe a bit of blackberry."

"So you know your wines?" She tilted her head, surprised.

"A bit. I actually worked in a vineyard over in France for a couple of years."

"There's so much about you that I don't know."

"I'm an open book. Ask me anything."

"I don't even know where to start." She

paused, then continued. "You're getting closer to your nephew now?"

"Now that I even know that I have one?" He grinned. "It's a bit of an adjustment knowing I have family again. I… I like it. And yes, we're getting close. Though, Brent spends most of his time with Darlene's granddaughter, Felicity. I think he cares greatly for her."

She traced the rim of her wineglass with her finger. "Young love is so different, isn't it? They're willing to rush headlong into everything. Like Brent and Felicity, with their whole lives ahead of them."

"Were we so different at that age?" Jonah's eyes held a warmth she remembered from decades ago.

"No, I suppose not." She paused, considering. "Though we didn't get what we wanted back then. And now…" She lifted one shoulder in a slight shrug. "Now there are so many layers to everything. So many years of habits and routines."

"And walls we've built around ourselves," he added. He shifted in Theodore's old chair, and she forced herself not to think about how strange it felt seeing him there.

"Exactly. I've lived alone for so many years

now. I have my routines. My quiet mornings with Winston. My garden. My committees." She took another sip of wine. "And you've had your travels, your freedom."

"Freedom can get lonely." His voice was soft, thoughtful. "Watching Brent with Felicity reminds me of that. Young love doesn't question itself, it just moves forward, full steam ahead."

She nodded. "While we sit here analyzing every little thing." She let out a small laugh. "Though perhaps that's wisdom rather than hesitation."

"Or perhaps it's fear dressed up as wisdom." His gaze met hers. "We're not exactly young anymore, Ellie. We don't have the luxury of endless time ahead of us."

"No, we don't." She smoothed her skirt, then settled her hand when she realized what she was doing. "But we do have experience. We know how easily things can go wrong, how complicated relationships can become."

"True. But we also know what matters. The problems that seemed so important in youth don't mean much anymore, do they?"

Winston got up from his bed and padded over to Eleanor's chair, resting his head on her knee. She scratched behind his ears, grateful for the familiar comfort of his presence.

"No, they don't," she agreed. "But starting over at our age… It's different from young love. There's no blank slate. We bring our whole lives with us—our children, our memories, our losses."

"Maybe that's not such a bad thing," he said. "Those experiences made us who we are. I'd like to think they made us better equipped for love, not worse."

"Maybe." She rose, hoping to break up the serious discussion. "I'll go take up our dinner."

"Can I help?"

"Could you refill our wine glasses? Then just head across the hall to the dining room. I'll be there in a minute with our food."

She turned and hurried off to the kitchen while Jonah headed to the bar cart, their serious conversation firmly set aside. For now.

Jonah carried the wine bottle into the elegant dining room and carefully refilled their glasses. The crystal stemware caught the light from the chandelier overhead, creating delicate patterns on the polished mahogany table. Ornately carved chairs sat around the table, each with richly upholstered seats.

His gaze traveled over the formal place settings, the silver candlesticks, and the ornate china cabinet displaying what he guessed were family heirlooms. The wallpaper featured a subtle damask pattern that complemented the heavy drapes framing bay windows that overlooked the garden.

"This is quite a dining room," he said, setting the wine bottle on a silver coaster as Ellie entered the room and set their plates on the table.

"It's the same table that's been in our family for generations." She sat down gracefully and smoothed her napkin across her lap. "Mother always said every proper home needed one."

He thought of his own modest cottage on Wisteria Street with its small eating nook and basic furnishings. He'd spent his career as a craftsman, working with his hands, either fixing things at the ports he'd worked at or his woodworking hobby. But his own place had always been simple, functional.

And he'd never actually met Ellie's mother. The Whitmores were old money, with generations of influence in the community. He'd known that even as a young man, but sitting here now, the differences in their backgrounds felt more pronounced.

"Your house is beautiful, Ellie." He slipped into the seat across from her.

"It's just a house," she said, but her eyes softened as she gazed around the room. "Though I suppose I've grown rather attached to it."

The evening light filtered through the windows, casting a warm glow across the antique sideboard where family photos in silver frames captured moments of Ellie's life with Theodore. Their wedding day, holidays, vacations—a whole history displayed with careful precision.

He sat up straight in his chair, feeling the weight of the years between them. He'd built a good life for himself, but it was worlds away from Ellie's refined existence. She'd been surrounded by family while he'd been alone.

The question that had nagged at him since reconnecting with her surfaced again—could two people from such different worlds find common ground after all this time?

CHAPTER 6

Mark descended the stairs early the next morning, lured by the aroma of fresh coffee and something cinnamony baking in the kitchen. The familiar scents reminded him of mornings with Sarah, but today the memory didn't crush him quite as heavily as usual.

In the dining room, soft morning light filtered through the windows with a warm, cheerful glow. A few early risers occupied tables near the windows, speaking in hushed tones over steaming mugs.

Darlene looked up from arranging fresh flowers on one of the empty tables. "Good morning, Mr. Donovan. You're up early today."

"Mark, please."

"That's right. Mark." She smiled.

"I thought I'd take your advice about exploring the island." The words felt strange, like trying on an old jacket that didn't quite fit anymore. Since Sarah's death, his world had shrunk to his desk and blank pages or pacing around his house. Not going out and roaming an island to see what it held in store for him.

"Coffee first?" Darlene gestured to the carafe on the sideboard.

He poured himself a cup, savoring the rich scent. "I could use some suggestions on where to start."

"The lighthouse is beautiful this time of morning." Darlene moved to the counter and pulled out a fresh batch of yeasty cinnamon rolls from the warming drawer. "The view from up there puts everything in perspective. Or if you prefer staying at sea level and don't want to climb all the stairs, the boardwalk's perfect for a morning walk. Lots of cute shops along the way."

"The lighthouse might be good." Mark accepted a cinnamon roll, remembering how Sarah used to joke about his sweet tooth. "I could probably use a new perspective."

"It's about a twenty-minute walk from here. Head out to Main Street and cut over to Seaside

Avenue, walk to the end. You can't miss it." Her eyes crinkled with warmth. "And if you get hungry later, after all that exercise, Coastal Coffee is right on the boardwalk. It's an excellent place to grab a bite of lunch."

"Thank you." He settled at a small table by the window, watching early morning sunlight dance across the bay in the distance. Maybe Darlene was right. Maybe what he needed wasn't to force the words, but to look at the world differently. A new perspective.

He finished his breakfast, tucked his notebook into his jacket pocket more out of habit than intention, waved to Darlene, and stepped out into the warm morning air. For the first time in he didn't know how long, he felt a flutter of something that *might* have been anticipation.

Darlene watched Mark leave. He'd seemed to relax as he'd eaten his meal and gave her a friendly wave as he left. She hoped he had a good time exploring today, though she wasn't sure if she'd pushed him into it, or whether it truly was a good idea for him. She knew nothing about writer's block. But she did know about sometimes needing a day for herself. Not that she got many of those, owning the B&B.

She picked up his empty plate, noting how he'd cleaned it completely. At least his appetite seemed healthy enough. The morning sun streamed through the bay windows, highlighting the fresh flowers she'd placed on the tables. A good breakfast could do wonders for the spirit—her grandmother had taught her that—and she'd seen it proven true countless times over her years running Bayside.

"More coffee, Mrs. Clifton?" she asked the elderly woman at the corner table.

"Yes, thank you, dear." The woman hesitated, then continued. "I was wondering… I'm enjoying the island. I thought I might stay longer. Would it be possible to keep my room for a few more weeks? I have some… decisions to make and need more time."

"Yes, of course. We do have the availability. I'll put you down for, say, two more weeks? You let me know if you need longer."

"Thank you." Mrs. Clifton smiled, then turned her attention to her newly filled coffee cup.

She wasn't sure what was up with Mrs.

Clifton. She'd been here two weeks. In and out most days. The woman mentioned some long beach walks and browsing around on the boardwalk.

Maybe another guest looking for something or just needing a break.

She gathered a few more dishes and carried them to the kitchen. The routine of running the B&B kept her grounded, even as her thoughts drifted to her newest guest, Mark. There was an air about him that reminded her of herself after losing her husband at a young age—that lost look, the way he seemed to be searching for something he couldn't quite find or maybe he didn't even know what he was looking for.

The sound of Felicity's footsteps as she entered the kitchen broke through her reverie.

"Morning, Gran. Need help with those dishes?"

"I've got them, sweetheart."

"No, let me help." Felicity grabbed a dish towel anyway, falling into their familiar rhythm of wash and dry. "Was that Mr. Donovan I saw heading out?"

"Yes, I suggested he might enjoy exploring the island today."

"You and your suggestions." Felicity bumped

her shoulder playfully. "Always trying to fix everyone who comes through those doors."

"I do not." Darlene handed her another plate, then grinned. "Well, maybe I do. But I simply believe everyone deserves a chance to find what they're looking for. Even if they don't know what that is yet."

The door to the lighthouse creaked as Mark stepped inside. Sunlight filtered through the narrow windows, casting geometric patterns on the weathered steps that spiraled upward. His footsteps echoed in the confined space as he began his ascent, one hand trailing along the curved wall.

By the third turn, his breathing grew slightly labored. Sarah would have teased him about needing more exercise. The thought *almost* came naturally now, without the usual sharp edge of grief. And that surprised him. He paused, letting the observation settle over him—and to catch his breath.

He continued and climbed higher and higher until he reached the door to the observation platform encircling the structure.

He stepped out, and a gust of wind buffeted him, tugging at his shirt and tousling his graying hair. He gripped the railing, steadying himself against the sudden force.

From this vantage point, the vast expanse of the sea stretched out before him, an endless view of turquoise blue fading into the distance as the sea met the horizon. Sunlight glinted off the water, creating a shimmering glow that danced with each gentle wave. The rhythmic sound of the surf against the rocks below filled his ears, a constant and soothing melody.

As he gazed out at the ocean, a sense of peace settled over him, as if the wind was gently washing away the jumbled thoughts and heavy emotions that were weighing him down. The grief that had clung to him like a second skin seemed to loosen its grip, allowing him to breathe a little easier.

In this moment, it felt like it was just him, the ocean, and the brilliant sunshine. The rest of the world faded away, and the pressures of his writing career and the expectations of others disappeared. He closed his eyes, inhaling the salty air deeply, letting it fill his lungs and invigorate his senses.

As the wind continued to whip around him,

his thoughts drifted to Sarah and the countless memories they had shared. The ache of her absence was still there, a dull throb in his chest, but somehow, in the presence of the vast ocean and the endless sky, it felt more bearable.

He wondered what Sarah would have thought of this place, with its quaint charm and natural beauty. She had always been his anchor, his guiding light, and he knew she would have wanted him to find his way back to the passion that had once driven him. To make a life for himself.

He lifted his face skyward and reveled in the feeling of the wind and the sunshine on his skin. He stood still in the moment as a bit of lightness seeped through him. He opened his eyes again, taking in the vastness spread before him. This had been a good idea. To get outside. To explore the island. To get out of his head and his thoughts and all the pressure. He'd have to thank Darlene for the suggestion. She was a wise woman.

CHAPTER 7

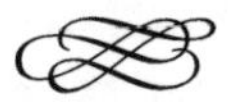

Darlene entered the back door of Coastal Coffee after closing time and found Beverly finishing up in the kitchen.

"Darlene, great to see you. What brings you here?" Beverly set down a tray of dishes.

"I'm just headed to the market to get a few things. Thought I'd pop in and say hi."

"I'm glad you did. I still have some sweet tea made up. Would you like a glass?"

"Sure, that sounds nice."

Beverly poured two glasses and led her over to a small table in the corner of the kitchen. They sat down, and Beverly let out a small sigh. "That feels good to get off my feet. Busy day today."

"I wish I could say I was that busy. We haven't been completely full of guests for weeks."

"I'm sure it will pick up. It's the end-of-summer lull is all." Beverly took a sip of her tea. "Oh, one of your guests came in today. He said you recommended the cafe to him. Mark Donovan. He was quiet, but friendly. He seemed like kind of a lost soul."

"You picked up on that too?"

Beverly nodded. "And he seemed familiar. I finally put two and two together and figured out he's that mystery author."

"He is. Though he told me he's having a bit of writer's block, which was why I suggested he put it aside and just explore the island for a bit."

"Always a good suggestion. Wandering the island always helps one sort things out."

"It does. Not that I've had much time for that. Felicity has been busy with Brent. Helping him with some research."

"You should hire someone part-time. Everyone needs a break sometimes. It really helps that Maxine is here and helping me with the cafe. I even took a full day off the other day." Beverly's mouth rose into a wry smile.

Darlene laughed. "Really? Well, good for you. Owning your own business isn't for sissies. It's a lot of work, a lot of hours."

"It is. But I wouldn't have it any other way." Beverly leaned back and stretched out her legs. "Say, did you hear about the new inn opening up?"

"Felicity mentioned it."

"It opens this weekend. They're calling it Sea View Inn." Beverly looked at her closely. "You worried at all about it?"

"No, I don't think so. It sounds like it will appeal to a different clientele than the guests who come to my B&B."

"You're probably right. And the wine bar they have—with something called small plates?—won't compete with Coastal Coffee because I'm only open for breakfast and lunch, not happy hour."

"As much as I like things to stay the same here on the island, I know that's not possible." She frowned. "Any more news about Cliff and the high-rise he wants to put at the end of the boardwalk?"

Beverly scowled. "Not that I've heard. I think it's stuck in some kind of re-planning stage. Trying to get it to squeeze past approval with the planning committee. I think they're having another open council meeting soon. I plan on going and voicing my opinion that a structure like that has no business on this island." She shrugged. "Anyway, I suggested to Cliff that he no longer come into Coastal Coffee. I have no desire to see him. There are other places he can frequent if he needs to eat out."

"Eleanor is pretty mad at him about the whole thing. She told me she didn't know where she went wrong in raising him. He should know better than to try to change the whole small-town atmosphere of Magnolia Key."

"Well, Cliff has always done what he wants. What's best for him. Never considering other people." Beverly's words came harsh, clipped.

"Hopefully, we can convince the town council to reject his plans."

"Hopefully. But he does have a few buddies on the council. And quite often, a Griffin or a Whitmore gets what they want."

Darlene smiled. "But have you ever seen Eleanor not get what she wants? And she sure doesn't want that high-rise."

Beverly laughed. "There is that."

She rose. “I should get to the store and back to the B&B.”

Beverly took the glasses and put them in the sink. “I’m glad you stopped by. Don’t be a stranger.”

She waved and slipped out the back door, eager to get her groceries and back to the B&B.

Darlene pulled into her usual parking spot behind Bayside B&B, then gathered the grocery bags from the trunk. The late afternoon sun cast long shadows across the wraparound porch, where Mark sat in one of the white rocking chairs, a notebook open on his lap.

“Good afternoon, Mark. Did you enjoy exploring the island?”

He looked up, closing the notebook. “I did. The lighthouse was exactly what I needed today. Thank you for the suggestion. Oh, and I had a late lunch at Coastal Coffee. Another good suggestion.”

She didn’t mention that she already knew that because she’d stopped by to see Beverly. His smile seemed more genuine. He stood and stepped forward. "Here, let me help you with those bags."

"That's very kind of you." She handed him two of the lighter ones. "I was just about to set out some wine and appetizers for the guests. Would you care for a glass?"

"That sounds wonderful, actually." He followed her to the door. "Would you consider joining me? I'd love to hear more about the island."

"I could take a few minutes, yes." She led the way into the kitchen, setting her bags on the counter. "Just give me a few minutes to arrange everything."

He placed his bags next to hers. "Can I help?"

"You're sweet to offer, but you're my guest. Please, make yourself comfortable on the porch. I'll bring everything out shortly."

He nodded and headed back outside while she began unpacking the groceries. She pulled out the cheese she'd purchased, along with fresh grapes, crackers, and two bottles of wine. Within minutes, she had arranged everything on her grandmother's silver serving tray.

Darlene balanced the silver tray as she stepped onto the porch. The late afternoon breeze carried the scent of jasmine from her garden, and the setting sun painted the sky in soft peach and rose. Mrs. Clifton and the Hendersons sat at the far end, deep in conversation about local restaurants.

"Would anyone care for some wine?" she asked, approaching them first. Mrs. Clifton accepted a glass of white wine with a warm smile, while the Hendersons declined politely, explaining they had dinner reservations in town.

Darlene made her way to where Mark sat, the tray now lighter. "I have a lovely cabernet or a crisp sauvignon blanc. Do you have a preference?"

"The cabernet would be perfect, thank you." Mark closed his notebook and set it aside.

She poured his wine, then settled into the chair beside him with her own glass of sauvignon blanc. The wooden rocker creaked softly as she found her rhythm, matching the gentle sway of the porch fans overhead.

Mark lifted his glass. "To Magnolia Key and all it has to offer."

"To Magnolia Key." She clinked her glass softly with his.

Darlene settled deeper into her rocker, watching Mark take a thoughtful sip of his wine.

The tension he'd carried in his shoulders when he first arrived had eased somewhat.

"The view from up at the top of the lighthouse…" He paused, swiveling his gaze out to the bay before turning back to her. "I spent nearly two hours just watching the waves. The boats coming and going. It gave me space to breathe."

"Sometimes that's all we need." She sampled a grape from the cheese plate. "A change of perspective."

"I even opened my notebook." He glanced at the leather-bound journal beside his chair. "Didn't write anything yet, but it's the first time in… a very long time… I've felt like I could."

"The island has a way of making people slow down. Relax." She smiled, remembering countless guests who'd found their own piece of solace here. "Some people come here looking for answers, others just need rest. The key is letting go of expectations."

"Sarah would have loved it here." His voice softened. "She always said I worked too hard, that I needed to slow down more."

"Sarah?"

But before he could answer, Felicity walked

up to them. "Hey Gran. Glad to see you sitting down for a change."

"Felicity, this is Mark Donovan. Mark, this is my granddaughter, Felicity. She's been helping me run the B&B this summer."

Mark rose and held out his hand. "Good to meet you, Felicity. Your grandmother has been incredibly welcoming."

"That's Gran for you. And it's nice to meet you too." Felicity shook his hand. "I hope you're enjoying your stay so far?"

"Very much. The lighthouse visit today was exactly what I needed."

"Oh, the lighthouse is one of my favorite spots." Felicity's face brightened. "Have you tried the walking trail that circles the small wildlife area beside it? The wildflowers are beautiful this time of year."

"Not yet, but I'll add it to my list." He smiled, and Darlene noted how the expression reached his eyes this time. He turned to her. "I was wondering if after breakfast tomorrow you might like to go with me and do some more exploring."

"Oh, I don't know. There's always so much to do."

"And luckily, I'm here to help you," Felicity

interrupted. "Gran, you should go. You deserve to take a break. I'll be here at the B&B and can handle anything that comes up."

"You sure?"

"I'm sure."

"Then thank you. Would you like to sit and join us and have some wine?"

"Thanks, Gran, but I'm meeting Brent for dinner." Felicity squeezed her grandmother's shoulder. "Just wanted to let you know everything's ready for the morning."

"Thanks, dear. You and Brent have a nice time tonight."

"I'm sure we will." Felicity headed back inside.

"Must be nice having her here helping you." Mark nodded toward Felicity's retreating back.

"It has been. She was a teacher. Well, still is, but she's not returning to the classroom this school year. She's suffered some burnout." Darlene smiled. "And she's met a nice young man, Brent Dunn. They've been dating. I like seeing her so happy like she is now."

"Well, I'm pleased she'll watch the B&B for you tomorrow and that you decided to join me on some more exploring."

"We could go to the wildlife area Felicity

mentioned, and then if we head back towards the bay, there's a pretty little cove." She paused and looked at him. "We could… maybe… pack a lunch and have a picnic?" Suddenly, she was unsure of her spontaneous suggestion.

He hesitated the tiniest bit, nodded, then answered, "Yes, I'd like that."

CHAPTER 8

The next morning after breakfast, Darlene wiped down the counter, the scent of maple syrup and coffee still lingering in the kitchen. Felicity loaded the dishwasher, humming softly under her breath. It was comforting to have her company even if they mostly worked silently side by side.

"I think that's everything from breakfast." Felicity closed the dishwasher and turned it on. "What are you packing for your picnic with Mr. Donovan?"

"Just a few sandwiches and some fruit." She placed the items in a wicker basket. "I don't want to make a fuss."

"Gran, it's okay to enjoy yourself." Felicity smiled. "You deserve a break."

"I know, but running the B&B is a full-time job."

"And I'm here to help." Felicity squeezed her grandmother's hand. "Go, have fun. Explore the island with Mr. Donovan."

She hesitated, then nodded. "Thank you, dear."

Just then, Mark popped his head into the kitchen. "Good morning, Darlene. Felicity."

"Good morning, Mark." She finished packing the basket, tucking in a small container of cookies and a thermos of lemonade.

Felicity dried her hands on a towel. "Perfect timing, Mr. Donovan. Gran was just finishing up your picnic lunch."

"Please, call me Mark." He smiled. "And thank you, Darlene. You didn't have to go to all this trouble."

"It's no trouble at all." She picked up the basket.

"Gran, go." Felicity made a shooing motion with her hands. "I'll finish up here."

"Are you sure?"

"Positive." Felicity grinned. "Now, you two have a wonderful time."

She glanced at Mark, who offered her a

reassuring smile. She untied her apron and hung it on the hook by the door.

"Shall we?" Mark gestured toward the door.

Darlene nodded, feeling a flutter of—*what?* — in her chest. She couldn't remember the last time she'd taken a day for herself. As they walked out of the kitchen, she glanced back at Felicity, who waved encouragingly.

The door creaked open, and she blinked against the bright morning sunlight. He held the screen door for her, his tall frame casting a shadow across the porch steps. She paused to breathe in the fresh coastal air, letting it calm her unexpected nerves. The familiar weight of the picnic basket grounded her as Mark led the way to where his car sat in the gravel driveway. His rental car gleamed in the morning sun, its silver paint job reflecting the cloudless sky above. A pair of cardinals darted past, red feathers bright against the green hedges bordering the driveway.

"Beautiful morning for a drive," he commented, opening the car door for her with an old-fashioned courtesy that made her smile despite herself. The gesture reminded her of gentler times, when such manners were commonplace rather than remarkable.

"I'm really looking forward to this day trip. I appreciate you taking the time to show me around," he said, his voice carrying a note of enthusiasm that made her earlier hesitation begin to fade. His genuine warmth helped ease the strange tension in her shoulders.

Darlene slid into the passenger seat of his car, and he placed the wicker picnic basket and the beach blanket she'd grabbed in the back seat. As they drove toward the boardwalk, a comfortable silence settled between them, punctuated only by the soft hum of the engine and the distant cry of seagulls. The morning sun sparkled on the water, and a light breeze carried the scent of salt and seagrass through her open window.

He parked the car, and they got out. "The trailhead starts just past those trees," she said, pointing to a wooden archway. "It's an easy walk, perfect for spotting wildlife."

They followed the sandy path, walking in comfortable silence. The air was filled with the gentle rustling of palm fronds and the chirping of birds. She breathed in the scent of wildflowers as the warm breeze surrounded them.

When was the last time she'd been here? She

couldn't even remember. She really should take a bit more time to smell the roses… or, in this case, the jasmine and free sea air.

They walked along the trail, side by side, and she pointed out various plants and trees, sharing tidbits of knowledge she'd gathered over the years. As they rounded a bend in the trail, Mark suddenly stopped, pointing toward the sky. "Look," he whispered.

She followed his gaze and gasped. There, soaring majestically above the treetops, was a bald eagle. Its white head and tail gleamed in the sunlight as it circled lazily overhead.

"Isn't it beautiful?" he murmured, his eyes never leaving the bird.

She nodded, transfixed by the sight. They watched in silence until the eagle disappeared from view, its presence lingering in the air like a whispered secret.

They continued wandering along the trails, enjoying the wildlife and the views, then headed back to the car. After retrieving the picnic basket, she led him along a narrow path that curved around the point of the island.

"Most tourists stick to the ocean side," she explained as they walked. "But this is my favorite spot."

The path opened onto a secluded cove, where gentle waves lapped at a crescent of sandy beach. A gnarled live oak spread its branches over a shaded area, creating a natural canopy.

"This is perfect," he said as he looked around the area with appreciation.

They spread the blanket under the oak tree and Mark set down the basket. The breeze carried the softer, calmer scents of the bay—more brackish and earthy than the ocean side. She settled onto the blanket and opened the basket, laying out their simple lunch.

"I hope you like turkey sandwiches," she said, unwrapping them from their paper. "And I brought some fresh fruit from the farmers' market."

"That sounds great."

She poured them both a cup of lemonade and set her sandwich on a cloth napkin, watching the gentle waves of the bay lap at the shore. The peaceful setting made her feel at ease, despite the weight of running the B&B that usually sat on her shoulders.

"This is wonderful," he said, biting into his sandwich. "Thank you for bringing me here."

"Sometimes we forget to appreciate what's

right in our backyard." She smiled, pulling out the container of fresh strawberries.

A flash of movement caught her eye, and she pointed toward the water. "Oh, look!"

Two dolphins broke the surface, their sleek bodies arcing gracefully through the air before they slipped back into the water. They played in the gentle waves, seeming to dance together in perfect synchronization.

He set down his sandwich, absorbed in watching them. "Nature's best entertainment."

As the dolphins disappeared beneath the water, a blue heron landed near the shoreline, its long legs carrying it through the shallow water with gangly steps.

"The wildlife here never fails to amaze me," she said. Her thoughts drifted to their conversation the previous evening. "Mark, you mentioned someone named Sarah last night before Felicity came and interrupted us."

He stilled, his sandwich forgotten on the napkin in front of him. The silence stretched between them, broken only by the soft splash of waves.

"Ah..." He cleared his throat. "Sarah was my wife." His voice was quiet, barely audible above the water. "She passed away two years ago."

"Oh, Mark. I'm so sorry." She wanted to reach out to offer comfort, but held back.

"Cancer." He picked up a strawberry but didn't eat it. "It happened so fast. One day she was fine, and then…" He set the strawberry down. "She always believed in my writing more than I did. Even at the end, she gave me a notebook, told me to keep writing."

"That must have been very difficult."

"I haven't written a word since she died." He looked out at the water. "Every time I try, I remember how she used to be my first reader, how she'd curl up in her favorite chair with my latest chapters." His voice cracked slightly. "I just can't seem to find the words anymore."

The blue heron took flight, spreading its wings wide as it disappeared around the curve of the shoreline. Mark stared after it, as if he wanted to flee with the majestic bird.

"I'm so sorry," she said again softly.

He turned to her and smiled slightly. "Thank you. I know she'd want me to move on. To find a life without her. I just haven't figured out how yet."

"These things take time. Sometimes it takes

us a while to figure things out when life throws us a big curve we weren't expecting."

He nodded.

She watched the water lap at the shore, giving him a moment with his thoughts. The breeze rustled through the oak leaves above them, creating dancing shadows on their picnic blanket. She understood loss—maybe not the same kind, but loss nonetheless. The way it hollowed you out and changed your whole world.

"I'm sorry you're having such a hard time finding your words again. Sometimes we need a fresh perspective, a new place to help us see things differently." She smoothed a wrinkle from the blanket. "Maybe being here on the island will help."

He picked up another strawberry, this time taking a small bite. "I hope so." He gazed out at the water. "My agent keeps calling, asking about the next book. But every time I sit down to write..." He shook his head. "The words just aren't there."

"Give yourself time. The island has its own rhythm, its own pace. Sometimes slowing down helps us find what we've lost."

"I hope you're right." He finished the

strawberry. "Sarah would have loved this place. The quiet, the wildlife, even this little cove." A small smile touched his lips. "She always did prefer the hidden gems to tourist spots."

She watched as a pair of sandpipers scurried along the water's edge on thin legs that moved in quick steps. "I think I would have liked your Sarah."

He smiled at her. "I think she would have liked you, too."

"Well, you're welcome to stay here on the island as long as you need," she said. "Sometimes finding our way back takes longer than we expect."

CHAPTER 9

The next morning, Mark settled into the weathered balcony chair, his leather notebook open. The tiniest germ of an idea for a new story had seeped into his mind in the shower this morning. Not much yet, but at least the seed. Just a whisper of possibility, but still a possibility.

He took out his fountain pen and let it hover over the blank page, then slowly began to write. His pen scratched against the paper, leaving behind a trail of hesitant words. Then a few more. He picked up the pen and stared at the words on the page. Dark ink against cream paper. The sight looked so familiar, and yet so foreign. The familiar loops of his handwriting filled the once-empty page, yet reading the words, he felt like an interloper who discovered someone's journal.

He stared at the words he'd written, doubt creeping in. Was this idea good enough? Could it sustain an entire novel? He'd had countless ideas over the past two years, but none had taken root. They'd all withered away, leaving him with nothing but frustration and blank pages.

But this idea… it nagged at him, refusing to let go. He picked up his pen again, jotting down a few more notes. The setting came into focus. A small coastal town not unlike this one. The main character began to take shape—a woman with a mysterious past who kept to herself.

As he wrote, the story started to unfold in his mind. Plot points, twists, and turns. And then, like a bolt of lightning, the perfect villain appeared. A character so complex and multi-layered that his hand flew across the page, desperate to capture every detail before it slipped away.

He wrote furiously, filling page after page with notes, character sketches, and snippets of dialogue. The villain's backstory, motivations, and secrets poured out of him, as if the character had been waiting in the wings all along, just waiting for Mark to bring him to life.

When he finally set down his pen and notebook, he leaned back in his chair, a sense of accomplishment washing over him. For the first time in years, he felt the familiar spark of excitement that came with a new story. The doubts that had plagued him for so long began to slowly recede, at least a little bit.

As he closed his eyes, savoring the moment, he swore he heard Sarah's voice whispering in his ear. "Way to go," she seemed to say. "I knew you could do it."

A smile tugged at the corners of his mouth. Sarah had always believed in him, even when he doubted himself. She'd been his biggest cheerleader, his most honest critic, and his unwavering support. Losing her had been like losing a part of himself, and for a long time, he'd wondered if he'd ever be able to write again.

But now, sitting on this balcony with the sea breeze blowing his hair and a new story taking shape in his mind, he felt a glimmer of hope. Maybe, just maybe, he could find his way back to the writer he'd once been. And maybe, in the process, he could honor Sarah's memory by doing what he loved most—telling stories that touched people's hearts with mysteries that kept people guessing until the very end.

With renewed resolve, he opened his eyes and reached for his notebook once more. He had a lot of work ahead of him, but for the first time in ever so long, he was ready to face the blank page. And somewhere, he knew, Sarah was smiling down on him, cheering him on every step of the way.

CHAPTER 10

For the next week or so, Darlene found herself taking a bit more time off and going on long walks with Mark. He accompanied her on the ferry to the mainland when she needed to do a larger shopping trip to restock items for the B&B. They often sat out on the porch after she served drinks and snacks to the guests for happy hour. They talked about their lives, their childhoods, their favorite foods. Slowly, she got a glimpse into the man he was before he lost his wife. An easy smile here and there, a laugh, a slight spryness to his step.

Tonight he sat with her in the front room as she knitted, while they both enjoyed an after-dinner glass of wine.

Her fingers moved deftly, the soft click of

her knitting needles punctuating the comfortable silence. She glanced up at him, noting the pensive expression on his face as he swirled the wine in his glass.

"So I have a bit of news I've been meaning to tell you," Mark began, his voice low and thoughtful. "I think I finally have the bones of a new book."

Her eyebrows rose in pleasant surprise. "That's wonderful. I know how much your writing means to you."

He nodded, a hint of a smile tugging at the corners of his mouth. "It's still in the early stages, but I've got a lot of it planned out. Characters, plot, setting… It's all starting to come together."

"I'm so glad to hear that." She set her knitting aside, giving him her full attention. "How many chapters have you written?"

He shrugged. "That's the problem. I haven't written any words. Just worked on planning out the book."

"What's holding you back from starting the actual writing process?"

His gaze dropped to his wineglass, his fingers tightening around the stem. "It's just… I feel a bit disloyal to Sarah, starting a book without her."

Her heart ached for him. She reached out, placing a comforting hand on his knee. "I understand how you must feel, but I don't think Sarah would want you to put your life on hold forever. She loved you and your writing. I'm sure she'd be thrilled to see you finding your passion again."

He met her gaze, his eyes filled with pain and a bit of hope. "You really think so?"

"I do." She gave his knee a gentle squeeze before withdrawing her hand. "Sarah will always be a part of you, and I believe she'd want you to embrace this new chapter in your life. Writing this book doesn't lessen what you had with her. It's a tribute to the love and support she always gave you."

He took a deep breath, his shoulders relaxing as he exhaled. "You're right. I know you're right. It's just hard sometimes, moving forward without her."

"Of course it is. Grief is a process, and everyone moves through it at their own pace. But I have faith in you. You have a gift, and I truly believe Sarah would want you to share it with the world." She grinned at him guiltily. "I have to admit, I downloaded a few of your books and I've been reading them at night. You're keeping me up way too late. They're very good. You keep me guessing until the very end."

A wide smile spread across his face. "Thank you. I love to hear when readers enjoy my books." He paused, looked directly into her eyes, and continued. "And… you've been a big help. Just spending time with me. Letting me work through all this. Your encouragement."

"Anytime." She picked up her knitting again, the familiar motion soothing her. "If you ever need a sounding board or a friendly ear, I'm always here."

He raised his glass in a toast. "To new beginnings and cherished memories."

She retrieved her glass and clinked it against his, the soft chime echoing in the cozy room. As they sipped their wine, a comfortable silence settled over them once more, broken only by the gentle rhythm of her knitting needles. She was getting quite used to spending time with him. And she wasn't sure if that was a good thing or not…

Later that night, Darlene moved through her nightly ritual, counting place settings and coffee cups for tomorrow's breakfast crowd. Four rooms occupied—Mrs. Clifton and Mark among them—barely warranted the term crowd.

Two couples had canceled their reservation, and she had a sneaking suspicion they'd gotten rooms at the new Sea View Inn. She pictured them sipping wine at the new, trendy wine bar or enjoying their luxurious whirlpool tubs.

The kitchen clock's soft tick punctuated her steps as she turned off the overhead light. A single lamp cast a warm glow across the worn floor tiles as she retreated to her suite. After changing into her favorite nightgown, she nestled into her bed and rested against the down pillows. Her e-reader cast a gentle blue light across her face as she found her place in Mark's novel, eager to lose herself in his words.

Before long, she set her e-reader on the nightstand, Mark's words swimming before her eyes. She'd read the same paragraph three times without absorbing a single detail. Her thoughts kept drifting to the time she spent with him and the easy conversation between them. How much he seemed to enjoy just sitting on the porch with her, chatting away, or the way his eyes had brightened when he spotted that eagle soaring overhead, or his appreciation of a simple picnic at the cove.

"Stop it," she whispered to herself in the quiet bedroom.

She'd lived on Magnolia Key long enough to know how these things played out. The summer visitors came and went. The winter guests drifted through like the tide. Even the most charming ones packed their bags, eventually.

Mark belonged to a different world. A world of book tours and publishing deadlines, of city lights and literary circles. He'd come here searching for his words, and once he found them, he'd return to that life.

The way he'd opened up about Sarah today, the raw grief still evident in his voice, made it clear his heart remained with his wife. That kind of love didn't fade quickly, if ever.

No, it was better to keep things simple. They could share morning coffee and pleasant conversation. She could recommend more walking trails and maybe show him a few more of the island's hidden spots. Just two people enjoying each other's company until his inevitable departure.

She reached for the lamp switch. She really should go to sleep. Tomorrow would bring its familiar rhythm of breakfast preparations, checking in with guests, and managing the countless details that kept the B&B running smoothly. That was her world, and it had served her well all these years.

She should concentrate on the B&B, especially with that new inn opening up. She needed to focus on what mattered. Keeping her business thriving and supporting Felicity. Those were the constants in her life, not temporary connections with passing guests, no matter how engaging they might be.

CHAPTER 11

Darlene knew exactly where to find Eleanor. This was Eleanor's regular morning to go to Coastal Coffee. Her own guests had eaten early, and she'd cleared the dishes and left them for later. She wanted a chat with her friend. The rumors had been flying that Eleanor and Jonah had often been seen about town.

She was certain her friend wouldn't be pleased about the gossip, but she hoped Eleanor and Jonah were working things out. They'd spent a lot of years apart after Eleanor had married Theodore… and what a mistake that had been. Just like Darlene marrying Dean had been. He'd left her in a hot minute when she got pregnant, never interested in knowing anything about their child. Both she and Eleanor had made poor choices in their youth. Hopefully, they were wiser now.

Darlene stepped into Coastal Coffee, the bell above the door announcing her arrival. The aroma of freshly brewed coffee and warm pastries welcomed her as she scanned the room. She spotted Eleanor at her usual table, engaged in conversation with Beverly.

She made her way over to join them, weaving between the tables and offering friendly smiles to the other patrons. As she approached, Beverly looked up and grinned.

"Well, look who's here! Good morning, Darlene. Care to join us?"

She nodded, pulling out a chair and sitting down across from Eleanor. "I'd love to, thanks."

Eleanor turned to her, a slight frown creasing her forehead. "It's good to see you, Darlene. How are things at the B&B? A bit worried about all the hoopla about the new Sea View Inn."

"I've had some cancellations, but I'm doing okay." She didn't want anyone worrying about her. She'd figure things out. She always did.

Beverly reached for a clean mug and held it up. "Coffee, Darlene?"

"Please," she replied, grateful for the offer.

As Beverly poured the steaming coffee, Darlene noticed the way Eleanor's fingers tapped lightly on the table, a habit she'd had for as long as Darlene could remember. It usually meant her friend had something on her mind.

"So, Eleanor," she began, accepting the mug from Beverly with a nod of thanks, "I've been hearing some interesting rumors around town lately."

Eleanor arched an eyebrow, her fingers stilling. "Oh? And what might those be?"

Darlene took a sip of her coffee, savoring the rich flavor before continuing. "Word has it that you and Jonah have been spending quite a bit of time together."

Eleanor scowled and glanced down at her mug. "Well, I suppose there's no hiding anything in this town, is there?"

Beverly chuckled, slipping into the chair beside Darlene. "You know how it is. Magnolia Key thrives on gossip."

She reached out and patted Eleanor's hand. "I know you value your privacy, but I hope you know that I'm here if you ever want to talk about it."

Eleanor met her gaze with a mixture of

gratitude and hesitation in her eyes. "Thank you. It's just… It's been so long, and we've both changed so much. I'm not sure what to make of it all."

"Take your time," she advised, her voice gentle. "There's no need to rush into anything. Just enjoy getting to know each other again."

Beverly nodded in agreement. "Darlene's right. You and Jonah have a lot of history, but that doesn't mean you can't start fresh."

Eleanor sighed, a small smile tugging at the corners of her mouth. "I suppose you're both right. It's just strange, navigating this at our age." Then Eleanor turned to her and pinned her with a gaze. "And how about you? I hear you've been seen about town with one of your guests. Frequently. A famous author, if I heard correctly."

"I'm just showing him around town a bit. He's had a bit of a rough go of things. Lost his wife a few years back."

"Oh, that's too bad." Beverly's eyes filled with sympathy.

"I think he's finally finding a way to deal with it." She shrugged.

Eleanor's eyes narrowed, and she tilted her head. "So… you like him?"

"What? No. It's not like that."

"Isn't it?" Eleanor raised an eyebrow.

She didn't answer her friend because she really had no idea what it was. Didn't know what was going on between her and Mark. Maybe it was just all in her mind. But it didn't really matter, she reminded herself. He was a famous author and soon he'd be off to bigger and better things.

"You're always taking care of everyone," Eleanor interrupted her thoughts. "You know, maybe it's time you did something for yourself. Go out with the man. Have some fun. Get to know him."

She looked over the rim of her mug at Eleanor. "I could say the same about you and Jonah."

Eleanor's lips tilted into the tiniest smile as if saying, touché.

The three women fell into a comfortable silence, sipping their coffee and lost in their own thoughts. Darlene felt a warm sense of camaraderie with her two friends, knowing that they'd all faced their share of challenges and heartaches over the years, but they'd found a way through them.

~

Darlene walked up the driveway of the B&B, still mulling over Eleanor's words at the cafe. She glanced at the wraparound porch and spotted Felicity chatting with Mark. Her granddaughter's animated gestures made her pause. She knew that look.

Felicity was up to something.

"Gran!" Felicity called out as Darlene walked up. "Perfect timing. I was just telling Mark about the theater opening their new show this weekend."

Mark turned in his chair, offering a warm smile that made her heart skip.

No. No, it didn't. She was just a bit out of breath from her quick walk back from the cafe.

"Your granddaughter speaks highly of their productions."

"Oh, they do wonderful work," Darlene said, climbing the porch steps. She noticed the manuscript pages spread across the small table beside Mark's chair. "I see you've been writing."

"Finally making progress," he admitted. "The words are coming easier now."

Felicity nodded her head emphatically.

"Which is exactly why you should celebrate by going to opening night. Both of you."

Darlene shot her granddaughter a warning look that clearly said stop meddling, but Felicity just grinned, completely undeterred.

"They're doing that new comedy," Felicity continued. "What was it called? 'The Late Bloomer' or something like that? I heard it's supposed to be hilarious."

"Felicity." Darlene's tone carried a warning.

"What? The theater needs support, and you both could use a night out." Felicity smiled innocently. "Besides, I already mentioned to Mark how much you love live theater, Gran."

She felt her cheeks warm as she gave Felicity another pointed look. Her granddaughter simply smiled, completely immune to the silent reprimand.

Mark cleared his throat. "It does sound interesting."

"See? I told you it was a good idea. Anyway, I should head out. Brent's waiting." Felicity moved toward the steps, then paused. "Oh, and the show starts at eight on Friday. Just in case anyone's interested." She practically skipped down the stairs, leaving Darlene shaking her head at her granddaughter's less-than-subtle matchmaking attempt.

Darlene turned to Mark, an apologetic smile on her face. "You'll have to excuse my granddaughter. She… ah… meddles. We don't have to go."

He paused, his expression thoughtful. "Actually, I think it sounds like a nice idea. Would you like to accompany me?"

She blinked, surprised by his invitation. "Oh, well, I suppose it could be fun." She hesitated, searching his face. "Are you sure? I don't want you to feel pressured into it."

He chuckled softly. "Not at all. I think a night out would be good for both of us. Unless you'd rather not?"

"No, no, I'd love to go," she assured him, feeling a flutter of excitement in her chest. "It's been a while since I've been to the theater."

He smiled, his brown eyes warming. "Then it's settled. We'll go together."

She nodded, returning his smile. "All right then. I'll let you get back to your writing. Just let me know if you need anything."

"I will. Thank you."

She turned and headed inside, her mind racing. As she stepped into the foyer, she took a deep breath, trying to calm her nerves. It's not a date, she told herself firmly. He just asked her to *accompany* him, that was all.

But as she walked into the kitchen, she felt a spark of anticipation. It had been so long since she'd gone out with anyone, let alone a man as charming and handsome as Mark. She shook her head, chiding herself for getting carried away.

"Get a hold of yourself, Darlene," she muttered, busying herself with the dishes in the sink. "You're just two friends going to see a play. Nothing more."

Yet even as she said the words, she wondered if there was something more between them. The way he looked at her, the easy conversation they shared—it felt different from just a friendship. But she couldn't let herself get swept up in romantic notions. He was still grieving, and she had her own baggage to deal with.

No, it was better to keep things simple. They would go to the theater, enjoy the show, and come back to the B&B as friends. That was all it could be.

She sighed, drying her hands on a dish towel. She glanced out the window, catching a glimpse of Mark on the porch, his head bent over his manuscript, jotting notes with a red pen. A small smile tugged at her lips. Even if they were just friends, she was grateful for his presence in her life. He brought a sense of warmth and companionship. Something she hadn't realized she was missing.

CHAPTER 12

Mark stood before the mirror in his room at Bayside Bed-and-Breakfast, adjusting his collar and smoothing down his hair. The reflection that stared back at him seemed almost unfamiliar—the gray that had crept into his hair over the past few years, the lines that now framed his eyes. Time had left its mark on him, a sure sign of the grief and struggles he'd endured since Sarah's passing.

As he prepared for the evening ahead, a flicker of uncertainty danced through his mind. Was attending the theater with Darlene a wise decision? It wasn't a date, he reminded himself firmly. He didn't date, not anymore. Not since Sarah. This was simply two friends enjoying each other's company, sharing in an experience they both appreciated.

Yet, even as he silently reassured himself, he couldn't ignore the faint stirring of anticipation in his chest. Darlene's presence had become a reassuring constant during his stay on the island, her warm smile and gentle encouragement a balm to his weariness. She seemed to understand the weight of loss, the struggle to find purpose and meaning in the wake of tragedy.

His gaze drifted to the notebook lying on the dresser, its pages filled with the beginnings of a new story, a tale inspired by the tranquility and rich history of the coastal town and the secrets he imagined lurking below the surface. Darlene's words ran through his mind, urging him to embrace the island's magic, to allow himself to rediscover the passion that had once driven his writing.

With a deep breath and one more look at his reflection, he turned away from the mirror. Tonight, he would step out of the shadows of his grief, if only for a few hours. He would allow himself to enjoy the company of a friend, to lose himself in the laughter and entertainment of the theater.

As he made his way downstairs, his thoughts lingered on Darlene. Her strength and her resilience in the face of her own challenges had become a source of admiration for him. In the midst of their shared experiences, a connection had begun to form. One, he had to admit, that went beyond the boundaries of a simple guest and innkeeper relationship.

But for now, he pushed aside the deeper implications, focusing instead on the evening ahead. A night of laughter, of companionship, of momentary escape from the weight of the past.

Darlene looked up from the bottom of the stairs, her eyes meeting Mark's appreciative gaze. A flutter of nerves danced through her as she took in his appearance. He wore a button-down shirt that accentuated his broad shoulders and trim waist, and his hair, threaded with silver, was neatly combed.

"You look very pretty tonight," he said, his voice warm and sincere.

She felt a blush creep up her neck. "You do too," she replied, then immediately cringed at her own words. She needed to pull her thoughts together.

Felicity, standing at Darlene's side, nudged her gently with an elbow. Darlene glanced at her granddaughter, who gave her an encouraging smile.

"I mean, you look very handsome," Darlene corrected herself, smoothing her hands over the skirt of her dress. She had chosen a simple navy blue dress for the opening night of the new comedy at the local theater. It had been years since she'd dressed up for a night out, and the unfamiliar sensation of butterflies in her stomach caught her off guard.

Mark descended the last few steps, his eyes never leaving Darlene's. "Thank you," he said, offering her his arm. "Shall we?"

She hesitated for a moment, her mind whirling with the implications of accepting his gesture. It was just a friendly outing, she reminded herself. There was no need to read too much into it. And yet, as she slipped her hand into the crook of his elbow, she couldn't deny the spark of electricity that seemed to pass between them.

Felicity stepped forward, handing Darlene her clutch purse. "You two have a wonderful time," she said, her eyes twinkling with mischief. "Don't worry about a thing here. I've got it all under control."

Darlene nodded, grateful for her granddaughter's support. She knew Felicity was up to something, playing matchmaker between her and Mark, but she couldn't find it in herself to be upset. Not when Mark was looking at her with such warmth and admiration.

As they stepped out into the warm evening air, she felt anticipation building within her. She knew it was foolish to hope for anything more than friendship with Mark. He was still grieving the loss of his wife, and he would eventually leave the island to return to his life in the city. But for now, she allowed herself to enjoy the moment, the feeling of his arm beneath her hand, and the promise of a lovely evening ahead.

The evening air held a hint of salt and honeysuckle as Darlene walked beside Mark down Main Street toward the theater. His steady presence at her side felt both comforting and unsettling.

The night had transformed the street into a scene from a vintage postcard. String lights twinkled between the lampposts, and couples young and old meandered along the sidewalks. The familiar storefronts of Main Street took on a magical quality in the evening light, and she found herself seeing them through new eyes. She turned to glance at Mark, only to find him already looking at her with a soft expression that made her heart flutter. When their eyes met, he gave her hand a gentle squeeze where it rested in the crook of his arm, and she felt some of her nervousness melt away.

As they approached the restored theater building with its gleaming marquee, Darlene spotted Tori standing near the entrance, greeting early arrivals. Her gray hair caught the light of the marquee, and her natural elegance showed in her perfectly tailored outfit.

Tori's eyebrows rose slightly as she caught sight of them, a knowing smile playing at her lips. Darlene's cheeks warmed. She knew that look—it was the same one Felicity had given her earlier.

"Darlene, what a wonderful surprise," Tori said, stepping forward to greet them.

"Tori, I'd like you to meet Mark Donovan. He's staying at the B&B." She gestured to Mark. "Mark, this is Tori. She purchased the theater last year."

"It's a pleasure to meet you," he said, extending his hand.

"The pleasure's mine." Tori paused as recognition dawned on her. "Mark Donovan, the author? I've read several of your books." Tori's eyes sparkled with interest as she shook his hand. "Darlene, I had no idea you were coming tonight. And with such a brilliant writer as your date."

"Oh, we're just…" She paused, unsure how to define their outing.

"Enjoying an evening of theater," Mark finished smoothly.

She nodded, grateful for his intervention. "Tori has done amazing work here. The theater was practically falling apart before she bought it. Now look at it." She gestured to the beautifully restored building. "She's brought life back to this place, along with wonderful shows for the community."

"It's been a labor of love," Tori said. "Though I must admit, it's nice to see the seats filling up again. Tonight's show is particularly special."

The marquee lights reflected in Mark's eyes as he studied the building's architecture. "The restoration work is remarkable. You've preserved the original character."

"That was exactly my goal," Tori said. She glanced at the growing line of theatergoers. "I should get back to greeting my guests, but please, enjoy the show. And Darlene…" She paused, her expression softening. "It's wonderful to see you out for the evening."

They stepped into the theater's restored lobby, the familiar space transformed by the evening crowd's energy. She recognized faces all around her and their curious glances and whispered conversations weren't lost on her. She ignored the stares—at least she tried to—as they made their way through the lobby.

"Your seat numbers?" the young usher asked, checking their tickets.

"Row F, seats six and seven," Mark replied.

As they made their way down the aisle, she felt the weight of dozens of eyes following their progress. She caught the Jenkins twins pointing, their heads bent together in whispered conversation. Heat crept up her neck.

"Are you all right?" he whispered, his hand settling briefly on her lower back as she slipped into their row.

"Just fine," she said as she quickly sat down.

"Small town, you know. Everyone notices everything."

"Ah." His understanding smile put her at ease. "I suppose I'm giving them something to talk about."

"We both are," she admitted. "I don't get out much these days."

The lights dimmed, and a hush fell over the audience. She took a deep breath and tried to relax. In the darkness, she became aware of Mark's presence beside her—the subtle scent of his cologne, the way his arm rested next to hers on their shared armrest.

The show began, a clever comedy about mistaken identities in a small coastal town. The dialogue sparkled with wit, and the local actors brought their characters to life with enthusiasm. She found herself laughing more than she had in months.

During a particularly funny scene, she turned to share her amusement with Mark and found him already looking at her, his expression soft in the reflected stage lights. Her laughter faded into a smile, and for a moment, the rest of the theater seemed to fade away.

When the final act concluded, the audience erupted in applause. Darlene and Mark rose with everyone else, joining in the standing ovation.

Her heart felt lighter than it had in ages, buoyed by the evening's entertainment and Mark's companionable presence beside her. As the cast took their final bows, she caught herself stealing glances at him, touched by the genuine enthusiasm in his expression. After three curtain calls, the heavy velvet curtain finally swooped closed for good, and the house lights gradually brightened.

"Brilliant performances," Mark commented as he turned to her. She nodded in agreement, fumbling slightly with her wrap as the excitement of the evening still bubbled through her. He took the wrap and placed it gently around her shoulders, his hand brushing her skin momentarily, and she was honestly surprised not to see sparks flying between them.

She needed to get her thoughts under control. She took a step back as they waited patiently for the rows ahead of them to empty. They walked slowly up the aisle to the lobby. The theater doors were open, releasing a stream of chattering patrons into the warm evening air. She stepped out beside Mark, her smile lingering from the delightful performance. The sidewalk buzzed with energy as people gathered in small groups, discussing their favorite moments from the show.

Through the crowd, she spotted Eleanor and Jonah approaching. Eleanor's hand rested gently on Jonah's arm. Eleanor's elegant dress and Jonah's sharp sports coat suggested they'd made an evening of it too.

Eleanor caught her eye and raised an eyebrow, her lips curving into a knowing smile. Darlene returned the look, acknowledging their shared understanding of stepping out of their comfort zones.

"Eleanor, Jonah," Darlene waved. "I'd like you to meet Mark Donovan. He's staying at the B&B." She turned to Mark. "Mark, this is Eleanor Griffin and Jonah Burton, dear friends of mine."

Mark stepped forward, extending his hand. "A pleasure to meet you both."

"Likewise," Jonah said, giving Mark's hand a firm shake. "Did you enjoy the show?"

While the men exchanged pleasantries, Eleanor leaned close to Darlene's ear. "Good for you," she whispered, her eyes sparkling. "It's nice to see you out on a date."

"It's not a date," Darlene whispered back,

though her cheeks warmed at the assumption. She glanced at Mark, who was deep in conversation with Jonah about the theater's architecture. "I'm glad to see you out with Jonah."

"We're on an *official* date." Eleanor smiled. "You might be too, and you just don't know it."

"Shh…" she said quickly as the men turned back to them. She nodded at Mark. "We should probably get back home. I have to get up early tomorrow and get breakfast going for my guests."

"It was good to see you, Darlene. Maybe the four of us could go out sometime," Jonah suggested.

"I… uh…"

"Sounds like I good idea," Mark said agreeably as he turned to her and placed her hand on his arm. "Let's get you back home."

Darlene and Mark walked up the steps to the B&B's porch, the old boards creaking beneath their feet. The evening had been magical, filled with laughter and a definite connection she couldn't deny. As they reached the door, she found herself reluctant to let the night end.

With her hand on the doorknob, she turned to Mark. “Would you maybe… like a nightcap? I have a lovely bottle of wine I’ve been saving for a special occasion.”

His smile was warm in the soft glow of the porch light. “I’d like that very much.”

Their footsteps echoed in the quiet house as they made their way to the kitchen. She retrieved two glasses and the promised bottle of wine, then poured them each a small measure, the rich ruby liquid catching the light.

They carried their glasses back outside, where a gentle breeze stirred the potted flowers lining the porch. She settled onto a glider, and after a moment’s hesitation, he sat down beside her.

“It was a wonderful evening,” she said as she raised her glass to her lips.

“It was. I’m glad we went. It was a wonderful production. And your friend, Tori, has done a really nice job with the restoration of the theater.”

They sipped their wine in comfortable silence broken only by the occasional call of a night bird ringing through the air. Mark set his glass on the side table and gently pushed off with his foot, setting the glider in motion.

The rhythmic swaying was soothing, and she felt herself relaxing, the warmth of the wine and Mark's presence easing the tension she hadn't realized she'd been carrying. She leaned back, her shoulder brushing against his.

"This is nice," she said softly. "I can't remember the last time I just sat and enjoyed the evening like this."

Mark hummed in agreement. "There's something about this place, about being here with you, that feels… right. Like I'm exactly where I'm supposed to be."

She turned to look at him, her heart fluttering at the sincerity in his eyes. "I feel the same way. It's been a long time since—" Should she go on? "Since I've connected with someone like this."

"Me, too." His hand found hers, and their fingers laced together.

The glider swayed in its gentle movement, and the air wrapped around them like a familiar melody.

He finally broke the silence. "I know we've talked about my past. But we haven't talked much about yours." His shoulder gently bumped hers. "Your… husband…?" The question hung in the air between them.

She let out a long sigh. "That would be Dean." She paused, trying to form the words. She rarely talked about him. Or the pain. "We were very young when we got married. I was so in love with him. I thought he was my whole world." She shrugged. "Then I got pregnant with my son. Dean didn't want anything to do with a child. Or me, at that point. He just up and left without a word."

"While you were pregnant?" Mark squeezed her hand. "I'm sorry. That must have been hard."

"It was." The memories flooded back. Being so frightened and wondering what she was going to do as her life exploded around her. "Eleanor was there for me back then. Encouraging me. Helping me. She's been a good friend."

"I'm glad you had her."

"Anyway, I found ways to make it work. I worked two jobs and luckily found people to help watch my son and jobs where I could take him with me. We did okay. I scrimped and saved and eventually bought the B&B. My son grew up, got married, and they had Felicity, the light of my life. I had no idea how much joy a grandchild could bring. She'd come and stay with me every summer."

"Ah, that's why you two are so close. And do you ever hear from Dean?"

"No. Never. He never met his son or Felicity. Last I heard, he was somewhere in Montana. But that was maybe ten or fifteen years ago."

"I'm so sorry you went through that. It's… it's hard to lose someone unexpectedly."

"It was. I felt so deserted."

He looked into her eyes and there it was again, that undeniable connection. He pulled her hand close to his chest. "Darlene, I…"

The sound of a car door slamming interrupted them. She pulled her hand away, suddenly self-conscious, the moment broken. She stood, smoothing her skirt.

"That's probably Felicity and Brent," she said, slightly breathless. "I should go and ask about her evening."

He stood as well, his expression understanding. "Of course. I should probably turn in, anyway. Want to get an early start on the book tomorrow."

She walked him to the door, and they stepped inside. "Thank you for a lovely evening. I had a wonderful time."

"The pleasure was all mine," he said, his eyes holding hers. She stared into their depths, trying to read his thoughts.

He just smiled at her, then turned and disappeared up the stairs, leaving her alone in the entryway with a million thoughts ricocheting through her mind. She took a deep breath, trying to calm the riot of emotions swirling within her.

She knew she was treading on dangerous ground, allowing herself to feel this way about a guest, about a man who was still grieving for his late wife. She decided to slip upstairs without going to find Felicity. She'd give her some privacy to say goodnight to Brent. And if she was being honest with herself, she wasn't quite ready for her granddaughter's inevitable barrage of questions.

CHAPTER 13

Eleanor tugged Winston's leash and steered him in a new direction today on their walk. She deliberately headed in the opposite direction of Wisteria Street and Jonah's cottage, the usual path she'd come to take over the last week or so. Her chin lifted as she recalled the stares of the townspeople when she'd gone to the theater with Jonah last night. So many of them craning their necks, watching Jonah and her find their seats.

Not that it was anyone's business what she did. But the Whitmore reputation had survived generations of scrutiny in this town. She wouldn't be the one to change that now.

Even though she hadn't been a Whitmore since she was a young girl. But the Griffin name was *almost* as respected as Whitmore and part of the reason her father had been so determined that she marry Theodore.

It had been such a loveless marriage. He'd never shown her any affection, except occasionally when they were in public. At parties, he would rest his hand on her back and smile at her—a performance for the guests, not true affection. The cold silence afterward felt sharper after the tiny glimpse of the pretense of warmth.

At home he'd sit in his leather armchair, newspaper lifted like a shield between them. No holding hands. No quiet moments discussing their days. No praise when she pulled off a fancy dinner party for him.

What would her life have been like if only…

She shook her head. Dwelling in the past was for dreamers and romantics. She'd made her choice all those years ago, signed her name on that marriage certificate in flowing script. The ink had long since dried.

If-onlys were for fools. Everyone chose their path and lived with the consequences of their decisions. She couldn't go back.

She paused as Winston pulled on his leash so

he could snuffle along the base of a fence. She patiently waited for him to finish.

Her fingers traced the worn leather of Winston's leash, a comfort she'd relied on through so many seasons of change. Memories of last night's theater performance flickered through her mind—Jonah's warm smile, his gentle hand at her elbow as they walked up the steps. Such proper, innocent gestures, yet they'd set tongues wagging all over town. She squared her shoulders against the memory.

She was too old, too set in her ways for this sort of attention. The peaceful routine of her daily walks with Winston felt safer and more appropriate for a woman like her. At her age, she should be well past such foolishness as romance. The whole town probably thought the same—their whispers followed her like a dried palm frond skittering down the sidewalk.

She was Eleanor Griffin, née Whitmore, after all. The thought settled heavily on her shoulders, the familiar weight of expectations and propriety crushing down on her.

And these butterfly feelings when Jonah smiled at her? Surely they were just another misstep waiting to happen. Maybe all this with Jonah was a mistake now too.

Winston finished his exploration and turned to trot down the sidewalk. She clenched his leash a bit tighter as she thought about this morning. She'd gone to the market and heard two checkout girls talking. They were talking about her.

And Jonah.

"Do you hear that he used to be a dockworker? What is she doing going out with a *dockworker*?" one of the young girls had said.

"They're too old to be dating, anyway." The other girl shrugged.

She'd pushed her cart up to the checkout, given them both a hard stare—which at least caused them to blush—and stood silently as the girl rang up her purchases.

But they were just two of the many people who were talking about her, she was certain.

She and Winston rounded the corner back to her house. Her heart skipped a beat as she saw Jonah standing on her front porch, leaning against the railing, his hands tucked into his pockets and a welcoming smile on his face. She approached cautiously, Winston trotting alongside her, his tail wagging at the sight of a familiar face.

"Jonah, what are you doing here?" she asked.

He took a step forward, his eyes filled with concern. "I just wanted to check on you, Ellie. I noticed the stares last night at the theater. I wanted to make sure you were okay."

She felt a lump form in her throat. She'd hoped Jonah hadn't noticed the whispers and sideways glances, but of course, he had. He was observant, always attuned to her feelings, even after all these years.

She hesitated, unsure of how to respond. Part of her wanted to brush it off, to pretend that everything was fine. But standing there, with his warm gaze fixed upon her, she found herself unable to lie.

"I… I'm not sure," she admitted. "I don't like gossip associated with the Whitmore name. And I don't like change, Jonah. I like my routines. It's how I've survived my life."

He nodded, understanding etched in the depths of his eyes. He took another step closer, reaching out and gently touching her arm. "But merely surviving isn't the point, is it, Ellie? We have one life to live. Shouldn't we live it to the fullest? Do what brings us joy?"

Tears pricked at the corners of her eyes—totally catching her off guard because she never cried. Ever.

Jonah's words struck a chord deep within her. Still, she was unsure. And being unsure of something unnerved her. "Maybe we should take a step back."

"Ellie, we've barely taken a step forward." A crestfallen look swept over his face, but he quickly recovered. "But if you need space, need time, I can do that."

"Thank you. I think that's best."

He shook his head slowly. "But one thing is certain. I'm not giving up this time. I'm not walking away. I'll change your mind and show you we're meant to be." He reached out and took her hand. "Because we are, Ellie. We are. We are meant to be together. I can be patient until you realize that too."

He let go of her hand and walked down the stairs, giving her a brief wave as he headed down the street. Away from her…

But she'd made the right decision, hadn't she? This was just all too much. Too fast. Too… different.

"Winston, let's go in."

He looked up at her with a reproachful glance before stepping away from her and heading inside. Even Winston was questioning her decisions now.

CHAPTER 14

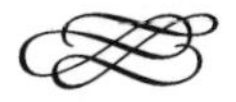

Darlene bustled around the kitchen, preparing breakfast for her guests. The aroma of freshly brewed coffee and sizzling bacon filled the air. As she flipped the pancakes, Felicity entered the room, an expectant smile on her face.

"Good morning, Gran," Felicity chirped, reaching for a mug from the cupboard. "How was your date last night?"

She felt her cheeks flush as she turned to face her granddaughter. "It wasn't a date. Mark and I just went to the theater as friends."

Felicity's grin widened as she poured herself a cup of coffee. "Whatever you say, Gran," she teased, her eyes twinkling with amusement.

She shook her head, focusing on the

pancakes to avoid Felicity's knowing gaze. She couldn't deny the connection she felt with Mark, but the thought of pursuing something more than friendship made her heart race with both excitement and… fear.

Felicity's expression turned serious as she leaned against the counter. "Gran, I have some bad news. Two more reservations have canceled."

Her heart sank. The B&B had been struggling lately, and she feared the new Seaside Inn was drawing away their guests. She took a deep breath, trying to maintain a positive outlook.

"I think it might be because of the new inn," Felicity continued, confirming Darlene's suspicions. "But don't worry, Gran. I have an idea."

Darlene raised an eyebrow, curious to hear her granddaughter's suggestion.

"Why don't we fix things up around the B&B?" Felicity proposed, her eyes sparkling with enthusiasm. "We could give the rooms a fresh coat of paint, update the decor, and maybe even add some new amenities. It might help us attract more guests."

She forced a smile, appreciating her

granddaughter's enthusiasm, but she knew the truth behind the B&B's financial situation. The cancellations and dwindling reservations had taken a toll on their income, and the thought of investing in renovations made her stomach clench with worry.

"That's a lovely idea, dear," she said, trying to keep her voice steady. "But I think the B&B is just fine the way it is. We've always prided ourselves on our cozy, homey atmosphere."

Felicity's brow creased, and Darlene could see the concern in her granddaughter's eyes. "But Gran, if we don't do something to compete with the new inn, we might lose even more guests."

She reached out and patted Felicity's hand, hoping to reassure her. "Don't you worry about that, sweetheart. We've weathered tough times before, and we'll get through this too."

Felicity didn't seem entirely convinced, but she nodded, trusting her grandmother's judgment. "If you say so, Gran."

Darlene turned back to the stove, flipping the last pancake onto a plate. She didn't want to burden Felicity with the financial struggles of the B&B. Her granddaughter had already sacrificed so much to help her run the place, and Darlene couldn't bear the thought of causing her more stress. Besides, Felicity had her own life to live. She had her new romance with Brent. She didn't need to get bogged down in the B&B's day-to-day struggles.

As she set the food out on the warming trays in the dining room, her mind wandered to the mounting bills and the dwindling savings account. She'd always managed to keep the B&B afloat, but with the new competition in town, she feared for the future of her beloved business. And what if Clint's high-rise got approved at the end of the boardwalk? What would that do to the B&B's reservations?

The sound of footsteps on the stairs pulled her from her thoughts. She looked up to see Mark entering the dining room, a warm smile on his face. "Good morning, Darlene. Something smells delicious."

She returned his smile, feeling a flutter in her chest at the sight of him. "Morning. I hope you're hungry. We've got pancakes, bacon, and fresh fruit this morning."

As Mark took a seat at one of the tables, Felicity walked past, shooting Darlene a knowing look. "Gran, I'm off to meet up with Brent if you don't need me anymore."

"I've got it, hon. You go and have a good time."

"We're working on some new research. It's fascinating the things that Brent can dig up."

Darlene poured coffee into Mark's cup, her hands steady despite the flutter in her chest. The dining room door opened, and Mrs. Clifton walked in, her silver hair neatly styled and her face bright with a wide smile.

"Good morning," Mrs. Clifton said, settling into a chair at the table next to Mark's. "The weather is perfect today."

"It does look like it will be a nice day." She filled another coffee cup and placed it in front of Mrs. Clifton. "Would you like pancakes this morning?"

"That sounds lovely." Mrs. Clifton's eyes sparkled. "And I wanted to tell you that I've made a decision. I'm thinking about finding a place to rent here on the island."

Darlene paused in her serving. "Really?"

"Yes, I've fallen in love with this island." Mrs. Clifton gazed out the window at the morning sunshine. "There's something special about it. The pace, the people, the sea air."

"That's wonderful news." Darlene set a plate

of pancakes in front of her. "The island does have a way of enticing people to stay."

Her gaze drifted to Mark, who was focused on buttering his pancakes. He glanced up, catching her eye, and she quickly looked away. Of course, Mark had his own life waiting for him—book tours, signings, events. His world moved at a much faster pace than their quiet island. But she couldn't help but wish it was Mark telling her he was staying on the island.

She pushed the thoughts away and busied herself with refilling coffee cups, but it was hard to ignore the odd ache in her chest at the thought of Mark's eventual departure.

He finished his breakfast and rose. "I'm headed out to the porch to write a bit." He pointed to his laptop case. "I want to finish the chapter I'm working out, then print it out for revisions. I'm old-school that way. I revise on paper."

"I'm glad the words are coming again."

"So is my agent." He laughed. "I sent him the first part of the book and he's really excited. Now if I can just pull it off."

"I'm sure you will." Not that she really knew what was involved in writing a book, especially a mystery with all its twists and turns. "Good luck with it."

Mark headed out to the porch, laptop case in hand, while she gathered up the plates and utensils from the table and carried them to the sink. The familiar routine that usually gave her such comfort felt a bit empty today.

Felicity was busy doing research with Brent. Mark was writing a new book. Even Mrs. Clifton was contemplating a new life. But here she was, doing the same thing, day after day. And now, with the added worry of finances.

She shook her head as she placed the dishes in the sink. It wasn't like her to feel sorry for herself. Enough of these thoughts. She was a lucky woman. Owner of a lovely B&B and she had a wonderful granddaughter. Her blessings were many.

Darlene tried to remember the feeling of how she was so blessed as she wrestled with the leaky kitchen faucet. No matter what she tried, she couldn't quite get the leak to stop and it was driving her crazy. Not to mention she wasn't one to waste water. And leaky faucets led to higher water bills.

She stood up and stretched, her hand on her back. And after she got this fixed—if she got it fixed—she needed to go work on the balcony door in room ten. The last guests had mentioned it was hard to open and wasn't closing properly. She couldn't bear to think of guests thinking the Bayside wasn't kept up properly. A B&B with reviews that said it was cozy could quickly turn into a B&B with reviews that said it was run-down.

She sighed, staring at the stubborn faucet that refused to cooperate. She heard footsteps behind her and turned to see Mark entering the kitchen. His eyebrows rose as he took in the scene before him.

"Everything all right?" he asked, his voice laced with concern.

She straightened up, wiping her hands on a dishcloth. "Oh, just trying to fix this leaky faucet. It's been driving me crazy, but I can't seem to get it to stop."

He stepped closer, examining the faucet. "Mind if I take a look?"

She hesitated for a moment, not wanting to trouble him—he was her guest after all—but the offer was tempting. She handed him the wrench. "Be my guest. I've been at it for a while now with no luck."

He rolled up his sleeves and got to work, his forehead creased in concentration. She watched, impressed by his focus and the confident way he handled the tools. It was a side of him she hadn't seen before, a glimpse beyond the grieving widower or famous author.

As he worked, she found herself studying his features. The way his salt-and-pepper hair fell across his forehead, and the intensity in his eyes as he tackled the problem at hand.

After a few minutes, he straightened up, a triumphant smile on his face. "There, that should do it. Give it a try."

She turned on the faucet, holding her breath. She turned it back off, and to her relief, there wasn't a single drip. She beamed at him. "You fixed it! Thank you so much. I don't know what I would have done without your help."

He shrugged, a hint of a smile playing at the corners of his mouth. "It's the least I could do. You've been such a gracious host, and I know running a B&B isn't easy."

A warmth spread through her at his words. It was rare for someone to acknowledge the challenges of her job, and even rarer for a guest to offer assistance. "Well, I appreciate it more than you know. It's been a bit of a struggle lately, trying to keep up with everything."

He nodded, his eyes full of understanding. "I can only imagine. If there's anything else I can do to help, please don't hesitate to ask."

She so wanted to ask how he was with cantankerous doors.

He must have noticed her hesitation. "Come on. Tell me. You've got something else that needs to be fixed, don't you?"

She gave him a sheepish grin. "There is this one balcony door…"

"Lead the way."

She grabbed the toolbox and led him up the stairs to room ten, grateful for his willingness to help. She opened the door to the room and gestured to the balcony. "It's just out there. The guest said it was sticking and not closing properly."

He stepped out onto the balcony, examining the door. He ran his fingers along the frame, testing the hinges. "I think I see the problem. It just needs a little adjustment."

He retrieved a screwdriver from the toolbox and set to work. She watched, impressed by his handiness. It was a pleasant surprise to discover this side of him.

Within minutes, he had the door gliding smoothly and closing securely. He turned to her with a satisfied smile. "There, that should do it. What's next on your list?"

"Oh, you've done more than enough. I'm sure you have writing to get back to."

"Have you ever been around a writer who is procrastinating? That's what I'm doing now. Procrastinating. I've written myself into a corner. I find if I step back and do something non-writing related, the solution will usually come. So I'm at your service this afternoon."

She hesitated, not wanting to impose, but the loose step on the front porch had been nagging at her. "Well, there is one more thing, if you don't mind."

He followed her downstairs and out to the front porch. She pointed out the wobbly step, and he crouched down to take a closer look. "Ah, I see. The board just needs to be secured. Do you have a hammer and some nails?"

She fetched the tools, and he quickly fixed the step. As he hammered the last nail in place, a guest emerged from the B&B, nodding approvingly at the repair.

As they headed back inside, she remembered one last issue that had been bothering her. “I hate to ask, but there’s a ceiling fan in the front room that’s been making an annoying noise. I don’t suppose you’d be willing to take a look?”

He chuckled. “Lead the way. I’m on a roll now.”

In the front room, Mark climbed up on a ladder and examined the fan. He tightened a few screws and gave the blades a gentle spin. The fan whirred to life, silent and smooth.

She clapped her hands in delight. “You’re a miracle worker! I can’t thank you enough for all your help today.”

He climbed down the ladder, wiping his hands on his jeans. “It’s my pleasure. I’m happy to lend a hand.”

She felt a sudden urge to repay his kindness. “Let me make you dinner tonight, as a thank you. It’s the least I can do after all you’ve done.”

He looked surprised, but a smile tugged at the corners of his mouth. “That’s very kind of you, but you don’t have to go to any trouble.”

She waved off his protest. “It’s no trouble at all. I love cooking, and it would be my pleasure to make dinner for you.”

He hesitated for a moment, then nodded. "In that case, I'd be delighted. Thank you, Darlene."

She felt a flutter of excitement. The prospect of cooking dinner for Mark and sharing a meal together appealed to her greatly.

"Oh, and I did think of a way out of the spot I wrote myself into. I'm just going to pop upstairs and make some notes."

"Okay, I'll have dinner ready about six, if that works for you."

She bustled into the kitchen, her mind already whirling with menu ideas. She couldn't remember the last time she'd looked forward to making dinner for someone, but somehow, with Mark, it felt different. Special.

CHAPTER 15

Felicity wandered into the kitchen about five-thirty and stared at Darlene. "Gran, what are you doing?"

Darlene blushed. "What does it look like? I'm making dinner."

"Gran, I'm sorry. I thought I told you. I have plans to go out with Brent and his uncle, Jonah."

"Yes, I remember."

Felicity frowned. "So, you're making all this for you?"

She turned to face Felicity, hands on hips. "If you must know, I'm making dinner for Mark. He helped out with a few repairs around here, and I thought this was the least I could do to repay him."

Her granddaughter made a weak attempt at hiding her smile. "Ah, yes. The least you can do. Well, you two lovebirds have fun."

"Felicity," she warned.

Felicity laughed out loud. "Just teasing. No, really. I hope you have a nice evening. I'll be home late. Don't wait up."

"Have fun." Darlene turned back to the final preparations for dinner. At five before six, she looked at the table. She'd set the table in the kitchen instead of out in the dining room where another guest might disturb them. Placemats and a vase of flowers from her garden made the table look fancier. She'd pulled out some of her china she rarely used, along with two nice crystal wineglasses.

Suddenly, she worried that she'd gone overboard.

The door to the kitchen opened and Mark stepped in. Too late to change anything now.

"Wow, it smells wonderful in here."

"Oh, just stuffed chicken breasts, some pasta, and a side salad," she said like she hadn't toiled tirelessly this afternoon getting it all ready. "Oh, and I made a pie. Peach."

"Love peach pie. And I don't remember the last time I had a home-cooked meal like this."

He grinned at her. "Well, except for your delicious breakfasts. Thank you for doing this for me."

"Thanks for all the help with repairs." She motioned to the table. "Sit down and I'll dish everything up."

She anxiously watched Mark's expression as he took his first bite of the stuffed chicken breast. His eyes widened, and a smile spread across his face.

"Darlene, this is absolutely delicious," he said, reaching for his wineglass. "You've outdone yourself."

She felt a flush of pride at his compliment. "Thank you. I'm glad you're enjoying it."

As they ate their meal, they chatted about the upcoming storm that was predicted to come in the next few days as well as the play they'd enjoyed so much at the theater. She enjoyed just sitting and chatting with him. It was easy and fun and… she really liked it. Liked *him*.

She sat back for a moment, letting that thought sink in. Admitting the truth to herself.

He interrupted her thoughts and asked, "So, tell me, what's it like running the B&B? It seems like a lot of work for one person."

She brought her thoughts back to his

question, ignoring the truth she'd just admitted to herself. "It can be challenging at times, but I love it. It's been my life for so long now, I can't imagine doing anything else."

"Do you ever take a break? A vacation?"

She paused, her fork hovering over her plate. When was the last time she had taken a real vacation? She couldn't remember. "I… I guess it's been a while. Years, maybe." Or maybe she couldn't ever remember taking one since she bought the B&B.

Mark's eyes filled with concern. "That's a long time to go without a break. Don't you ever feel like you need some time for yourself?"

She shrugged, pushing a cherry tomato around her salad plate. "Sometimes, but the B&B is my life. It's hard to step away from it, even for a little while."

As the words left her mouth, a realization struck her. Had she really let the B&B consume her entire life? She thought about all the invitations from friends she had declined, the vacations she had put off, and even the quiet moments alone she had sacrificed.

He seemed to sense her thoughts. "It's important to take care of yourself sometimes too. You deserve a break now and then."

She appreciated his concern. "You're right. Maybe it's time I start thinking about taking some time for myself." Although she had no idea how to make that happen.

They continued their meal, the conversation flowing easily between them while she steadfastly ignored the truth she'd discovered. She liked Mark Donovan. Liked him a lot.

After they finished their dinner, she cleared the plates and brought out the peach pie. His eyes lit up at the sight of the golden crust and the aroma of cinnamon and ripe peaches.

"This looks amazing," he said, accepting a slice from Darlene.

She smiled, pleased with his reaction. It had been a long time since she'd shared a meal like this with someone, and she realized how much she had missed the simple pleasure of good food and good company.

Mark stood at the end of the meal and gathered his dishes. "Let me help with these."

"How about I just rinse them and set them in the sink? I'll deal with them later when I'm getting things prepped for breakfast tomorrow."

"Are you sure?" He really wouldn't mind helping. He wasn't quite ready to call it an evening.

"I'm sure."

"Well, would you like to go out and sit on the porch for a bit?"

"That sounds lovely."

Relief swept through him that the evening wasn't over yet.

They headed outside, and Darlene settled onto the glider. The evening air was warm and heavy with the scent of honeysuckle, and the gentle sound of the water lapping at the shore of the bay created a soothing backdrop. He eased down beside her. The glider creaked and swayed gently as they found their balance together.

"It's a beautiful night," he said, resorting to small talk, even though he wanted to ask her questions and learn more about her. About her life here on Magnolia Key. What she thought about so many things. Her hobbies, her favorite color. So much he didn't know.

She nodded, her eyes scanning the horizon, where the evening darkened and the stars began to dot the sky. "It is. I love this time of day, when everything starts to slow down, and the world feels a little more peaceful."

They sat in comfortable silence for a few moments, enjoying the serenity of the evening. He found himself stealing glances at her, admiring the way the fading light played across her features. She looked relaxed and content.

"Thank you again for dinner," he said, breaking the silence. "It was delicious." Why would his mind only give him small talk? He wanted to ask her questions. Endless questions.

She smiled, turning to face him. "It was my pleasure. It's nice to cook for someone who appreciates it."

"I more than appreciate it. You're a fantastic cook." He hesitated, not sure he should say it, then added, "And a wonderful friend."

Her smile softened, and she reached out to pat his hand. "You're a good friend too, Mark. I'm glad you came to stay at the B&B."

A feeling of *something* spread through him at her words. He'd come to the island seeking solitude and inspiration, but he'd found something even more valuable in Darlene's friendship. She understood his grief and his struggle to move forward. Her presence brought comfort and belonging. Two things he'd been missing.

"I'm glad too," he said softly, covering her hand with his own. "I didn't know what to expect when I arrived here, but you've made me feel more at home than I have in a long time."

Her eyes glistened in the fading light, and she gave his hand a gentle squeeze. "That's what I want for all my guests, but especially for you. You've been through so much, and you deserve to find peace and happiness again."

He swallowed past the lump in his throat, touched by her words. "I'm starting to believe that's possible, thanks to you."

He chased away any remnants of guilt as they slowly swayed back and forth. It felt so right, sitting here beside Darlene.

They lapsed into silence again, their hands still clasped together as they watched the night darkened and the stars began to dot the sky. He knew that, eventually, he would have to leave the island and return to his life in the city. But for now, he was content to sit beside Darlene, enjoying the simple pleasure of her company and the beauty of the evening around them.

As they sat on the porch glider, the evening breeze gently rustled through the nearby magnolia trees. A sound so familiar, yet somehow it sounded more magical tonight to Darlene.

A feeling of being in the exact right place at the exact right time settled over her. As they watched the night sky, their hands remained clasped together, a simple and subtle gesture highlighting the connection they shared.

Her heart skittered as she realized the depth of her feelings for Mark. It frightened her, the thought of opening her heart again after so many years of focusing solely on the B&B and her granddaughter. She knew Mark was still in love with his late wife, Sarah, and that his stay on Magnolia Key was temporary. Yet, in this moment, none of that seemed to matter.

Mark turned to face her, his eyes filled with a tenderness that made her breath catch in her throat. "Darlene, I…" His voice was soft and filled with emotion. "I can't thank you enough for everything you've done for me. Your friendship, your support… It's meant more to me than I can express."

She swallowed, hard, as she gazed into his eyes. "You don't have to thank me. Having you here, seeing you find peace, and hearing that you're writing again… well, it's made my heart happy."

They leaned closer, drawn to each other like two stars caught in a gravitational spin. Her heart pounded as his face drew nearer, his breath warm against her skin. Just as their lips were about to meet, the sound of the screen door slamming jolted them apart.

"Gran, I—oh!" Felicity stood in the doorway, her eyes wide as she took in the scene before her. "I'm so sorry. I didn't mean to interrupt."

She felt her cheeks flush as she quickly jumped up, her hands shaking as she shoved them in her pockets. "It's all right, dear. Did you need something?"

Felicity shook her head, a knowing smile playing at the corners of her mouth. "I wanted to talk. But it can wait. I'll see you in the morning. Night, Gran. Good night, Mark."

As Felicity disappeared back into the house, Darlene turned to face Mark, her heart still racing. The moment had passed, but the electricity between them remained, a crackling force that neither could ignore.

"I should probably head up to bed, too," he

said softly, his eyes never leaving hers. "Thank you for a wonderful evening."

Not trusting herself to speak, she only nodded. As he stood and made his way to the door, a pang of longing poked at her, and the desire to reach out and pull him back to her was strong. But she remained rooted to the spot, watching him disappear into the house, the screen door closing gently behind him.

Alone on the porch, Darlene let out a shaky breath, her mind reeling from the events of the evening. She couldn't lie to herself anymore. She cared for Mark more deeply than she'd ever anticipated. The future was uncertain, but in this moment, that didn't matter to her. All that mattered was she was certain—fairly certain—no, *certain*—that Mark had feelings for her too.

CHAPTER 16

The next morning, Darlene was in the kitchen, tidying up the remnants of breakfast, when Felicity walked in. Her granddaughter's eyes sparkled with mischief as she grabbed a dishcloth and started wiping down the counters.

"So, Gran," Felicity began, her tone light and teasing, "you and Mark seemed pretty cozy last night on the porch."

She felt her cheeks warm as she focused intently on scrubbing a particularly stubborn spot on the frying pan. "We were just enjoying the evening. It was a beautiful night."

"It looked like more than just enjoying the evening to me. Did he kiss you?"

The question hung in the air, and her heart

skipped a beat as she recalled the moment on the porch, the electricity that had crackled between them. She set the pan down and turned to face her granddaughter, her expression serious.

"No, he didn't kiss me," she said softly. "But I'm positive he was going to, right before you interrupted us."

"Oh, Gran, I'm so sorry! I didn't mean to ruin the moment. I feel terrible."

She shook her head, a small smile tugging at her lips. "It's all right. These things happen. And maybe it's for the best. Mark and I… well, it's complicated."

Felicity set down the dishcloth and moved closer. "Gran, I know you care about him. And from what I've seen, he cares about you too. Don't let fear hold you back from something that could be wonderful."

She sighed. "I know you're right. But Mark is still grieving for his wife, and his stay here is only temporary. I don't want to get my hopes up for something that might not be possible."

Felicity reached out and took her grandmother's hand, giving it a reassuring squeeze. "I understand, Gran. But don't close yourself off to the possibility of happiness, even if it's just for a little while. You deserve to be loved and cherished, and if Mark can give you that, even for a short time, isn't it worth taking a chance?"

She stared out the kitchen window, watching the palm fronds sway in the breeze and the dancing shadows below them. Felicity's words struck a chord, but the reality of her situation with Mark remained complicated.

"I appreciate what you're saying, sweetheart." She turned back to the task at hand, running fresh water over the breakfast dishes. "But at my age, taking chances isn't as simple as it used to be."

Mark's presence here had awakened something she'd thought long dormant. Their easy conversations, shared laughter, and quiet moments felt precious. Natural. But her practical side couldn't ignore the temporary nature of their connection.

"The B&B needs my full attention right now," she said, more to convince herself than Felicity. "With the new inn opening and bookings down, I can't afford distractions."

"Gran, the B&B will still be here whether you allow yourself to be happy or not."

Darlene dried her hands on a kitchen towel

and walked to the coffeepot, where she poured herself a fresh cup. The familiar aroma steadied her thoughts. "You know, when your grandfather left, I promised myself I'd never depend on anyone else again. The B&B became my anchor, my purpose."

"But Mark isn't Dean." Felicity's gentle words hit home.

No, Mark definitely wasn't Dean. Where Dean had been restless and unreliable, Mark was steady and thoughtful. His grief for Sarah spoke of a man capable of deep love and commitment.

She took a sip of coffee, letting the warmth spread through her. "You're right about that. Mark is different. But he has his own life waiting for him back in the city. Publishers, deadlines, book tours. That's his world, not our quiet little island."

The memory of last night on the porch flooded back—the way Mark's hand had found hers, how natural it felt to lean into him, the current of possibility that had sparked between them. But along with those sweet memories came the shadow of doubt.

"I spent years building this life, creating something stable and meaningful. The idea of disrupting that balance, of opening myself up to…" She paused, searching for the right words. "To disappointment. It's frightening."

"Oh, Gran." Felicity wrapped an arm around Darlene's shoulders. "Being scared just means it matters."

"Maybe," she said, unable to commit to anything. Uncertainty still swirled in her mind like cream in coffee, refusing to settle into any clear pattern or answer.

She shook her head, clearing her thoughts. "New topic. Now, last night you said you came looking for me because you wanted to talk to me. What's up?"

Felicity frowned. "Maybe now isn't a good time."

"Of course it is. My situation with Mark isn't going to change in the next few minutes. Sit. Tell me whatever it is you wanted to talk about."

Felicity sat down at the kitchen table, her expression tentative and uncertain. She could sense that whatever Felicity wanted to discuss was serious.

"What is it, sweetheart?" she asked, taking a seat across from her. "You know you can tell me anything."

Felicity took a deep breath and fidgeted with the placemat in front of her. "Brent and I have been discussing something. He has another research project coming up. He's headed out for California. And…" She paused, her eyes meeting Darlene's. "He's asked me to come along."

She felt a sudden tightness in her chest, a combination of surprise and a twinge of sadness. She had grown accustomed to having Felicity around, to the laughter and energy she brought to the B&B. The thought of her granddaughter leaving, even temporarily, was difficult to process.

"But I told him I have to talk to you," Felicity continued, her words tumbling out in a rush. "I know you've gotten used to my help around here. I can't bear to think of you doing all this alone again. I've learned how much work it is to run the B&B. And with the new inn opening and bookings being down, I feel awful leaving you to handle it all on your own."

She reached across the table and took her granddaughter's hand in her own. She could see the concern etched on Felicity's face, the worry that she might be letting her down.

"Oh, hon," she said softly, giving her hand a

gentle squeeze. "You know I love having you here. Your help has been invaluable, and I've cherished every moment we've spent together."

She paused, gathering her thoughts. As much as she wanted to keep Felicity close, she knew that her granddaughter had her own life to live, her own dreams to pursue. "Listen to me. You have your whole life ahead of you. If Brent is asking you to go with him, it means he cares about you and wants you by his side. That's a precious thing, and I don't want you to miss out on it because of me. If going to California with Brent is something you want to do, then I want you to do it."

"But I feel like I'm abandoning you."

"You could never abandon me. You've been such a help these past few months, and I'm grateful for every minute we've had together. But I managed the B&B on my own for years before you came to stay. I can do it again. You should go with Brent."

Felicity's eyes widened as a mix of surprise and relief washed over her features. "Really? You sure you're okay with that?"

She smiled, hoping to reassure her. "Of course I am. I want you to be happy, to experience new things, and follow your heart.

And if that means going on this adventure with Brent, then I support you completely."

Felicity's eyes filled with tears, and she stood up, moving around the table to wrap her in a hug. "Thank you, Gran. You have no idea how much that means to me. I love you so much."

"I love you too, sweetheart," she murmured.

She held her granddaughter close, leaning into the warmth of the embrace. She knew that letting Felicity go wouldn't be easy, that the B&B would feel emptier without her here. But she also knew that it was the right thing to do.

As they pulled apart, she cupped Felicity's face in her hands, looking into her eyes. "I'm so proud of the woman you've become. No matter where you go or what you do, remember that you always have a home here with me."

Felicity nodded. "And I promise, I'll come back to visit as often as I can."

She felt a bittersweet mix of emotions as she watched Felicity wipe away her tears, a newfound excitement shining in her eyes. Change was never easy, but it was a part of life. And as much as she would miss her granddaughter, she was grateful for the time they'd had together, and she wanted Felicity to feel free to live her own life.

She smiled at her granddaughter. "Now, run along and tell Brent the good news."

Felicity kissed her quickly, a smile spreading across her lips. "I will. Thanks, Gran."

Felicity rushed out of the kitchen, and Darlene sat there trying to figure out her thoughts. So much had happened over the last day. Her feelings for Mark. The almost-kiss. And now finding out Felicity was leaving.

She finally stood, picked up her coffee mug, and walked over to the sink. Life had a way of throwing curve balls when least expected. She hadn't expected Mark to come into her life, nor had she expected Felicity to leave.

One of her grandmother's sayings ran through her mind. "Trust the journey, even if the destination is unclear."

CHAPTER 17

Darlene sat on the porch, her hands wrapped around an ice-cold glass of tea, her thoughts a tangled web of emotions. The sun was shining brightly this afternoon, but it did little to ease the heaviness in her heart.

She heard the creak of the porch steps and looked up to see Mark approaching. He offered her a gentle smile as he sat down beside her on the glider.

"Mind if I join you?" he asked softly.

She shook her head, managing a small smile in return. "Not at all."

They sat without speaking for a moment, the only sound the gentle creak of the glider and the distant cry of seagulls. She could feel Mark's gaze on her, could sense his concern.

"Is everything all right?" he asked finally, his voice laced with worry. "You seem… troubled."

She sighed and stared down into her glass. She wasn't sure how to put her feelings into words, how to explain the turmoil that had taken root in her mind.

"I'm just… processing a lot right now," she said quietly. "Felicity told me that she's leaving. Going to California with Brent for a while."

"Oh, I'm so sorry." He reached out to lay a hand on her arm. "I know how much she means to you, how much you've enjoyed having her here."

She nodded. "I'm happy for her, truly. But I'd begun to think she would make Magnolia Key her home now. It's hard to imagine the B&B without her. And with everything else going on…"

She trailed off, unsure how to broach the subject of their almost-kiss, the feelings that had been growing between them.

Mark was quiet for a moment, mindlessly rubbing his thumb back and forth on her arm. "Darlene," he said softly, "about last night…"

She looked up at him, her heart fluttering. "Mark, I…"

"I understand if you think we're moving too

quickly." His eyes searched hers. "If you're not ready for whatever this is between us. I don't want to pressure you or make you uncomfortable."

She shook her head, reaching out to cover his hand with her own. "It's not that. It's just... I'm surprised. Surprised by whatever it is. But I'm also scared."

"Scared of what?" he asked gently.

"Of getting hurt again. Of losing someone else I care about. I've been alone for so long, and the thought of opening my heart again... It's terrifying."

His expression softened, and he shifted closer to her on the glider. "I care about you too. More than I ever expected to. It caught me by surprise. And I know we both have our fears, our wounds from the past. But I've also learned that life is short. Too short to let fear hold us back."

She gazed into his eyes, seeing the sincerity there, the gentle warmth that had drawn her in over these past weeks. His words echoed Felicity's advice from the night before. The same message—don't let fear stand in the way of happiness.

Her breath caught as he lifted his hand and

brushed his fingers over her cheek with such tenderness it made her heart ache. The warmth of his touch sent a shiver through her, despite the afternoon heat.

"Can't we at least try to see where this is leading?" he asked softly, his voice filled with a quiet yearning.

Her thoughts bounced around in her mind until they finally settled and she knew what she wanted to say. She opened her mouth to respond, but the sound of footsteps on the sidewalk path drew her attention. A woman was walking toward the porch. She was tall and elegant, strikingly beautiful, her long dark hair perfectly styled despite the humidity.

The change in Mark was immediate and unmistakable. His hand dropped from her face as if burned, and he stiffened beside her. The color drained from his face, guilt written clear as day across his features.

"Savannah," he said, the single word falling between them like a stone.

Something cold and heavy settled in her stomach as she looked between Mark and the woman on her porch steps. The moment of warmth and possibility that had existed just seconds ago shattered like fine china dropped on an unforgiving tile floor.

Her heart plummeted as she took in the scene before her. The way Mark had reacted, the guilt etched into his expression… it could only mean one thing. This woman, Savannah, was someone from his past. Someone important.

"Savannah, what are you doing here?" He stood and stepped toward the woman.

The woman smiled, but there was a hint of sadness in her eyes. "I needed to see you," she said softly. "I heard you were staying here, and I… I needed to talk to you. It's important."

Darlene felt like an intruder, witnessing a moment that was clearly private. She stood, her legs shaky beneath her, and managed to find her voice. "I should go inside," she said quietly, not meeting Mark's eyes. "You two plainly have some things to discuss."

She turned to leave, her heart heavy, barely able to breathe, but Mark's hand shot out, grasping her wrist gently.

"Darlene, wait," he said.

She shook her head, pulling away from his touch. "It's okay." She forced a smile. "I'll give you two some privacy."

She turned and walked away. She didn't look back, didn't want to see the way Mark looked at Savannah, the bond that clearly existed between them.

As she stepped into the B&B, Darlene leaned against the closed door, trying to compose herself. She had allowed herself to hope, to dream of a future with Mark. But there was no denying the connection between Savannah and Mark. It was like an almost visible magnetic force between them.

She took a deep, shuddering breath, trying to compose herself. She just had to focus on the B&B and the guests who needed her. She couldn't let her personal feelings interfere with her responsibilities. What had she been thinking? Getting involved with a guest? She knew better.

But she felt like her chance for change, for happiness, was slipping slowly through her fingers like tiny grains of sand.

CHAPTER 18

Mark stared at Savannah standing at the bottom of the stairs. Always self-assured. Always doing what she wanted, even when he'd told her he was leaving and needed some space. Needed a change.

She *never* listened to him.

"Aren't you going to ask me to join you?" She tilted her head, eyeing him.

"I thought we agreed that I needed some space."

"I know you said that… but I need to talk to you. You're not answering my calls or texts."

"Isn't that the definition of needing space?" he asked dryly.

She laughed softly, then climbed the stairs to

stand right in front of him. "But this is important."

He let out a long sigh. "Okay, come sit. What is that you want? Then after you have your say, will you just let me… be?" His words came out harsher than he'd meant. But Savannah arriving at the precise moment she did? Right when he was talking to Darlene? Well, she couldn't have come at a worse time.

He led the way to the chairs at the end of the porch where they'd be assured of some privacy. He sank into one of the chairs and Savannah sat in the chair beside him, gracefully tucking her long legs and straightening her skirt.

When he'd first met her, he thought she should be a model with the way she moved and her undeniable beauty. But she'd laughed at him when he'd said that. Said the artificial world of fashion and beauty wasn't for her. And as he got to know her, he realized she was right. She was very down-to-earth and practical.

He leaned back in his chair, waiting, unease settling over him. She'd come a long way for… something. And her arrival had disrupted the peace he'd found here. A peace he was reluctant to give up.

And Savannah? All she would do was drag him back into the past.

"So, I came to ask you a favor." She leaned toward him.

"A favor." He kept his voice neutral, though his jaw clenched. The last thing he wanted was to be pulled back into the world he'd left behind. Here on Magnolia Key, he'd found something different. Something healing.

"And if you won't do it for me. I hope you'll do it for… Sarah."

"Savannah…" he warned her.

She reached out and touched his hand. "No, hear me out. The literary festival, the one Sarah always organized. We want you to be the keynote speaker this year. Sarah always said you were the best speaker she knew. The way you connected with the audience, made them laugh—"

"Stop." The word came out sharp, cutting through her praise. "I can't."

A sharp stabbing pain slashed through him. Sarah had poured her heart and soul into that festival, using it as a platform to promote literacy and inspire writers. After her death, he had distanced himself from anything that reminded him too vividly of her, the pain of her absence too raw and all-consuming.

"Get someone else." The words were laced with ice, full of finality.

"We could… but… I think Sarah would want you to do this. You could talk about how involved she was with this cause. How much she helped your career. It might do you good to talk about it."

"Not a chance." He glared at her.

"I think you should consider it." Savannah reached out and touched his hand. "You know, I miss her too. She wasn't only my sister, she was my best friend."

Her words were like a strong slap, bringing him out of his self-absorbed thoughts and words. He knew what she said was the truth. Sarah and Savannah had always been inseparable, almost like twins at only eleven months apart in age. Sarah's death had hit Savannah hard.

He let out a deep sigh, sorry for his harsh words to her. "I know you miss her too." He squeezed her hand, and she smiled gently.

He looked out over the bay, trying to reel in his emotions.

"Mark, it's been two years." Her voice

softened. "Sarah wouldn't want you hiding away forever. The festival meant everything to her. You know how passionate she was about literacy programs and making sure everyone had access to books."

He rubbed his face as memories washed over him. Sarah at the podium, her eyes bright as she introduced authors. Sarah working late into the night, planning every detail. Sarah's laugh reverberating through their home as she practiced her speeches with him.

He looked over at his sister-in-law. "That's not fair, Savannah."

"What's not fair is letting her legacy fade away. The festival needs you. The literacy programs need you." She paused. "And maybe you need this too."

"Savannah, I honestly don't know if I can..." He trailed off, his gaze drifting to the distant horizon.

Memories of Sarah flooded his mind. Her passion for books and her staunch belief in the power of storytelling. She'd always been his biggest supporter, his guiding light. And now, with the spark of inspiration slowly rekindling within him, the words flowing once more, he couldn't deny the feeling that she would want him to do this.

"I'll think about it," he said finally, his voice thick with emotion.

"Thank you. That's all I ask." She smiled, but he could see the tears she was trying so hard to hold back.

They sat in silence for a moment, the weight of shared grief and memories hanging between them. She finally turned to him again and asked softly, "How are you doing? Has it been… helpful… to get away for a while?"

He nodded slowly. "It has. I've managed to find a bit of peace here."

"You know I've been worried about you. Your agent's been worried. A lot of people care about you. Are you… are you writing again?"

"Some." He shifted in his chair. "It's different now."

"Different can be good. Sarah would be proud of you, you know. For finding your words again."

He nodded, a bittersweet smile tugging at his lips. "She always believed in me, even when I didn't believe in myself."

"I should get going," Savannah said, rising

from her chair. "But please, consider the festival. It would mean so much to everyone."

He stood as well, walking her to the steps. "I will. And Savannah… Thank you for coming. I know it couldn't have been easy."

She smiled, a hint of sadness in her eyes. "We're family, Mark. I'll always be here for you." She gave him a little wave and disappeared down the sidewalk.

He stood there looking out at the bay as wave after wave of emotion rolled over him. He'd just found the peace he so desperately needed here on Magnolia Key. He didn't think he was ready to be sucked back into his old life. Go back to his old home. Deal with the memories in every corner of every room. But he didn't want to disappoint Savannah. And in a way, if he said no, he felt like he'd be disappointing Sarah too. He couldn't ignore all the energy she'd put into this annual festival.

Guilt ran through him when he admitted he wanted to say no to the talk. He should do it for his wife's memory. But then it also made him feel guilty about the idea of moving on from his wife's memory and starting whatever this was with Darlene.

He stared out at the bay, at the peaceful water that refused to give him answers.

CHAPTER 19

Darlene hid out in her room that night, telling Felicity she had a headache. Then when Felicity offered to take over breakfast the next morning, to her granddaughter's surprise, she rapidly agreed.

She slipped out of the B&B in the early morning, not wanting to run into Mark. She wasn't ready to see him. Not ready to talk to him. She headed to Coastal Coffee.

The familiar atmosphere greeted her as she walked through the door. Beverly looked at her in surprise, frowned, and hurried over. "What are you doing here so early? What about breakfast at the B&B?"

"Felicity's handling it for me today. I just… I just needed a break."

"Well, come in and sit. I'll get you some coffee. Let me wait on that other table and I'll be back in a jif."

Darlene settled at a table at the back as the cafe buzzed with locals grabbing their breakfast, so different from the quiet, intimate atmosphere of her own dining room at the B&B.

Beverly slid a steaming mug of coffee in front of her. "You look like you need this. How about a fresh, hot cinnamon roll? Or maybe pancakes?"

"The cinnamon roll sounds great." She wrapped her hands around the warm mug and breathed in the rich aroma. How many mornings had she served coffee to others, making sure their cups stayed full? Now here she sat, on the other side of breakfast service.

A hint of guilt crept through her at the thought of Felicity handling everything back at the B&B this morning. But her granddaughter had grown into such a capable young woman. But soon she'd be off to California with Brent, pursuing her own dreams. The B&B would feel emptier without Felicity's cheerful presence, her easy way with the guests, and her help with all the little tasks that kept the B&B running smoothly.

Beverly returned with a cinnamon roll and slipped into the chair across from her. "Here you go. Now spill it. What's got you hiding out here this morning?"

"I'm not hiding," she protested, but even she didn't believe it. She poked at the cinnamon roll with her fork. "Just needed a change of scenery, I suppose."

"And?"

She sighed. "So, Felicity told me she's leaving with Brent. They're headed for California for I'm not sure how long. Quite a while. Another research trip for a book for him."

"Oh, I'm sorry. I know you've loved having her around. And it was nice for you to have help with the B&B."

"I have loved it. But Felicity needs to go live her own life."

"She does." Beverly nodded. "But it doesn't mean the change is going to be easy. But you've run the place on your own before. You'll manage it again."

"I will."

Eleanor walked up to the table. "What's going on here? Why the serious faces?"

"Felicity is leaving. Going to California with Brent," Beverly explained.

Eleanor frowned. "Brent is leaving? Jonah didn't mention it."

"When was the last time you saw him?" Beverly eyed her.

"Well… I told him we needed to take our time. I've turned him down the last few times he suggested we do something."

Beverly rolled her eyes. "You really should give the man a break. Go out with him again."

Eleanor sat down beside her. "Maybe I'm just too old for his. Too many changes."

"I know what you mean," Darlene nodded.

"You do?"

"I was just getting… ah… closer to Mark."

"I knew it." Beverly grinned.

"But then, this woman came to see him. She was beautiful. Self-assured. And there was definitely a strong bond between them."

"So who was she?"

She shrugged. "I'm not sure. Maybe someone he met after his wife died? But there's something between them. It was obvious."

Eleanor tapped her finger on the table. "So why don't you ask him who she was?"

Beverly's mouth rose in a sassy grin. "Because she's too busy hiding out here avoiding him."

"I'm not—" But she stopped because the fact was, she was hiding out.

Beverly shook her head. "I love you both… but sometimes…" She sighed. "It's a full-time job just getting you two to think straight."

"Miss Eleanor, you should give Jonah a chance. It's obvious he cares about you, and you care about him." Beverly turned to Darlene. "And you. Quit hiding. Go talk to the man. Why give up without really even trying?"

Beverly pushed her chair back, its legs scraping on the wooden floor. "And that's all that I'm saying about that. I have customers to wait on. And Miss Eleanor, I'll bring you your coffee and cream."

Darlene walked slowly back to the B&B, thinking about what Beverly had said. But then, Beverly hadn't seen the obvious connection between Mark and Savannah. Each step that brought her closer to home punctuated her indecision on her next move.

She finally reached the B&B and slipped in the back door to the kitchen. Felicity looked up, her sleeves rolled up as she loaded the last of the breakfast dishes into the dishwasher.

"I can finish that up," she said as she grabbed an apron.

"I was starting to worry." Felicity closed the dishwasher door. "Mark was asking for you earlier. Said he wanted to talk to you about something."

A knot formed in Darlene's stomach. "Oh? Did he say what about?"

"No, but he seemed…" Felicity studied her grandmother's face. "Is everything okay? First, you had that headache last night and went to bed early. Then this morning, you actually let me handle breakfast service without hovering nearby to make sure I didn't mess anything up."

"I don't hover."

"Gran." Felicity crossed her arms. "You absolutely hover. Every morning. But today you disappeared completely."

"I just went to have coffee with Beverly." Darlene busied herself wiping down the already spotless counter.

"At the busiest time of the morning? When you never leave the B&B during breakfast?" Felicity gently took the cloth from Darlene's hands. "What's really going on?"

She sank onto one of the kitchen stools. "I saw Mark with a woman yesterday. There was clearly something going on between them."

"Did you ask him about her?"

"No." Darlene smoothed invisible wrinkles from the placemat in front of her. "I didn't want to intrude."

"So instead, you're avoiding him completely?" Felicity shook her head. "That doesn't sound like my Gran at all. The woman who taught me to face my problems head-on. You should go find him. Talk to him."

"That's what Beverly said."

"Beverly's a smart woman," Felicity said. "So am I. It's good advice."

"I don't know..."

Felicity sat down beside her. "You know, Gran. I was thinking. I'm not sure now is a good time to leave with Brent. And he'll be so busy with his research. I mean, I'll have the online classes I'm teaching, but—"

She held up her hand. "Stop right there. I am not your responsibility. And you will not stay here because of me. Of course you're going with Brent. That's all there is to it."

"But, Gran—"

"No buts." She sat back in her chair, her

resolve growing. "And you're right. I'll go talk to Mark. At least then I'll know what's going on."

Darlene stepped onto the porch, her heart beating faster when she saw Mark in his usual spot, writing in his notebook. A gentle breeze rustled the pages.

He looked up at her approach, his face brightening. He set his notebook aside and rose from his chair. "I've been looking for you."

"I know." She clasped her hands together. "Felicity told me."

The silence stretched between them, filled only by the distant call of seabirds and the sound of the breeze rustling the leaves on the magnolia trees.

She took a deep breath. "Truth is, I've been avoiding you."

His forehead creased. "Why? I know we got interrupted yesterday, but I was hoping we could talk."

She looked down at her hands, still locked together. "I saw you yesterday. With that woman. Savannah." The name felt strange on her tongue. "You seemed… close." She looked up at him, meeting his eyes. "It's obvious there's a bond between the two of you."

The boards creaked beneath his feet as he took a step toward her. She forced herself to continue to meet his gaze, steeling herself for whatever explanation he might offer. The connection they'd built over these past weeks felt fragile now, like a soap bubble ready to burst at the slightest touch.

"I wanted to explain."

Darlene nodded, her throat tight. Part of her wanted to run back inside, to protect herself from whatever truth might follow. But she stayed rooted to the spot, remembering her own advice to Felicity about facing problems head-on.

"I do have a special bond with Savannah."

Her heart sank, and she swallowed.

"Savannah is my sister-in-law. Sarah's sister."

Shock bounced through her. "Sarah's sister?"

He nodded. "And we are close. But when I came here, I told her I needed to get away from everything. That included her. I love her, and she has a big heart, but she's quite the force of nature. Always trying to get me to move on. Hovering over me. Asking me too many questions. I needed to go somewhere away from all that. The memories. The questions. The prodding to move on."

"So she came here to see how you were doing?"

"Partially. And she asked me a favor. She wants me to give the keynote speech at the literary festival. Sarah was the one who started the festival and organized it each year. Savannah thinks I should give a speech. About literacy. About writing. About books. About… Sarah and what the festival meant to her."

She stepped back, her mind whirling with this new information. Sarah's sister. Of course. The pieces clicked into place—Mark's reaction when Savannah arrived, the bond between them. She sank into the porch chair, processing what it meant.

Heat rose to her cheeks as she recalled her assumptions. She'd jumped to conclusions, letting her old fears take control. Dean's betrayal had left deeper scars than she'd realized.

"I should have told you sooner about Savannah," Mark said, settling into the chair beside her. "I just… It's complicated. Talking about Sarah, about that part of my life."

She glanced out at the bay, buying time to gather her thoughts. The literary festival. No wonder Mark had seemed so conflicted. Speaking about Sarah in front of all those people would force him to confront his grief in such a public way.

"That's quite a request your sister-in-law's made," she said softly.

"It is." His shoulders looked weighted down with responsibility. "Sarah loved that festival. She poured her heart into it every year. I told Savannah I'd think about it. I'm just not sure I can be pulled back into that world…"

The breeze carried the scent of magnolia blossoms across the porch. She thought about her own experience with loss and how even years later, certain memories could catch her off guard. But Mark's situation was different—he'd be standing in front of a crowd, speaking about the woman he'd loved completely and lost to death.

"I've been sitting out here trying to write that speech in my head," he admitted. "Every time I start, I see Sarah's face. I hear her voice. She was so passionate about bringing authors and readers together. Make books accessible to everyone."

Darlene's heart ached for him. She understood now. He wasn't just dealing with their growing feelings for each other—he was wrestling with how to honor Sarah's memory while allowing himself to move forward.

He sank into the chair beside her. "And then there is… us. Whatever this is." He reached out and took her hand.

She stared down at his hand for a moment, then looked at him. "Maybe now isn't the time for us to figure out what this is. Maybe our timing is off." She tried to slip on a smile. "It sounds like you still have things to figure out. Decisions to make."

"Maybe you're right. I need to figure myself out before I can drag another person through all my baggage and into my life."

Those were not the words she wanted to hear, but they were practical words. They held a thread of truth in them. How can anyone move on if they don't sort out their past? Hadn't she jumped to conclusions about Mark and Savannah because of Dean? She hadn't sorted out her past, either.

She pulled her hand from his and pushed up

out of her seat. "I've got things to do in the kitchen. I'll leave you out here to…"

He looked up at her with sadness lurking in his eyes as he simply nodded.

She hurried inside, trying not to look like she was running away. Hiding. Because she was just being practical, right?

CHAPTER 20

Darlene threw herself into her work at the B&B. She scrubbed the kitchen counters until they gleamed, dusted every windowsill twice, and reorganized the guest welcome baskets multiple times so there was no room for wandering thoughts. The distance between her and Mark had grown with each day, a wall erected by their shared understanding that now was not the time to explore their feelings. She moved through her daily tasks mechanically, trying to keep her mind from constantly drifting to the moments they had shared and the potential future that now seemed just out of reach.

At breakfast, they exchanged polite smiles and small talk, but the warmth and ease of their previous interactions had been replaced by a cautious reserve. One afternoon, they found themselves sharing a glass of iced tea on the porch, but the conversation felt strained, both carefully avoiding the topic that hung in the air between them.

Felicity noticed the change in her. She approached Darlene one evening as she was folding laundry in the utility room.

"Gran, are you okay?" Felicity asked, her eyes full of concern.

She forced a smile. "Of course, dear. Why wouldn't I be?"

Felicity sat down beside her, taking a towel from the basket and folding it. "You seem… different lately. Ever since Mark's sister-in-law visited."

She set aside the sheet she had been folding. "It's complicated, sweetheart."

"Do you love him?"

The question hung in the air, and she felt her heart constrict. She had been avoiding putting a name to her feelings, but hearing it spoken aloud made it impossible to deny.

"Maybe I do," she admitted softly. "But sometimes, loving someone means doing what's right for them. And right now, Mark has things he needs to figure out."

"Like the literary festival and dealing with his late wife's memory?"

"Exactly." She picked up another towel, focusing on the task at hand. "He's still wrestling with his grief and trying to find his way forward. It wouldn't be fair of me to add to that burden."

"But what about your happiness, Gran? Don't you deserve a chance at love too?"

She smiled sadly. "Of course I do, dear. Everyone does. But sometimes, the timing just isn't right. Mark needs space to sort through his feelings and make decisions about his future. And I need to respect that, even if it means putting my own feelings aside for now."

She smoothed the wrinkles from a pillowcase with practiced precision. "And I suppose I have my own issues to work through too."

"You mean Dad's father? Dean?"

The familiar ache spread through her at the mention of her ex-husband. She set the pillowcase aside, her hands falling still in her lap. "Yes. Dean left before your father was even born. I was so young, so excited about the baby, about our future together."

"What happened? You don't really ever talk about it." Felicity asked, sliding closer on the bench.

"One day he said he was going to the store for cigarettes." Her voice caught. "He never came back. No note, no explanation. Just… gone."

She picked up another towel, needing the distraction. "I kept thinking I'd done something wrong, that if I'd been different somehow, he would have stayed. It took me years to realize it wasn't my fault."

"Oh, Gran."

"The truth is, Dean's leaving changed everything about how I approach relationships. I built this B&B and made it my whole world because buildings don't walk away. They're constant, dependable." She gestured at the walls around them. "But people? People leave. Your father moved across the country."

"And now I'm leaving for California." Felicity's eyes filled with pain.

"That's different. You're not abandoning me."

"And I'll come visit all the time. And after Brent is finished, we'll be back."

"I know that, sweetheart. In my head, I

know. But my heart?" She pressed her hand to her chest. "My heart still expects everyone to leave eventually. And with Mark…" She shook her head. "He has his own life waiting for him back in the city. His publisher, his career. Even if things were different between us, even if the timing was right, he'd still leave now that the island has given him his words back."

"You don't know that for sure."

"The point is, I've let that one moment with Dean color every relationship since. I've used it as an excuse to keep people at arm's length, to protect myself." Darlene picked at a loose thread on the towel. "Maybe it's time I dealt with that."

"I just feel like it's the wrong time to leave you."

"We'll have no more talk about you staying. You'll have a grand time with Brent. I'm sure we'll find time for frequent visits."

Felicity got up and hugged her tightly. "I just want you to be happy, Gran. You've spent so long taking care of everyone else. It's time for you to focus on yourself too."

Darlene returned the embrace, feeling a surge of love and gratitude for her granddaughter's support. "I know, sweetheart.

And I will. But for now, I need to give Mark the space he needs and work on my own issues too. Make peace with what happened with Dean and not let it color my decisions." She pulled back. "Now, you run along. Go find Brent. Or I'm sure you have packing to do."

"You sure you're okay?" Felicity asked softly.

"I will be. Don't worry."

Mark sat at the small writing desk in his room, staring at his laptop screen. The words came easier now, but something felt off. He'd taken to working upstairs instead of on the wraparound porch where the ocean breeze and familiar creaking of the wooden boards had become part of his writing routine.

His fingers hovered over the keyboard. The story was there, but his mind kept drifting to Darlene's smile, the way her eyes crinkled at the corners when she laughed. He'd caught glimpses of her moving through the B&B, but they'd barely spoken since Savannah's visit.

"You would have liked her, Sarah," he whispered to the empty room as guilt settled heavily in his chest. Sarah had been his lighthouse, guiding him through the darkness of writer's block, celebrating each published book. Now Darlene had somehow slipped past his defenses, showing him a different kind of light.

He pushed back from the desk and walked to the window. The late afternoon sun danced across the waves in the bay. Two years had passed since Sarah's death, yet some days the loss felt as fresh as yesterday. He'd found peace here on Magnolia Key and rediscovered his voice as a writer. But at what cost?

The festival keynote speech hung over his head like a pending storm cloud. How could he stand at that podium, in the space Sarah had made her own, and pretend he was ready to move forward? Each time he saw Darlene in passing, their eyes would meet briefly before one of them looked away. The easy friendship they'd built had crumbled into awkward silences.

He returned to his laptop, but the words refused to come. The mystery he'd been crafting felt hollow now, missing the spark that had ignited when he first arrived. He'd found inspiration in Darlene's quiet strength, her dedication to the B&B, and the way she nurtured not just the building but everyone who passed through its doors. She was always taking care of others, but who took care of her?

But he wasn't ready. The ring on his finger still felt right, even after all this time. His love for Sarah was woven into every story he'd written, every character he'd created. Opening his heart to Darlene meant accepting that Sarah was truly gone, and he wasn't sure he could do that yet.

The ringing of his phone caught his attention, and he glanced at it as Savannah's name flashed on the screen. He let it ring twice more before reluctantly answering. "Hi, Savannah."

"Hey. How are you doing?"

"I bet you didn't call just to chat about how I'm doing."

She laughed. "No, not really, but I do care how you're doing. And I know you said you needed time to think about the keynote, but we really need an answer. And, you know, giving this speech might bring a boost to your career too. Get your name out there again." Her voice carried that familiar tone—the same one Sarah had used when she wouldn't take no for an answer.

He stood and walked to the window, watching a pair of seagulls circle over the water.

"I don't know if I can do it justice, Savannah. Sarah always made it special."

"That's exactly why it needs to be you. No one understood her vision better." Savannah paused. "She would have wanted you there."

Mark pressed his forehead against the cool glass. The weight of Sarah's absence pressed against his chest. But maybe Savannah was right. Maybe it was time to honor Sarah's memory instead of hiding from it.

"Okay," he said quietly. "I'll do it."

"Really?" The relief in her voice was unmistakable. "Oh, Mark, thank you. This means so much."

"Just…" He swallowed hard. "Send me the details. I'll need time to prepare something worthy of her memory."

After saying goodbye, he set the phone down on the desk. The cursor on his laptop screen still blinked accusingly at him, but now his mind was filled with memories of Sarah at the podium, her face glowing as she introduced each year's keynote speaker. She wouldn't be there to introduce him.

He scrubbed his hand over his face. What had he gotten himself into?

CHAPTER 21

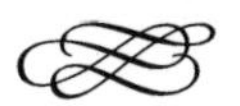

Mark lingered by the window in his room, tracking Darlene's path to the storage shed. She disappeared inside, then emerged moments later, arms laden with a box. His stomach knotted. He'd spent days finding reasons to stay in his room, postponing the inevitable conversation. But he couldn't put off telling her about his decision any longer.

Taking a deep breath, he made his way downstairs and pushed through the screen door onto the porch. A slight breeze coming off the bay stirred the humid air.

He caught her as she was coming up the porch steps. "Need any help?"

Darlene paused and shifted the box she was

carrying to her other hip, her eyes meeting his briefly. "I've got it."

"Could we talk for a minute?"

She set the box down on the porch and turned to face him, her expression carefully neutral. "Of course."

"I spoke with Savannah again." He shifted his weight, searching for the right words. "She convinced me to give the keynote speech at the literary festival. Says it might give a boost to my career too. Get my name out there again since I haven't published a new book in a few years."

"Oh." A flash of disappointment crossed her features before she smoothed it away with a small smile. "That's wonderful. Sarah would be proud."

"And my agent set up some interviews for me. Trying to stir up some excitement for the new book."

"That's probably a good idea." She glanced away from him, suddenly interested in the flowers lining the porch railing.

"I'll be heading back home next week." His words scraped against his throat, dry as beach sand. The familiar view of the bay blurred at the edges as he studied a point past her shoulder. "I just wanted you to know."

"Of course, you need to go." She turned and picked up the box again and squared her shoulders, her expression giving not even the tiniest hint of what she was feeling. "It's a big opportunity."

"Darlene—" He wanted to say more but knew there was really nothing else to say. He'd made his choice. His wedding ring pressed cold against his finger as he curled his hand into a fist, Sarah's memory drawing him back like the tide. He'd chosen the familiar weight of his grief over the uncertain promise of something new.

"I really need to get back to work." She turned away from him but paused when Felicity walked out onto the porch.

"Gran, are those the other vases you wanted to use?"

"Yes, I found them in the storage shed."

Felicity looked at him, then Darlene. "I can take those in for you, Gran, if you two need to talk."

"No, I'm good. Mark was just telling me that he'll be leaving soon. Going back home."

"Oh." Felicity glanced at him again. "We'll be sorry to see you go."

"I'm sorry to leave. I've really enjoyed my

time on the island." He tried to slip on a convincing smile. "Well, I should go in and get back to work." He quickly retreated inside, trying to convince himself he was just going back to work. Not running away.

CHAPTER 22

Felicity crossed the porch and draped her arm around her grandmother. "Are you okay?"

Darlene slipped on a smile and nodded, but she could tell Felicity wasn't convinced. "I'm fine, sweetheart. We knew he was leaving eventually."

"I know… but it seems so final. So definite now. And before you two…"

"It just is what it is." She shrugged.

"You could ask him to stay."

She shook her head. "No, he has to do what he needs to do. And he needs to do this. Maybe it will help him move on with his life."

They both turned at the sound of someone approaching up the walkway. Darlene frowned, trying to focus her vision. Because it couldn't be…

She froze as he walked up the sidewalk, the late afternoon sun catching the streaks of gray in his hair. But he looked the same—just as handsome as the day he'd walked out on her. Her heart stuttered, and she gripped the porch railing.

"Gran?" Felicity's voice seemed far away. "Who is that?"

She couldn't find her voice. The years melted away in an instant. The same confident stride, the same strong jawline, the same blue eyes that had once promised her the world. Only the silver at his temples and the lines around his eyes marked the passage of time.

"It's Dean," she finally managed the words.

Felicity's grip tightened on her shoulder. "What? But you said he's never come back—"

"I know what I said." She straightened her spine, drawing on every ounce of strength she possessed. The young, heartbroken girl she'd been was long gone, replaced by a woman who'd built her own life, raised her son alone, and created a successful business.

Dean stopped at the bottom of the porch steps, his hands shoved in his pockets—the same nervous gesture she remembered from their youth. His gaze moved between her and Felicity, lingering on their similar features.

"Hello, Darlene." His voice was deeper, raspier than she remembered. "It's been a long time."

She felt Felicity's protective presence beside her as she lifted her chin. "Yes. Yes, it has."

Her fingers curled around the porch railing as she studied the man who'd left her pregnant and alone all those years ago. Dean's scrutiny made her skin prickle, especially the way his gaze kept darting between her and Felicity, no doubt noting their shared features.

She resisted the urge to smooth her hair or adjust her blouse. She wouldn't give him the satisfaction of seeing her flustered. Instead, she drew herself up, channeling the strength that had carried her through raising her son on her own.

"What are you doing here, Dean?" The words came out steadier than she felt.

His eyes settled on Felicity again. "Is this—"

"This is my granddaughter." Her tone held a hint of pride, mixed with warning. "Felicity."

Dean's expression softened. "My granddaughter?"

"No. *My* granddaughter. You are not part of our family." She felt Felicity's hand squeeze her shoulder. The gesture steadied her, reminded her that she wasn't that vulnerable young woman anymore. "You still haven't answered my question. Why are you here?"

He shifted his weight, looking exactly like the uncertain young man who'd promised her forever, then vanished before dawn. "I've been thinking about the past. About choices I made." He glanced down at his shoes. "Bad choices."

Her heart thundered in her chest, but she kept her voice level. "That's quite an understatement."

"I know." He looked up, meeting her eyes. "I know it is. Anyway, we need to talk."

"I don't *need* to do anything you say."

"Darlene, don't be like that."

"And you don't get to tell me how to act, how to feel, what to do." She snapped at him as anger surged through her.

Dean climbed the stairs and turned to Felicity. "Felicity, can you talk some sense into your grandmother?"

Heat seared through Darlene at Dean's presumption. How dare he try to manipulate

Felicity against her? But before she could speak, Felicity stepped forward, her eyes flashing.

"Gran always does what she wants. She does what's right, even if it's hard." Felicity's voice rang with conviction. "She's raised an amazing family and built a wonderful life here without any help from you."

Pride swelled in her chest. Her granddaughter stood tall and strong, defending her with the same fierce determination that had gotten Darlene through those early years alone.

Dean blinked, taken aback by Felicity's response. He shifted his weight uncertainly.

Felicity planted her hands on her hips. "Do you know what Gran did after you left? She worked two jobs while carrying my father. She saved every penny to buy this place. She turned it into something beautiful."

She placed her hand on Felicity's arm, touched by her fierce protectiveness. She'd never wanted her family to carry the weight of that old hurt, but here was her granddaughter, defending her with such passion.

"And you don't get to waltz in here after all these years and act like you have any right to tell her what to do." Felicity's words carried the heat of long-simmering anger. "Gran taught us what real strength looks like. What real love looks like."

"And you know what else?" Felicity continued. "She never once let your abandonment turn her bitter. She taught me to be kind, to be brave, to believe in myself."

Tears filled the corner of her eyes. She'd spent so many years wondering if she'd done enough, been enough. Now, listening to her granddaughter, she realized just how much her choices had mattered.

Dean scuffed his shoe against the porch floorboards as a swatch of red swept over his face. He finally looked at Felicity. "I… I deserved that. And so much more."

He turned to Darlene. "I know saying I'm sorry won't help after all these years. But I am. I was young, scared, and foolish."

"And you don't think I was scared? And you left me all alone to deal with it."

He nodded. "I did. And it's my biggest regret in life."

"Telling Gran you're sorry doesn't change anything. You never even wanted to meet my father. Or me."

A wistful look came over Dean's face. "I did come looking for you once. Saw you out on the beach with Darlene and your dad and mom. I spent an hour watching my son playing with you in the waves. You were just a little thing then."

"Why didn't you come over to us? Say something?"

"It just looked like things had turned out fine for everyone without me." He shrugged. "And…" He turned to Darlene. "I couldn't quite face your Gran."

"So you left without saying a word." Felicity's tone was cold and accusing.

"I did. But I'd like to say a few things now. If… if Darlene will let me talk to her." He shook his head. "But it's your choice, Darlene. I don't blame you if you don't want to speak to me."

She studied Dean's face, searching for traces of the young man she'd loved, the one who'd promised her the world and then disappeared with only a scribbled note she found days later. The years had changed him—silver threaded through his dark hair, and there were lines etched around his mouth and eyes. But something in his expression reminded her of that young boy who'd made her heart flutter so many years ago.

"Fine." She bobbed her head once, then

turned to Felicity. "Would you mind giving us a few minutes?"

Felicity's protectiveness flashed across her face. "Are you sure?"

"Yes, sweetheart. I'll be fine." Darlene squeezed her granddaughter's hand.

"I'll be in the kitchen if you need me." Felicity shot Dean a warning look before heading inside.

Darlene gestured to the porch chairs, and after he sat down, she took one across from him. She wouldn't sit next to him, wouldn't let him that close.

"You have fifteen minutes," she said. "Then I need to start prep for tomorrow's breakfast."

"The B&B looks amazing." He glanced around the wraparound porch. "You've done well for yourself."

"I didn't have much choice." The words came out sharp and clipped. "A single mother needs to provide."

Dean's shoulders slumped. "I know I hurt you badly. Left you in an impossible situation."

"You left me with nothing but a note saying you couldn't handle being a father." The old pain rose in her chest. "Do you know how many nights I cried myself to sleep? How scared I was?"

"I was a coward." He met her eyes. "Plain and simple. I've spent over forty years knowing that."

She wrapped her arms around herself, fighting the urge to flee inside where Felicity waited. But she'd spent too many years wondering why. Maybe it was time to hear his explanation.

"Say what you came to say, Dean."

He leaned forward, elbows on his knees. "I got remarried. Had two more kids." He paused. "My wife passed last year. Makes you think about things differently. About mistakes you've made."

"I'm sorry for your loss," she said quietly. Despite everything, she meant it.

"Cancer." He cleared his throat. "Before she died, she made me promise to try to make things right with my first family. Said no one should leave this world with regrets that big."

Her throat tightened. All these years, she'd imagined him living carefree, unburdened by the choices he'd made. Instead, he'd carried this weight too.

"I don't expect forgiveness," Dean

continued. "I just wanted you to know how sorry I am. For everything."

Her fingers traced the arm of her chair as Dean's words settled around her. The life he'd built after leaving her—a new wife, more children—it was everything he'd run from when he'd abandoned her. Her chest ached with an old, familiar pain.

"So you weren't too young for a family after all," she said bitterly. "Just too young for one with me."

He shook his head. "I was different back then. Selfish. Scared. By the time I met Janet, I'd grown up enough to handle it."

The casual mention of his wife's name stung more than she expected. This woman had shared his life, raised his children, grown old with him—everything that should have been hers.

"I saw an article about our son in the business magazine." Dean's voice held a note of pride that made her bristle. "The tech company he founded…"

"You've kept tabs on us?" The thought unsettled her.

"Just… checking in from afar." He shifted in his seat. "I wanted to know you were okay."

She let out a harsh laugh. "We were okay because we had to be. Because I made sure we were."

The sound of Felicity moving around in the kitchen drifted through the screen door, grounding Darlene in the present. Her granddaughter's presence reminded her of all she'd built from the ashes of Dean's abandonment.

"You know what's ironic?" She ran her finger over the smooth wood of her chair, needing something to do with her hands. "I spent years wondering what I did wrong, why I wasn't enough. But here you are, telling me you managed just fine with another family."

"Darlene—"

"No, let me finish." She held up her hand. "I just realized I don't need your explanations anymore."

But even as she said the words, she recognized the lie in them. Part of her—that young, pregnant girl he'd left behind—had always needed to know why. But now she had her answer, and it was both better and worse than she'd imagined. He hadn't wanted a family with her. Hadn't wanted her enough to stay and raise their son.

"Now that we both agree what an incredible fool I was, and what a terrible person I am, have one more thing to tell you, then I'll leave."

She stiffened, eyeing him suspiciously.

"And I'm not bragging here, honestly. But I've built quite a successful business. Real estate development. Made some good investments along the way."

"Good for you." She kept her voice flat, unimpressed.

"I want to make things right." He pulled an envelope from his jacket pocket. "I've set up a trust fund. It's substantial. Here is the paperwork."

The words hit her like a physical blow. After all these years, he thought money could fix what he'd broken? Her hands clenched in her lap as anger bubbled up inside her.

"I don't want your money." The words came out sharp enough to cut. "I didn't need it then, and I certainly don't need it now."

"The paperwork's already done." He held out the envelope. "Take it. Give it to Felicity if you want. Donate it to charity. I don't care what you do with it—it's yours to decide."

"You think you can just throw money at this and make everything okay?" Her voice shook.

"That you can buy your way out of more than forty years of absence?"

"No." He set the envelope on the small table between them. "But I can try to leave something good behind. Something that might help make up for what I didn't give before."

Darlene stared at the envelope, her throat tight with emotion. All those years of struggling to make ends meet, of pinching pennies to give their son everything he needed—and now Dean wanted to sweep in with his money like some fairy godfather?

"Take it," he said softly. "Please. Even if you never forgive me, take it."

He shoved the envelope into her hands, and she stared down at it.

"And… one more thing."

She looked back up at him as a strange expression crossed his features.

"Just so you know, the money is payable upon my death. And you'll get the money soon. My doctors have given me only a few months to live."

His words took her breath away as she stared at the haunted look in his eyes.

"So I know that I had to make one last try to… I don't know. Make amends. Not that I think the money will do that. Nothing can change what I did. I had to come and say I'm sorry. I am so very sorry."

She tried to breathe as she studied Dean's face more carefully. Now she noticed the pallor beneath his tan, the slight tremor in his hands, the way his jacket hung loose on his frame. The signs had been there, but she hadn't wanted to see them.

"Cancer?" The word slipped out before she could stop it.

He nodded. "Same thing that took Janet. Guess there's some justice in that."

The bitterness she'd carried for so long shifted inside her chest, making room for something else—not quite forgiveness, but perhaps understanding. She thought of all the times she'd imagined confronting him, telling him exactly how much pain he'd caused. Now, faced with his mortality, those rehearsed speeches felt hollow.

"I don't want you to die thinking I hate you," she said softly. "I did, for a long time. But I learned to let that go. Had to, for my own sake."

"You're a better person than I ever was." His smile was weak, but genuine. "I watched you build this place, raise our son, become someone amazing. I was too much of a coward to even say hello."

Her fingers brushed against the envelope. Part of her wanted to throw it back at him, tell him to take his guilt money and go. But she saw the desperation in his eyes, his need to leave something behind that might help balance the scales.

She rose from her seat. "I expect you're hungry after your trip. Come inside and I'll get you something to eat. We'll get you a room for the night. You look tired."

CHAPTER 23

Darlene watched from the kitchen window as Dean and Felicity sat on the porch, sharing stories over lemonade. His face lit up when she laughed, a shadow of the young man she'd once known peeking through his tired features.

Three days had passed since his arrival, and each evening he excused himself early, clearly drained from his illness. But during the daylight hours, he made every effort to engage with their granddaughter, asking about her teaching and her plans for California.

The familiar ache in her chest had softened. She'd spent so many years carrying the weight of his abandonment, but seeing him now—frail and seeking connection in his final days—she found her anger dissolving like sugar in hot tea.

"Gran?" Felicity stepped into the kitchen. "Dean's taking a nap. He said the morning wiped him out."

She nodded, continuing to fold napkins for tomorrow's breakfast. "He's pushing himself too hard, trying to make up for lost time."

"I thought I'd hate him." Felicity leaned against the counter. "But he's different than I imagined. More… human, I guess."

"Time has a way of changing people. Sometimes it takes facing the end to realize what matters." She set down the napkins and turned to her granddaughter. "What happened between Dean and me—that's our past. It shaped us, but it doesn't have to define us. I know that now."

Through the window, she could see the empty porch chairs where Dean had spent the morning sharing stories about his travels. His laughter had carried through the screen door, mingling with the sound of waves in the distance. It wasn't forgiveness exactly, but something closer to acceptance had settled over her during these past few days. The bitterness she'd carried for over forty years had begun to feel like an old sweater that no longer fit—still familiar, but unnecessary to hold on to.

The next morning, the air held a gentle, warm caress as Darlene stood on the lawn with Dean and Felicity.

Felicity shifted beside her, twisting her hands together the way she had since childhood when emotions ran high. In the past few days, something had changed between them all. The weight of decades of hurt had lifted, leaving room for something new to grow in its place.

"I'll miss our talks, Dean… Granddad," Felicity said, her voice catching slightly.

Dean's eyes filled with tears, his weathered face softening at the word he'd never expected to hear. He opened his arms, and Felicity stepped into them, holding him close.

"Thank you," he whispered into her hair. "That means more than you know."

When they separated, he turned to her. She studied his face—the deep lines around his eyes, the gray at his temples, the gentle slope of his shoulders. Somewhere beneath the changes time had carved into him, she could still see traces of the young man who'd captured her heart so long ago. The same man who'd broken it just as thoroughly.

But now, looking at him, she felt the last remnants of her anger dissolve. Without a word, she reached out and took his hand in hers.

"I forgive you, Dean," she said softly.

His shoulders sagged with visible relief, and a tear tracked down his cheek. Before she could think too hard about it, Darlene stepped forward and hugged him. His arms came around her, tentatively at first, then holding on as if to anchor himself against the tide of emotion.

She stepped back. "Goodbye, Dean." She paused and smiled at him. "I'm really glad you came. That we—"

"Me, too." He smiled sadly. "Me, too."

He turned and walked away and she had to fight to keep back her tears.

Felicity's eyes filled with tears as she slipped her arm around Darlene's waist. "Are you okay?"

"I am. I think I'm better than I've been in a long time. I'm at peace with Dean." She let out a little sigh. "I'm just sorry that finding that peace came with such a price for him."

CHAPTER 24

Darlene stepped onto the front porch the next morning. Her heart squeezed at the sight of Felicity's and Brent's luggage lined up near the top of the steps, each bag a reminder of the imminent goodbye.

Felicity turned to her, eyes bright with unshed tears. "Are you sure you'll be all right, Gran?"

She pulled her granddaughter into a fierce hug, breathing in the familiar scent of her shampoo. "Of course I will." She smoothed Felicity's hair, just as she had done when her granddaughter was small. "This is your adventure. Your chance to spread your wings."

"But with everything that's happened—

Dean, and now Mark leaving soon…" Her voice wavered.

"Life keeps moving forward, sweetheart." She pulled back to look at her granddaughter's face. "These past weeks have taught me that change isn't always bad. Sometimes it's exactly what we need."

Brent picked up their bags and took them out to his car. The sound of the trunk closing echoed across the quiet morning.

"The B&B—" Felicity started.

"Has survived plenty of seasons, and will survive plenty more." She squeezed her granddaughter's hands. "You've given so much of yourself to this place. Now it's time for you to chase your own dreams."

Felicity's eyes welled up. "I love you, Gran."

"I love you too, sweet girl." Her voice grew thick with emotion. She looked at Brent, who stood respectfully to the side. "Take care of each other out there in California."

"We will. And we'll be back soon to visit. I promise," Brent assured her.

Her arms tightened around Felicity one last time. She breathed deeply, storing away this moment, knowing her granddaughter was no longer the little girl who needed her, but a woman ready to forge her own path with the man she loved.

She waved as they pulled away, a smile firmly placed on her lips until they drove out of sight. It was hard to feel sorry for herself when Felicity was so happy. Off on her great adventure. She turned to head inside. There was work to be done. Always work to be done.

Darlene looked up from where she was folding napkins in the kitchen when the door opened. Mark stood in the doorway.

"Are you busy?"

"Just finishing up some chores." She motioned to the stack of napkins before her.

He took a step into the room. "So I noticed that new guest you had the last few days. That man." Mark shifted from foot to foot. "And… um… I saw you, Felicity, and him the other morning when he was leaving. I didn't mean to be watching… I was just looking out the window and saw you."

She set down the napkin she was folding. Her heart skipped a beat. Of course, Mark would have noticed Dean's presence over the past few days. She drew in a deep breath. "That was Dean." She paused, gathering her thoughts.

Mark's eyebrows shot up. "Your ex-husband?"

"Yes. He showed up unexpectedly." She absentmindedly smoothed the napkin beneath her fingers. "He wanted to make amends before…" She swallowed hard. "He's dying."

"Oh. I'm sorry." He walked over and sat on the chair beside her.

"I am too." She stared at the stack of napkins before her. "He needed to make peace with what he did all those years ago. For leaving me when I was pregnant with Felicity's father." The old pain surfaced, but it felt different now—duller, more distant. "I hadn't seen or spoken to him in over forty years."

"That must have been difficult."

"It was." She picked up a napkin again, finding comfort in the familiar motion of folding them. "But… I think we made our peace. I gave him what he came for."

"What was that?"

"My forgiveness. And Felicity got a chance to get to know her grandfather. I'll never regret that."

"And you're okay?" He reached out and

almost—*almost*—took her hand before snatching his hand back and resting it on the table.

"I am okay. All that bitterness and pain has eased. I think I've finally made peace with my past."

"I'm happy for you."

"And now, maybe you can make peace with your past too." She looked at him.

His gaze met hers. Sadness hovered in the depths of his eyes. "Maybe. It feels like it never will let go of its stranglehold on me."

"I hope you find a way to change that." She kept herself from reaching out to comfort him.

He gave her a small smile and stood up. "I hope so too. Anyway, I came to tell you that I'm leaving tomorrow."

Tomorrow. Well, she knew the day was coming soon. She rose from her chair. "Well, I'm glad you came to Magnolia Key and glad you found your words again."

"Darlene—I—" He stopped and just stared at her for a moment. "I'm glad I came here too. I'm leaving very early tomorrow to catch the first ferry. I have an early flight. So… I guess this is goodbye."

"Goodbye, Mark." The finality of the words hung between them.

"Goodbye, Darlene… I…" He gave a little half-shrug. "Good night."

He disappeared out the door, and she sat down, staring at the napkins waiting to be folded. Even her familiar tasks, which usually brought her comfort, couldn't help her now. Felicity left this morning and now Mark was leaving tomorrow.

CHAPTER 25

Darlene pulled out a stack of plates from the cabinet and set them on the counter with unnecessary care. She scrubbed the shelf, placed the plates back in the cabinet, then moved on to the next shelf. The methodical work kept her hands busy and her mind off the emptiness in the kitchen.

The back door creaked open, and Eleanor stepped into the kitchen. "I thought I'd find you here." She glanced at all the open cabinets. "Cleaning, are we? You always did clean when you were upset."

"I'm not upset."

"I know Felicity and Brent left yesterday," Eleanor said, settling onto one of the chairs at the table. "How are you holding up?"

She picked up the plates again, moving them to a different shelf. "Oh, I'm fine. Just catching up on some organizing that needed to be done."

"These cabinets were perfectly organized last week when I saw you put away those new coffee mugs." Eleanor's knowing look made Darlene pause.

"Well, maybe I wanted to try a different system." She straightened a stack of bowls that didn't need straightening.

"Darlene Bond, stop fussing with those dishes and sit down with me for a minute."

With a sigh, she set down the bowl she'd been holding and took the seat next to Eleanor. "It's just so quiet now. I keep expecting to hear Felicity's footsteps on the stairs or her voice calling out about something she needs help with."

"Of course you do. She's been here all summer." Eleanor reached over and patted Darlene's hand. "And now Mark's leaving soon too, isn't he?"

"He left this morning." She stood back up, unable to keep still. She picked up a dishcloth and wiped down the already-clean counter. "But that's fine. He was always going to leave. He has his writing career to get back to, and the keynote speech to prepare for."

"And that's not all, is it? I heard Dean was in town."

She headed over to the stove to put the teakettle on. "Yes, Dean was here too. He came to… to say he was sorry."

"After all these years? Too little, too late."

She returned to her seat beside Eleanor. "He really was sorry. And he was making amends, trying to find some peace with what he did all those years ago… because he's dying."

Eleanor's eyes narrowed. "Dying?"

"Yes, and he set up a trust fund for me. Or I can give it to Felicity or give the money away. I'm not sure what I'll do with it."

"You'll take it and fix up the B&B, that's what you'll do with it. It's the least the man owes you."

"Eleanor, he's dying."

"Yes, that's what you said. And I'm sorry for him. But money won't fix what he did to you. I was right beside you back then. You were devastated."

"But I made it through it all. And now I'm here. I'm fine. And… well, I've finally made peace with what happened." She got up to pour them some tea.

"I am glad you've made your peace." Eleanor watched her closely. "But that's a lot of people leaving in a short time."

"I'm fine."

"So your clean and well-organized cabinets say." Eleanor shook her head.

She brought their teacups over to the table and sat down. "I *will* be fine."

Eleanor leaned forward. "You will be fine. I know. But I also know your greatest fear."

"What's that?"

"That people you love will leave you. And now Felicity and Mark—and don't deny it, I know you have feelings for him—have left."

"You've known me too many years, my friend." She smiled slightly as she stirred some sugar into her tea. "But I'm doing okay. Felicity will come visit. And Mark had to do what he had to do."

"You could have asked him to stay. Told him how you felt about him."

"I needed to let him go and deal with his past."

Eleanor scowled. "You still could have told

him how you felt. Let him take that into consideration with his decision to leave."

"Can we talk about something else?" She stirred her tea again even though the sugar had long dissolved.

"Yes, we can." Eleanor bobbed her head. "Are your bookings up at all?"

She frowned. "They are up a bit. Or at least we're not getting as many cancellations. Why?"

"I heard that Seaside Inn isn't filling up like they'd hoped. They've gotten some poor reviews online about their service." Eleanor smiled. "Beverly told me there's even a couple of reviews saying their beds are horrible and impossible to get a good night's sleep on. Oh, and complaints their whirlpool tubs aren't working."

"Oh, I hadn't heard anything about it."

"See, you just keep doing what you do here at Bayside. The guests will come. You've got the nicest place to stay on the island."

"But I don't have anything fancy here like whirlpool tubs or wine bars."

"You don't need them. It seems the people coming to Magnolia Key like more of an old Florida feel. Why do you think Anna Maria Island

and Sanibel are so popular? They've tried hard to keep some of that same old Florida atmosphere instead of lining all the beaches with high-rises like Miami and Tampa. People like what you offer."

"I am glad to see my occupancy rise, I admit."

"Now, you just have to get someone to help you. It's silly to try and run this B&B all alone."

"I have for years."

"Yes, but you don't have to, you know."

After Eleanor left, Darlene went out to get the dining room ready for breakfast tomorrow. The more work she could do today, the easier the breakfast rush would be for her to handle alone tomorrow.

She adjusted the white hydrangeas in the crystal vases, centering them just so on each table. The familiar motions of setting out plates and silverware filled her evening, a rhythm she'd perfected over the years. The clink of silverware echoed in the quiet room.

"There you are." Mrs. Clifton's voice carried from the doorway. "I hoped I'd catch you before turning in."

She placed the last fork down. "Is everything all right with your room?"

"Oh yes, perfect as always." Mrs. Clifton stepped into the dining room, her gray hair neatly styled despite the late hour. "I wanted to let you know I've made my decision. I'm staying on Magnolia Key."

"That's wonderful news." She moved to the next table, spreading a fresh tablecloth.

"Now I just need to find the right place to live." Mrs. Clifton smoothed her hand over the back of a chair. "I heard Felicity left for California."

"Yes, she did." Darlene focused on arranging the napkins, trying to keep her voice steady.

"You must be missing her already." Mrs. Clifton paused. "Have you considered hiring someone part-time to help? I noticed you're doing everything yourself now."

She straightened. "You're the second person to suggest that today. And you both might be right. It would be nice to have an extra pair of hands, especially during breakfast service."

"Well, if you decide to look for someone, I'd love to be considered to work here. I even have some experience. I used to work in a small inn. I could help out with whatever you needed. Breakfast, getting rooms ready, checking people in." Mrs. Clifton smiled. "This place is special. I'd love to work here."

"Are you sure?"

"Yes, I'm positive."

"In that case, you're hired. And if you want it, there's a small studio apartment on the first floor. It's not much. It does have a small kitchenette in it, though you're free to use the full kitchen. You can stay there as long as you like, or until you find somewhere else you'd rather stay."

"Oh, that sounds perfect." Mrs. Clifton's eyes lit up. "I'll move my things tomorrow if that's okay with you."

"It sounds wonderful."

"I'll be downstairs first thing tomorrow and you can start showing me the ropes."

"I'll see you in the morning, then."

Mrs. Clifton headed upstairs, and Darlene sank into one of the dining room chairs. And just like that, one of her problems was solved.

She grinned to herself. Eleanor had wanted her to get some help with the B&B. And Eleanor always got what she wanted.

CHAPTER 26

Mark opened the door to his apartment, holding his breath, unable to actually step over the threshold.

He pushed the door wider but remained frozen in the doorway. The apartment sat exactly as he'd left it when he headed to Magnolia Key—Sarah's favorite throw draped over the arm of the sofa, her reading glasses still perched on the side table next to her usual spot. He'd never been able to actually pick them up and put them away.

The late afternoon sunlight streamed through the windows, catching dust dancing in the air. His chest tightened as he finally stepped inside, his footsteps echoing in the stillness.

"I'm home," he whispered, a habit he

couldn't break even after two years. Sarah used to call back from wherever she was, usually her office or the kitchen.

The silence pressed in around him. Her presence lingered everywhere—in the carefully arranged bookshelf where she'd organized their collections by genre and color, in the small potted herbs that had long since withered on the kitchen windowsill.

He moved through the living room, trailing his fingers along the back of her armchair. The fabric held the phantom impression of countless evenings she'd curled up there, reading his latest chapters and offering gentle critiques.

In the kitchen, her favorite coffee mug still sat on the counter. He'd never put it away, but couldn't actually bring himself to use it.

Their bedroom door stood slightly ajar. He paused, his hand resting on the doorframe. Sarah's perfume bottles lined her dresser, gathering dust. Her robe hung on the back of the door—as it had for two years—and for a moment, he could almost see her wearing it, padding around their bedroom on lazy Sunday mornings.

The bed remained perfectly made, hospital corners crisp, just the way Sarah insisted upon.

She'd always teased him about his messier tendencies, lovingly smoothing the wrinkles he left behind.

"I miss you," he said softly, sinking onto the edge of the mattress. "Every day, I miss you."

The bedroom walls held their shared life—photos from their travels, the framed cover of his first novel that Sarah had surprised him with, and her diplomas alongside his awards. All those years of memories surrounded him, each one both precious and painful.

A knock sounded at the door and he got up, wondering who even knew he was back in town. He crossed the rooms and opened the door.

Savannah held up a bag. Its enticing aroma immediately surrounded them. "I got takeout from Frank's. Your favorite. Pastrami sandwiches."

"How did you know I was here?"

"Your agent told me. Are you going to ask me in?"

"Sure, come on in." He stepped aside and led her into the kitchen. "Wine?"

"Yes." She nodded as she grabbed some plates out of the cabinet and he poured them some wine. They sat down at the table and he stared at the food. A meal he'd shared with Sarah so many times.

He attempted a smile and picked up the sandwich. Savannah had no way of knowing he hadn't had a pastrami sandwich from Frank's since Sarah died. They ate in silence for a while. He was grateful she wasn't peppering him with questions.

She finally leaned back in her chair, sipping on her wine. "So… you're back."

"I'm back."

"Do you think you should be back?"

"What are you talking about? You're the one who insisted I come back and give the keynote speech."

"I do want you to give the speech. I think it will be good for you. Maybe bring you some closure. But…"

"But what?" He glared at her.

"But… you're never going to move on if you don't get rid of this apartment."

"Get rid of it?"

"It's like some kind of memorial or monument to Sarah. You still have all her things out. It's like she's… like she's still here." Savannah reached over and took his hand. "But she's not here. Not anymore. You need to… to try and move on."

Tears gathered in his eyes. "I'm not sure that I can."

"You can. You just need to take that first step. And believe in yourself."

Mark stared at his half-eaten sandwich, his appetite gone. Savannah's words struck a chord he'd been trying to ignore. The apartment had become exactly what she'd said—a shrine to Sarah, preserving every detail of their life together as if freezing it could somehow keep her memory alive.

His gaze swept across the kitchen, noting all the places where Sarah's presence still dominated. Her collection of pottery bowls lined the open shelves, gathering dust. The drawer of her favorite cooking utensils remained untouched, just as she'd left them.

"I know you're right," he said quietly. "But every time I think about boxing up her things or changing anything, it feels like I'm erasing her."

"Sarah would want you to live, Mark. Really live, not just exist in this museum of memories."

He thought of Darlene and how alive he'd felt on Magnolia Key. How the weight of his grief had lifted for a while, allowing him to breathe again, to write again. To feel again.

Savannah stood, gathering her purse. "Just think about it. That's all I'm asking." She placed a gentle hand on his shoulder. "The speech isn't for another few weeks. Take some time to consider what you really want."

"I will." He nodded, unable to meet her eyes.

"And Mark?" She paused at the door. "Sarah loved you enough to want you to be happy. Remember that."

After she left, Mark sat in the quiet kitchen, surrounded by the remnants of his life with Sarah. For the first time, he allowed himself to imagine what it might be like to live differently, to create a space that honored Sarah's memory without being consumed by it.

He walked over to the counter and picked up Sarah's mug. He held it in his hands and felt its weight. He slowly opened the cabinet and put her mug away.

He walked into the living and spotted Sarah's reading glasses. He picked them up, staring at them for a moment, then tugged open the drawer on the side table and slipped the glasses inside.

Small steps. He could do small steps.

CHAPTER 27

Darlene and Mrs. Clifton fell into a routine at the B&B. Mrs. Clifton was a great help and Darlene was grateful she had found her. As the days went on, she started to adjust to the fact that Felicity and Mark were gone. Or, at the very least, convinced herself she'd gotten used to it.

She pushed into the kitchen with a tray of dishes. "Only one table left and they're just finishing up."

"Why don't you let me handle them and clean up this mess? You go out for a bit. Maybe visit with some friends. I'm supposed to be giving you a break somctimes, remember?" The woman smiled at her.

"You know. I think I will," she said,

surprising herself. She hung up her apron. "I won't be too long."

"Take as long as you want. I'll be fine."

She headed out into the morning sunshine, feeling it wash over her. Warm her.

Darlene walked down the sidewalk toward Coastal Coffee, her feet carrying her along the familiar path without much thought. The morning breeze caught her hair, and she tucked a loose strand behind her ear.

The bell chimed as she opened the door. She spotted Eleanor at her regular table and waved, threading her way through the tables to join her.

"Well, look who finally came up for air," Eleanor said as Darlene slid into the seat across from her.

"Mrs. Clifton practically pushed me out the door." She settled into the chair. "Said I needed a break."

"I told you it was a good idea to hire some help." Eleanor gave her a self-satisfied smile.

Beverly appeared at their table, coffeepot in hand. She poured a steaming cup and set it in front of Darlene. "Glad to see you. It's been a while."

"Thanks." Darlene wrapped her hands around the warm mug, breathing in the familiar aroma. "I've been busy with the B&B."

Eleanor folded her newspaper and set it aside. "How are you holding up? Really?"

"I'm fine." She took a sip of her coffee. At Eleanor's raised eyebrow, she added, "Or I will be. The B&B keeps me busy enough not to think too much. And Felicity will be here for a visit at the end of the month."

"Have you heard anything from Mark?"

"No, and I don't expect to."

Just then, Jonah walked up to the table. "Good morning, ladies."

"Morning." Beverly and Darlene greeted him. She looked at Eleanor, waiting for her to speak.

"Jonah." Eleanor nodded slightly.

"I'm just going to go grab a cup of coffee at the counter. I'll leave you ladies to it." He walked away and slid onto a stool at the counter, where Maxine poured him a cup of coffee.

"You really should give the man a break. He comes in here all the time when he knows you're here. He cares about you. You can tell from the way he looks at you. Don't you think it's time you quit stalling?" Beverly said as she leaned forward.

"I'm not stalling." Eleanor insisted.

"You know, you really do have to give the guy credit. He's wooing you as best he can," Darlene added.

"We're too old for that."

"But are you? Really? Is anyone ever too old for love?" Beverly gave Eleanor a hard stare.

"I—"

"Mother, I've been looking for you." Cliff Griffin appeared at their table, his gaze traveling from Eleanor to Jonah and back. "Why is that man always around you these days?"

"What man?" Eleanor asked innocently.

"That Jonah fellow. I've heard the gossip." Cliff's voice got louder.

Darlene glanced toward the counter. Jonah was looking over at them and frowning.

"Why are you dating that man? I can't figure out what you see in him or what you're doing with him. You know he's probably just after your money."

Jonah rose and walked over to the table. "Is there a problem here?"

"No, not at all. And maybe stay out of private conversations." Cliff glared at him.

Jonah stood his ground. "Well, I don't take kindly to people upsetting Ellie."

"Ellie? Ellie?" Cliff looked incredulously at Jonah. "You call her Ellie?"

Eleanor slowly rose from her seat. "Cliff, you don't get to tell me what to do with my life. I decide. No one else makes any decisions for me ever again."

"Mother, you're not thinking straight."

Beverly stood. "Cliff, I think you should leave. I told you that you're not welcome here at Coastal Coffee."

Cliff ignored Beverly. "Mother, come on. Let's leave. I'll walk you home."

"No, I think not. I'm staying." Eleanor slipped her hand through the crook of Jonah's elbow. "With Jonah. I decide what I want. And I want Jonah."

Jonah's mouth dropped open in surprise. "Ellie?"

Eleanor turned and looked up at him. "I've been an old fool. I've wasted time worrying about things that don't matter. What people think. How old we are. I do want you. And I don't care who knows it."

"Oh, Ellie." Jonah reached out and touched her facc gcntly.

Cliff frowned. "Mother, if he thinks things are getting serious, you need to see a lawyer.

Protect your assets. If he asks you to marry him, get a prenup."

Eleanor turned slowly to Cliff, pinning him with her famous Miss Eleanor stare. "Cliff, you should go. And if you ever talk about Jonah like that again, or suggest something ridiculous like a prenuptial, I'll disown you. Do you understand? Never tell me what to do again."

Cliff's face turned bright red. "Mother, you're not thinking clearly."

"No, I'm actually thinking very clearly And I know what I want. And I want you to leave now."

Cliff glared at Jonah, shook his head, and stormed out of the cafe.

Darlene leaned back in her chair, smiling. "Well, it looks like I picked a good day to finally take some time off. Wouldn't have wanted to miss that."

They all laughed.

Eleanor sat down in her seat and looked up at Jonah, a new sparkle in her eyes. "Well?"

His forehead creased, and his eyes clouded with confusion. "Well, what?"

"Aren't you going to ask me out again?"

The corners of his eyes crinkled as his smile

lit up his whole face. "I sure am. Ellie, will you go out with me?"

Eleanor's eyes softened and her lips curved into a smile that made her look decades younger. "Yes. We'll go out on Friday. Pick me up at six."

"Yes, ma'am," Jonah said, his eyes twinkling. He dropped some bills on the table for his coffee, then turned and headed out. But not before one last look back at Eleanor with a bemused smile on his face.

"Well, that was quite the morning," Beverly said as she sat back down. "Guess I was right about no one is too old for a second chance at love."

"Let's talk about something else," Miss Eleanor said brusquely. "Jonah and I—and our relationship—are not up for discussion."

"But we all like to think that love can strike a second time, don't we?" Beverly asked softly.

Darlene looked over at Miss Eleanor, deeply engrossed in staring absentmindedly at her coffee. Maybe love came a second time for some people. But she'd lost her chance with Mark. If only she had told him how she felt. Maybe things would have been different. But she'd let that opportunity slip away.

CHAPTER 28

Mark took one last look around his apartment. It looked different now with so many of Sarah's things packed away. Boxes of her clothes sat by the door to be donated to a woman's shelter. Sarah would want someone else to get use out of her belongings. He donated cartons of her books to the library in a small town nearby. He couldn't quite give her favorite coffee mug away, but it stayed in the cabinet now.

He patted his pocket again to make sure he had his notes. As he walked out of the apartment, he turned back. "I'll make you proud, Sarah."

A half-hour later, he stepped into the bustling auditorium and scanned the rows of seats that were quickly filling with eager literary enthusiasts. The familiar scene and excitement brought back memories of past festivals where Sarah had commanded the stage with her magnetic presence.

Savannah appeared at his side and placed a gentle hand on his arm. "You nervous?"

"Yes." His voice came out rougher than intended. The thought of following in Sarah's footsteps was a constant pressure on his shoulders.

"You'll do fine." Savannah squeezed his arm before stepping back.

The festival coordinator introduced him, her voice echoing through the space. His footsteps were heavy on the wooden stage as he made his way to the lectern. The audience fell silent, faces turned expectantly toward him. The spotlight warmed his face as he pulled his carefully prepared notes from his pocket.

He looked down at the words he'd written, meant to honor Sarah's memory and her contribution to the literary festival. His throat tightened. The pages trembled in his hands.

"I..." He cleared his throat. The words on the page blurred together, feeling hollow and inadequate. With a deliberate movement, he folded the papers and slipped them back into his pocket.

He gripped the edges of the lectern and looked out at the sea of faces. "When my wife Sarah stood on this stage, she never needed notes. She spoke from her heart about the power of stories to change lives. Today, I'd like to do the same."

The room was so quiet he swore he could hear a pin drop. He loosened his grip and drew in a deep breath, drawing strength from the memories of Sarah's passionate speeches in this very spot. "As some of you know, my wife, Sarah, passed away a few years ago."

A whisper went through the crowd. He took a moment to gather his thoughts before continuing. "Sarah organized the first literary festival here. She believed that books were more than just entertainment. They were doorways to understanding, to empathy, to knowledge. She used to tell me that every person deserves the chance to open those doors."

His voice grew stronger as he spoke about the cause so dear to his wife's heart. "Sarah picked new and upcoming authors to introduce each year, giving them her full support. She worked tirelessly to ensure that children in under-funded schools had access to books. That adults who struggled with reading could find the resources they needed. That libraries in small towns could keep their doors open."

The familiar faces in the crowd nodded, many of them having worked alongside Sarah over the years.

"The funds we raise today will continue that mission. Every dollar goes toward putting books in the hands of those who need them most. To funding literacy programs in communities that might otherwise go without. To keeping Sarah's dream alive."

He paused, once again gripping the podium. "I've spent the past two years unable to write, lost without Sarah's guiding light. But recently, I discovered something important. The best way to honor her memory isn't to stop creating stories, but to ensure that everyone has the chance to read them."

A quiet murmur of agreement rippled through the audience.

He looked out over the crowd, to the many people who'd come out to support the festival and everything Sarah had made it. The final words he needed to say came to him.

"Writing has been my solace, my way of

making sense of the world. When Sarah passed away, I lost my way. I couldn't find the words to express the grief and emptiness I felt. But then I discovered a place, a small town called Magnolia Key, where I found the strength to start anew. To write my stories."

A sense of peace, of rightness, settled over him. "Sarah always said that stories connect us, heal us, and show us who we can become. Today, we're not just raising money—we're investing in futures, in dreams, in possibilities. We're carrying forward Sarah's vision of a world where everyone can experience the magic of reading."

His voice softened with emotion. "These programs meant everything to Sarah. And I hope they mean everything to you too."

The crowd rose, and thunderous applause swept through the auditorium.

As the applause washed over him, he stepped back from the podium. His heart hammered in his chest, and for a moment, he could almost feel Sarah's presence beside him, see her bright smile encouraging him as she had done so many times before. The standing ovation continued, faces beaming up at him with genuine appreciation.

He managed a small wave, his legs unsteady as he made his way off the stage. In the darkness of the wings, he leaned against the wall and closed his eyes, letting out a long breath. The speech had taken more out of him than he'd expected, but in its wake, he felt lighter somehow.

"Mark?" Savannah's voice cut through the lingering applause. She appeared at his side, her eyes bright with tears. "That was beautiful. Sarah would have loved it."

"You think so?" His voice came out hoarse.

"I know so." Savannah pulled him into a tight hug. "You spoke from your heart, just like she always did."

He returned the embrace, grateful for this connection to Sarah, this shared understanding of who she had been. When they pulled apart, Savannah dabbed at her eyes with a tissue.

"I wasn't sure I could do it," he admitted. "Standing up there, where she used to stand."

"But you did." She squeezed his arm. "And you didn't just talk about Sarah's legacy—you showed everyone that you're ready to be part of it again."

He nodded, surprised to find that the crushing weight of grief that usually accompanied thoughts of Sarah felt different now. Still present, but transformed into something else. Something that propelled him forward rather than holding him back.

"And one more thing." Savannah looked directly at him. "I think you should go back to Magnolia Key. Sell your place here. Move on. Start a new life."

He stared at his sister-in-law, shocked by her words. The bustling activity of the literary festival faded into the background as he processed what she'd said.

"What? You want me to move away?" He stepped back, looking at her closely.

"Yes. I'll miss you, but it's time. I saw how you came alive talking about Magnolia Key." Her expression softened. "Sarah wouldn't want you living in your apartment surrounded by memories. She'd want you to be happy."

"I don't know if I can—"

"Mark, when you talked about finding your words again on that island, your whole face lit up. I haven't seen that spark in your eyes since before Sarah died."

He walked to a nearby chair and sank into it, his legs suddenly weak. The truth of her words hit him square in the chest. Every morning at the B&B, he'd woken up eager to write. To talk with Darlene. To explore the island.

"But what about… Sarah?" His voice came out barely above a whisper.

"Sarah's memory lives in your heart, not in that apartment." Savannah pulled up a chair next to him. "You can honor her by living fully, by writing again, by opening yourself to new possibilities."

He thought of Darlene's warm smile, her quiet strength, and the way she'd helped him find his creativity again without even trying. He remembered the way she understood his grief without pitying him, the comfortable silence they shared, and their almost-kiss on the porch.

"The festival will go on without you here," Savannah continued. "I'll make sure of that. Where you need to go is where the words come to you. Where your heart is leading you. "

"To Magnolia Key," he said slowly, the words feeling right as they left his mouth.

"To Magnolia Key," Savannah agreed. "And to whatever—or whoever—is waiting for you there."

CHAPTER 29

Darlene swept the porch of debris that had been blown onto the floorboards during last night's storm, her mind drifting to the rhythmic motion of the broom against the wood. The sun filtered through the branches of the large magnolia tree, casting dancing shadows across Bayside's wraparound porch.

The soft scrape of footsteps made her look up. Her breath caught. Mark stood at the bottom of the steps, his silver hair catching the sunlight, wearing the same blue button-down shirt he'd had on the day they met.

Her heart skipped, joy flooding through her before she forced it down. She'd already said goodbye once. She didn't need to do it again.

"Mr. Donovan," she said, gripping the broom handle tighter. "What brings you back to Magnolia Key?"

His eyes held hers, gentle and warm. "I gave the speech at Sarah's literary festival."

"That's nice. I hope it went well." She focused on sweeping, though there wasn't much left to clear.

"It did. But that's not why I'm here, Darlene."

The way he said her name made her pause. She straightened, finally letting herself really look at him. He appeared different somehow—lighter, as if he'd set down a heavy burden.

"Why are you here, then?"

Her pulse quickened as he climbed the steps to stand beside her. The familiar scent of his aftershave brought back memories of their morning walks and shared time out here on the porch.

"I tried to stay away," he said. "I went back to my apartment. And… well, eventually, I packed up Sarah's things."

She looked at him in surprise.

"And I gave the speech at the festival. It was something I needed to do. To give me closure. But something kept pulling me back here."

She set the broom against the railing. "What about your writing? Your career in the city?"

"I can write anywhere." His blue eyes crinkled at the corners. "In fact, I wrote more while I was here than I had in the last two years. But when I went back home? Not another word. There's something about this place—the rhythm of the waves, the quiet mornings."

"The cinnamon rolls?" She allowed herself a small smile.

He laughed. "Those too. But mostly it's the peace I've found here. For the first time since Sarah died, I feel like I can breathe again. Like I can write without guilt."

"And what does Savannah think about all this?"

"She's the one who suggested it. Said she hasn't seen me this happy in years." He stepped closer. "I've found a small cottage near the lighthouse. It needs work, but the view of the ocean is perfect for writing."

Her heart skipped a beat. "So you're staying? On the island?"

"If that's all right with you." His hand found hers, warm and steady. "I'd like to see where this could go, Darlene. No rush, no pressure. Just two people sharing meals, taking walks, and getting to know each other better. I've learned that it's possible to honor Sarah's memory while still embracing joy." He squeezed her hand. "And being here, with you—that brings me joy."

She blinked rapidly as tears threatened to spill. Her gaze met his, and the warmth she found there made her heart do cartwheels. His eyes held such hope, such possibility—everything she'd been afraid to dream about since he'd first arrived at Bayside.

She drew in a deep breath, steadying herself. His hand still held hers, anchoring her to this moment.

"Then there's something I need to tell you," she said, her voice soft but steady. "That I should have told you before you left, but I was… afraid. Afraid of opening up my heart again."

Her fingers tightened around his, drawing strength from his presence. Years of keeping her heart carefully guarded had become second nature after Dean left. But standing here with Mark, feeling the gentle way he held her hand, she realized she didn't want to hide anymore.

The words she'd held back for so long sat ready on her tongue. She'd spent decades building walls to protect herself, teaching herself not to need anyone. But Mark had slowly worked his way past those defenses with his quiet kindness and gentle understanding.

After Dean's recent visit and the peace she'd made with their past, she finally understood that holding onto old hurts only prevented new joys from taking root. Mark waited patiently, his thumb brushing softly across her knuckles, giving her the time she needed to find her voice.

"I realized something while you were gone," she said, her voice soft but clear. "It wasn't planned. It wasn't something I was looking for." She met his gaze, drawing courage from the warmth she found there. "I found myself falling in love with you. Between the walks and talks and quiet evenings on this porch—it just happened."

Her heart thundered in her chest as the words hung in the air between them. She'd spent so many years keeping her feelings carefully contained, but now they spilled out like waves crashing on the shore.

A smile spread across Mark's face, reaching all the way to his eyes. He stepped forward and drew her into his arms, pulling her into his embrace. She relaxed against his chest.

"That's good to hear," he murmured, his voice rich with emotion, "because I've fallen in love with you too."

She closed her eyes and savored his words, the steady beat of his heart against her cheek. All the worry and doubt she'd carried these past weeks melted away in the safety of his arms.

Mark pulled back slightly and cupped her cheek in his hand. His lips brushed against hers, soft and sweet. Her heart soared as she melted into the kiss, letting go of years of careful restraint. His gentle touch held more tenderness than she'd ever imagined possible, and she found herself responding with all the love she'd kept locked away.

His arms remained gently anchored around her waist as their lips parted. She drew in a slow breath, capturing this perfect moment in her memory—his steady heartbeat against her cheek, the distant call of the seagulls, the sun and shadows dancing around them.

"I'm finally home," Mark whispered against her hair.

His words reached deep into her soul. After all these years of taking care of others, of running the B&B alone, of keeping her heart protected behind carefully constructed walls, she'd found someone who understood her completely. Someone who saw her strength and her vulnerability and cherished both equally.

And she was finally home too.

CHAPTER 30

Eleanor smoothed her skirt and checked her reflection in the hall mirror one last time. Winston sat at her feet, his tail thumping against the hardwood floor as footsteps approached the front door.

"Someone's coming," she told Winston, who perked up his ears.

Through the window, she spotted Jonah walking up the brick pathway, his silver hair catching the porch light. His smile stretched wide across his face, making her heart skip.

She opened the door before he could knock. "You're right on time."

Winston padded over and nosed Jonah's hand in greeting. "Evening, Ellie." He scratched behind Winston's ears. "And hello to you too, old boy."

"Would you like to come in for a drink before we leave?"

"I would."

She led him into the front room and poured two glasses of wine. Jonah stood by the window, looking out.

"Aren't you going to sit down?" She walked over and handed him his glass.

He turned around slowly. "You know, it took everything in my power not to come over before today. Three days you made me wait. You said Friday, so I waited. But Ellie, I have to know."

"Know what?"

"Know if you meant what you said. That you… that you want me. That you don't care who knows." He looked down at his wineglass before looking back at her. "Because I lost you to Theodore once. You chose him over me."

She took his glass back and carefully set both their glasses on a table. "I did do that. I was young and foolish."

"But you've been doing your best to avoid me since I've returned. We've only gone out a few times. And… just like before… you're so worried about what other people think."

"Jonah, you listen to me now. Yes, I meant what I said at Coastal Coffee. I'm sorry how I've acted since you returned. Sometimes..." She grimaced. "Sometimes I can just be an old fool. Set in my ways."

His hand was warm as he clasped hers, his fingers slightly rough against her skin. Her heart skipped a beat at the contact.

"I hope you truly mean it this time. That you're choosing me." The hint of vulnerability in his voice made her ache deep inside.

The familiar scent of his aftershave brought back memories of stolen moments all those years ago. Moments they'd shared before she let her family's expectations guide her down a different path. Standing here now, in her formal living room with Winston dozing nearby, she knew with absolute clarity that she'd finally made the right decision.

She studied his familiar face—the laugh lines around his eyes, the distinguished silver of his hair, the same kind expression he'd worn all those years ago. Without hesitation, she reached out with her free hand and touched his cheek, feeling the slight stubble beneath her fingertips.

"Yes, Jonah. I choose you. I'm certain of this choice." She paused, her own insecurities bubbling to the surface. “I just hope you haven’t changed your mind.”

“I haven’t changed, Ellie. Not in the ways that matter.” His voice was soft, but sure. “I’ve loved you since that first summer day I saw you.”

The admission she’d held back for decades rose in her throat. She squeezed his hand, gathering her courage. “I loved you too, Jonah. Even when we were apart. I’ve loved you through all these years.” Her voice cracked slightly. “I never stopped.”

Winston shifted in his sleep, sighing contentedly by the window. The familiar tick of the grandfather clock marked this moment, this confession that had waited so long to be spoken.

Jonah stepped closer, his free hand coming up to cup her cheek. “Then don’t you think we should do something about it?”

“What did you have in mind?”

“I thought…” He gave her the impish smile she remembered so well. “I thought we might start with a kiss.”

Her heart fluttered as his lips met hers. His touch was feather-light, almost reverent, and she closed her eyes, savoring the sweetness of the moment. The years fell away, and she was transported back to that first stolen kiss behind the marina so many summers ago.

His fingers traced along her jaw as he pulled back, his eyes bright with emotion. "I've been waiting so many years to do that again."

Her hands trembled as she smoothed his lapel, needing something to ground her in this moment. All those wasted years, all the times she'd chosen what others expected over what her heart wanted, none of it mattered now.

Winston let out a soft snore from his spot by the window, breaking the spell. She laughed softly, feeling like a teenager again despite her silver hair and sensible shoes.

"Was it worth the wait?" she asked, surprising herself with her boldness.

"Every minute." His thumb brushed across her cheek. "Though I'd rather not wait another fifty years for the next one."

"I don't intend to make you wait at all." The words came easily now, all her earlier hesitation gone. This was Jonah—her Jonah—and she was tired of denying what they both wanted.

His eyes twinkled as he smiled, and her heart skipped. That smile had always been her undoing, even back when she thought she needed to be sensible and proper and make the expected choice.

"Good," he said simply, drawing her closer. "Because I have a lot of lost time to make up for."

I hope you enjoyed Seaside Sunshine. Are you ready for the final book in the Magnolia Key series? Book seven is Boardwalk Breezes. Yes, Beverly will finally get her book! I hope you've enjoyed reading this series as much as I've enjoyed writing it.

As always, thanks for reading my stories. I truly appreciate all my readers. — Kay

ALSO BY KAY CORRELL

COMFORT CROSSING ~ THE SERIES

The Shop on Main - Book One

The Memory Box - Book Two

The Christmas Cottage - A Holiday Novella (Book 2.5)

The Letter - Book Three

The Christmas Scarf - A Holiday Novella (Book 3.5)

The Magnolia Cafe - Book Four

The Unexpected Wedding - Book Five

The Wedding in the Grove (crossover short story between series - Josephine and Paul from The Letter.)

LIGHTHOUSE POINT ~ THE SERIES

Wish Upon a Shell - Book One

Wedding on the Beach - Book Two

Love at the Lighthouse - Book Three

Cottage near the Point - Book Four

Return to the Island - Book Five

Bungalow by the Bay - Book Six

Christmas Comes to Lighthouse Point - Book Seven

CHARMING INN ~ Return to Lighthouse Point

One Simple Wish - Book One

Two of a Kind - Book Two

Three Little Things - Book Three

Four Short Weeks - Book Four

Five Years or So - Book Five

Six Hours Away - Book Six

Charming Christmas - Book Seven

SWEET RIVER ~ THE SERIES

A Dream to Believe in - Book One

A Memory to Cherish - Book Two

A Song to Remember - Book Three

A Time to Forgive - Book Four

A Summer of Secrets - Book Five

A Moment in the Moonlight - Book Six

MOONBEAM BAY ~ THE SERIES

The Parker Women - Book One

The Parker Cafe - Book Two

A Heather Parker Original - Book Three

The Parker Family Secret - Book Four

Grace Parker's Peach Pie - Book Five

The Perks of Being a Parker - Book Six

BLUE HERON COTTAGES ~ THE SERIES

Memories of the Beach - Book One

Walks along the Shore - Book Two

Bookshop near the Coast - Book Three

Restaurant on the Wharf - Book Four

Lilacs by the Sea - Book Five

Flower Shop on Magnolia - Book Six

Christmas by the Bay - Book Seven

Sea Glass from the Past - Book Eight

MAGNOLIA KEY ~ THE SERIES

Saltwater Sunrise - Book One

Encore Echoes - Book Two

Coastal Candlelight - Book Three

Tidal Treasures - Book Four

Bayside Beginnings - Book Five

Seaside Sunshine - Book Six

Boardwalk Breezes - Book Seven

CHRISTMAS SEASHELLS AND

SNOWFLAKES

Seaside Christmas Wishes

WIND CHIME BEACH ~ A stand-alone novel

INDIGO BAY ~

Sweet Days by the Bay - Kay's complete collection of stories in the Indigo Bay series

ABOUT THE AUTHOR

Kay Correll is a USA Today bestselling author of sweet, heartwarming stories that are a cross between women's fiction and contemporary romance. She is known for her charming small towns, quirky townsfolk, and the enduring strong friendships between the women in her books.

Kay splits her time between the southwest coast of Florida and the Midwest of the U.S. and can often be found out and about with her camera, taking a myriad of photographs, often incorporating them into her book covers. When not lost in her writing or photography, she can be found spending time with her ever-supportive husband, knitting, or playing with her puppies - a cavalier who is too cute for his own good and a naughty but adorable Australian shepherd. Their five boys are all grown now and while she misses the rowdy boy-noise chaos, she is thoroughly enjoying her empty nest years.

Learn more about Kay and her books at kaycorrell.com

While you're there, sign up for her newsletter to hear about new releases, sales, and giveaways.

WHERE TO FIND ME:
My shop: shop.kaycorrell.com
My author website: kaycorrell.com
authorcontact@kaycorrell.com

Join my Facebook Reader Group. We have lots of fun and you'll hear about sales and new releases first!
www.facebook.com/groups/KayCorrell/

I love to hear from my readers. Feel free to contact me at authorcontact@kaycorrell.com

facebook.com/KayCorrellAuthor
instagram.com/kaycorrell
pinterest.com/kaycorrellauthor
amazon.com/author/kaycorrell
bookbub.com/authors/kay-correll

Made in the USA
Middletown, DE
28 June 2025